W9-BMP-629

LOVE'S ENCHANTMENT

Valor gawked at the naked woman dancing a wild pagan dance with a flock of butterflies.

Raena—naked—lovely—Raena—was dancing with butterflies.

Butterflies that moved in unison with her, sweeping down and up, around and around her body as if they were compelled to dance to the same silent music that moved her. It seemed her power of enchantment was not limited to humans. She had the power to seduce every living creature, no matter how low or how mighty.

Suddenly fearing he might not be alone, Valor tore his gaze from Raena and stood in his saddle to look around, but there was no one to be seen. Thank heaven for that or for certain he'd be fighting his way out of the meadow by now. For what man could gaze upon this sight without desiring to make her his own?

Certainly not he.

When he cantered toward her, the butterfly spell was broken. The butterflies flew away, rising from her body like miniature rainbows until the splendid beauty of her body was completely revealed to him.

Anger and desire battled within him as he drew up to her, staring at the graceful curves of her body. "You fool. Don't you know the danger you've put yourself in, prancing around naked?"

"Danger, my lord? Dancing with butterflies? Am I then in danger of being tickled to death by the velvet touch of their wings on my skin?"

That all-too-vivid image made Valor leap from his horse. "Danger of being ravished by any rutting male who happens by!"

"But you are the only male who has happened by. Am I in danger of being ravished by you?"

"Imminent danger," he answered huskily as he moved toward her.

* * *

"A perfect book!"

—*Affaire de Coeur* on
THE HEART REMEMBERS

THE PAPERBACK EXCHANGE
102 W. Walnut
Watseka IL 60970

SPINE TINGLING ROMANCE
FROM STELLA CAMERON!

PURE DELIGHTS   (0-8217-4798-3, $5.99)

SHEER PLEASURES   (0-8217-5093-3, $5.99)

TRUE BLISS   (0-8217-5369-X, $5.99)

Available wherever paperbacks are sold, or order direct from the Publisher. Send cover price plus 50¢ per copy for mailing and handling to Penguin USA, P.O. Box 999, c/o Dept. 17109, Bergenfield, NJ 07621. Residents of New York and Tennessee must include sales tax. DO NOT SEND CASH.

THE ENCHANTING

Sandra Davidson

Zebra Books
Kensington Publishing Corp.

http://www.zebrabooks.com

ZEBRA BOOKS are published by

Kensington Publishing Corp.
850 Third Avenue
New York, NY 10022

Copyright © 1997 by Sandra Davidson

All rights reserved. No part of this book may be reproduced
in any form or by any means without the prior written consent of the Publisher, excepting brief quotes used in re-
views.

If you purchased this book without a cover, you should be
aware that this book is stolen property. It was reported as
"unsold and destroyed" to the Publisher and neither the
Author nor the Publisher has received any payment for this
"stripped book."

Zebra and the Z logo Reg. U.S. Pat. & TM Off.

First Printing: October, 1997
10 9 8 7 6 5 4 3 2 1

Printed in the United States of America

Prologue

England, 1175

Lady Eleanor was in a devilishly daring mood this morn. Having slipped away from her bothersome entourage unnoticed whilst they rode after the hounds, she made her way toward the shelter of the ravine where she would meet her lover.

No doubt, when the hunting party discovered her missing they would report it to Henry straight away. So be it. She would endure his stern lecture, then play the contrite little wife and pout prettily for him. He would forget his anger after that.

She knew well how to handle him. Though he was more than thirty years her senior, his knowledge of women wasn't very keen.

And she *was* a woman, despite her tender years. She had such womanly longings for the touch of a firm young man, she thought she would perish of it. But, ah, very soon she would know that pleasure in Rolf's strong arms.

She reined in her mount at the top of the ravine. Her heart pounded with excitement as she dismounted, hastily tying her horse to a tree. Glancing quickly down the road to see if she had been followed, she laughed triumphantly and started down the steep path overgrown with ferns and tangled vines.

Although this was the first time she had ever been unfaithful, she knew instinctively she had picked the perfect spot to meet her lover. The gigantic circle of stones nestled at the bottom of the ravine was thought to be enchanted.

Few people dared go there. And of those few brave souls who did, none dared breach the sanctity of the mysterious circle.

A shiver of fear coursed through her as she stared down at the stones from a vantage point halfway down the incline. They looked ominous. But surely she was in no danger here. The stories she had heard of this place were but old women's exaggerations.

And yet, she had to admit, it did make her heart beat madly to see rocks of such size placed in a perfect circle. No human hands could have achieved such a tremendous feat. Each boulder stood twice as tall as a man and three times as wide. Indeed, it had been said the faery folk had built this place for their indecent pagan rituals.

Mmmn, she would soon indulge in a few indecent rituals of her own. If only Rolf would come. Squinting up at the bright sky, she sucked nervously at her lower lip. She had told Rolf she would meet him here when the sun reached its highest position in the sky. And it was most certainly there now.

For the first time since she had initiated this clandestine meeting it occurred to her that he might not come at all. She couldn't help remembering how reluctant he had been to meet her at the faery stones. He had told her he wanted a luxurious soft bed under him; and at the time, she had thought he was just trying to be romantic. But now, now, she wondered if he were too afraid to come to this lonely place.

That wouldn't do. She deserved a real man and wouldn't settle for some gutless, fainthearted mouse afraid of an extinct tribe of silly pagan creatures.

Faery folk no longer existed. Everyone but fools knew that. The once-powerful magical people had died out long ago after some terrible scourge that affected only those of their race. Naught was left of them but the mysterious faery mounds and faery circles that dotted the land.

Reaching the bottom of the ravine at last, she looked around at the steep, verdant walls surrounding the stone circle. 'Twas an odd force of nature to make such a deep dimple in the earth, but no doubt the protection it offered was the very reason the stone circle had been built here, for it could not be seen by anyone traveling on the road above.

She was counting on that.

A tiny pinch of guilt tweaked her conscience at the thought of the wicked thing she was about to do, but she pushed it easily from her mind. She was young, alive, and sick to death of the company of her ancient husband and the tedious people who occupied Caldwell Castle. Sick, too, of the servants who shadowed her every footstep, following her everywhere but into her husband's bedchamber.

They might as well have followed her there, too, for there was not much activity in her marriage bed. Not that Henry didn't try. She shuddered at the thought of his groping, liver-spotted hands on her body, his half-soft manhood that had to be stroked and stroked to be of any use at all.

She wanted a man as upright as the standing rocks of the faery circle. And she thought she had found such a man in Rolf. Surely, she hadn't imagined the incredible hardness of his body rubbing against her on the occasions when he found her alone in the castle's dark hallways or when he stood behind her at the monthly jousts.

In truth, his rod felt every bit as lethal as the steel lances wielded by the knights on their giant steeds. But where was this man of steel? It wasn't very flattering to be kept waiting. She'd make him pay for it by teasing him unmercifully before she opened her thighs to him.

Then, thinking—hoping—he was, indeed, teasing her, hiding behind one of the giant stones only to spring out at her when she passed by, she laughed out loud and called his name.

"Rolf?"

Her voice echoed through the ravine, startling her. It sounded so lonely, so hollow, she knew she must be alone. Swallowing her disappointment, she decided to tarry awhile in the hope he might still come. In sooth, she couldn't bear to return to the castle just yet. And whilst she waited for Rolf, she could explore this strange, wild place.

She had always been fascinated by tales of the faery circle and had tried on many occasions to visit the stones, but her ever-present escorts always prevented her from doing so. If nothing else came of her ride out here, at least she would have satisfied her curiosity about this legendary place.

Reaching out to fondle the cold, hard surface of one of the standing rocks, she felt a puff of hot air across her face, and a hushed voice whispered, "Beware."

She spun around, but there was no one there.

Had she imagined it? Of course, she had. Her imagination was getting the better of her. She would not fall prey to the superstitions of the ignorant castle folk.

Jutting out her chin determinedly, she touched the cold rock again. The hushed voice sounded louder. "Beware!"

She withdrew her hand as quickly as if it had been burnt.

What strange magic is this?

For a moment, she almost bolted, but the thought of retreating to her husband's castle like a frightened doe stiffened her spine. She would not be dissuaded from her goal. She would not have constraints put upon her by some bodiless spirit. She was verily tired of being told what to do, where to go, even what morsels of food she should eat.

Gathering her courage, she made her way between two boulders, emerging inside the stone circle.

A sudden rush of wind engulfed her, taking her breath away and almost knocking her off her feet. Just as suddenly it ended, and an eerie stillness surrounded her. It was as if the very land itself had paused to listen, to watch what would happen next.

Mayhap . . . she had been foolish to come here. Mayhap there was good reason why no one ventured here. Gazing at the silent sentinel stones surrounding her, she felt a tingle of fear.

The air seemed so much heavier here, pressing in on her like an ardent lover. And the silence, the terrible silence, was almost more than she could bear.

But still . . . still . . . there was something about this place that thrilled her heart with excitement. Something . . . sensual, and *alive*. Something that gave her the courage to keep from fleeing. She would not leave until she discovered the source of such unexpected exhilaration. She couldn't remember the last time she had felt so good.

She laughed nervously to herself, thinking surely her imagination was getting the best of her now. There was nothing to fear in this sterile place of stone. But just to be sure, she gazed around at her surroundings, cautiously studying each stone in turn.

The huge boulders that made up the perfect circle she stood in were standing upright, but there were other, smaller rocks inside the circle that looked like some sort of primitive seating, and one in particular that must surely have been an altar for some ancient pagan ceremony.

She shivered, imagining what must have taken place there, and decided she had tarried long enough.

She was about to turn and leave when she caught a trace of a tantalizing fragrance wafting her way. She sniffed curiously at the air. What was that strange, delicious aroma? It pulsated through her nostrils, teasing her with its wonderfully intoxicating perfume, infusing her with a sense of well-being.

What exotic flower gave off such an enticing smell? Taking another deeper whiff of it, she felt suddenly aroused.

How very odd.

How very, very lovely.

Giving in to the exquisite sensations that washed over her, she closed her eyes and slid her hands down her body, seeking the place between her legs where such heat as she had never known before was emanating.

The sudden tinkle of bells halted her. Spinning around, she cried, "Who . . . who goes there?"

The bells tinkled again, and she realized with a start it was laughter.

"What manner of creature are you? Reveal yourself to me at once."

Something pulled at the hem of her gown.

Startled, she looked down to see the velvet fabric rise as if clutched in invisible hands. She gasped, tugging harder at it, and the invisible force released its hold.

The tinkle of laughter rang out again and she knew no human voice had ever sounded like that. Her heart pounded so hard, she feared it would leave her chest. Placing a hand over her heart, she took in a deep breath to calm herself.

Her hand was suddenly flung away, replaced by an invisible one that tweaked at her breast.

She jumped, crying out more in shock than in pain.

The invisible hand was joined by another, roaming over her breasts boldly, then moving down to grasp her waist while she stood rooted to the spot, too frozen with fear to move.

Her breath came in quick little spurts as the hands continued their journey around to her back, where they started working at unlacing her.

Her arms flailed out, seeking some solid, though invisible, form; but she fought nothing but air. At the same time, the erotic aroma grew stronger and, despite her fear, her arousal became intense.

How could that be? What was happening to her?

Before she knew it, her wimple was flying through the air as if it were a bird on wing, her tunic was in a heap at her feet, and her form-hugging brown velvet underdress was yanked violently from her body. It happened so fast, she had no time to think. She was naked, and the hands were on her again, this time more gently, moving over her body in a slow, seductive manner.

She trembled every bit as violently as a wild bird she had once held in her hand, but her fear soon subsided in the intoxication of the erotic aroma that filled her senses. Her feeling of well-being returned, and with it, the certain knowledge that whoever her invisible assailant was meant only to pleasure her, not to hurt her.

That was the last clear thought she had. It was as if her mind was being lulled to sleep whilst at the same time her body was awakening most deliciously. She rolled her head slowly, undulating her torso, as the touch of invisible hands became increasingly pleasurable. So very . . . very . . . pleasurable.

The touch of a hot tongue on her most intimate female part sent a jolt of sheer ecstasy soaring inside her and she pleaded, "Ohhh, who are you? I pray you make yourself known to me so that I might see my seducer."

Her eyes opened in wonder as the most splendid of creatures appeared before her. He was kneeling at her feet, his dragonfly wings of purple, green, and gold unfurled in a fantastic display. She drew in her breath.

A faery! So the stories were true. But why had there been no mention of how very beautiful they were to gaze upon?

The incredible creature looked up at her with a dazzling smile upon his face and her heart melted away. Never had she seen a more angelic, yet masculine face. And his eyes—ohhh, his fabulous, shimmering eyes—were an exquisite shade of purple, the color of the richest lavender silk.

He rose to his feet gracefully, effortlessly, and she stared into the depths of his strange, shimmering eyes and was lost. He had but to command, and she would gladly, eagerly, do anything he asked.

Oh, yes. She would do anything for such a creature as he. Flawlessly structured with fine bones and lean muscles, he stood no taller than she, but his lack of height didn't matter a whit for he was more manly than all the great hulking knights of her acquaintance.

When he stood, she realized that he was naked, without a single hair to blemish his sleek, pale, body, and he was so generously gifted that the sight of him took her breath away.

She feasted with her eyes as her lust for him grew out of bounds. With a man like that inside her, she could surely become the most thoroughly sated female in all the land.

Tearing her gaze away from that awesome sight, she focused on his beautiful faery-face framed with long hair, as black as the night, that accented his purple eyes so very becomingly.

He was looking at her with great interest, his head tilting from side to side as he stared at her. Nay, 'twas much more than that. He looked at her as a man looks at a female he is about to bed; and she wished it were so, for she felt such an overwhelming compulsion to mate with him that she knew she couldn't bear it if she didn't join with him soon.

What was happening to her? How could any male have such powers to seduce? Could she be under some erotic enchantment?

He caressed her cheek, causing her to shiver, for she knew his hands had never left his side. She felt her breasts being grasped most boldly, and still, his hands never moved. Oh, yes, she was most certainly under an enchantment. An otherworldly enchantment of immense proportions. For no man from her dreary world could ever bring her to this extreme state of sexual excitement.

She felt herself responding most eagerly to his phantom touch, knowing it would be impossible to fight it. Indeed, she had no desire to even try, for what she was experiencing was the most wonderfully exciting thing that had ever happened to her in all her life.

A sly smile captured her lips as she looked down at the part of him that would be embedded in her. No human male had an instrument of pleasure such as that. But then, he wasn't human, was he? Not with those beautiful wings. Not with those shimmering, purple eyes.

Remembering tales of the extraordinary prowess of faerie men, she squirmed with delicious anticipation, knowing the stories were far from mythical, for here was proof. Ah, yes, she had come to the faery circle to lie with a man, and it seemed she would not be disappointed.

His hands moved to her breasts again, and she felt seared by the touch. In a daze, she gazed down and saw that this time the touch was real. What she had felt before was nothing in comparison to what she was feeling now. Lightning bolts of desire shot through her body to the very center of her being.

And still, not a word was spoken between them.

His hands caressed her breasts, exploring every inch of them with soft, supple fingers that moved in perfect unison; and she wanted to close her eyes to enjoy it all the more, but she couldn't bear not gazing into his enchanting eyes.

When he had his fill of her breasts, his hands wandered down to her waist, and then to her hips, stopping only long enough to explore her navel most curiously with one finger whilst she waited, breathless, for him to continue what he had started with his tongue.

For sooth, he must have read her mind, for he slowly knelt before her, his fingers trailing down her body, leaving streaks of heat in their wake. She trembled, knowing what was to come.

His hands moved between her legs, parting her most gently; and when she felt the heat of his breath, a jolt of desire radiated from her until she thought she would come right then and there.

His tongue flicked into her opening so quickly, so deeply, she cried out in surprise. Grasping his head with her hands, she drew him closer, opening her legs wider to receive him all the better. Deep, raw pleasure coursed through her—so great, she was sure her body would be rent in two with the intensity of it; and she cried out, unable to hold it all within.

Her voice echoed through the ravine, bouncing off each stone in turn, reverberating back to her in a seductive rhapsody as she cried out yet again.

Then, before she could comprehend what was happening, he was standing, lifting her up by her waist as easily as if she were made from air, and impaling her on his magnificent phallus.

A jolt of desire raked through her, turning her body to liquid heat as she grasped him around his neck for support. In the blinking of an eye, he levitated off the ground, locked tight inside her, and she cried out in fear and excitement, surprise and joy, as she felt her body rise from the ground.

There was no time to contemplate what was happening as he took her higher and higher over the faery stones. But she didn't care. She was beyond reason now—so filled with the need, she could think of nothing but the tremendous sensations that engulfed her.

So tight did he fill her, it was impossible for him to retreat, impossible for any thrusting inside her; but that didn't matter to either of them.

As they soared up over the faery circle, he undulated his body against hers and she against his, locking her legs around him to hold him tight. His manhood throbbed so strongly inside her, each fervid pulse pushed her closer to the edge of rapture.

Surely the magnitude of passion was more than any mortal woman could stand! Surely she would go mad if she had to endure another moment of such terrible want, such enormous craving to become one with her glorious mate!

And then the world turned to a blazing red flame as ecstasy claimed her. She felt herself tumbling over and over in the air, locked tight to the faery prince, until the world below her was no more than a blur. The only thing that kept her from falling was the part of him that was joined to her and her hands and legs holding him tight.

They spun through the air, their bodies entwined, whilst her soul-splitting release shattered the very essence of her being in a brilliant flash of purple, red, and pink. She was melting into him, opening up a part of her to receive him that she had never known existed.

He must have known, for at that very moment his seed exploded inside her in wave after wave of rapture until, at the very height of it, the intensity of feeling was too great and she fainted dead away.

She awoke to find her arms fluttering at her side as if they were wings, her body still locked in the faery's embrace, her head tilted backwards so that she stared up into the bright sky. They were still aloft over the faery circle, her legs dangling freely beneath her; only his hands supporting her back and the still-tight fit of his manhood kept her from falling.

Shuddering from the residual excitement that still coursed through her, she stared up at his face, knowing she would be condemned to madness if she could not be with him forever.

They descended, lower and lower, then touched down at the center of the circle. Still locked inside her, he lowered her to the ground, then pulled himself free of her as the searing heat once again claimed her.

She reached up for him, urging him with pleading eyes not to leave her. She wanted him with her always. *Always.*

Anything else would be unbearable.

But that was not to be, for she heard his faery voice whisper to her, "Remember me. I am Prince Ohreinn of the people of Dawne, the last living tribe of Faerie."

His eyes grazed over her one last, lingering time, and then his body faded away until there was nothing left of him.

She lay there for a long time, too weak to stand, too disheartened over losing her beautiful lover to do anything but stare at the spot where he had been.

"Ohreinn." The name spoken out loud was as beautiful and sensuous as the creature who bore it.

And then, a strange sensation inside her made her gasp. She knew the moment his faery seed found the source of fertility inside her womb, for she felt a hot rush of bliss at the same moment a voice inside her head whispered, "It is done."

One

In restless torment, Raena watched from her tower window as arrows of rain pelted the castle walls. Lush streams of water cascading from the ramparts to the drenched earth below formed crystal waterfalls she found hard to resist.

She yearned to open her mouth and taste the rain on her tongue, to quench her thirst with a deep, satisfying gulp; but more than anything, she longed to tear off her clothes, dash out into the night, and race with the summer storm.

But, alas, she could not.

Here in her father's home, she must control that wild impulse and act with the constraint expected of civilized castle folk.

She would abide, hard though it might be, for she had no desire to be sent back to Sherwood Forest. Not with her father so ill. Though he was not the one to sire her, she loved him just as much as if he were, and it hurt to see him suffer so.

'Twas a hard thing to know that the only reason her father had ended her seven-year exile in the forest was because he didn't expect to live much longer.

Still, she couldn't resent him for banishing her . . .

for he had sent her away not to punish her, but to protect her from being ravaged.

She felt no resentment toward any other man either, though they were the reason for her banishment. How could she blame them? 'Twas not as if they had any choice in the matter. The faery aura and faery scent that she was cursed with, passed down to her from the wild faery creature who had sired her, was to blame for it all. No male of any age or any station of life could resist its lure.

When her adopted father had seen how irresistibly attractive she was to males, even at the tender age of eleven, he had removed her from their presence until she could learn to control the seductive effect she had on them.

She tried not to think of the faery prince who had fathered her, for it hurt too much to be reminded that because of his powers of seduction, her mother had been driven completely mad and had leapt to her death from the ramparts of the castle shortly after Raena's birth.

And it pleased her not to discover she favored her faery father in the loathsome ability to enchant. In truth, she wished she were as ignorant of the existence of faeries as the rest of humankind.

Oh, there were a few who knew of them, but they were wise enough to keep that knowledge to themselves for fear of retribution, or ridicule.

In time, she had learned to accept that she was different. Through the years, under Wiggles's patient guidance and wisdom, she had learned to cloak the scent that drove men to act like stags in rut and had all but mastered the ability to hide her radiant aura.

In some ways it was easier to control those irksome qualities than to keep her wild nature under control. In the forest she had been free to be herself. Free to run naked in the rain, dance with the butterflies in the sunlit clearing of Wiggles's cottage, or accompany birds in their morning song.

Ah, how she missed that freedom now.

She was half faery, after all.

A low, muffled rumble pulled her from her reverie—the familiar sound of the drawbridge being lowered. How curious. Why would her father admit anyone to the castle so late at night?

Awareness prickled at her spine. Something was going to happen that would change her life forever. She knew not what it was or how it would happen, she only knew that it would.

Through her years in exile she had learned to listen to the strange thoughts that came to her unbidden, for along with her other qualities, she was graced, or cursed, with fey knowledge beyond human understanding.

Lightning crackled across the midnight sky, illuminating, for a moment, a small party of riders making their way over the drawbridge. They were hunched over to protect their faces from the rain, and she couldn't make out who they were.

Curious, she ran down the narrow, winding tower stairs that led to her sitting room and then out the door to the landing above the great hall.

Kneeling to conceal her presence, she gazed through the sturdy wooden rails and saw the bedraggled men making their way inside.

Her eyes opened wide at the sight of white surcoats emblazoned with red crosses.

Crusaders.

No wonder her father had admitted them. No one in all of England would turn away the soldiers of Christ.

Never before had she seen with her own eyes the

fearless knights who rode to the ends of the earth to fight the powerful Saladin, but she had heard the great tales of their derring-do.

She counted but three men and, remembering her premonition, wondered which of them would play a part in changing her life. She thought about that whilst she watched her father lead them to the roaring fire to dry themselves.

One of the men was bent over as if injured and he had to be helped to a chair. Her heart went out to him. Was he the one?

Her gaze took in the man who supported his injured comrade, helping him into a chair, but his face was hidden from view.

Shifting her attention to the last of the three men, she saw the solemn robes of a priest and felt a shiver of fear. Wiggles had told her that priests were the natural enemies of faeries.

Surely he was not the one.

Her gaze returned to the second figure, now standing with his back to the fire. He was young, bearded, his stance and demeanor that of a man who had fought many battles and had emerged victorious. In this noble knight she saw the very essence of masculinity, and it was exceedingly appealing to her man-starved eyes.

The fire flared, casting a halo of light around his head, making his flaxen hair shimmer with gold; and her heart fluttered with excitement, knowing it was a potent omen.

This was the one.

This was the man who would change her life.

Baron Henry Caldwell gazed with interest at the virile young knight and was well pleased with what he saw. Sir Valor Godwin stood as straight as an arrow despite his obvious weariness. In sooth, the Crusades had forged this son of his old friend into an exceptional young man, as strong and as straight as a mighty oak.

Though his youth was still evident, the slim mustache and fine golden beard that adorned his face added character, and the Celtic blood of his Scottish grandmother, prominently displayed in his cheekbones, provided the finishing touch. No one who saw him could mistake him for anything but a good and noble man.

He envied his friend Ambrose for being gifted with four amazingly strong and healthy sons; 'twas a rarity, indeed, in a time when disease claimed more children than ever it spared.

Stephan, the wounded one, was the eldest. The priest, Matthew, was the second son, whilst Valor was the third. Avery, the youngest, had been too young to accompany his brothers on the Crusade.

The Godwin brothers lineage was one of the most respected lines in all of England, having to its credit many brave and noble knights; and it suddenly came to Henry that Valor, the most gallant knight of all, could be the answer to a dying man's prayers.

Seeing the concern on the young knight's face as Henry's servants led his injured brother from the hall, he said, "Fear not, my servants will look after Sir Stephan. There's a warm fire and comfortable bed waiting for him. For you and Father Matthew as well. 'Tis been a long time since Godwin men have slept under my roof."

Almost dazed from lack of sleep, Valor answered, "In truth, a long time since we've slept in a real bed. I look forward to it most earnestly."

Henry shook his head. "My poor fellow. You've

had a rough time of it, haven't you? But tonight, you shall sleep on down mattresses."

"Not until I know my brother is comfortable."

"Be assured, Sir Valor. I've sent a woman wise in the knowledge of medicinal herbs to care for your brother. He's in good hands."

Valor closed his eyes, savoring the baron's words. "I pray you're right, for I fear nothing less than a miracle will save Stephan from the fever that rages through him. But then, seeing the faint lights from Caldwell Castle through the miserable rain was very nearly a miracle in itself. Until that moment, I feared my brother would not last the night."

"You say he has a fever?"

"Never fear. Upon my sword, I swear 'tis not the plague. A zealous Arab knight, reluctant to concede the war was over, stabbed him ere we headed back to England. The wound festered on the long journey, growing worse each day. I had hoped to make it home by now, but Stephan became delirious this morn and it became impossible for him to sit a horse any longer."

"God's blood. What rotten luck, to be so grievously wounded after the war ended. Set you down, sir, and I'll have a supper prepared for you. You look in need of a repast."

Valor was reluctant to leave the warmth of the fire, but the grumbling in his stomach was too powerful to ignore. " 'Twould be very welcome."

Turning to the priest, Henry gazed at the hard-bodied holy man. Matthew had a face weathered beyond his young years and a gaze that seemed to pierce one's soul. If not for his priestly garb, he could easily have been mistaken for the fiercest of warriors. Indeed, he probably had fought as valiantly as any of them. "Father, what is your need? How can I best serve you?"

"Lead me to your feather bed, and I shall think I've died and gone to heaven."

Smiling, Henry answered. "Done. If you'll follow my servant, she'll take you to your chamber. God grant you a restful night."

Nodding his head wearily, the priest followed a maidservant up the stairs.

Alone with the young knight, Henry led him to a trestle table and sat with him. The room was deserted at this late hour and the lighting, dim—except for the fire in the hearth and the glow of the reed torches mounted on the four corners of the walls. The only sound that could be heard was the sputtering and hiss of the fire.

Gathering his thoughts before he spoke, Henry said, "News reached us months ago that the Crusade had ended. We rejoiced to hear that Jerusalem is now open to Christian pilgrims. Your father's very proud of your part in that. He spoke of it to me on many occasions."

A goblet of mead was placed before Valor, and his hands closed round it in anticipation. "I find it hard to imagine my father boasting of anything I do. Stephan has always been the favored son."

"Not so. Your father has always been proud of all his sons."

"Forgive me, I mean no disrespect. I'm tired and irritable and more than a little worried about my brother. As for the Crusade, I can only say, the blood and carnage was not to my liking. If not for my liege, King Richard, I would have turned back."

"Ah, yes, 'twas a pity the king should live through the war only to be captured on his way home to England."

"Has not his ransom been paid yet? Surely, he'll be released soon."

"I fear not. John will not lightly give up a hundred thousand marks. Not after the expense of financing the Crusades. It is said that when Richard was raising money for the venture, he went so far as to offer up London Town for sale. Nay, don't look to John for that kind of dedication. He's a frugal man. Richard's release will not be soon."

Valor swallowed the mead thirstily, then set the goblet on the table. It was quickly filled again. "I pray you're wrong. I only wish 'twas in my power to raise an army to free the king."

"You've seen enough fighting, methinks. Your father will be glad to see you home. Tell me. . . . Does my memory serve me? You have no wife to greet you with fond kisses?"

Valor smiled. "No wife. But my betrothed awaits me at Godwin Castle. I sent my squire on ahead to let Lady Elizabeth and my father know where we were and what delayed our return."

Henry pondered that a moment. "I see. Your betrothal . . . was it a love match?"

"Love match?" Laughter rumbled from Valor's throat. "Nay, nothing as romantic as that. My father arranged the marriage in the usual way. I've only laid eyes on Elizabeth once. 'Twas not exactly the most tender moment of my life. She was six at the time, ungainly, with two missing front teeth and a sour look upon her face. Most unbecoming. I'm hoping her looks have improved since then."

Henry's face lit up. Perhaps, this gallant knight would yet be the answer to his prayers. "Drink up, Sir Knight. Drink up. If you'll excuse me, I'll see to it your supper is brought to you. You must be famished for a tasty meal."

After seeing to the knight's supper, Henry ascended the staircase, surprising his daughter, who was busy gawking at the young knight below. She scrambled to her feet when he cleared his throat rather loudly.

"You find our guest fascinating, I see."

Raena blushed. "Do you blame me, Father? I've not been privileged to be in the company of men for several years. 'Tis only natural I should be curious about the strange creatures."

"I'm not here to chastise you, child. I've come to ask a favor of you."

"Then ask away. You know I'd do anything to please you."

Beaming, Henry said, "You're a good and loving daughter. I'm well pleased with the way you've turned out."

Gazing down at Sir Valor sitting hunched over the table, he grasped Raena's arm and pulled her away from the railing. "But, come, I needs must speak to you in the privacy of your chamber."

They passed through her sitting room and up the stairs, then entered Raena's tower room. Wiggles was sitting by the bed, her arms crossed. The colorful clothing she wore of purple-and-red-striped bodice and hunter-green skirt trimmed with gold braiding belied her grumpy demeanor.

"So, there you are, you willful child. I returned from nursing the injured knight to find you gone. I'm sorry, my lord. I'll see to it she doesn't bother you anymore this night."

"Saera, dear woman, hush. My daughter is never a bother to me. And neither are you, my dearest friend. Now, rid yourself of your ill humor and tell me how Sir Stephan fares."

Brushing back a stray lock of coarse, curly, rust-colored hair, Saera answered, "Ah, he's very sick. His wound infested badly, but I bathed it in my special concoction and wrapped it with clean linens. If he lasts the night, I'll be more optimistic about his future. Lady Raena and I can take turns attending him; that is, if she can tear herself away from staring after that virile young knight who has come to us in the night like some wayward Celtic god."

"Aye, and who's to blame for that? If you hadn't kept me away from men all these years, I wouldn't feel the need to study them so closely at every opportunity."

"Raena, enough. Saera, dress Lady Raena in her most becoming garment. I wish her to entertain my guest down in the great hall."

"My lord?" Saera asked incredulously.

"Don't look so surprised. The answer to our prayers is waiting below, though he is certainly unaware of it. Sir Valor Godwin is the perfect choice of husband for Raena. With that strong and godly man as her mate, she'll be safe from those who would harm her."

Raena's eyes opened wide. "My husband? Oh, Father, is my company so hateful to you that you must marry me off to rid yourself of my presence?"

"Sweet child, you have it wrong. I love you most dearly. Surely you know that. Whatever I do, I do to protect you."

"Then I don't understand. You have no reason to worry. Have I not done well learning to control my faery nature?"

Stroking her cheek gently, he murmured, "You've done exceedingly well, my child. But it isn't nearly enough to keep you from harm. You need a righteous, faithful man to be your husband, to protect you, watch over you. Someone good and honorable.

Such a man as that has come to us most timely, and he brings his priestly brother along. Don't you see? 'Tis a powerful omen."

Taking her in his arms, Henry said, "Raena, I haven't much time left. Let me die in peace, knowing you are safely married to a good man."

Raena knew he spoke the truth. Wiggles had tried to prepare her for his death. But it hurt so much more hearing it from his own lips.

If it would give him some small measure of happiness before he died, then how could she deny him? It was not in her to be that selfish.

In truth, she would have to marry sooner or later. Who knew what pompous ancient lord she might end up with in the future. 'Twas not as if she had any say in the matter. At least, this one was exceedingly pleasing to the eye. More importantly, with this one, she would be giving her father the gift of peace.

"I'll do it. And then, when I'm safely married, 'twill be such a relief to you that your health shall improve most astonishingly."

Henry smiled sadly. "Dance for Sir Valor, Raena. Uncloak your faery scent, display your beautiful aura, and let us see what astonishing things happen."

In shock, Raena cried, "Father! After all these years of struggling to learn how to control those very things, you wish me to let them loose? I don't know if I can. It frightens me to think of what could happen."

"Child, you have nothing to fear. No one will be present but Saera, two female servants armed with swords, and myself. Trust in me. I'll not let anything happen to you."

"Then, oh, Father, if I can make your last days happy, of course, I'll gladly do as you wish."

"Excellent. Now, hurry and change. I'll keep him busy until you come."

As soon as her father left the chamber, Raena began to cry. Saera Wigglesworth folded her to her abundant breast as she had since she was a small child, and she was comforted by the touch.

"Hush, child. Dry your eyes. 'Twill not be such a tragedy, I'm thinking, married to a handsome knight such as he."

"Oh, Wiggles, you don't understand. I'm not crying for myself, but for my father. He must be very near to dying if he wants me to marry so soon."

"Don't think of that. Think of the joy you'll bring him knowing you are taken care of."

Pulling herself from Wiggles's arms, Raena said, "If only I could give him the precious gift of peace of mind—but, oh, Wiggles, what if I fail? What if the knight doesn't want me as his wife?"

Saera smiled wisely. "Child, pretend you are in a great wide meadow dancing with the butterflies as you are wont to do, and I promise you, he'll not resist."

Smiling mischievously, she added, "He's only human, after all."

Two

Tired and irritable with the baron for keeping him waiting alone at the table far longer than was polite, Valor was about to search for a servant to guide him to a bedchamber when Henry Caldwell returned.

Rising unsteadily to his feet, he said, "Forgive me, my lord, I'm rather tired and would take my leave of you. Methinks I drank too much of your good mead and ate too much of your delicious mutton."

"Ah, but who could blame you after your long arduous journey? Join me in one more tankard of mead before you retire. There's someone very special I wish you to meet."

Valor groaned inwardly, wishing nothing more than to be able to sleep. "I'm not fit company for anyone this eve."

"You'll not find it an unpleasant chore, I assure you. I've arranged for a little entertainment. Someone wishes to dance for you." With that, Henry gestured to the dark form of a plump old woman at the top of the stairs and a strange, eerie pipe music began.

Not wanting to offend his host, Valor sank back wearily into the chair. What could it hurt to please the old man? He couldn't help but notice how frail and ill the baron looked and remembered his father's telling him that his old friend was dying a slow and agonizing death.

Aye, what could it hurt to be kind? He would suffer the awkward stepping of some silly wench, then bid the baron good night and sleep the sleep of the dead.

Valor watched as the old woman made her way down the stairs, playing all the while on a reed pipe. There was something very odd about her, but he was at a loss to understand what it was.

Her face was lined with wrinkles, and yet, she still walked with the strong, youthful demeanor of a woman much younger and lighter.

His attention was suddenly transferred to the glitter of gold at the top of the steps, and his gaze focused on a bewitching sight.

A young maiden in the first blush of womanhood was standing there, staring down at him with an intent look upon her beautiful face.

He blinked twice, thinking she could not be real, knowing that in all his days he had never seen a more lovely vision. Was this some ghostly apparition brought on by his weariness?

Adorned in a loose garment of translucent material that shimmered with a golden essence, her slender shapely form was tantalizingly outlined through the dress.

Shadows of soft spheres and gentle curves were revealed to his gaze only to disappear, then reappear with each step that she took. He strained his eyes to see as much as he could of her until, in frustration, he felt the urge to tear the diabolical cloth from her body and feast his eyes on her fully.

Fighting to control the urge, he shifted his gaze to her face, but found no relief there. Her face was every bit as enticing as the rest of her. Endowed with lustrous, long dark hair that swept down to her waist and a pert mouth that teased him with a beguiling smile, he had to resist the temptation to tangle his fingers in her hair, draw her up against him until he could feel the heat of her, and taste the nectar of her lips.

She lifted the hem of her dress as she descended the stairs and he noticed that she was barefoot, with circlets of tiny bells around her slim ankles.

He watched as she walked across the great hall with a lithe grace, the miniature bells tinkling softly to the rhythm of her steps, and he was so entranced he forgot to breathe until the baron's earnest voice broke through his senses.

With a twinkling in his eyes, Henry said, "Sir Valor, if you still wish to leave, I won't force you to suffer my little entertainment. I realize how tired you must be."

Dismissing that notion with a restless wave of his hand, Valor never let his eyes waver from the beautiful form. "No, no. Really, I shall be happy for your entertainment. Who is she? Who is that dazzling maid?"

A strange smile crossed the baron's face, but Valor didn't see it, for, at that moment, the girl began to dance.

It was as if he were lost in some waking dream, watching the enchanting creature move about the great hall. A dream so deliciously real, so incredibly sensual it brought a lump to his throat.

Her hips undulated softly, sensuously, but 'twas a natural movement as if she were unaware of the erotic effect she was having on him. She danced to the pipe as if she were born to do so, using her body to express the mood of the music, her arms and legs, shoulders and hips moving in graceful abandonment.

And the pipe music. Never had he heard such a strange tune. It conjured up visions of spring meadows and butterflies, of wild bodies and wild hearts beating to an exhilarating rhythm. It was as if the music had been made for her alone, for no one but she could have danced to it so perfectly.

She was beauty and grace personified, and he wanted her. Wanted her as he had never wanted a woman before. But that couldn't be. He must remember what awaited him at Godwin Castle.

Elizabeth and all that she stood for.

He would—must—marry Elizabeth as his father wanted so he could achieve the rich future denied him by his birth order.

As third son, he had no chance to inherit from his father. Marriage to Elizabeth would bring him great wealth which, in turn, would afford him the power needed to protect himself and his family in these turbulent times.

He must forget this young seductress.

If only he could.

If only he could tear his gaze from her lovely face, glowing with youth and beauty and vibrant life. But look at her, rising on the tips of her toes. See her gathering up the luminous fabric of her dress and leaping high above the floor, her beautifully sculpted legs stretched far apart.

See the way she glides through the air, weightless, as if on invisible wings. She must surely be the goddess of love, for to look at her was to desire her. His need to mate with her was growing stronger with every beat of his heart. So strong, he suddenly became exceedingly uneasy. Why had the baron sent her to him?

There could be but one reason.

The baron wanted him to have her.

Have her . . .

Oh, yes, he must have her . . .

He *must* have her or die. Nothing else mattered. Nothing . . .

Nothing . . .

No! Fight it. Fight it, or be damned.

Fight it or break the blood vow to take no woman to bed until his wedding night.

But the seductive creature was dancing in front of him, smiling at him as no woman had ever smiled at him before, and he could not deny the compulsion to reach for her.

She laughed gaily and easily moved out of his reach. Raising her arms over her head, she swayed back and forth, her hips seeming to move independently of her body, and his desire for her grew out of bounds.

In a daze, he rose from his chair and took a step toward her. She laughed and blew him a kiss, then, still in step with the music, backed away from his reach. She was pure magic, pure bliss, and he wanted her more than he wanted to eat or sleep or even breathe.

Through a thick, purple mist he heard someone shout, "My lord. Name your price for the girl."

The words floated in the air for one long, drawn-out moment before he realized it was he who had spoken.

He hadn't meant to say that.

But, what matter? Nothing mattered anymore but to lie with this enticing creature.

The baron barely breathed. This was the moment he had been waiting for. Trying to sound indignant, he answered, "Price? You speak of my daughter, sir. I wouldn't sell my daughter's favors to Richard the Lionhearted himself."

That was the last thing Valor expected to hear. "Surely you jest? She cannot be your daughter. You would never allow your daughter to dance in such a seductive manner."

"I tell you, sir, she is, and no man but her husband shall bed her."

Valor felt the blood rush to his face. Never in his life had he been so incensed. Not in the thick of battle, not even when his brother had been so badly wounded.

This old man had deliberately teased him with the seductive presence of the enticing girl and now he was denying him access to her without the vows of marriage.

Ah, but what was so wrong with marrying her?

He could wed this beautiful girl who danced like a goddess. Wake up each morn to her enchanting face.

Realizing how close he was to giving in, Valor suspected he must be under some potent spell, for 'twas certain his judgment was being clouded. A sense of urgency came over him.

He must escape her presence immediately, or be lost.

Pushing the baron out of the way, he started for the door, when suddenly the most exotically lovely smell drifted to his nostrils. He stopped and looked at the girl, a quizzical expression on his face. She gazed back in such a sweet, poignant way, his heart went out to her.

Nay, it wasn't his heart that reached for her, but the area of his groin, for a powerful erection was making itself known inside his chain mail.

Whatever desire he had felt for her before was nothing to what he was feeling now. It was so strong, so overwhelming that he wanted to take her right then. *Right there.*

What was wrong with him?

He was an honorable knight, not some base animal, and yet surely what he felt was more animal-like than human.

He moved toward her with a desperate need to touch her, be with her, and she suddenly backed away, a frightened look in her eyes. He realized that his obvious lust frightened her, but he couldn't stop. He had no control over his wild passion. He was a puppet, dancing to the command of his erotic mistress.

The distinctive sound of metal on metal suddenly broke through to his feverish brain as two servant women crossed swords to block his way. Infuriated, he knocked them away with a sweep of his arm, but the touch of a dagger point at his spine brought him quickly to a halt.

"Sir Valor. You'll do the honorable thing. You'll marry her before you make her yours. She is a virgin and will not consent to lie with you any other way."

Rage began to build inside Valor. He was compelled to be with this woman by a force too strong to resist. He couldn't fight it. The need to mate with her was too overwhelming.

Dagger or not, he must have her.

He started toward her again, but suddenly the swords in the hands of the female servants were jabbing at him, moving up his chest to the exposed skin of his neck.

The baron's voice boomed. "Desist. I warn you. If you touch her, I've instructed my servants to run you through."

Raena let out a small cry of alarm.

"Don't be frightened, daughter. This man will not harm you. He's too honorable to take you without benefit of a priest."

Raena wasn't worried about her safety—but, rather, the knight's. If he came after her, the servants would most certainly run him through. And even if he didn't try to take her, he'd still suffer.

Staring into the knight's eyes, she saw they were glazed with pain. She knew how hard he was trying to fight the enchantment, and she wanted to ease his pain, wanted to turn off her faery glamour.

Her gaze shifted to her father's. "Let me end his pain, Father. I cannot bear this."

"No, child. You must go through with it."

Then let it be quick, she thought.

Concentrating hard, she let her aura escape its banishment from deep within her. She felt it radiate from her body, reaching out along with her faery scent to entrap the knight. He tried to fight it, but she knew he would give in.

Valor felt the prick of the sword tip dig deeper into his skin as his madness for the girl took him to the point of no return. He must have her, even if it meant his very life. Moaning loudly, he rolled his head in agony, his suffering beyond his endurance.

The baron spoke, knowing that the time was right. Knowing that if it didn't happen soon, Raena would soon tire and her faery glamour would weaken and fade. "What say you now, Sir Knight? Will you take a wife?"

Blood pulsated through Valor in a strong surge of desire. Nothing mattered anymore but his need for release, and the baron was offering him a way.

In a tormented rage, he cried, "Send for the priest."

Three

Raena stared at the crazed knight in stunned silence. She had had no idea how powerful her faery glamour truly was until this moment. In truth, she wished she were still ignorant of it, for it was too awesome a thing.

If not for the dagger held by her father and the swords in the hands of the two female servants holding Sir Valor at bay, she would have been ravaged right there on the very spot where she stood.

'Twas overwhelming to know that she had the power to compel a man near twice her size and several times her physical strength to do her bidding, and she realized her powers must have increased tenfold since she was eleven. That knowledge frightened her much more than the threat from this poor, bedeviled knight.

For what if, having unleashed her scent and aura, she could not control them again? Nay, that wasn't possible—else she would be destroyed in the process. Surely faery glamour was meant to protect faeries, not destroy them.

Watching as the appealing young knight strained against the blades, his face flushed and beaded with sweat, she felt her heart go out to him. She wanted to give him ease, but dared not. She must keep up her faery glamour until the priest read the Christian words that would seal their union.

For as much as she wanted to help this worthy knight, her desire to help her beloved father was greater yet.

The door of the great hall was suddenly flung open and Matthew Godwin stumbled in, rubbing the sleep from his eyes. "What is this urgent need of a priest?"

Then seeing Valor being held at sword point by two women, he cried, "Have you lost your minds? Release my brother, immediately."

The servants lowered their swords instantly, and the baron himself gave in to the priest, letting the hand that held the dagger fall helplessly to his side.

He could not bring himself to defy a holy man.

Valor tore his gaze from the enchantress and focused on his brother. "Bind me to this woman in marriage immediately."

"You can't be serious, Val. Are you too drunk to remember that Lady Elizabeth is to be your wife? Well, you may have forgotten, but I have not. Go to bed and sleep it off. You'll feel differently in the morning." Matthew turned to leave, but Valor stopped him with his tortured pleading.

"For God's sake, Matt, there's no time for discussion. Do it. *Now!*"

Matthew stared intently at his brother. Never, on the long bloody road to Jerusalem and back, had he ever seen his brother so agitated.

What evil magic was at work here?

And, then, in an instant, he knew the answer.

An uncommonly pleasant smell was teasing his nostrils, bringing with it a feeling of euphoria and then a powerful arousal.

He was all-too-familiar with that provocative scent.

"Brother, you are under a faery enchantment. You must resist it with all your will."

But in his heart Matthew knew that was all but impossible. Although he himself was not the subject of the glamour, he still felt the residual effects most strongly. God alone knew if he would have been able to fight the faery glamour if it had been directed at him.

In truth, he wondered if any mortal man could.

Valor heard his brother speak, his voice sounding far away. Dear God, he was fast losing his strength. There was no time to reason with Matthew. There was only one way to make it happen.

Grasping the baron's dagger from his limp hand, he pointed the blade at his own throat.

"Waste no more breath. Bind me to this girl this very moment or live with the knowledge that you could have saved me from death, for I tell you that if I don't have the girl immediately I have no wish to live. For God's sake, wed us so I'll not burn in the fires of hell."

Seeing that Val was too far gone to respond to reason, Matthew dared not refuse, for in his state he might indeed kill himself. But that didn't mean he wouldn't try to stop this abomination.

Valor had too much to lose if he wed this girl.

He would watch carefully for an opportunity to save his brother. "Very well. Baron, lead us to your chapel. Mayhap, in the sacred house of our lord, Sir Valor will come to his senses."

Carrying a torch to see through the darkness of the night, Henry tried to hide his great joy as he led the small party out into the bailey. The only sound to be heard on the short journey to the chapel was the torches sizzling in the stream of water still descending from the heavens.

Henry was thankful for the rain, for it had brought Valor to him and had even provided a priest to perform the holy ceremony.

Surely this marriage was preordained, for if not for Father Matthew, the marriage could never have taken place. The castle's own priest had died a short time ago. But still, he would not take an easy breath until the two were united.

Peering into the chapel, he saw that no one was about. Good. He wanted no witnesses to this forced marriage. Holding his daughter by the arm, he led her down the narrow aisle to the ornate altar.

The priest and Valor followed after them; and standing in front of the altar, Henry could see the tension on the knight's face as he watched them approach. Pray God he doesn't come to his senses before the vows can be taken.

Matthew started to plead with Valor, but quickly changed his mind when his brother dug the dagger point into the skin of his neck a little farther, piercing it.

The ribbon of blood trickling down Valor's neck was more than enough to convince Matthew that it was useless to reason with him in his craven state.

In agony, Valor cried, "Say the cursed words and make it brief. Oh, God, make it brief. I cannot last much longer."

Raena gazed around the chapel almost dazed. The scene seemed more a dream than reality. Dim lights winked at her from the altar, but the rest of the small room was lost in dark shadows.

All but for Sir Valor.

Dressed in his white tunic emblazoned with a red cross, he stood out from the rest as if the lights of heaven were shining on him. He looked so noble, so pure of spirit, her heart went out to him. How could she continue this? How could she torture him so?

Losing her courage to continue, she took a step away from the knight, but he grabbed her roughly by the arm and forced her back to his side. "Come here."

Raena stared up at the knight's face and saw pain etched in his eyes. Staring back at her, his fervent gaze pierced her soul and for one brief moment—oh, stars in heaven!—for one brief moment, she saw the faces of children illuminated in their blue depths. Nay, not just *any* children. Her future children were reflected there.

Had she imagined it? Pray not, for if she truly saw them, then it would mean that she and Valor were destined to be together and that what she did now was not so very terrible after all.

Matthew saw the looks exchanged by Val and Lady Raena and knew it would be useless to defy his brother. He spoke the words that would join Val to the pagan faery, the dagger still pointed at Valor's throat, and when he was finished, he said solemnly, " 'Tis done. You are joined."

Val gave out an anguished cry that pierced Matthew's heart. He couldn't leave his brother to this dismal fate. He'd do whatever he could to save him. It wasn't too late. Not yet. Not until the consummation. This godly man deserved better than to have a pagan bride forced upon him.

Godly . . . man. Hmm . . . indeed, he was. That could be his salvation. There was still a way to save him.

Turning to the girl's father, he said, "Let us leave them alone for a moment so that the sacredness of their joining will be felt."

The baron looked at him curiously, but nodded

his head and started for the door. Matthew's heart began to race. Excellent. He suspected nothing. There was still a chance.

Following after the others, he hurried down the aisle, then quickly stepped outside, closing the door behind him. Looking around, he saw a cache of sturdy lances propped against the wall and took one, forcing it through the great iron handles of the doors. When Val tried to open the door, he would find it barred.

The baron looked at him as if he were dim-witted. "What do you hope to gain by locking them inside? The deed is done; they are lawfully joined."

The priest was triumphant. "Not yet, they're not. Their union has not been consummated. My brother is a godly man, and no matter the enchantment he's under, he will not lie with a woman in that holy place. I know of her kind. Her faery glamour will weaken and fade long before his strong will is broken."

"How . . . how did you know?"

"I have heard the confessions of poor tormented souls who were seduced by faeries and I am familiar with the intoxicating aroma that surrounds them. Even without the telltale scent in the air, 'twould be clear to me your daughter has faery blood, for nothing less could compel my brother to act this way."

Henry's senses were flooded with shock and understanding. This holy man had personal knowledge of faery folk; and it was certainly true that if the marriage wasn't consummated, it would not be binding. That was the law.

But it had to be consummated or Raena was lost.

In a panic, the baron started for the door, halting when the priest held out his hand in warning. "The only way you can open that door is through me. Do you dare touch my person? I am God's holy representative on earth, and I say to you that you'll surely burn in hell if you do me harm."

"Father Matthew, you don't understand. This marriage must be consummated. My daughter's future is at stake."

"My *brother's* future is at stake."

Henry knew he was defeated. The priest would fight to the death to keep him or anyone else from freeing Sir Valor and, not even for his daughter's sake, could he harm a holy man. He couldn't die with that grave sin upon his soul.

His only chance now was that Raena's pagan faery blood would be stronger than the will of the Christian knight. Sinking wearily to the stone steps leading into the chapel, he began his vigil.

Four

Alone with the object of his obsession, Valor's full concentration was on fulfilling the overwhelming need that consumed him. With one bold sweep, he lifted the girl, swinging her over his shoulder as if she were no more than a sack of grain, and started for the door.

The desire to mate with her was so powerful now, every moment spent holding back was torture of the cruelest kind, and he prayed he had enough self-control left to make it to his seductress's bedchamber.

Grasping an ornate handle of one of the heavy double doors with his free hand, he pulled on it, but it would not give. Impatient, he tugged at it again, using all his strength, but it stood firm.

What the . . . what was going on?

Impatience turned to instant anger as he yanked on it once again, and when it didn't give, suspicion flooded his brain.

Matthew. He was responsible. He had deliberately locked him in.

In torment, he shouted, "Matthew! Don't do this to me. For God's sake, open the door."

His brother's muted voice drifted to him through

the thickness of the wood. "Forgive me, Val. For *God's* sake, I must keep you in there."

Raena had no understanding of what was happening. What had the Christian God to do with this? For that matter, why would the priest lock them in the chapel? It seemed such an odd thing to do. But something inside her told her this did not bode well for her union with the knight.

When there was no further answer from his brother, Valor set her down and began to beat on the door with his fists.

Bewildered, she reached out to touch his shoulder gently. " 'Tis of no consequence. We'll spend the night here. Methinks it's as good a place as any for our wedding night."

Valor turned on her with such force she recoiled. "Only a pagan could have no understanding of my dilemma. I cannot take you here. All the magic spells in the world can't make me defile this holy place."

"Defile? Is that what you truly think you'd be doing to make me your wife? I offer my virginity to my husband. Tell me, where is the evil in that?"

He wanted to believe her. She could see it in his eyes. His desire for her was so great now, surely it wouldn't take much to convince him. And indeed, he reached for her, pulling her into his arms and kissing her hard, his lips grinding into hers as a low, tortured moan escaped his throat. Once again, she marveled at the power of her faery glamour.

But she, too, was under a spell, for she hadn't counted on the intense desire that coursed through her at the touch of a man's lips.

Nay, not just any man's. His.

She felt her body grow weak and for the first time

understood the powerful need to mate. In truth, it was a wondrous thing.

But not to him, it seemed. For he pushed her away, crying, "Father, give me the strength to resist this unholy temptation."

His words might as well have been a dagger through her heart for they hurt every bit as much. "Unholy? My husband, our union will be as natural as the butterflies and the bees, as holy as the mating of any of your God's creatures. Why do you fight it? Why must you make something evil of it?"

Frustrated and impatient for the act to begin that would bind him to her for all time, she opened her arms to him whilst at the same time letting loose her aura completely. It pulsated from her body, spreading out to encompass the knight.

He would give in now.

No human could resist the full thrust of her power. She watched in awe as he tried to fight it, his soul at war with his body. Never had she seen such terrible agony. Forsooth, it was too much for her to bear. She wanted to set him free, but the thought of her father's grave disappointment kept her from it.

Surely this good knight would give in soon. Surely his ordeal would end quickly so she could release him. Oh, please let it be so. She couldn't take much more of his suffering. She hadn't known it would be so terrible.

But it seemed that she would not be spared his pain, for she watched in shock as he lowered his head and butted the door, slamming into it with such great force she was sure he must have fractured his head. As he backed away, she saw the determination in his eyes and a cold horror crept over her. *He was going to do it again.*

"No!" She cried, grasping him by the arm.

At her touch, Valor's body began to shake. He looked down at her with eyes glazed with pain, and something else . . . something akin to sadness emanated from his blue eyes, turning them to somber gray. She knew he had reached the limit of self-control.

He was going to give in.

Give in.

Give . . . in.

Suddenly, she couldn't bear for this noble man, this exemplary knight to lose his soul. Without knowing she was going to do so, she turned off her faery charm.

Melancholy spread over her like a shroud. Without the consummation, there would be no marriage. He could very easily get an annulment. But what did it matter? Their marriage was already doomed, for deep in her heart she knew that if he had been forced to take her in this holy place, he would never have forgiven her. He would have hated her forever and a day.

Knowing that, she had had no choice but to set him free. Not even for her father would she spend the rest of her life tied to a man who despised her for forcing him to betray his faith. It was too much to ask of anyone. There was nothing left to do but explain and pray that her father understood.

For a moment, Val stared at the enchantress in disbelief; and then a large shudder shook his body, his eyes rolled up in his head, and he sank to the floor at her feet.

Raena knelt by his side and gently caressed the pain from his face with her hand. In a moment he was in a deep, exhausted sleep. Smoothing his golden beard with her fingers, she gazed at his exquisitely carved features, and a wave of longing washed over her.

He was so very beautiful to look upon, so heart-breakingly splendid to touch, that she grieved for his loss already. In truth, she felt his loss so deeply, it was as if he had died instead of just fainted.

Ah, but he was, indeed, dead to her now. Oh, why did he have to be such a goodly knight? Why couldn't he have given in to her will without a struggle like any other man? She almost regretted setting him free, for every fiber of her being told her that it wouldn't be hard to love such a man as he.

Everything about him spoke of manhood; and yet, even with all that masculine power, the battle for his soul had drained him of all his strength. When he awoke, would he hate her for showing him his vulnerability?

Gathering her own remaining strength, she rose to her feet. The hardest part was yet ahead of her. She would have to face her father.

Rapping lightly on the door, she said, "Priest, open the door. You and your stubborn God have won."

Five

Valor awoke to the sound of bird-song; and for one sweet moment, all was right with the world. But when he opened his eyes and saw the dark-clad form of Matthew staring down at him like the wrath of God, bits and pieces of the night before swam through his mind.

Groaning, he tried to sit up, but the pain was too great. "Ohhh, my head. Did someone use it for a battering ram?"

A faint smile played across Matthew's face, then his countenance became somber once more.

Valor remembered it all then, and an uneasy feeling crept through him. Forgetting his pain, he climbed to his feet. "Where is she? Where's the witch?"

"Your *wife* left you to my care last evening."

"My wife? What are you saying? Surely . . . I couldn't have. . . . For God's sake, Matthew, did I take her? Was I so driven out of my mind, I have no recollection of it?"

"Nay, there's no harm done. I stood outside the door, preventing anyone from freeing you; and when you were done with your ranting and raving, I unlocked the door and found you sleeping. Lady Raena assured me you had not touched her. Remarkably, the girl took pity on you and released you from her spell. She'll not fight an annulment." Looking Valor straight in the eye, he added, "If that is your wish."

"Can there be any doubt what I wish? My future has been planned since I was a boy. Upon my sword, I'll not have it destroyed because some toothsome girl took a notion to wed me."

Shaking his head sadly, Matthew answered, "You were always the most ambitious of us all, Valor. You should have been the firstborn. Stephan has not half the desire for worldly goods as you."

"Stephan has never had the need. He's always known he would inherit. Don't dare compare me to my brother."

"You've yet to ask about his health. Since I've taken a vow of poverty, if he dies everything will be yours. Is that what you want?"

Clenching his fists, Valor spoke through gritted teeth. "Your priestly clothing will not save you from my fists if you as much as hint of that again. You know I love Stephan."

Then, fearing Matthew's words had some deeper meaning, Valor asked anxiously, "What prompted you to speak so? Is his condition worsening?"

"Nay. Thanks to your new wife, he's on the mend. She went to him as soon as I released her from the chapel and has been with him through the night."

"What?" Close to panic, Valor shouted, "You left her alone with Stephan! Are you mad?"

Forgetting the pain in his head, he strode out of the chapel, stopping only long enough to ask directions to Stephan's bedchamber from a passing servant.

Matthew followed him, amused that Val should be

so worried about what Raena might do to Stephan. He had much to learn about his faery wife.

But then, Valor was ignorant of anything pertaining to the Fair Ones. In truth, not many humans were even aware of their existence. Would that he himself had no knowledge of them. . . . Life would be far less complicated.

Bursting into Stephan's bedchamber unannounced, Valor saw Raena bending over his brother's bed, her head so close to his, she must surely be kissing him.

Enraged, he grabbed her arm and pulled her away. "Leave my brother be, witch. Have you no conscience at all, trying to seduce a sick man?"

"Valor! What in God's name has gotten into you? Lady Raena was just helping me sit up."

Gazing at Stephan, Val was surprised to see how well he looked. Then, turning to the girl, he saw the shocked, hurt expression on her face and knew how grievously he had wounded her. "I misunderstood. Forgive me. It's just . . ."

Her voice was tight and choked when she spoke. "You thought I wanted to seduce my husband's brother? How could you think such a thing?"

Lying in bed, Stephan's puzzled gaze traveled from Lady Raena's face to Val's and then to the one person he trusted who could explain what was happening, his brother Matthew. "What's this all about, Matt? Val calls Lady Raena a witch. She calls him her husband. Methinks I must still be delirious."

Matthew smiled ruefully. "Valor is the only delirious one in this chamber at the moment. That's his only excuse for being so ungracious toward the woman who saved your life, Stephan. If he had seen her minister to you throughout the night, he wouldn't be so quick to condemn her."

Valor looked at Matthew in disbelief. How could he—of all people—defend this pagan creature? Then the words sank into his head and he exclaimed, " 'Tis she who brought forth this miracle cure?"

"Aye," Stephan answered. "She was by my side all night with her cool compresses and endless tankards of water to flush out my sickness. Never complaining, not even when all that lifegiving water caused me to have to relieve myself in the earthen bowl she provided. She was here, seeing to my needs like an angel from heaven."

Torn between his gratitude to Raena for saving Stephan and his rage at having been enchanted, Val lashed out, "Do not put her with the angels, brother. She is surely from a much lower place. Methinks she is, indeed, a witch."

Raena's hurt was compounded by his insensitivity to her feelings. Striking back, she cried, "I wish I were, for I'd turn you into an ugly toad and have done with you."

With that, she stormed out of the room and headed for the stable. She needed to get away from Valor Godwin. Away from everyone in the confining castle. She'd ride to the faery circle, the only place she could call her own.

Saera Wigglesworth watched from the tower window as Raena rode away, knowing full well where she was headed. There was yet a chance for saving this union between the reluctant young couple.

Making her way into Stephan's chamber, she approached Sir Valor with great boldness. "Lady Raena has ridden off alone. Must you be reminded that she's your responsibility now? If anything happens to that poor child 'twill be on your head."

Valor looked in turn at each face in the silent

chamber and felt their disapproval. Turning his back to them, he tried to block them out, but there was no way he could block out the image of the girl.

When he became a knight, he had taken a sacred vow to protect the weak and the helpless; he couldn't turn his back on Raena, riding the countryside alone. Anything could happen to the girl.

"Where shall I seek her?"

Saera smiled triumphantly.

Six

All was still, Raena thought, sighing in contentment. It was ever so when she came to the faery stones. After the jarring noise of the castle, it was sweet music to her ears. In truth, she enjoyed the silence as if it were the grandest song played by master musicians.

Being here always brought back memories of Sherwood Forest. There, she had thrived on the soft rustle of leaves when the wind came to visit, the crystal clear sound of bird-song in the morn. Interspersed with pure stillness, those pleasant sounds had for years been her comfortable companions as she strode through the woods and danced in the meadows.

If not for missing her father, she would have been happy to live there forever with no one but her beloved Wiggles for company and her dear friend Robin of Locksley, who visited her there from time to time. She smiled, thinking of him. Though he was a few years older than she, he was always eager to roam the woods with her, climb with her to the top of the highest trees, where they would talk for hours or at least until Wiggles found them, as she always did.

She enjoyed Robin's company, for he paid no attention at all to the faery part of her—or even, for that matter, to the fact that she was female.

'Twas as if he were immune to her faery glamour, and she was glad for that. In truth, it had never been spoken of between them and she had no idea if he even knew she was a half-ling child.

She was thirteen the last she saw of him. Wiggles had told her he didn't come anymore because he had outgrown childish play, that he had grown up much sooner than he should and was making a name for himself through all of England as the savior of the poor and downtrodden.

She was neither poor nor downtrodden, but he would surely be her savior if he would only come to her now. She was certain no one but he could possibly understand what it was like to be so different from everyone else.

No wonder she thought of the faery stones as her refuge. Here, she could be herself. Here, she could dance and play, think and dream. Here, she could inhale the wild beauty and be at peace. She had found this place by accident on a long walk and had told no one of it, save for Wiggles, from whom she kept no secrets.

She dared not tell her father. He might lock her up or send her back to Sherwood Forest. But she couldn't blame him for that, considering what had happened here, at this very spot, so very long ago.

Wiggles had told her that none but those with faery blood could enter the faery circle and escape unscathed, that being here was a dangerous undertaking for mortal man. Woman, too, she thought, thinking of her dead mother.

She often thought of her mother when she came here. Indeed, it was the only time she dared let herself think of her. She had been just a babe when her mother jumped from the tall ramparts of the castle.

'Twas most fortunate Raena had not tumbled into the sea as well, for 'twas said her mother had held her clutched tight in her arms up to the very moment that she jumped.

She often wondered what had compelled her mother to set her safely down. A moment of clarity in her muddled, tortured mind? Wiggles had tried to explain that her mother had been driven mad by her desire to be with the Prince of Dawne, the tempting faery who had seduced her, but 'twas hard to fathom that.

'Twas hard for her to think of that faery prince as her natural father. In truth, she had tried to bury all thoughts of him. Because of him, her mother was dead, lost to the sea, her body never found.

If only she had been born to Henry Caldwell. If only she had no trace of faery blood in her veins. Because of it, she was doomed to a life of loneliness, separated from the people of Caldwell Castle as if there were an invisible wall between them.

But enough of this melancholy. It was a useless thing. Mayhap she would try one of the chants Wiggles had taught her, for that special music was the way to communicate with her faery kin.

Nay, not this day. She would rather concentrate on the extraordinary man who was her reluctant bridegroom.

Closing her eyes, she leaned up against a standing rock and envisioned his handsome face. Of certain, he was a man among men. For who else but he could have fought against her faery glamour so well? It bespoke his courage that he would even try.

She knew little of men, but one thing was all too clear. She had learned early in life that the part of them between their legs was their greatest weakness. 'Twas no wonder it was so easy to charm them into bed.

"There you are!"

Startled, Raena looked up to see Valor standing between two of the standing rocks. One more step and he would be inside the circle.

"No!" she cried, rushing into his arms, propelling him outside the circle with the force of her body.

Caught off guard, he tumbled backwards, landing with a thud on the ground, Raena sprawled on top of him. Catching his breath, he said, "I wasn't expecting such an enthusiastic welcoming."

Compelled to action by the sudden armful of soft female, he closed his arms around her and reveled in the sweet touch of her, despite himself. Gazing into her eyes, such a short distance away, he was struck by their vibrant, lavender color. "You've got the strangest eyes I've ever seen."

Once again Raena was forced to remember how very different she was from everyone else. She tried to struggle out of his arms; but he held her so tight, she could barely breathe. "And you've got the strangest way of showing gallantry that I've ever had the misfortune of witnessing. Let me up. I have no desire to be in your rude company."

"Not until you tell me what compelled you to knock me down like that. I could have fractured my skull."

"And if you had, you'd still be better off than if I had let you enter the circle."

"Let me? *Let* me? Do you think you have control over everything I say or do? Not even your infernal faery glamour is as powerful as that."

"Is that the gratitude I get for saving you from going mad? Surely you know the folly of entering a faery circle. Everyone raised around here knows of the danger."

Val laughed heartily. "Is that what this is all about? You were saving me from a fate worse than death? Such irony. I thought I was saving you from that very same fate by riding out here after you. Don't you know, 'tis unwise for young maidens to travel the countryside alone?"

Gazing deep within his eyes, she felt a shiver of excitement. Her voice lowered to a husky purr when she answered, "The only danger I seem to be in at the moment is from you, Sir Knight."

Suddenly sober, Val abruptly pushed her off him and rose to his feet, brushing away the dried leaves and dirt that clung to his tunic. "Believe me, you're in no danger of being ravished. I mean to go ahead with the annulment of our altogether-illegal marriage. Hard though it might be to believe, your beauty is not nearly enough enticement to make me change my mind."

In righteous anger, Raena rose to her feet, standing with her hands on her hips. "You'd do well to reconsider. My father tells me you're a third-born son and, therefore, not in any position to pick and choose. Marriage to me would bring you Caldwell Castle and all its holdings."

With a magnanimous sweep of her arms, she said, proudly, "The moment our marriage is consummated, all this will be yours."

Val tried to keep from laughing, but it spilled out anyway. "I'm sorry. I don't mean to laugh, seeing how serious you are; but 'tis plain you have no idea what wealth awaits me when I marry Lady Elizabeth Plantagenet. She's the favorite daughter of Prince John, though, in truth, she was born on the wrong side of the blanket. King John himself offered her, knowing that she'd be marrying into one of England's most respected families. That alone will afford me and my entire family entry into the court's inner circle. Tell me, what is Caldwell Castle in comparison to that?"

Raena's heart sank. All was lost if what he said was true. But still, for her father's sake, she was compelled to try one more time. "Well, I, too, am the daughter of a prince. A prince of the faery tribe of Dawne. I can bring you great knowledge. What is wealth in comparison to that?"

Val laughed again, but without derision. She was really an admirable young woman. But it wouldn't do to dwell on that. If he were to leave Caldwell a free man, he'd find it more profitable to keep her angry with him.

"Really? Do you actually believe you're a princess royal? I can see us now, being presented at court. Sir Valor Godwin and his lady wife, the faery princess of Dawne. Why, they'd laugh me out of the country!"

Swallowing her hurt, Raena tried to keep from crying. "It seems the valiant knight is not so very perfect after all, for, verily, he lacks one admirable trait. Gallantry."

Gathering her dignity, she smoothed down her clothing, then walked away from his ridicule with her chin stuck exceedingly high. She made her way up the path to the top of the ravine, her mind in turmoil. Her new husband clearly had no use for her and wanted to rid himself of her at first chance. That bothered her more than she cared to think about.

For it wasn't pride alone that made her resent his rejection, but knowing how heartbroken her father would be when he found out their marriage would not be consummated.

Oh, why had he picked that stubborn knight to be her husband? Wouldn't another have done just as well?

She knew the answer to that.

Her father had wisely picked the one man whose principles could not be compromised. From her father's point of view, that made Sir Valor the perfect choice.

As for her own view of the situation, much as she wished differently, she couldn't help but be impressed by the man. He did stand out. A man amongst men. If she had to be wife to any man, then let it be to Sir Valor Godwin.

Well, there it was. Her father needed to see her married to a good man before he died, and he had chosen one so superior that even she could see the merit in marrying him. That left but one choice.

She must use her faery glamour once again.

But this time, this time, she would be sure it happened in a more fitting place for Christian and pagan alike.

Valor watched as Lady Raena walked away, almost regretting to see her go. Despite everything, she was a delightful handful of femininity. Even so, he had deliberately made her angry and was pleased to know that he, too, had a weapon to use against her bewitchment. Ah, if only anger would work as well on him. Whenever he was near her, he had to force himself to keep from taking her in his arms.

Even now, hours after she had broken the erotic spell over him, she still had a devastating effect on him.

Following after her, he mounted his horse to escort her back to the castle. He rode in silence, angry with himself and with her for the desire that rode between them as if it were a palpable, living thing.

He knew in the sweet temptation of her soft lips, the exotic beauty of her lavender eyes, he would be fighting a greater war than ever he had fought against Saladin. For he battled for his very soul.

Seven

Surreptitiously, Raena glanced over at Valor as he galloped down the road ahead of her. Her body still tingled from their close contact, a few moments ago, and her mind—oh, dear—her mind kept wandering to thoughts of what it would be like to mate with him.

Though she was still a virgin, she had no fear of lying with him. Her faery spirit was too strong to fear anything of nature. And mating must surely be one of nature's most enjoyable acts, else there wouldn't be so much of it going on.

In Sherwood Forest, she had witnessed all manner of creatures procreating and knew what to expect. And, too, her dear Wiggles had more than prepared her for the moment of her own deflowering. And then . . . there had been the night of the Beltaine festival. . . .

She would never forget that strange event as long as she lived. She had been all of thirteen when Wiggles took her and Robin to the edge of the forest to watch the secret pagan ceremony . . .

Hiding in a thicket, they witnessed a godlike man with a thick white beard and long hair the same color standing naked before a stone altar bedecked only with the antlers of a stag fastened to his head.

She watched from her hiding place in complete awe whilst Wiggles explained in a low whisper what was going on. The man was no god, but a powerful duke who on this pagan festival day each year doffed his Christian clothes and Christian demeanor and took on the appearance of a pagan deity.

In days of yore, high lords such as he had the right to deflower any virgin of their choice on Beltaine Day, and it seemed that ceremony continued even now under the cover of secrecy and the dark of night.

The duke took two virgins that night, right there in front of their parents and the other villagers, and then pressed a coin into the hands of each of the girls' fathers when he was done. Watching, Raena could only wonder if the poor folk permitted the ceremony because they were still pagans at heart or whether the color of the duke's coin had mesmerized them. Most likely they had no say in the matter, for a duke's power was all-reaching.

Later, on the way back to their cottage, Wiggles had prompted, "Tell me, children, what you learned this night."

Raena thought it over before she answered, wanting to be sure what she said would not sound too childish. "I learned that being deflowered is not pleasant but can be endured."

Wiggles nodded her head solemnly, although it seemed to Raena that there was mirth in her eyes. "Ah, yes. That is a good lesson to learn. And what about you, Robin? What have you learned?"

Through gritted teeth Robin answered, "I learned that the powerful prey on the weak and force them to their will."

Raena was surprised that Robin should come to that conclusion and began to understand how deep his feelings of resentment were toward those with wealth and power.

Wiggles patted Robin on the shoulder, letting him know that she sympathized with him, then turning to Raena, *she asked, "Can you think of anything else you've learned?"*

Thinking of the duke in his pagan attire, she said, tentatively, "That people are not always what they seem to be?"

"Bright girl. Remember that lesson. It will keep you in good stead."

"Wiggles?"

"Yes, child?"

"Are you what you seem?"

"Not entirely. For my protection I appear to all who gaze upon me as a harmless, crooked old woman, and so I must appear to you and Robin, too."

"Oh, but you are so much more than that. You are beautiful and wise, lithe of foot and strong of will."

Wiggles bestowed a rare smile upon her. "Aye, you see me with love's eyes, which is another thing entirely."

Robin, however, had a question. "I don't understand, Saera," he pondered. "Why do you feel the need to hide your true self?"

"Because elven and faery folk have been all but driven from this land. First by a terrible scourge that decimated the fey people and then by the superstitious fears of humans. For our very survival we must stay hidden. That's why we live, for the most part, underground, away from the vigilance of humans who want to erase our kind from the earth."

"But why is that? Why cannot both peoples share the world we live in? Why do they hate you so?"

" 'Tis not hate that motivates them, but fear. Humans fear what they do not know or understand. What they cannot see or touch or taste. That's why they persecute beings who have developed their natural abilities to a higher state."

"Higher state?" Robin asked in wonderment.

"Aye. What seems like magic to humans is in reality

nothing more than using the mind and body to the very highest degree. Had humans not been so fearful, they, too, might have evolved much further. But there's no use speaking of what might have been. We must deal with the reality of what is."

Robin pondered what Wiggles said for a while, then said, "I understand all you have said, Wiggles, but there is one thing that puzzles me. Why do you live amongst humans? Are you not afraid they'll discover you are elven?"

"Because, Robin, I've been sworn to protect our little Raena. And when you are grown, I do dare hope you'll protect her, too."

"But what need is there to protect her? Who would want to harm a little girl?"

"Ah, Robin, the truth is that you and she are very special, in different ways, of course. But I cannot speak of the rhyme and reason of it now, for I've been sworn to secrecy. You'll know soon enough, I ken, when you are old enough to understand."

Satisfied with that answer, Robin pranced ahead until he was out of sight. In a conspiratorial tone, Wiggles leaned closer to Raena and, speaking barely above a whisper, said, "As for living amongst the humans, I have little fear of them, having spent my life studying their kind. No, 'tis not they that I fear, but extinction. You see, child, elves and faeries are superior to humans in every way save the most important way. The ability to reproduce.

"Between the terrible scourge and being forced to live underground away from the life-giving warmth of the sun, females have all but lost their ability to give birth to healthy children."

Looking Raena directly in the eyes, she murmured, "For our survival, our males have been forced to mate with human females in an attempt to keep our race alive."

"Is that why Prince Ohreinn seduced my mother?"

Patting her lovingly on her shoulder, Wiggles answered, "Aye, child. Your birth was precious to our cause, for few human females can bear a faery child for the full span of incubation. Half are aborted very early on; and of those who are not, none with wings have been born alive."

"How sad. It must be glorious to have wings. To have such wonderful freedom. To be able to soar with the falcons and hawks. I wish I had been born with wings."

"I, too. 'Tis lamentable that elven people have none. I fear that's why our nature is so earthy whilst that of the faery is so airy and wild. And now, it seems, even the faeries will be denied that gift."

"But surely, surely you have not given up hope that it might still happen? That a human female will give birth to a child with wings?"

"We do dare hope for that miracle birth, else faeries will be forever lost. 'Twould be a far less vibrant world without them."

"Oh, why couldn't I have been born with wings? I would so love to save the faeries."

"Child, though you are wingless, you do give us hope. You were born with all the special gifts of your kind, save that one. You have all the best traits of Faerie, even down to your beautiful, lavender eyes. And who knows, someday when you're grown, you may be the one to give birth to a winged one. It is my most fervent hope."

Seeing Robin running back toward them, his arms outstretched as if he were flying, Wiggles laid a hand on her shoulder and whispered, "What I've said is for your ears only. Not even Robin knows that you are faery, and 'tis best to leave it that way."

Robin came to a stop in front of them and, puffed up with pride, announced, "Never fear, I shall protect you, Raena. For you are special to me, too. You have only to call out my name, and wherever I am, I shall fly to your side though I have not wings."

Remembering that day made Raena more determined than ever to make Valor her husband. It would take a strong man, a good and noble knight such as he, to protect her from humankind. For what if Wiggles's wish were granted? What if she gave birth to a winged child? She couldn't count on Robin for, despite his vow that day, he was too busy protecting the poor to come to her—and she would have it no other way. What were her small troubles compared to those of others?

Suddenly, an uneasy thought came to mind. If Wiggles were so keen on her giving birth to a faery, why had she agreed to this union with a human? Surely mating with another faery would be far more likely to produce winged offspring.

Had Wiggles given in to her father's will? Knowing her mentor's stubborn elven nature, Raena couldn't believe that. Ah, but what did it matter? She trusted Wiggles. She knew her better than she knew her father, for she had been in Saera Wigglesworth's care all her life.

The two of them had lived alone in Sherwood Forest with none but wild creatures for companions, save for Robin. She would push that troubling thought from her mind and concentrate on what she must do now.

Consummate her marriage to Sir Valor Godwin.

Riding back to her father's castle alongside Valor, she was surprised and chagrined to find an entourage of riders carrying the Godwin banner of crimson and cream in the bailey. Her heart lurched. Had Lady Elizabeth come to claim Valor?

Valor must have wondered the same, for as soon as he helped her dismount he accosted a squire. "I sent you to my father's house to tell him of our circumstance," he said with a trace of impatience.

"Why have you returned? Did my father and Lady Elizabeth travel with you?"

"Nay, Sir Valor, 'tis Lady Caroline who insisted on journeying here immediately upon learning of her husband's condition. I had a devil of a time persuading her to wait until this morning to make the journey. She's with Sir Stephan this very moment."

Raena could see that Valor was relieved, but was it because her father wasn't here or was it Lady Elizabeth's absence that made him happy? She wanted to believe it was the latter. Ah, yes, but it was certainly understandable that he wouldn't be eager to explain to Lady Elizabeth why he had married another.

Hiking the hem of her underdress up, she ran after Valor as he made his way into the castle and up the stairs. "Wait for me. I want to meet Lady Caroline."

Valor laughed sarcastically. "Are you sure that's what you want? My brother's wife will hardly greet you with kind words, considering how intimately you nursed her husband. She might think you wish to steal him away from her."

Raena paused on the steps, afraid that what he said might be true, but the expression on his face gave his true feelings away. "Look in your heart, knight, for 'tis jealousy that makes you say that. Admit it. You don't truly think I did wrong."

"Ah, but I do, and so will Caroline. She'll want to know why you didn't engage a servant to see to such things as would make a virgin blush. That's what servants and old women are for, after all."

"Well, I don't care. I still wish to meet her. After all, she is part of my family now."

Valor gave her a withering look, then continued up the stairs and into the bedchamber.

She followed him inside, but held back near the door, suddenly timid in the presence of the beautiful lady who filled the chamber with her gracious presence.

Lady Caroline was fair of face and fair of hair and looked so angelic it fairly took Raena's breath away. Dressed most becomingly in a gown of a delicate fabric of pale blue and rose swirled together and accented with delicate gold trim, she exemplified womanhood, making Raena happy to be of the same sex as that lovely creature.

Bent over her husband, she lovingly caressed his hair. When Caroline tilted her face up to see who had entered, Raena was taken aback by the pure, unadulterated love that shone in her eyes.

Never before had she seen such an open display of affection. It radiated from Caroline, reaching into the darkest corners of the room and warming Raena's heart so thoroughly she almost gasped aloud and found herself instantly adoring her sister-in-law. And as for her sick husband, Sir Stephan was beaming brightly in the glow of all that love, How lucky he was to have her as his wife.

Upon seeing Valor, Caroline ran to him and was enveloped in his arms. Suddenly, it was Raena's turn to be jealous. How could anyone resist Lady Caroline's charms? Who could compete with all that radiance?

She spoke and—oh!—her voice was as heavenly as the rest of her. "Valor, 'tis good to see you looking so well, and my own Stephan, too. I came thinking to find him on death's door, and instead I find him on the mend thanks to the ministrations of two extraordinary women, so I've been told."

Then glancing over her shoulder to the dark-haired beauty who accompanied Valor, she murmured, "Is this Lady Raena?" Valor answered with a grim nod of his head.

Breaking free of his embrace, Caroline approached Raena with a fervent look in her eyes.

Raena held her breath, not knowing what to expect, when suddenly Caroline fell to her knees in front of her. Taking Raena's hands in hers, she kissed them in turn, sobbing loudly.

Astounded and completely disarmed, Raena let her gaze travel from Stephan on the bed, tears glistening in his eyes, to the priest Matthew, whose countenance she could not read, and then to Valor, who seemed as astonished as she at Caroline's unexpected action.

Matthew, the first one to recover, gently helped Caroline to her feet.

Unaware of anyone in the room but Lady Raena, Caroline murmured, "Thank you for nursing my Stephan. Without you and your wonderful Saera Wigglesworth, he would surely have died."

A hard lump formed in Raena's throat. Never had she ever been the recipient of such affection from a noblewoman—or any woman, for that matter, but her dear Wiggles. Staring into the beautiful, pale-blue eyes of the Lady Caroline, Raena could only nod her head. But, oh, she would remember this always.

Valor spoke then, breaking the sacredness of the moment with his bitter pronouncement. "Do not place her with the angels, for her powers are unholy."

Staring Valor down, Caroline answered, "I don't care if her powers come from the very devil himself. All that matters is, she saved my husband; and I will always be in her debt."

Raena, in awe of the powerful, unconditional love

Lady Caroline expressed for her husband, suddenly realized what a wonderful, magical force love could be. She envied Caroline and wished with all her heart that she, too, could share that kind of love with someone.

No, not just any someone, with Valor.

If she could be granted that one wish, she would never ask for anything again.

Stephan laughed merrily, lightening the mood in the chamber. "Methinks, Caroline and Raena will get along just fine. How different this scene would be if Elizabeth were present."

Valor stood silent and stone-faced.

"I don't mind telling you, I'm happy you came to your senses and married for love instead of wealth. 'Tis the greatest gift a man can have." Stephan reached out his hand for Caroline, and she walked to his bedside and clasped it in her own, beaming in turn at Raena and Valor.

Deeply moved and disturbed by Caroline's loving demeanor toward Raena, Valor fought his emotions. Could he be wrong about this stranger he was married to? But no, it wasn't worth contemplating; he couldn't so easily give up the future his father had planned for him. "You've been sadly misinformed. It wasn't love that drove me to marry Lady Raena so recklessly, but a witch's enchantment. I'm off to write a letter this very moment that will free me of this unholy alliance. Since there was no consummation, I doubt I'll have any trouble." With those cruel words, he left the bedchamber.

Saddened by Valor's brusque manner, Raena questioned whether she should go on with her plan to bind Valor to her. Would he hate her for it? That seemed more than likely. Oh, why couldn't he be more like his brother Stephan, who valued his wife above all else? But it was unfair to compare Valor to his brother. Who wouldn't adore the beautiful Caroline? And, too, it was possible Stephan would act the same way if he were third-born instead of first.

Feeling an arm on her shoulder, Raena turned and looked into Caroline's eyes. "Don't take what he said too much to heart. Valor doesn't know yet what he truly wants. He's spent his life under his father's influence, but I suspect that when he finally sorts things out, he'll be happy he has you instead of that lady of ice, Elizabeth."

Raena smiled. "Ah, but there's the rub, you see. There's been no consummation. He'll be free to go to her all too soon."

Wrapping her arm around Raena's shoulder, Caroline escorted her out to the hall. Then, squeezing her hand in a conspiratorial manner, she said, "You can remedy that. Go. Join him in his bedchamber. Give him reason not to write that letter."

Raena left, buoyed by Caroline's unexpected support. Her hope renewed, she had a tray of food made up to take to Val. After all, they hadn't eaten since breakfast.

Waiting nervously in the great hall for Esther to clear scraps of food from the table to the floor before concocting a tray for two, Raena noticed her father sitting forlornly by the fire. A shiver of fear winnowed through her. He seemed so frail and small, she knew his illness must be much worse.

Going to him, she knelt at his feet. "Father, are you in pain? Tell me what I can do for you?"

Henry looked up at her and a faint smile crossed his face. "Ah, 'tis just a minor twinge. It'll pass in a moment. There, you see, it's gone. I needed only to gaze upon your face to ease my pain."

Raena knew he was just saying that for her sake and loved him all the more for his consideration, but she hurt for him. If she could have taken on some of his pain to give him ease, she wouldn't have hesitated to do so.

"Child, I'm glad you're here. I was just now thinking about you and praying that you haven't abandoned hope of making your marriage binding."

"Oh, no, Father. Far from it. I've thought it over and have come to the conclusion that you are, indeed, wise to want me joined to Valor. He is an exemplary man. I swear to you upon my life that Sir Valor Godwin will become my devoted and loving husband before this night is done."

Seeing the pale glimmer of hope in her father's eyes, she knew she had pleased him with her words. He took her hand and pressed his lips to it, murmuring, "Then I shall rest in peace."

Raising her hands to sandwich his face between them, she tilted his head down and gently kissed his brow as she had done when she was little. "Rest now, Father; and when you awake, I will be Valor's wife in fact."

With that she rose, and with one last backward glance at him before she left the hall, she carried the tray of food up the stairs to Valor's chamber. Her father's words echoed in her mind uneasily. *Rest in peace.* Something about the way he'd said it gave her pause and she almost turned back; but as she came to a stop outside Valor's chamber, her heart quickened and everything left her mind but the task before her.

She knocked on the door and heard a muffled "Enter."

Swallowing hard, she opened the door and walked inside. Valor had taken off his tunic and was comfortably dressed in a shirt opened down the front. When he saw her, he immediately jumped up. "What are you doing here?"

Putting on an air of confidence she did not truly possess, she swallowed hard and said, "Is it so unusual for a wife to bring her husband food? Come sit at the table and eat. I'll join you, for I'm famished."

Valor looked at her suspiciously, then his face relaxed and he said. "Aye. We have things that must be discussed. We must reach an understanding, you and I."

Setting the tray of food on the small table by the hearth, she tried to take her mind from the sensuous sight he presented, but she couldn't help noticing how well he filled his shirt. She had the sudden desire to run her fingers beneath the fabric of his shirt and caress his beautiful, hard, muscled chest. "Uh, yes, I agree, but first, let's break bread and drink wine. I assure you, I'll be in a much more agreeable state after I've eaten."

The suspicious look came back. Taking a goblet of wine from the table, Valor sniffed it.

Raena smiled sweetly. "What is it, husband? Do you fear I've poisoned your wine?"

"The thought crossed my mind."

"Ah, but surely you know by now faeries have no need for artificial means. We can accomplish what we like with our natural powers." As soon as she said the words, she was sorry. She didn't mean to rub it in that she could force him to her will whenever she wanted.

"Is that why you're here? Do you still dare hope to consummate our marriage?"

"Oh, Valor, would that be so very terrible?"

She spoke so softly, so movingly, it stirred up his mixed emotions. He saw her in his mind's eye the way she had looked when she'd danced so magically, so erotically for him. It had haunted him ever since. No, making love to her would not be so very terrible.

Disarmed and vulnerable, he spoke to her from his heart, hoping, needing for her to understand how it must be. "Upon my sword, I cannot deny that you are the most beautiful and desirable creature I've ever seen or will ever see again. I'd give up anything to be with you, to lie between your soft thighs. Anything, that is, but my honor. That I cannot give up. I beseech you, don't make me betray everything I stand for. *Leave me in peace.*"

Ah, so it came down to that. Just moments ago her father had said he would rest in peace when the marriage was consummated, and now her husband was telling her he would be in peace if it was not.

She must choose between them. Gazing at the manly form of her husband, she sighed deeply.

Eight

In truth, there was no choice to be made.

Her father's peace was more important than anything else. She would not have him go to the grave without it.

But, oh, how she wished she could spare this lovely man. How she wished she could let him have his dignity and his blasted honor since they were so very important to him. But since that could not be, there was no reason to delay what must be done any longer.

"Valor . . . husband, if there were any other way my father could have a peaceful death, I'd give you up to your Lady Elizabeth; but alas, there is none. My father cannot last much longer, and I'll not allow him to die worrying about the fate of his daughter. I pray you can understand a daughter's devotion and forgive me."

Seeing the alarm that flashed across Valor's face, she knew he understood what was going to happen; and fearing he would flee before she could conquer his will, she let out her powerful scent in one tremendous explosion.

Valor staggered backwards, feeling the full magnitude of her enchantment, and a loud, unearthly moan escaped his lips. It was the sound of a man condemned to give in to the drive that engulfed him.

"Damn you, witch, don't do this. Don't destroy my future."

Gritting her teeth, she tried to block out the emotion that swept over her at his words and opened up her faery aura completely.

Never before had she dared to do that, and she feared the consequences. But she had no time for finesse. No time at all. She had to make Valor truly her husband before it was too late.

And then, strangely, an unexpected restlessness came over her. The erotic scent she had unleashed began to affect her as well until she worried that she might lose control of her own emotions.

Yet, still she let it happen. She had no choice, no goal but to bind Valor to her.

Her restlessness grew, surging like anger within her as the urge to mate with Valor became paramount. Something inside her had shifted, changed, altering her, and she sensed it was the very essence of her faery nature. What she felt now was, most certainly, alien to the part of her that was human.

All thought of sparing Valor vanished from her mind, replaced by her own needs and desires. It was the faery way, she knew, to be selfish, to care only about survival of their own, and for the first time in her life she truly felt one with the tribe of Dawne.

Valor watched the transformation from virgin to faery in horror. Precious blood of Jesus! He didn't have a chance. She had changed before his very eyes. Had become a wild, powerful creature, immune to any human pleading.

That she had given in to her faery nature was frightening and yet terribly exciting at the same time. The desirable creature she had been before was nothing to what she was now, and he barely noticed the erotic scent anymore, so overwhelmed was he by this new sensual being.

He had such great need to take her that it became impossible to think of anything else. Too far gone to care, he didn't even try. Nothing mattered but to be with her—in her—a part of her. And—oh, God—most of all, to drive his seed into her.

She began to disrobe, and he held his breath in awe. It was going to happen. Oh, God, after a lifetime of dreaming what it would be like to make love to a woman, it was finally going to happen. He stripped off his clothing, adoring her body with his eyes.

He was in tune to every beat of her heart, every breath that escaped her body, and he moved closer to her in desperate need to join with her in every way that was physically possible.

Reaching out, he pulled her to him with such force that she slammed into his chest, her breath escaping in a soft, fragrant whoosh.

He opened his mouth to capture it all and tasted her erotic scent. It nourished him, yet made him ravenous for more; and responding to the demand, his lips came down on hers in a fierce kiss.

Feeling Valor's naked skin against hers sent Raena reeling. Never had she felt such an exquisite need, an exquisite ache that had to be fulfilled. When his lips ground into hers, she almost fainted, the intense feeling too great to handle. Then, working on instinct alone, her hand found his manhood and tightened around it as if it were a lifeline.

And it was.

Without it, she feared she would dissolve into nothingness in the heat of her desire.

Valor cried out as if he were in pain and she released him instantly, but he took her hand and forced it back on his hardness once again. He wanted her to touch him, and she was most eager to do so for she had never felt anything akin to his enticing, velvet hardness.

And, oh, she knew where she wanted it.

She knew where it belonged.

But first—oh, yes, first—she wanted to do homage to this incredible man who would be her mate. Pulling herself free of him, she knelt at his feet and took that wonderful instrument into her mouth.

The taste and scent of him was every bit as intoxicating as her own faery scent, and she closed her mouth around it, wanting, needing, to savor all of it.

The hot, wet touch of her was too much for Valor, and he came in a violent convulsion that shook him to his core, spewing his seed down her throat and crying out like a wounded animal as a huge orgasm shook him.

At the same time he felt great victory.

He had escaped the consummation that would doom him to a dismal future.

He almost laughed out loud in triumph that she had done the one thing that could free him of her. But though he savored his freedom, he did not wish to humiliate her and he smothered his laughter.

Still caught inside the hot wetness of her mouth, he undulated his hips, savoring the lingering effects of the powerful rapture he had experienced; but then—oh merciful heavens—before he could even catch his breath, the need for her overwhelmed him again.

"Nooooo!"

She slid up his body like the serpent from the

Garden of Eden and he felt the touch of her breasts and nipples searing him with erotic heat.

He wanted her again, his need so strong, so powerful, it was impossible to deny.

She was standing before him now, and he was reaching for her breasts, fondling them, sinking his fingers into their sweet softness, reveling in the most wondrous of sensations.

His hands ventured out to seek other treasures, and he rejoiced in everything he found. This female, this splendid woman, was paradise, was home, was all the world he would ever need.

What was wealth or position next to this?

What was food or wine or the very air he breathed next to the thrill of her body?

Lost in her scent and aura, the erotic touch of her, Valor lowered her to the bed, the need to mate with her banishing all other thoughts from his mind. It was as if he were born this very moment. Born to take this woman, born to become one with her, to unite with her or die.

Raena felt the softness of the bed beneath her and sheer joy coursed through her body. Valor would be hers, and oh, how she wanted it to be so. The touch of his hands and mouth upon her was so much more wonderful than she could ever have imagined. She wanted him to go on forever and ever, exploring her body; and yet, at the same time, she wanted him to end her agony. She wanted to feel the rhythm of his body as he thrust into her over and over again.

Why couldn't she have both?

Surely he could go on touching her while he claimed her body. Surely this incredible ecstasy would not have to end at the consummation.

Sinking into the softness of the mattress, with the

contrasting hardness of his body on top of her, she marveled at the splendid sensations rippling through her body. She opened for him, wet with desire. She couldn't wait to feel him inside her and cried, "Valor, now, I need you inside me now."

Her voice penetrated Valor's senses and for one brief moment he realized fully the consequences of his actions.

If he didn't stop now, all would be lost.

If he didn't stop now, he could never claim his future in Prince John's court.

But the enchantment he was under moved over him again in a cloud of rapture so strong he forgot everything but the woman under him.

With one powerful lunge, he thrust inside her, his eyes closed tight as he rode the wave of desire that took him. Sensation after wonderful sensation thrilled through him, and virgin no more, he savored them all, knowing that for the rest of his life he would remember this moment.

Raena had expected to feel the pain Wiggles had told her was inevitable; but if there was any, it was hidden beneath the greater ache to mate with him, a much more potent pain than anything she had ever experienced before. Her muscles contracted involuntarily as she felt him push into her as far as he could go, and the enormity of feeling verily took her breath away.

Valor shuddered, feeling her close around him. With a groan, he retreated then pushed against her once more, carried away by such intense emotion it felt as if he were being ripped asunder.

Raena cried out from joy and ecstasy, from the overwhelming satisfaction of feeling him inside her. But no, the satisfaction she felt was not complete, for there was such a hunger for him to continue moving inside her she could not just lie there and wait. She wanted to participate in the act. To give as well as take.

She urged him on, moving under him, encircling his body with her arms and legs, pulling him closer to her until it truly felt as if they had merged into one erotic creature.

Seeing how wildly she responded, Valor gave himself up completely, holding nothing back. There was nothing timid about their lovemaking—nothing but pure bliss, and the feeling that what they did was what they had been born to do.

Having been satisfied earlier made it easier for him to go on longer now, and he was glad of that. He wanted to enjoy the lovely, slippery exploration of her body as long as he possibly could.

But Raena wouldn't allow that. Her need was becoming too great. She was crying for her release now, tears spilling down her cheeks. Giving in to her, he stepped up his thrusting until she tightened so hard around him he knew she was ready to come.

Raena felt his thrusts quicken and she thought she would explode. And then she did, and the aftershock took her to a place where she had never gone before.

She felt herself join with him body and soul, faery spirit and humankind melded into one magnificent being; and her exquisite joy spilled out in a voice that cried out to the heavens.

Valor heard her cry and felt jubilant that he could bring her such pleasure. And then he was cresting the wave of rapture, too, swept away in such bliss as he had never known existed. The tears he had tried so hard to hold back now fell to his cheeks as wave after wave of ecstasy raked over him. Drained of his strength, he collapsed on top of Raena.

All was still. Raena lay under Valor, exhausted and struggling for breath, in awe of what had transpired, but afraid, too. Afraid of what Valor would say to her now that he was no longer under her spell. Too cowardly to face him, she escaped quickly into a deep sleep.

A loud pounding on the door awoke her and Raena cried out her husband's name. She opened her eyes and in the dim light saw Valor standing by the door, his head buried in his hands. Her heart went out to him, knowing why he was so upset. He didn't want to open the door. Once it was discovered that they had been together, his bright future in Prince John's court was lost.

A voice from the other side of the door called out. "Valor, it's me. I need to speak to you."

Raena recognized the voice of Valor's priestly brother and she shriveled up inside when she saw the look of abject despair Valor gave her before he opened the door.

Stepping into the chamber, the priest said, "I was hoping to find you here. I'm looking for Lady Raena. Do you know where she is?"

Valor nodded toward his bed in silent resignation.

The priest took one look at her and groaned. "Too late. Too late. I should have known when the baron died so suddenly it was God's punishment on Raena for enchanting you into her bed."

A loud ringing sounded in Raena's ears. Surely she hadn't heard him right. With voice choking, she murmured, "My father . . . dead?"

Matthew saw her crumble and still he spoke harshly. Because of her, his brother's future was ruined. "Yes. Dead. God's punishment on you for your wicked enchantment."

For just a moment, Valor felt a bittersweet shard of vindication at his brother's words, but it vanished quickly at the sight of Raena's stricken expression. "For God's sake, man, where's your compassion?"

"Buried under the resentment I feel for what she's done to you. Don't you realize your future is lost now? If you hadn't bedded her, the marriage could have easily been annulled. Now things have become . . . complicated."

Raena pulled the covers over her head and willed the two men to leave. They spoke of the future when all she could think of was this terrible swift sense of great loss. She wanted to be alone in her grief, to mourn for her father. But her sorrow was tempered by an awareness that he had known before he died that she was safely married.

She was so glad that she had promised her father that Valor would be her true husband. It was the last thing she had ever said to him. It occurred to her then that he had surely taken that to heart, that he had been holding off death until he had been sure that Valor was committed to taking care of her. What must it have cost him to hold on for so long? How much pain had he kept hidden from her these past weeks?

She gave silent thanks to her new husband for coming into her life when he was most needed, for the knowledge that her adopted father had died in peace made it possible for her to go on with her life.

She didn't believe for a moment that the Christian God was punishing her. What the priest and Valor thought made no difference to her.

Feeling gentle hands through the blanket that

covered her, Raena knew they belonged to Wiggles. "Child, I'm here."

Throwing off the cover, Raena buried her face in Wiggles's bony shoulder. "Is it true? Is my father dead?"

"Yes, my child. He died a peaceful death, sitting by the fire in the great hall, a smile upon his face. It happened swiftly, mercifully; one moment he was sitting there talking to me, joking about the fine children you and Valor would make, the next moment he was gone."

"Then he knew I was well married to Valor?"

"Ah, yes, he knew. He had me follow you upstairs and report back to him when it was done."

Her eyes sought out Valor, who had become very quiet; and with her gaze locked onto his, she boldly proclaimed, "Then I have no regrets."

Nine

Her father was buried on a warm cloudless day when flowers carpeted the surrounding hills and the air was filled with bird-song. Raena took it as an omen that her father, indeed, was resting in peace, else the day would surely have been cloudy and stormy, the air rent with thunder instead of the cheery symphony of nature.

She took comfort from that, gratefully, for there was small comfort to be taken from her husband. Valor was of little use to her at the burial ceremony. Oh, he did give her use of his shoulder and arm for support, 'twas true. But though he lent her his strong body, she did not have that which she needed most, the compassion of his heart, the solace of his voice. In sooth, he had barely uttered a word to her since the moment they had been found together in his chamber.

Stephan was silent, too. Able to walk and move about now, he seemed puzzled by what was going on between her and Valor. 'Twas obvious Valor had not confided in him.

It was Wiggles and Lady Caroline who helped her make it through the sorrowful day without breaking down, but even those gentle women couldn't keep her from feeling so terribly alone in the world.

But late one night, under cover of darkness, Robin of Locksley, her childhood companion, slipped into the castle unseen and, for a short time, she was able to forget her grief.

All of England called him Robin Hood now, and she had heard there was a price on his head; yet still he had come to her.

When she got over the shock of seeing him, she flew into his arms, crying, "Robin, oh, Robin, I wish I were a child of thirteen again, immune to such terrible heartache."

Safely supported in Robin's strong arms, she let all the emotion she had been holding back pour out. She cried a long time, her head pressed against his manly shoulder, and it gave her the comfort that her own husband had denied her.

" 'Tis a hard place, this world we live in. But, Raena, you and I are strong. We'll both prevail, I promise you."

Hearing the hurt in his voice, she knew he was speaking of his own past suffering, too. His life had not been easy. Forgetting her own troubles, she couldn't help but worry over him and prayed that this act of kindness toward her would not cause him any harm.

They stood entwined in each other's arms for a long time without speaking, for, indeed, no words were necessary. Each knew what the other felt. Each derived comfort from the other as only lifelong friends can.

She inhaled his familiar, special scent that spoke of sunshine and trees, of velvet-green moss and all that was masculine and wonderful and felt a great contentment. She hadn't realized how much she missed her friend.

Tilting her head back to look in her eyes, he said,

"Raena, I promise you your grief will pass and one day soon you'll remember your father as he was in his prime and forget how he looked when he was so ill. Be comforted that he'll feel no more pain. Death sometimes comes as a friend."

"I know you're right, Robin, and I am comforted that Father is at last free of the terrible pain that racked his body. But I feel such loneliness already, I don't know if I can bear it."

"Why should you feel so lonely when you have a new husband to care for you?"

Bitterness permeated Raena's voice. "My husband? I doubt he'll ever truly be my husband."

Robin laughed merrily. "No man could resist you for long."

"You did."

"I was a boy then, and you a scrawny little faery child."

"Then you knew all along."

"I knew."

"But . . . but I never told you I was faery and I'm certain Wiggles never did. How did you know?"

Mischief sparkled in his eyes. "Someday you'll know the answer to that, but not now. I want you to have something to look forward to when next we meet."

"Oh, Robin, take me with you. Don't leave me alone with these cold castle folk. I want to go back to Sherwood Forest. I need to go back there. There's nothing for me here now that Father's dead."

Robin's face transformed from gaiety to compassion. "Ah, I wish I could. Truly. And I would, if I thought that was what you truly wanted. But methinks you are hurting too much right now to know what you want. Give your marriage a chance. Stay

with your husband for a time; and if you still feel
the need for Sherwood Forest at winter solstice,
you've only to send a messenger to me and I'll come
and bring you back with me."

Raena knew Robin was right. She was hurting too
much now to know what she truly wanted. She
would do as he asked and see the way things developed between her and Valor before she gave up on
him.

After Robin left, as surreptitiously as he had
come, Raena remembered that he hadn't answered
her when she'd asked him how he knew that she
was part faery. He had been deliberately evasive. But
why? Pondering that mystery gave her something
else to think of for a time.

She spent the night alone, as she had every night
since her father's death, and she dared to hope that
the reason her husband didn't join her was because
he didn't want to impose upon her in her time of
grief. But somewhere deep within, she feared it was
because he still would not accept that they were
truly man and wife.

Awaking the next morn, Raena was surprised to
find her nursemaid waiting patiently at her bedside.

"Wiggles, how long have you been standing
there?"

"For a time, but then what else have I to do?"

"Verily, you seem out of sorts. What troubles
you?"

"Hmph, when have you ever seen me out of
sorts?" She grinned wickedly and Raena smiled, assured that all was well.

"Gosling, you must prepare yourself. The castle
is alive with activity. Your husband and his kin have
ordered an inventory of all the baron's possessions

and are about it this very moment. Never in my life have I seen a castle so torn asunder."

Wiping the sleep from her eyes, Raena said, "I don't understand. Why is Valor doing that? It all belongs to him now. Isn't it enough for him to know that?"

"Evidently not." Leaning close to Raena, Wiggles whispered, "But there is one room they shall never inventory. One chamber secret from everyone but your father and me, and now you."

Pulling a leather cord from around her neck, Wiggles dangled it in front of Raena. "This golden key unlocks the secret room where your tribal birthright gifts are kept."

"Birthright gifts? This is the first I've heard any mention of them."

"You'll know of them now, for I shall show you everything bestowed upon you by the elders of the elves and faery tribes."

"Why was I never told?"

"Your father and I thought it best not to parade those treasures in front of the castle and town folk. It could have caused all manner of troubles if word had gotten back to Prince John."

"Are the gifts so very precious then?"

"Some are, for amongst our kind you are a princess of royal blood, revered by all. Some of the gifts are precious only to those of our tribe—made from things of the earth and sky, the trees and flowers."

"And what am I to do with these gifts?"

"Do? Why anything you wish. Or nothing at all. 'Tis your choice."

"May I see them? Where is this secret chamber?"

"Get dressed and I'll show you. You needs must know how to find it in case something happens to me."

"Oh, do not speak of that. I couldn't bear to lose you, too."

"Oh, my sweet Gosling, wipe away your tears. I'm not in danger of perishing just yet. It's just that you need to know what I alone know, else that knowledge be forever lost. Do you understand?"

Raena nodded her head, then scrambled to her feet, eager for the adventure ahead.

Saera Wigglesworth shook her head in wonder. It had always been so; the volatile girl had always had the ability to go from abject misery to sheer joy in the twinkling of an eye. 'Twas her faery blood that made it so.

Raena dressed quickly, then followed Wiggles down the stairs to the great hall. Valor was seated at a trestle table, a charger of food in front of him. Averting her eyes, she marched by him, not wanting to confront him at this awkward moment. She found it hard to reconcile his need for such a speedy inventory of her father's possessions.

Valor watched his wife pass by, surprised when she didn't acknowledge his presence. It was as if she didn't even see him. She seemed intent on following the old one through a narrow door. His gaze followed her, raking over her comely form.

Evidently faeries had no use for mourning clothes, for she was dressed in a soft, clinging dress of sleek, silver velvet. That it hugged her curves down to her hips was not lost on him, and he felt himself grow hard just gazing at all that exquisite femininity.

The sleeves of her dress were long and slender, coming to a point at the apex of her fingers, and— oh, wondrous to behold!—her head was free of a wimple, her hair cascading down to her waist in a magnificent black cloud. The only adornment on her head was a bronze circlet of entwining Celtic knots.

He rose, determined to follow her, but Matthew stopped him with a tug on his arm.

"Valor, the inventory has begun in earnest. I've assigned a man for every chamber, every nook and cranny in the castle. And I myself will scribe everything into a book." Seeing where his brother's attention lay, he added, "I think it wise that you take your mind off the very thing that caused all this trouble and participate in the inventory personally."

"Hmm? Oh, yes, I want to survey everything myself so I can have some idea of how very little I'm worth."

"Do I detect a note of bitterness in your voice, brother? Actually, I think you'll find the baron was more affluent than we've been led to believe."

"Oh? Tell me his estate is worth half as much as Lady Elizabeth's and I'll be more than content."

"You know that's not true, but I have discovered one bit of cheery news. Caldwell Castle is in much better repair than our father's castle. That's one thing to be thankful for."

"I'll try to remember that when father is shunned by the king and makes my life more miserable than ever with his complaints."

Raena followed Wiggles down the steps that led to the storerooms. She was surprised when Wiggles made a sudden sharp turn, stopping before a carved wall with strange markings on it.

"Halfway between the darkness and the light. That's where we be. This secret place was chosen for its symbolic location."

Raena's excitement grew as she watched Wiggles take out the golden key and place it in one of the markings. Before her very eyes, a hidden door squeaked and groaned its way open.

Wide-eyed with wonder, Raena entered the secret chamber and was immediately struck by the truly unusual gifts of gold and silver, wood and metal, and all manner of substances she had never seen before.

Amongst all the splendor, a few objects stood out. Over there was a miniature chair carved from wood with intricate flowers and animals painted on it. And, oh, yes, there was a golden cart embedded with rubies and emeralds.

And there, hanging from the low ceiling, was a mantle of feathers from some exotic bird, soft and vibrant with color. And there on the floor were tiny shoes made from a fabulous, shimmering fabric, embellished with infinitesimal flowers that still looked fresh and new.

"Oh, Wiggles, how wonderful! How extraordinary! I love them all." Then, spying a small ornate mirror with a handle carved from ivory, she turned it over to look at the beautiful carvings of wood nymphs on the back. "May I have it? Am I allowed to take it from here?"

"It's yours, but be careful with it, child. Be careful of whom you allow to gaze into it. For that mirror is from your Aunt Edainn, the powerful and dangerous Faery Queen. It has great magic about it. Whosoever gazes into it shall see themselves as they truly are."

"But what is so dangerous about that?" Raena had never gazed into a looking glass before. The closest she had come to seeing herself as others saw her was in the reflection of water and, suddenly eager, she turned it over and gazed into the silvery pool of light.

Staring at her reflection, Raena was surprised at the vivid color of her eyes. The girl who stared back at her was familiar, yet strange. She had never realized how high her cheekbones were. How straight her nose. "Oh, Wiggles, is that what I truly look like?"

"Yes, Gosling. Your beauty radiates out from within. In truth, you are no different when you look into the mirror because you are good through and through. There is no darker side to you. But others who gaze into the mirror might find their true selves much changed from the image they portray for the world."

"Oh, do look in it, Wiggles. I want to see your true self."

Wiggles smiled sadly. "For you I will do it this one time, but I prefer not to be reminded of my true self. Not as long as I must keep it hidden from humankind."

Taking the mirror from Raena, Wiggles gazed into it.

A lovely young face gazed back.

Seeing the beautiful image brought tears to Raena's eyes. "Oh, Wiggles, whenever I dream of you, that's the way I see you. How can you willingly give up that beautiful countenance just to care for me? 'Tis too much to ask of you. Too much to ask of anyone."

Tears glistened in the eyes reflected in the mirror. " 'Tis my choice, Gosling. Don't pity me. You are the future of our race. You and a few others who have survived. 'Tis an honor to be chosen to care for you. And now, you're doubly protected, for you have that good knight to watch over you. He wasn't the one *I* chose for you; but no matter, together he and I will keep you safe."

A sudden thudding echoed through the chamber, and Saera Wigglesworth put a finger over her mouth.

Raena understood and became silent. Someone was on the stairs outside. A muffled voice drifted through the walls of stone and wood.

"I don't understand. I could have sworn she came down here with her nursemaid. Where could they have vanished to?"

"You must have been mistaken, Valor. 'Tis dark as pitch down here," Matthew answered irritably. "Why do you seek her anyway? I'd think you'd not be so anxious to find her after what she's done to you."

"Matthew, for God's sake, what's done is done. There's no use in dwelling on it."

"No use? No use? Are you still under a spell? Have you not thought of father? You'll have to face him sooner or later, you know. And Elizabeth, too. The sooner 'tis done, the better. I hate to think what would happen if father found out from someone else."

"Do you think I've thought of anything else? I can't sleep at night for worrying about it. But you're right. We'll leave at first light for Godwin Castle. I'll tell father and face the consequences once and for all and be done with it."

"And what of your new bride? Will she be accompanying you?"

"Would you bring her home to father if she belonged to you?"

"Not if I wanted to keep her. Knowing father's temper, he's liable to kill her in rage. And if not he, than surely Elizabeth would."

"Ah, a point well taken. However, I have no choice but to keep her. I can't risk losing the assets she's brought to the marriage, meager though they be. As for Elizabeth, she'll not suffer long. Her list of suitors will grow longer every day."

Raena heard it all and wept silent tears. How ironic. She sat but a few feet from her husband, surrounded by the kind of wealth he craved so desperately, and she knew she could never show him this treasure.

For though he might be happier about their marriage if he knew, he would never come to love her for herself alone. Selfish though it might be, she wanted to be the only treasure Valor desired.

She wanted to be loved. But not even her faery enchantments could make that happen.

Ten

Determined not to be left behind like some dusty moth-eaten tapestry upon the wall, Raena clutched her mirror to her chest and made her way up the spiral stairs to her bedchamber. She immediately set about packing everything she would need at Godwin Castle.

Her mind was set.

She would go with Valor whether he wanted her to or not. He would not so easily escape his duty. Quickly filling a large wooden chest, she sat down on top of it and folded her arms in her lap, breathless with exhaustion and frustration. Just let him try and stop her. Why she'd—she'd use her faery glamour right in front of everyone, if she must, to get her way.

A light rapping sounded on the door and her heart quickened, sensing it was he. Coming to tell her goodbye, was he? Well, she'd just see about that. Hiding her anger behind a deceivingly temperate voice, she called out, "You may enter."

Valor opened the door, pausing awkwardly just inside. "I, uh, I've come to tell you that I'll be leaving at first light for my father's castle and . . ."

Raena's jaw tightened, ready for the argument ahead. "I know. I've already packed for the journey."

Valor saw her determination, and though he tried to fight it, he was moved by her forlorn aspect. She looked like an abandoned puppy though she hid it behind a brave front. "Have you now? How did you know I was leaving?"

"I know many, many things, husband, for I am a princess of the tribe of Dawne."

A frown furrowed his brow. "No need to remind me of that. 'Twould be hard to forget. In any case, I'll be leaving very early and will be traveling light, so no more than two attendants may accompany you."

Raena couldn't believe her ears. "You—you want me to go with you? I thought. . . . I mean, yes, of course, I shall be ready."

Seeing he had caught her off guard, Valor smiled to himself. It was nice knowing that he could have the upper hand with this strong-willed creature. "The visit will be brief. In fact, father may turn us away at the door when he hears the news of our marriage. He's worked and schemed to make my marriage to Elizabeth a reality, and he's been counting on the great advantage it would give him in his dealings with Prince John. So, I must warn you, it may not be pleasant meeting him."

Remembering what she had overheard him say when she was in the treasure room, she couldn't help but wonder why he had changed his mind and now wanted her to brave his father's anger.

"Then pray tell me why you want me to accompany you. Mayhap, you hope your father will do away with me so you'll be free to marry Lady Elizabeth."

"Without a doubt, you are the most contrary female it's ever been my misfortune to know. If you knew me better, you'd know I take my responsibilities seriously. No harm will come to you in my care, I promise you. If you'll not take me at my word, then I'll swear upon my sword. Surely that should convince you that I speak the truth. No knight worth his salt would ever give a sacred oath lightly."

Ashamed of her wicked thought, Raena's heart melted. She could feel his sadness, his resignation, and yes, his anger, though his face showed none of that.

She deeply regretted that he had to suffer so much. "That won't be necessary. I know you to be an honorable man." Aye, he was that, and so much more. "Valor . . ." Reaching out to touch his sleeve, she tried to speak though her voice was choked with emotion. "I'm so very sorry for the grief I've caused you. I wish . . ."

Valor turned and left without saying a word, leaving Raena feeling lonelier than ever.

The journey to Godwin Castle was so surprisingly short, Raena couldn't help but think of how close destiny had come to depriving her of Valor.

If Stephan had been able to travel but a few hours longer, they would have made it to Godwin Castle and the future would have been so different for them all.

Was it possible that destiny had brought him to her when she had such great need of him? She wanted so to believe that, for it would mean that they were meant to be together and that what she had done to him was not so terrible after all.

Short though the journey was, she was grateful it was no longer, for the sun beat unmercifully down on them. She wished to fling off her wimple and let the air caress her hair and skin, but she couldn't.

She had to look her proper best when she met her new family.

Especially Valor's father. The thought of his reaction when he learned that she had ruined his plans sent a cold shiver up her spine that even the hot sun could not warm.

Glancing over at Valor riding beside her, she thought he looked so cool and calm that the gods must surely be playing a trick on her, sending the heat only to her and sparing him. But she knew that was just her foolish imagination at work.

She continued to stare at Valor, struck by his handsome features. He was so fair of face, so light of hair, so opposite of herself, 'twas like the difference between night and day. But she liked it that way.

'Twas true her skin was pale, but her hair was as dark as midnight, contrasting mightily to Valor's. She wondered how that great contrast would affect the children she would have someday. She hoped for fair sons as beautiful and strong as their father.

Remembering she was half faery, she felt suddenly uneasy. Tall strong sons—or wispy, frail, winged boys that would not survive? What was their fate?

The sudden bleat of a horn brought her from her reverie and she looked up and caught her first glimpse of Godwin Castle in the distance. She was surprised to see a rather ordinary castle on a green motte, very much like other castles she had observed in her travel from Sherwood Forest.

What had she expected? That because the Godwins were a well-respected family in England, their home would reflect a superior status? It was a surprise to realize that one could be respected and not extraordinarily wealthy.

But Sir Ambrose Godwin was an ambitious man

who desired wealth, and because of her, it would be denied him. A feeling of dread coursed through her veins, and she wished she could turn back; but no, she would be brave for her husband's sake.

She consoled herself with the thought that there was yet another son who could marry well for his father. The youngest son, Avery. All was not lost. Ambrose would realize that, wouldn't he? She would face him bravely, show no fear, for her future depended on it. Her future as Valor's wife.

The horn sounded again, a signal to lower the drawbridge; and by the time they reached it, it was in position for them to ride over.

The sound of pounding hooves on the wooden bridge drowned out Valor's words to her, and she asked him to repeat what he had said as they rode beneath the portcullis into the bailey. "I said, 'I bid you welcome to my father's home.' "

He spoke so bitterly, so sarcastically, her stomach churned and her heart beat with the rhythm of the pounding hooves. Her horse carried her into the bailey at great speed and she tried to hold it back with a jerk of the reins, feeling that she had no control, that she was being swept to her fate. Her sudden action made the animal rear, almost tumbling her from the seat, and she screamed.

Valor jumped from his mount and was at her side in an instant, steadying the animal with a hard tug on the bridle. When the horse was finally calmed, he walked to its side and, grasping her waist, lowered her quickly to the ground.

Valor saw Raena's chin tremble and once again he reluctantly felt compassion for her. She had no idea what she was in for, but still she faced it bravely. "Stay close to me and you'll be safe."

She had every intention of doing just that. As

soon as Stephan was helped from his horse and Matthew had helped Lady Caroline from hers, they all walked slowly toward the keep. She had the oddest feeling that none of the Godwins were eager to enter their home. Did it have something to do with the castle's fierce lord?

Raena was sure her knees would collapse after so long a ride and so fearful a walk up the unfamiliar stairs into the great hall, but she managed it, staying close to her husband's side. But when Valor suddenly tensed and pushed her behind him, she shivered in terrible anticipation.

A booming voice called out, and Raena peered around her husband's broad back to see a short, stout man with a red beard. Valor gently pushed her behind him again, but held onto her hand to comfort her.

"My sons' triumphant return. Hallelujah! God is good."

Valor squeezed tight on Raena's hand. "Father. 'Tis good to see you. You're looking well."

Barely glancing at Valor, Ambrose strode up to Stephan and embraced him heartily. "Son, the sight of you brings me great joy. How fares your wound?"

"I'm almost fully recovered, Father, thanks to the help of—"

"Good. Good. Good."

Valor's pressure on her hand increased until she felt as if all the blood had vanished from it. Raena realized the tightness of his hold had nothing to do with comforting her, but everything to do with Sir Ambrose. Valor was as nervous about facing his father as she was.

Matthew and Valor stood watching in awkward silence, and Raena couldn't help but wonder why

Lord Ambrose had not greeted them as warmly as he had his eldest.

As if he had heard her thoughts, Ambrose turned to his other two sons and held out his arms. "Sons. Embrace your father, who has missed you dearly."

Valor slowly released his hold on her hand, and Raena sensed a reluctance on his part to go to his father. She understood that very well. Ambrose had gone to Stephan, but he wanted his other sons to come to him. That left no doubt in her mind which son was favored.

The two brothers obeyed their father, and in the midst of their awkward embrace, Ambrose suddenly became aware of Raena. "And what is this sweet little bundle?"

A female voice answered, "My lord, 'tis obvious my betrothed has brought me back a little Muslim slave. How like him to be so thoughtful."

Raena searched the throng of people for the source of that deep-throated, sensuous voice, and her gaze found the woman who must surely be Lady Elizabeth Plantagenet.

Raena stared at the one who had more claim to her husband than she and was pleased to discover that, though she was dressed in a beautiful gown of wine-colored velvet trimmed with gold and though the wimple she wore was the finest she had ever seen, Lady Elizabeth was not much of a beauty. She knew it was wrong to feel that way, but she couldn't help it. This was the woman who could yet destroy her marriage.

Valor broke away from his father and beckoned to Raena to join him. With great trepidation she walked up to him, aware that every eye in the hall was upon her. When she reached his side, he took a deep breath and announced. "This is Lady Raena Caldwell . . . my wife."

The hall became awkwardly silent, but not for long.

Ambrose found his voice after a shocked silence. It exploded through the hall, building and building until it was a great shout. "Whhhaaaatt! Tell me this is some ungodly prank on your part. Dear God in heaven, tell me you haven't ruined my future!"

"Father, I wish I could tell you that with all my heart. But the truth is, I met Raena and was . . . ah . . . compelled to marry her."

The next thing Raena knew, Ambrose was descending on her in a blind rage and she felt the force of his hand against her cheek.

She staggered from the blow, but otherwise was too stunned to move or talk.

Valor lunged at his father, slamming his fist into his face. Ambrose rocked on his feet, then steadied himself, whilst Lady Caroline and Wiggles quickly escorted Raena from the hall.

"You dare to strike your father?" Ambrose roared.

"When you do harm to a helpless female, yes; and upon my sword, if you dare to touch her again, I'll lop off the hand that does her injury. She's my wife, and you'll treat her with respect."

Ambrose wiped his bloody mouth with his hand, shouting, "Respect? Look who asks for respect? A son as worthless today as the day he came into the world, howling and red-faced and eager to suck on his mother's teat."

Valor held in the words he wanted to spew out. But he wouldn't embarrass his father with them, for he knew what angered him, what had always angered him. The day Valor was born, his mother had vowed never to have marital relations with her husband again.

That she had yet another son after that had always puzzled Valor. It was something that was never spoken of. He only knew what had been told to him by Matthew and Stephan, that their mother chose to sleep alone in her own bedchamber after his birth.

All these years his father had resented him for taking her away from him. As if it were his fault. As if there were anything he could have done about it. But Ambrose Godwin was an unforgiving man. Valor only wondered why his father hadn't strangled him in his sleep when he was young and vulnerable.

He wanted to leave that very moment, but he had come to settle things and settle them he would, by God. "Will you hear me out now?"

"I'll hear you out in the privacy of my chamber."

Valor had forgotten all about Elizabeth in the fury of the moment. He turned to her now and spoke in a low voice.

"Lady Elizabeth, I beg of you to find it in your heart to forgive me. In all the months that I was at war, I was faithful to you and looked forward to the marriage we would have. I wanted nothing more from life than that, but destiny had other plans. I cannot explain my compulsion to marry Lady Raena in any way that you could possibly understand; I just pray you understand it was not a marriage of my choice. That's all I can say, for Raena is my wife now and I'll not say ill of her to anyone, not even you."

Elizabeth thought she knew what Valor meant. 'Twas obvious he had been seduced by the slut and got caught. Well, it served him right. But she wouldn't tell him that. She'd make him suffer all the more by pretending to be devastated. And she would have been, if she loved him.

But she had learned early in life that love was a luxury. All that mattered was position and wealth. She had both now, and had no need of a husband, too.

But her smug thoughts were ruined when she remembered the reason she had wanted to marry him in the first place. He could have saved her from the unholy spell her depraved lover had cast upon her.

Eleven

After speaking with his father a short time, Valor made his way upstairs to his bedchamber to see how Raena was. His stomach still churned when he thought of the vicious slap she had received.

He should have seen it coming. He had promised to protect her and he had failed miserably. Would she ever forgive him?

Opening the door, he peered inside and saw Caroline and a servant sitting vigilantly by the bed.

"How is she?"

The bedcovers stirred and Raena rolled over and gazed up at him with sorrowful eyes.

He was surprised to see no anger in her eyes, no reproachful glance, only softness and the tears that brimmed up and spilled over onto her cheeks.

"Can you ever forgive me for what I've done? When I forced you into marriage, it never occurred to me how many other people would suffer because of my selfishness."

Valor gazed at her lovely, pale face in astonishment. *She* was asking *him* to forgive her? He swallowed hard, overwhelmed with raw emotion.

"I know I can never make up for what I've done, but I promise you on my father's grave that I shall never, ever use my faery glamour on you again."

Reminded of his untenable situation, all compassion for her was smothered by his rising anger, anger that this tiny female could have such power over him. Anger that she had repented too late. "Your promise is of little use to me now."

She turned her face away from his wrath and he saw the angry red welt upon her cheek. His anger melted as quickly as butter on hot bread. Wincing at the sight, he turned from her as shame washed over him. Overwhelmed by frustration and conflicting emotions for the woman who had caused him such grief, he walked out of the chamber in need of escape.

The next thing he knew, he was standing on the ramparts of the castle, gazing out at the hills and valleys that were his father's domain. A domain that he would never inherit because he was the third-born son.

Oh, yes, he would have married Elizabeth though he had no fond feelings for her at all. 'Twas a harsh world he lived in. A world ruled by brute strength and unscrupulous power. A world where he had to scramble and struggle for survival to secure any kind of future for the sons he hoped to have someday.

It seemed incredible that he had come to this. He was a soldier of Christ who had done his part to free the Holy Land—and this forced marriage was the reward he got? This unholy alliance with a half-human female barely more than a child was his reward for over a year's worth of suffering and misery, blood and inhumanity?

Where was the justice in that?

A sudden breeze blew across his face, caressing his cheek with a sigh. With it came the remembrance of the fierce lovemaking between him and

Raena, and he couldn't deny that it had been the most incredible night of his life.

Was her sweet body his reward then, and not a punishment? No, 'twas sacrilegious to even think it. 'Twas her will and her will alone that had caused their coming together, and oh! how he hated to be reminded that her will was stronger than his.

Ah, but God's will was stronger than hers.

Could it be possible God wanted this union between Christian and pagan? Could it be possible their marriage was sanctified and holy after all?

No. 'Twould be much better to think of it as a terrible coincidence.

He laughed bitterly as the wind carried his voice, scattering it to the four winds. Whether it be God's will or destiny that had arranged this farce, the deed was done and he had a wife who awaited him in his bedchamber.

Ah, but he had a will, too, and he'd use it now to show her he was no mindless slave. He'd sleep elsewhere this night.

After a lonely supper in Valor's bedchamber with no one for company, not even her attendants, an uneasy Raena undressed and went to bed. She knew she wouldn't be able to sleep in this strange bed in the best of circumstances, and most certainly not after the blow she had suffered. It was possible Lord Ambrose might take it upon himself to come back and finish what he had begun to get her out of the way so that Valor would be free to marry Elizabeth.

No wonder she felt uneasy. Where was Valor? Why was he not watching over her as he had promised?

If only she could escape into sleep! Sleep would take her away from this unfriendly castle to a dream world where she had an attentive husband to dote on her. One who would make her feel beloved. One who would never have allowed his father to dictate his life and determine whom he should marry.

Voices drifted to her from the other side of the wall. Someone else who could not sleep. That reassured her until she remembered that Caroline had told her it was Elizabeth's bedchamber.

Just what she needed, another reminder that she was a usurper here—that if not for her, Valor would still be betrothed to Elizabeth. Now the cursed woman would keep her awake with her chattering.

A male's voice joined in, and with a pounding of her heart, Raena came to a sitting position. Whom was Elizabeth talking to on such intimate terms? She couldn't make out the words or even tell who it was that spoke, but she heard the masculine timbre of his voice, a voice much like that of Valor's.

Could it be he? Was he pleading with Elizabeth even now? Explaining to her what had happened, how he had been trapped? Was he telling her he would divorce his wife and marry her? Is that why he hadn't come to her this night?

It drove her mad not knowing for certain if it were he, and she was sorely tempted to press her ear against the wall to try to catch the spoken words, but she wasn't brave enough. In truth, if it were Val, she couldn't bear the heartache.

The voices fell silent, and feeling greatly relieved, Raena sank back into the soft bed. Then, a few heartbeats later, an unmistakable sound reached Raena's ears. It was the sound of a female in the throes of lovemaking. The sound of a woman begging for release.

Oh, no, please no. Not Valor. Not my husband.

But who else could it be? What other man would be welcome in Elizabeth's bedchamber?

Pulling the covers over her head, she tried to drown out the rapturous voice.

In the next chamber, Elizabeth's lover commanded, "Keep your voice down, else I'll not give you what you want."

"No, please, don't stop. Not now—not now. I need a taste of it so badly."

"And I need for people to keep on believing you're the exemplary woman they think you to be. There's yet hope marriage to that girl can be ended. But not if the whole world knows what a wanton you truly are."

"Then why did you come to me tonight, of all nights, when she is lying in the next chamber? Does it amuse you or is it just another form of torture?"

"Do you wish me gone?"

"No. Damn you. You know what I want. Please. I'll be quiet, you'll see. Finish what you've started, I beg of you."

Elizabeth writhed in anticipation as her lover took the riding crop and caressed her naked breasts with the sting of leather.

Twelve

Raena awoke next morn with a fierce desire to escape the dismal atmosphere of Godwin Castle and go back to her own, much friendlier home. But she was a married woman now and had no freedom to do as she wanted.

If only she had Valor's favor, she could have put up with her miserable surroundings. If only he had come to her last night, instead of to Elizabeth, she could have shown him that they were well suited for each other. That he'd never need any woman but her.

A soft rapping on the door sent a jolt of fear careening through her. Could it be Valor, come to confess he'd spent the night with Elizabeth? Oh, please, no. She wasn't ready to hear it. She would never be ready to hear that he had betrayed her. As long as she didn't know for certain that it was he, she could go on.

Pulling herself together, she willed herself not to cry, no matter what. "Come in."

Caroline entered with a tray of food. One glance at her, and Raena's composure crumbled in a shower of tears.

Setting the tray down on a chest, Caroline embraced her. "Poor little thing. Losing your father so recently. Cry it all out. Tears will help relieve your misery."

" 'Tis not for my father I cry. I've had months to prepare for his death, years in exile to mourn his loss. Grief is an old friend of mine when it comes to my father. 'Tis Valor I cry for now. Oh, Caroline, he didn't come to my bed last night and . . . I fear he went to Elizabeth's."

"Oh, no, Sweeting, no. He'd never betray you."

"But, 'tis true! Elizabeth did have a lover in her bed last eve, and I swear to you his voice sounded like Valor's. Though I wish it were not so, I'm certain that the cries I heard through the walls were the sounds of passion."

"Are you sure of this? It seems so unlike the cold and calculating Elizabeth I've come to know. Although, now that I think on it, she has been acting strangely distracted for some time now. 'Tis possible she has taken a lover."

"For some time now? If that's so, then mayhap I'm worrying needlessly. If she's had a lover for months, then it couldn't possibly be Valor, for he was off to war then, safely removed from her." Realizing fully the implications of what Caroline had said, she cried, "Oh, your news is very welcome to my ears. If Elizabeth has a lover, I'm thinking she'll not be so inclined to thwart my marriage."

"Why, Raena, can it be true? Yes, I see by the bright sparkle of your eyes, you love your husband. How splendid for him. How lovely for you."

"Love Valor?" Raena's eyes widened in surprise. "I've been so preoccupied with everything that's happened to even give it much thought. But 'tis true, I do feel much emotion for him, though it's too new for me to fully understand. But if love be measured by how much I want to be with him, then I must surely love him, for I don't want to lose him."

"You won't. The Godwin men are very loyal." With that, Caroline suddenly sobbed loudly and buried her head in her hands.

Raena was at a loss as to what to do. What had prompted this unexpected outburst of tears? "Caroline, pray tell me what's wrong? Have I said something to offend you?"

Raising her head, Caroline gazed at Raena with haunted eyes. " 'Tis not you, but I, who has done something wrong."

"Nay, you are too sweet and good."

"I wish that were true. I wish I could turn back time and make things right. Oh, Raena, I've done something terrible to my dearest friend in all the world whilst he was on the Holy Crusade, I . . . Oh, I am too shamed to tell you. When he finds out, and he will, very soon now, the great love he has for me will die."

"Surely you exaggerate. How terrible can it be? Stephan loves you dearly. He'll forgive you your little transgressions."

Caroline laughed bitterly. "Oh, Raena, you are truly an innocent. If you knew the truth, you wouldn't say that. You would despise me for my weakness."

Raena couldn't imagine what horrible thing Caroline could have done to the man she loved so much; and she preferred not to think of it, for, verily, it disturbed her to find out that love could be so complicated. So very, very, fragile. If a couple as devoted as Caroline and Stephan could have grave problems, what chance did she and Valor have?

Caroline left soon after that, in need of tending to Stephan. Wanting, needing, to find her own husband, Raena dressed and headed for the great hall. She wanted to see for herself that he hadn't been with Elizabeth. One look and she would know. However, since he had been avoiding her as if she were afflicted with the plague, she wasn't hopeful of finding him any time soon.

Deep in thought, she turned down a narrow corridor and almost bumped into Valor. They both came to a stop and stood looking at each other in awkward silence. Raena's gaze followed the lines of Val's broad chest up to his face, and a thrill of excitement coursed through her as their eyes met. He looked at her with such a damnably innocent expression, she knew that what she had so fervently hoped for was true. He had not been with another woman.

Jolted with the sudden desire that swept over her, she instantly lowered her gaze, not wanting her husband to see how much she wanted him.

Valor watched as Raena's eyelashes fluttered and her gaze lowered most demurely. A thrill of victory swept through him. He had despaired of ever being in a position of power over her. For certain, she had flaunted her superior will in his face on more than one occasion.

His groin tightened as the urge to pull her into his arms swept over him. But though he resisted the impulse and was triumphant that he could, it didn't keep him from wanting her all the more.

Damn her.

Even without an enchantment he ached for her. Composing himself, he murmured, "My lady, I pray you are weathering the visit well?"

Raena knew she should mimic his politeness, and she would have—if only he hadn't said the very thing certain to set off her anger. He had been neglecting her completely since they'd arrived and now he dared ask that? "Not very well, my lord. I miss my home—*our* home—and beg you to tell me when we shall return there."

Valor gritted his teeth, *There she goes again,* he thought, *exerting her will, demanding to have her way.* "We'll leave when I am good and ready and not a moment before." Then seeing the troubled look in her eyes, he felt shame for his pettiness.

"Raena, bide your time. This hated visit will not last much longer. I would have left straight away and told my father so, but he asked me to stay awhile longer. He has need of me to meet with various kinsmen on important matters since Stephan is still incapacitated. I pray you can see the awkward position that puts me in."

"Was it important matters that kept you from my bed last night?"

"Nay, that was my choice. But surely you weren't worried. I asked father to send a servant to you to let you know where you could find me in case you needed me."

"No one came to me."

"Blast him. I'd like to think it slipped his mind, but knowing father, I fear it was deliberate. I'm sorry. I should have seen to it myself."

Raena had no doubt his father had deliberately kept Valor's whereabouts from her. But still blissful that she had not been betrayed, she could feel no anger toward any human being, even the terrible Ambrose. "No need to apologize, I'm just glad you and your father have settled your differences."

"To a degree and no more. In truth, it would have been much easier to have left immediately, believe me. But he relies on me right now, and I feel

I owe him that much fidelity after everything that's happened. Can you understand that?"

Controlling her voice, she spoke in a much more civilized manner than she felt. "I'm glad your father finds favor with you enough to ask for your help, and that encourages me to ask if that might mean that he accepts our marriage now?"

Valor stared into her eyes for one long tortured moment before answering, "How can he, when I cannot?" With that, he stormed off, leaving Raena to ponder her future.

She was heartily sorry that she had promised not to use her faery glamour on him anymore, for at this moment she wanted nothing more than to bring him to his knees.

Angry and frustrated and desperate for some outlet for her pent-up energy, she decided to go for a ride somewhere, anywhere, away from the dismal castle and all the righteous and difficult-to-please Godwin men.

Making her way to the stable, she happened on a horse already saddled and, on impulse, mounted the animal as a man would. Before anyone could protest, she galloped out of the yard and over the drawbridge to the freedom of the road.

Exhilarated, she rode away, not knowing or caring where she was going. She only knew she couldn't spend another moment in that hated castle.

She rode as far as she dared in this strange countryside, stopping only when she came to a fork in the road. She hesitated, wondering if she should turn back; but the thought of going back to the cold, uncomfortable castle and those cold, uncomfortable people was too much to bear. Choosing the narrower, less-worn path, she started down it.

Before long, she came to a meadow adorned with

bright flowers and butterflies, and tears came to her eyes at all the natural beauty. She missed her stay in Sherwood Forest. She had been happier there than anywhere else she had lived.

There had been no constraints on her to act in a civilized manner there, and she had reveled in the freedom to do just as she desired. Just as her faery spirit demanded.

Oh, Father, I wish it hadn't been necessary to marry Valor. We'd all be so much happier. Valor could be with Elizabeth, and I would be free to go to Sherwood Forest and join Robin Hood and his band of merry men. What fun it would be in the company of creatures as wild as I.

Mayhap, she shouldn't wait for winter solstice. Mayhap, it was time to send a message to Robin, for she had all but given up on Valor's becoming a real and loving husband.

Dismounting, she tied the horse to a bush and ran into the tall grass of the meadow. 'Twas obvious no one had been here for some time, for the meadow was in a natural state, not mown or cultivated in any way. This was what she needed. This was what she craved. The freedom only nature could give her.

Birds sang in the trees that rimmed the meadow, inspiring her to dance, and she moved through the tall grass as it bent and swayed to her will. It had been too long since she had been this free.

But she was still not free enough. She felt hindered by her clothes and, without a thought, stripped them off, then continued her dance in wild abandonment. Yes, this was the way she wanted to be. Free. Free. Free!

And when she was done dancing, she would climb up to the top of the tallest tree; and after that, why, she'd find a body of water to swim and gambol in and . . . and she'd do whatever her heart desired.

Coming to a halt, she stared into space. But what if all her heart desired was to be with Valor? What then?

Pushing that sad thought from her head, she twirled 'round and 'round until, even when she was done moving, the earth still spun around her.

Back at the castle, a frustrated young serf approached Valor. "I hardly dare to tell you this, sir, but your lady wife has taken the horse I use to do my work and I am in need of it very soon, else your father will take a whip to my backside."

"Lady Raena? Are you certain it was she?"

"I'm certain. For who but she has eyes the color of heather on a rainy day?"

Who else, indeed? He should have known she would balk against the constraints of the castle. Her life at Caldwell Castle had been much more carefree. "Where did she go?"

"She rode away from the village without an escort. That's all I know, sir."

Valor groaned. She was alone. Damn her. Without a doubt, he'd have to go after her. God give him the strength to keep from beating her, for if ever a wife deserved it, she did.

After arranging for the serf to use another mount, Valor was on his way, riding like the wind to find Raena before some miscreant found her and . . . but he couldn't bear to think of what might happen to her and pushed it from his mind.

His gaze swept over the landscape as he rode, hoping for a glimpse of her raven hair, but she was naught to be seen anywhere. When he came to the fork in the road, he hesitated, thinking she couldn't have come so far, that he must have missed her somewhere along the way; but something told him to go on, to take the narrower, less-worn path, and so he rode down it, thinking that her wild, faery nature would take her away from civilization.

In the distance, he saw the wide meadow and, almost instantly, his wife. Relief flooded his brain as he halted his horse. But relief soon turned to shock as he gawked at the naked woman dancing a wild, pagan dance with a flock of butterflies.

Raena—naked—lovely—Raena, was dancing with butterflies.

Butterflies that moved in unison to her, sweeping down and up, around and around her body as if they were compelled to dance to the same silent music that moved Raena. He shook his head in wonder. It seemed her power of enchantment was not limited to humans. She had the power to seduce every living creature, no matter how low or mighty they might be.

Suddenly fearing he might not be the only spectator, Valor tore his gaze from Raena and stood in his saddle to look around, but there was no one to be seen. Thank heaven for that or for certain he'd be fighting his way out of the meadow by now. For what man could gaze upon this sight without desiring to make her his own?

Certainly not he.

Impeded by a powerful erection, he spurred his mount and cantered toward her, and instantly, the butterfly spell was broken. The butterflies flew away, rising from her body like miniature rainbows until the splendid beauty of her body was completely revealed to him.

Startled, Raena spun around and saw her husband upon a fine white steed. Her heart quickened.

Valor had come to her.

Oh, he had truly come to her; and by the look in his eyes, she knew he desired her. Knowing she had not used her faery glamour and that he was there of his own free will; a thrill coursed through her body. Mayhap, it was too early to give up. Mayhap, there was hope for them yet.

Anger and desire battled within Valor as he drew up to her, staring at the graceful curves of her lovely body. "You fool. Don't you know the danger you've put yourself in, prancing around naked?"

"Danger, my lord? Dancing with butterflies? Am I then in danger of being tickled to death by the velvet touch of their wings on my skin?"

That all-too-vivid image made Valor's erection harder yet. Jumping from his horse, he answered, "Danger of being ravished by any rutting male who happens by!"

"But, Sir Knight, you are the only male who has happened by. Am I in danger of being ravished by you?"

"Imminent danger," he answered huskily as he moved toward her.

Raena felt her knees weaken. He was going to make love to her without any need of an enchantment. Ah, but knowing what she did of Valor, she feared he would certainly gain his composure and restrain himself no matter how much he wanted her. She knew, firsthand, how stubborn he could be.

Oh, why did he have to be so confoundedly noble, so damnably honorable, so completely and utterly driven by his head and not his heart?

Giving in to the idea of defeat, she backed away.

So be it. At least she could try to save something of her dignity by covering herself.

She knelt to retrieve her clothes when suddenly his hand closed around her wrist. Her heart leapt in her throat as he pulled her to her feet, saying, "Nay, don't. I want to see you as God made you."

His grip was strong and yet completely gentle. A shiver of anticipation snaked through her body. Could it be? Was he truly going to make love to her?

In answer to her unspoken question, he said, "I have the right, do I not? You belong to me. You're my lawful wife. I can do anything I wish with you now. Beat you, starve you, whip you. 'Tis my choice."

"My lord, if you don't mind, I'd rather not be whipped or beaten."

A lump came to his throat. She had spoken so softly and sincerely. Did she think he truly meant those words? God's blood, what kind of monster did she take him for? "Sweet, little Raena, don't you know I'd never deliberately hurt you? I want only to touch you. To caress you into submission."

Raena thought she knew what he meant, but it seemed too good to be true. Untrusting of her instincts, she asked, "Pray tell me what you would have me submit to, I beg of you."

"Come to me and see." Holding out his arms, he willed her to come to him. And she did, floating into his arms as sweetly and softly as any butterfly.

He enveloped her in his arms and squeezed his eyes shut as the sweet thrill of her touch washed over him. He had longed for this moment since last she was in his arms.

A sudden surge of strength engulfed him and he lifted her over his head by her waist. Holding her aloft, he stared up at the wonder of her. "By my sword, you are the fairest of women, the wildest, sweetest . . ." Then, in need of action instead of words, he lowered her back to the ground and kissed her mightily.

The wind blew around them as they stood in the meadow locked in each other's embrace. Her hair fanned his face, caressing him with its silky fabric whilst the sweet smell of flowers intermingling with the scent of meadow grass wafted through his nostrils.

Scent . . . scent . . . what was it about scent? Ah, yes, 'twas her scent that had captured him, brought him to his knees. And here it was again. Did she think he wouldn't know when he was under an enchantment? Did she think she could trick him so easily?

'Twas true the scent was different this time, radiating slowly from her instead of all at once. And he had to admit he enjoyed it much more this way. Why not enjoy her offered body? It would be foolish to try to fight her. He might as well save his strength, for he was destined to lose in the end.

Why not, indeed? She was his wife now. He had the right to take her whenever he wished, and oh, he wished to take her now.

Tasting the nectar of her lips, he decided this enchantment was much different from the others. This time, he was aware of everything, and of nothing, as the sweet aching escalated and he delved into her mouth to taste her, revel in her, prepare her for yet another more potent invasion that was sure to come.

Raena endured the exploration of her mouth with great relish. Wiggles had never told her of such a thing as that. She was learning all manner of wonderful things from Valor.

And than his mouth was on her breast, pulling on her nipple, conjuring up enticing feelings, and she discovered yet another wonderful sensation. Was there no end to the sensuous parts of the body?

She closed her eyes, absorbing herself in this exquisite new pleasure. But as the feeling escalated, she felt the need to retaliate and ran her fingers through his golden beard.

Valor released his hold on one breast and started in on the other, discovering the taste was just as sweet as the first. He likened them to rosy berries and felt heady with power that he could make them harden and swell. And, oh, he knew of another rosy nub he wanted to swell and harden, and with that in mind, he pulled her down to lie with him in the sweet grass.

The grass was so tall and thick, it hid them completely and he was glad. He wanted no one to destroy this moment.

It felt good knowing he could take as long as he wanted to accomplish the act of making love, for he wanted it to take a long, long time.

But he panicked when Raena suddenly pushed him away. Oh, God, no, she couldn't be that cruel.

"Husband, will you disrobe for me? I want to enjoy the touch of your skin against mine."

Relief flooded his senses and a surge of great joy soon followed. Most eager to fulfill his wife's request, he had his clothes off in the blinking of an eye. Then, with one long, lingering view of her lying on the matted grass, he lowered himself onto her very slowly, reveling in her sweet touch.

Raena closed her eyes in pleasure when he descended on her and stroked his arms and shoulders, neck and back, in long, slow caresses. "You are so hard and strong, so filled with life's force, that I am compelled to honor thee."

Her strange words filled him with great satisfaction, and he felt pride that she should utter them to him.

"And you, wife, are so soft and delicate, as fresh and lovely as the most rare and precious flower, that I must honor thee."

"Honor me, then, with your body and with your soul."

Valor's eyes glittered with fervent light as he lowered his head to taste her lips. Her soft, sensual touch sent him reeling and he invaded her mouth with his tongue, eager to penetrate the very boundaries of her being. She took it with a great moan and arched her body up to meld with his.

He would have liked to linger, enjoying the stroking and exploring of her, but her hand had found his swollen part and she was maneuvering it between her legs.

Ah, well, there would be other times when he could tarry longer. Right now, it seemed prudent to let her have her way.

With one slippery motion he was inside her and she was crying out her pleasure. "Oh, Valor, you fit just right, as if you were made to pleasure me."

"Methinks 'twas you who were made to pleasure me," he groaned. Wriggling his body, he moved within her in a circular motion, and she rejoiced in his touch and begged for more with tiny, upward thrusts of her body.

He retreated and then plunged in all the deeper, and she took all of him with joy. It felt so good to be under him, to feel him move within her, that she wanted it to go on forever and ever. But, ah, no, she couldn't bear for it to go on much longer, for she had such need to crest the erotic tide that swept over her.

Valor's thrusts lost their playfulness as his desire for her made him concentrate all his efforts at finishing what he had begun. He was seriously at work now, lost in the rapture of her body, needing to bring her with him to that private world of ecstasy where only they two could go.

Raena reveled in the rhythmic thrusts that rent her with such intense pleasure that she raked her fingers down his back, digging into his skin to help him along. The closer they melded, the higher her need until, at last, at long last, she exploded into him and he into her and the union of their bodies was real and good and right and so very, very wonderful that she knew she had experienced the ultimate state of union with her husband.

When it was over, they lay quiet for a time, listening to the beat of each other's heart. The wind sighed through the grass, and the drone of a bee searching for nectar amongst the flowers added to the gentle symphony.

Deeply satisfied and content, Raena sighed. "I want to stay here forever in your arms. I want you to make love to me for all eternity."

Her innocent-sounding words touched his soul, disturbing him profoundly. For innocent though they sounded, they were a reminder to him that he was a slave to her demands. Pushing her out of his arms, he sat up, saying, "Then, by all means, let out your faery scent again. That way, I'll be compelled to service you again and again until you weary of mating me."

Raena stared at Valor in shock. "Surely . . . surely you don't think I used my faery glamour on you just now?"

" 'Tis useless to deny it. Your scent is unmistakable."

"But . . . but, I didn't. I swear to you, I didn't."

"Enough. I've accepted that I'm under an enchantment. In truth, I enjoyed it very much. No need to pretend what happened was natural."

Raena was stunned and hurt that he could believe that she had deliberately seduced him. "I'm not pretending. You have to believe me. I didn't use my faery glamour."

"Raena, I smell the scent even now."

"You smell the wildflowers and the meadow grass. That's all."

Puzzled, Valor shook his head. "Mayhap, you released your scent without being aware of it. It is part of you, after all."

Could it be true? Could she have released her glamour without even trying? Raena didn't want to believe that. She had worked so hard the past seven years learning how to control it.

But what if he were right? What if their lovemaking had not come about naturally? How could she ever be sure that Valor truly wanted her?

Thirteen

Feeling miserable and alone, Raena dressed and began walking down the road. So deep was her misery that she cared not where she was going or what she would do when she got there. She only knew that she could see no way out of her dilemma. Valor would always believe that he was under her spell, and there was nothing she could do about it.

Valor dressed in uneasy silence. Raena was acting very strange. Why had she set out without her mount? Grasping the reins of both their horses, he went after her, walking at double speed until he caught up to her. "Hey, there, where are you off to? It's a long way back to the castle."

Raena heard his words as if through a fog, but she didn't respond. Lost in her misery, she continued to walk.

Valor was truly uneasy now. What was wrong with her? All he had done was question whether she was using her faery glamour. Why should that upset her so? After all, he was the victim, not she.

Sounding more irritated than he meant to, he said, "Raena, I really wish you'd get on your horse. It will be dark by the time we get back to the castle. I don't know about you, but I'm getting hungry."

Reaching out, he took hold of her arm, stopping her from treading any farther.

Raena looked up at him in such a heartwrenching way, he couldn't stand it. With a groan, he pulled her into his arms. She was as pliable as a child's poppet, and that scared him all the more. Lifting her up, he set her on his horse and climbed up behind her.

Wrapping his arms around her, he grabbed the reins and cantered down the road. Raena leaned backwards against him as they moved to the rhythm of the horse, and they rode back to the castle in silence, their bodies rubbing against each other in a gentle, persistent caress.

Choked with emotion, Valor realized that this girl, this faery bride of his, was so much more than he'd ever expected, more than he'd ever dared dream of, and he couldn't bear for her to hurt like this. He wanted her to be happy, to look at him with her beautiful, purple eyes sparkling with life once again.

And yet . . . yet . . . he knew that because of her, everything that he had hoped for and planned for was now lost to him. He should hate her for that, but try as he might, he could not. He couldn't help feeling that some unknown force was at work, that she had become a part of his life for a reason. She moved him in mysterious ways, and somewhere deep within, he knew that he was more of a man for it.

Shading her eyes with her hand, Elizabeth surveyed the countryside from the ramparts of the castle. Seeing two black specks upon the landscape, she cried, "There! I see them coming, at last. But something's strange. Oh, I see now, her horse is riderless. Damn. He's carrying her on his mount. How intimate. Of certain, the she-devil has had her way with him again. They probably rutted in some grassy field like dogs in heat. I swear, she means to rub it in my face that he chose her over me."

Elizabeth's lover answered, "Obviously, she wants to be doubly certain everyone knows their marriage is binding. I'm told she went so far as to have her servant show Matthew the bloodied sheets from their wedding bed so there could be no doubt about the consummation."

"Curse her. Did she have to be a virgin? 'Twould have been much easier to be rid of her if she had not been so pure. I tell you, the more I learn about her, the more I want revenge."

"Not half as much as I do. 'Tis not as if you love Valor or need him to warm your bed. You have all the man you need in me." He circled her waist from behind, but she quickly escaped his grasp.

"Don't. Someone will see. As long as there's a chance I might still have Valor, our relationship must be kept secret."

"Methinks you grow more like your father every day, Elizabeth. Neither of you allows anything to be taken from you, even when 'tis something you don't want any longer."

Elizabeth smiled, but she was far from happy. She had good reason to want Valor as her husband. She had counted on that goodly knight to free her, for she had not the strength to break away from her lover's evil spell.

"But no need to worry," he continued. "You'll have your way on this matter, too. I have a plan."

"A plan?" A spark of hope lightened Elizabeth's heart. "It had best be a good one. Divorces are as rare as hen's teeth."

"Not if the bride were discovered in bed with her husband's father."

Elizabeth stared at Ambrose Godwin in horror. "Only you could think of something so vile."

"Was it not you who cried out so passionately for revenge but a moment ago?"

"Damn you. I don't hate the girl nearly enough to subject her to your *tender* touch."

"A touch that you crave."

Ambrose laughed and caressed the exposed area of her breasts with his ever-present riding crop. Elizabeth could not stop the shiver of pleasure that crawled up her spine.

"Mellicent did not have the heart for it, unfortunately, but it didn't take you long to learn to love the sting of leather on your skin."

The aphrodisiac scent of leather permeated the air, and Elizabeth's body responded whilst at the same time her mind silently cursed the day Ambrose had come into her life.

She had come to Caldwell Castle to wait for her betrothed's return from the Holy Lands, thinking it would be only a matter of weeks. Alas, it had turned out to be several months of waiting, several months of slow seductions.

She had been easy prey, for Ambrose had studied her well and knew just how to make her his creature. He had discovered what she had never dared admit even to herself, that the sting of pain brought her pleasure, that from submission came ecstasy.

Using the last of her willpower, she pushed away his hand that held the crop; then, escaping his clutch, she ran down the spiral steps, emerging in the bailey below.

Valor! He could still be her redemption. He could yet save her from the lord of depravity.

Running out into the bright light of day, she saw her savior helping his wife from the horse and she stopped to take in a deep breath and compose herself. "Valor."

Hearing his name called out in a breathless voice, Valor looked over Raena's shoulder to see Elizabeth standing a few feet away.

"Tarry with me awhile, Valor; I wish to speak with you."

Valor started toward Elizabeth, but was stopped by Raena's plaintive call. "Husband, walk with me to my bedchamber; I fear your father too much to go there alone."

A hard lump came to Elizabeth's throat as she heard the girl's words. She wanted to shout, "Never mind *her!* Save *me* from your father. *Save me.*" But knowing she could never tell him of her unholy alliance with Ambrose, she kept silent.

Valor was torn between the two women. He wanted to make amends with Elizabeth and was happy that she would give him that chance, whilst at the same time, he understood Raena's fear of his father.

It wasn't every day a gentle woman such as she was struck by a man. Looking from one woman to the other, he knew not what to do.

Seeing his indecision, Elizabeth grew angry. What was it about the girl that bewitched him so? It couldn't be her appearance. She had not meat enough upon her bones to feed a mouse. She supposed the girl could be considered comely in an odd sort of way, but she was no raving beauty to capture him in a silken web.

And yet, yet . . . Valor was, indeed, under her spell, every bit as much as she herself was under Ambrose's spell.

It would be only fitting for those two cursed enchanters to get together, for they deserved each other. Yes. Oh, yes! She would play matchmaker. She would tell Ambrose she had had a change of heart. She would help him with his plan. But first, she must keep Valor on her side.

"Valor, please, we must talk. I fear your father has concocted an evil plot to separate you from your new wife."

Valor made his way to Elizabeth and spoke to her in a low voice so Raena could not hear. "Has he confided this to you?"

"Aye, he thought I would be happy for revenge. But I'm not like that, Valor, surely you know that. If I cannot have you on honorable terms, I do not want you at all."

"Elizabeth, it warms my heart to hear you speak thus. You have every reason to hate me; and knowing you don't makes me admire you all the more. After what you've said, 'tis obvious I must leave my father's home as soon as possible, for I'll not allow anyone to harm my wife or try to interfere with my marriage. I mean to do my best to make this union work, for I truly believe God wishes it to be so."

Elizabeth wanted to puke. She had heard how religious Valor was, but hadn't thought much of it, until now. "I understand and hold no hard feelings toward you, though I am heartbroken that we cannot be together."

"No more than I. I've decided to return to Caldwell Castle on Saturday. I'd leave this very moment, but Mother and Avery will be returning home this evening and I'd like to see them before I go."

Elizabeth felt a moment of panic. *Saturday. He was leaving Saturday! Ambrose's seduction must take place immediately or all would be lost.*

Taking Elizabeth's hand, Valor kissed it fervently. "My lady, if you'll forgive me, my wife has need of me."

Raena watched as Valor kissed Elizabeth's hand and felt a sharp pain in her heart. If not for her faery glamour, Valor would be wed to Elizabeth now. If she had any decency at all, she'd give Valor up so he could marry the woman he wanted.

Valor turned and walked back to her then, and her heart beat with a fury. Never had he looked so appealing as at this moment when she thought of leaving him. The very sight of him was a blessing to her, and she knew she could never willingly give him up. Not as long as there was a chance he could come to love her.

"What did she say? What plot has your father concocted to separate us?"

"I didn't ask. There was no need, for whatever it is won't work."

His short, terse answer frustrated Raena, but she kept silent. She'd not make a scene in front of Elizabeth. "Then, you must stay with me."

Valor gritted his teeth together. Once again she was making him her slave. "I'm here, aren't I?"

"What I mean is, stay *near* me. I do fear your father so."

Valor's demeanor softened immediately. She needed him. That was enough for now. "I'm sorry for that. Raena, the man is not a monster. But if it makes you feel better, come, I'll walk you to your chamber. Did you know Mother and Avery will be returning at supper time? With her in the castle, you'll be safer than if you had a hundred knights watching over you."

"That's welcome news, my lord. I only wonder if

they'll receive me any more warmly than your father."

Valor laughed softly. "Take my word on this, Mother will love you. She has a penchant for strange creatures."

But Valor was wrong. For when Lady Mellicent and young Lord Avery came sweeping into the great hall at dusk, Valor's mother took one long look at Raena and gasped audibly.

"Mother, what is it?" Valor said. "You've grown so pale."

" 'Tis nothing, son. Just a twinge of pain, nothing more."

Raena knew better. 'Twas obvious her outcry had something to do with her. If only she had the gift of reading minds. She would dearly love to know what bothered Mellicent. Mayhap, it was just the sight of her purple eyes. They did tend to make a person look twice.

To make matters worse, the hall was filled with people. Stephan and Caroline were there, too, seated at the high table, along with Ambrose and Elizabeth. All were witness to Lady Mellicent's uncommon behavior. It seems I cannot please any of the Godwins, Raena thought bitterly.

But she dared to hope again when Avery, the youngest of the four brothers, came up to her and took her hand in his. Staring uncomfortably deep into her eyes, he murmured, "Have we met before?"

"No, I don't believe so." But Raena felt uneasy about her answer. There was something familiar about Avery, as if, indeed, they had met before—but when? Where? Nay, she would remember if she had ever met this one, for he was entirely too unforgettable.

From the moment he'd entered the hall, the attention of all had shifted to him. And it was attention well deserved, for never had she seen a more beautiful male in her life. He was by far the handsomest of the four brothers, and he carried himself like a prince.

In truth, all the brothers could have been born to different mothers, for they were each so very different. Whereas Valor's hair was blond like his mother's, Stephan and Matthew had reddish hair like their father. Avery resembled none of them, with hair as black as a moonless night.

His stature was smaller, despite his princely stance; but then, being only sixteen, he had some growing to do yet. His eyes were the color of smoke one moment, the color of pond water the next. And before she knew it, they were changing again, this time to the color of rich, fertile earth.

He had full, pouty lips and a perfect, straight nose; and although his face was beautiful, still there could be no doubt that he was all-male. The adoring gaze of every female in the hall, including herself, was proof of that.

Avery kissed her hand lightly, then, strangely, circled his nose delicately over it as if seeking to smell the very essence of her being. At length, he gazed into her eyes as if he had some amusing secret. "My brother is a lucky man. If I had seen you first, I would have claimed you for my own."

Breaking his hypnotic hold on her, Avery escorted his mother to the table, seating her next to his father. He leaned over her and whispered something into his mother's ear, whereupon Lady Mellicent nodded her head and said, "Will you join us at the table, Lady Raena?"

Surprised and a little frightened, Raena sat next to Lady Caroline.

It was then Avery saw Caroline for the first time, and Raena saw a nerve twitch in his cheek. Caroline turned ashen, and her pale-blue eyes took on a haunted look.

What was this tension between brother and sister-in-law? Were there hard feelings between them? If there were, Stephan was most certainly unaware of it, for he was even now welcoming his brother most warmly.

"Avery, how you've grown! When last I saw you, you were a boy; and now, indeed, you've turned into a man. Had I but known, I would have rested easier knowing you were here to watch over Caroline and mother."

Avery laughed and walked around the table to embrace his brother. "Stephan, 'tis been too long a time. But we're all together now. Our family united. Methinks that warrants a prayer of thanksgiving from Brother Matthew."

"Upon my sword, *brother,*" Matthew answered, " 'tis odd that you of all people should ask for a prayer of thanks. Has Caroline converted you to Catholicism whilst I was gone to war?"

"Would that please you?"

"It would depend on your reason for converting."

Ambrose suddenly pounded on the table with his fist, startling Raena. "There'll be no more talk of religion in my home. Not as long as I'm alive. Your mother has barely just arrived, and already the conversation turns to religion."

Mellicent seemed not to be disturbed by her husband's sudden outburst, but calmly lifted her spoon, saying, "Shall we eat? I'm famished after our long ride."

Valor was quiet throughout the meal and Raena sensed he was as uncomfortable as she. What kind of family had she had married into? From the moment Mellicent and Avery had arrived, the tension in the air had become so thick one could almost pierce it with a dagger.

But she had to admit, her curiosity was strong. There was much she had to learn about her new family.

In need of solitude after the meal was finished, Raena excused herself and was about to ask Valor to escort her to her chamber when Elizabeth stood and said she would accompany her upstairs. Raena had no wish to talk with Elizabeth, but she had no choice. It would seem pettish if she spurned Elizabeth's friendly offer.

Taking a torch of reeds to light the way, Elizabeth led her up the stairs. When they came to Raena's chamber, Elizabeth asked if she might speak with Raena in private.

Fearful of what she had to say, yet very curious, too, she nodded her head and opened the door, gesturing for Elizabeth to enter.

Once inside, Elizabeth wasted no time. "Valor confided in me today that he still hoped there could be a divorce so he would be free to marry me. He asked me if I would wait for him until that could be accomplished, and I said that I would, for I have always loved him."

Raena didn't want to believe what she had heard. "If this be true, why hasn't Valor made his wishes known to me? I spent the morning alone with him and he made no mention of it. In fact, if I may confess, he acted like an ardent lover, not a man who wished to be rid of me."

"Ah, yes, I'm sure he was very attentive. Can you blame him for taking advantage of the situation. After all, he's a man, like any other. But he probably had an attack of conscience afterward and found it awkward to speak so bluntly to you since he is as much at fault for your marriage as you."

"But I don't understand. It was not his fault. He had no choice in the matter."

Elizabeth was puzzled. How could Valor be completely innocent? Pressing on, she said, "That's neither here nor there. The fact of the matter is, he wishes to be with me and he hopes you'll understand and agree to a divorce."

"But how can there be a divorce? Our marriage is perfectly valid. Even if I were to agree, how could it be done legally?"

Elizabeth's eyes narrowed to a slit. "There . . . is a way."

"Yes? Go on. Tell me how."

Elizabeth drew herself up and took in a deep breath, staring down at Raena like some deadly cobra. "If you commit adultery. Valor will even provide the man for you to take to bed. When you are found together, no law in the land would refuse Valor a divorce."

Too stunned to speak, Raena stared at Elizabeth in horror. She could barely believe Valor would agree to such a despicable arrangement. No wonder he had sent Elizabeth to tell her. He couldn't face her himself. What had their tryst been all about this morning? One last fling with his eager little wife before he put her permanently aside?

"Well, what is your answer?"

Struggling to compose herself, Raena said,

"Surely you don't expect an answer from me this very moment. You've given me a lot to think on. I do want to make amends to Valor, but adultery is such a drastic measure. Surely there must be some other way."

Elizabeth knew she had her then. Using her softest voice, she said, "Ah, we all wish there were some other way. But alas, there is not. I can appreciate your reluctance, but 'twould be only once and would take only a few moments to accomplish. Surely that's not too much of a sacrifice after all the harm you've caused to so many?"

Too choked to answer, Raena sat down on the bed and buried her head in her hands. When she looked up again, Elizabeth was gone.

Oh, Valor, she thought, *why couldn't you at least try to make our marriage work? Why didn't you give it a chance? Is material wealth so important to you that you could ask your wife to spread her legs for another man?*

But she knew the answer to that. Obviously, material wealth was all Valor cared for. He had proven that to her long before today. Hearing a knock upon the door, Raena dried her tears and opened it.

Valor stood there.

'Twas obvious he'd been drinking, for he reeked of wine and was unsteady on his feet.

"Is that the only way you could face me? After imbibing in spirits? Well, I don't wonder."

"I'm here. What more do you want?"

"Me? What do *you* want? Everything has been settled. *Elizabeth* told me everything."

Valor was puzzled, then he remembered his speech to Elizabeth earlier. She must have repeated to Raena what he'd told her, that it was God's wish that he stay married. "Then you know why I'm here. 'Tis my duty to see that—"

"Your duty? Oh, yes, I see, *your duty.* Well, you can go to blazes. I release you from your blasted duty." Pushing him into the corridor, she slammed the door shut and burst into tears. She had no need for him to repeat what Elizabeth had just told her. Did he now feel ashamed at having sent another to do his dirty work?

Curse him and his duty. How dare he! How dare he think she would want him anywhere near her after he'd sent Elizabeth to her. Could he be that dense? That cold and unfeeling?

Apparently he could, else he wouldn't have asked that she perform such a base act. But she would go through with it all the same, for right now she wanted desperately to be rid of him and all the other miserable Godwins. But, oh, why did it have to hurt so terribly?

It was no more than she deserved. After all, she had wronged him first, hadn't she? Still, she had no regrets, for she had given her father an easier death and that was worth all the pain of this short and bitter union.

And, oh, there was great pain, for though she had married Valor for her father's sake, she realized now, when she was about to lose him, that she truly loved him.

Fourteen

Valor's mind was muddled, but not just because of the wine his father had plied him with. That was puzzling enough. In the past, his father had never been one to seek his company, preferring to break bread and drink mead with his minions or with Stephan. But tonight, he had kept him at the table talking and drinking for an uncommonly long time. And now Raena, who had been so loving to him this morning, was acting as if she loathed him. 'Twas as if the world were turning topsy-turvy.

Why had the mention of duty seemed so odious to Raena? What was wrong with feeling duty to one's wife? Surely that couldn't be the reason she had turned away from him. And why had she sounded so bitter at the mention of Elizabeth's name? Was it possible she was jealous of her?

Nay, to be jealous, one first had to have feelings for the object of that jealousy, and she had none. She had married him out of duty to her father and for no other reason.

Duty, there was that word again. A perfectly reasonable word. Why should she object to his doing his duty when she had done hers? She would be the one to benefit from it, not he. The girl was maddening and completely unreasonable.

But in all honesty, she wouldn't be the sole beneficiary of his sense of duty, for he couldn't help but remember what it was like to make love to her. The thought of sharing his bed with her every night made him eager for a thousand nights of loving.

In sooth, in all the years he had thought about marrying Elizabeth, he had never really envisioned her in a carnal way. With Raena as his wife, he contemplated nothing else.

What choice had he since he was under her enchantment?

Would he feel the same without it? What did it matter? She was his wife. He had every right to bed her; in fact, it was his duty.

Duty.

There it was again.

'Twas a word he cherished as right and good, and yet 'twas a word she despised. Surely it must be the faery in her that made her so contrary.

Turning down the hall that led to Matthew and Stephan's chambers, he met Caroline going the other way. Seeing her tearstained face, he was alarmed. "Caroline, how fares my brother?"

"All is well," she answered, wiping her eyes. "I'm just on my way to see your dear wife. Stephan is sleeping, so I pray you do not wake him."

"Nay. I'm going to Matthew's chamber."

For some strange reason that he could not fathom, his innocent words set Caroline to crying again. Through her tears she said, "Why do you sleep in your brother's chamber when you have a sweet and loving wife to warm your bed? I pray you come to your senses before it's too late."

With that, she continued down the hall, leaving Valor to stare after her in wonder. What was happening? Was everyone in the castle going completely mad?

Caroline knocked on Raena's door and tried to gather her courage about her. It wouldn't be easy telling Raena what she must, but Raena was the only one who could help her. Matthew had told her of the enchantment she had put on Valor. Surely she must have tremendous magical powers to do that. She was counting on those powers to help her out of her terrible predicament.

The door opened a crack, but when Raena saw it was Caroline standing there, she opened it wide and admitted her.

"Caroline! What is it? You look so distressed."

"Oh, Raena, I am in distress, nay, more than that; I am in dire trouble and need your help."

"Oh, Caroline, of course, I'll help. Tell me what troubles you so."

Caroline looked Raena straight in the eye for one fleeting moment before turning her face away and crying out, "I'm pregnant."

Raena stared at Caroline, barely comprehending what she'd said. "But I don't understand, how could you possibly know that so soon? Stephan has been away so . . . long. Oh . . . I see; at least, I think I do."

"Oh, Raena, it isn't his child." Facing Raena, Caroline continued, speaking in a haunted voice. "I know what you must think, that I was lonely, that I craved the attentions of a man, but that isn't so. I was content to wait for my beloved husband to return. I swear to you. I can't explain what came over me. I had this great compulsion to mate with Avery, and I couldn't fight it."

"Avery? The child you carry is Avery's?"

"Yes, but he's not to blame for this, 'tis entirely my fault. He's but a child yet. Barely sixteen. I took advantage of him."

"But how? Why? I don't understand. I've never seen a love as great as that which you share with Stephan. I cannot believe you'd betray that love."

Caroline covered her eyes with her hands, unable to look Raena in the eyes. "I don't know what came over me, Raena. I swear I don't. It happened without any warning."

Raena reached out to touch Caroline's shoulder, but the tormented girl shrugged her off and walked to the window, gazing out, but seeing nothing.

"Caroline, there's no need for you to continue if it's too painful to talk about. I'll . . ."

Twirling around, Caroline said, "Oh, but I must tell you. I have to tell someone. It's been gnawing at me ever since it happened, but who could I tell? Who would possibly understand, when I don't?"

Taking a deep shuddering breath, Caroline composed herself before continuing. "You see, Avery and I are both inclined to stay up late, and we had gotten into the habit of having a tankard of mead together before retiring. We usually chatted for a while and then went our separate ways. He is such a sweet and charming boy. I enjoyed our talks. But that night . . . one moment I was talking to him in a sisterly manner, and the next, I was embracing him in the throes of such a violent passion that I couldn't stop myself."

"Forgive me, Caroline, but that seems peculiar, to say the least. Had you been drinking?"

"Just our usual tankard, no more. I can't explain why it happened."

"And you became pregnant that one time?"

"Yes. And 'tis a waking nightmare to me. For very

soon I'll begin to show and Stephan will know of my betrayal. I can't let that happen, Raena. I can't. I don't want to hurt him like that. You must help me abort the child. Surely, with all your knowledge of magic, you know of some herb or medicine I can take to end this pregnancy."

Raena was aghast at Caroline's request. Help her abort her child? Avery's child? "Caroline, surely it doesn't have to come to that. Stephan will accept the child. He'll forgive you, for he loves you very much. Give him the chance."

"I can't. Don't you understand. I don't dare chance losing his love. And beyond that, I don't want him to suffer, knowing of my betrayal. It's too cruel. Please, Raena, you must help me. I have no one else I can turn to."

"I don't know what to say, Caroline. Really I don't. I do have the proper herbs to give you, for my nursemaid bestowed all her knowledge of cures and medicines upon me whilst we lived in Sherwood Forest, but I don't know if I'm capable of deliberately ending a precious life. I can't give you a decision tonight. I'm sorry, but you must give me time to think on it."

Taking Raena's hands in hers, Caroline murmured, "At least, you give me some hope. I can live on that for a while, but please don't wait too long. Stephan has already noticed my breasts are much fuller. Raena, sweet angel, you saved my husband's life; now, I pray you, save mine, for I couldn't go on living without my precious Stephan at my side."

Raena felt a cold chill at Caroline's words, and they echoed through her head long after the two women had parted company. Was Caroline truly capable of killing herself?

Giving up all hope of sleep, she concentrated on

trying to solve both Caroline's problem and her own, wishing she had someone to turn to. But Wiggles was not here, and there was no one else she could trust.

She wished with all her heart she were back in Caldwell Castle living a simple, uncomplicated life. But that life was gone now, and even when she did return there, it would never be the same.

When she tired of tossing and turning in her lonely bed, she arose and paced the floor. Whenever she had a problem to solve, frantic energy built inside her until she released it in a long walk or ride or swim.

But the castle was closed tight for the night, the drawbridge up, making escape impossible without climbing over the wall. Verily, she was almost desperate enough to do that, but it would solve nothing.

She would wait it out.

She had to wait it out if she wanted to free Valor. Elizabeth would send some knight to her and she would open her thighs to him and her life with Valor would be ended.

She almost hated Valor for asking it of her. She had thought him much too honorable, much too gallant, to demand such retribution of any woman. Mayhap, she didn't know what he was really like.

Ever since she'd witnessed the Beltaine festival and had seen the baron acting like a pagan, she'd realized that many people had a secret side to them, but not Valor, never him. No, it wasn't his nature to keep secrets. She admired that about him, for 'twas nice to know he was exactly as he appeared to be—which certainly seemed an uncommon thing for these treacherous times.

Surely desperation drove him to this. If he wanted her to lie with another, she'd do it, for he had suffered enough at her hands. She had to face reality.

Her dream of being loved by him was just that—an impossible dream.

When morning came, she dressed in her brightest garment in hope of bolstering her spirits and made her way down to the great hall for breakfast. Elizabeth was waiting for her, barely giving her time to catch her breath before asking her if she had reached a decision yet.

Forcing herself to say the words that would end her marriage, she answered, "Yes. I've decided to give Valor his freedom. I'll receive this man my husband has chosen. I trust he's picked someone . . . gentle."

"I have no idea whom Valor has chosen."

Raena didn't believe her, for Elizabeth acted cagy, but what matter whether she knew or not? She would accept whoever came to her and be done with it once and for all.

Elizabeth could hardly contain her glee. "I'll tell Valor of your decision. No need for you to speak to him. I know how painful that would be, under the circumstances."

Raena spoke through gritted teeth. "Thank you for your consideration, though, mayhap, 'tis more for Valor's sake than mine. But you may tell him he needn't worry. As soon as this awful business is over, I'll be on my way to Caldwell Castle. He'll never have to see me again."

"Very wise. I warrant you would have this done swiftly. I can arrange for your rendezvous at high noon if that meets with your approval."

Approval, she dared mention that word to her? She was not willingly taking a man to her bed. Then, remembering what she knew of Elizabeth, she lashed out, "In the harsh light of day? I understand, your lover comes to you in the dark of night."

Elizabeth stared at her in shock. "If you hope to turn Valor from me by telling him that, you're mistaken. Valor would never believe ill of me."

"I'm sure you're right. But I advise you to give up your lover if you hope to marry Valor. For if I find out you still dally with him, I'll make sure Valor finds out about it, and then we'll both be the lighter of a husband."

"You have my word on it. Valor is the only man I want in my bed."

Raena sensed that it was true. At least, she could be grateful for that much. Valor deserved a faithful wife.

"Then, if you've no objections to having the rendezvous at noon, I'll see to the arrangements."

Hearing a hearty laugh, Raena turned to see Valor entering the great hall with Stephan. He saw her standing with Elizabeth and slowed his steps, but the smile still shone brightly on his face.

It was a wonderful smile. A beautiful smile that made her heart ache. Every time she saw him, he looked more appealing than the last. 'Twould be good to be away from all that brightness, all that manly beauty, for it was too painful a thing—seeing him, but not having him as her own.

"Raena. There you are. I stopped by your chamber, but you were gone. I'd thought, mayhap, we could break our fast together this morning."

His voice was so warm and soft, it brought a lump to her throat. She was wrong. He was as deceptive as any man, for the friendly tone of his voice could only be an act. "Why, Valor? Do you want your kin and castle folk to see how devoted you are to me so that when the end comes, everyone will remember that you treated me with kindness?"

Valor swore he had never met such a perplexing

person in all his life. "Will someone tell me what she's talking about? Elizabeth? Stephan? Can you fathom what she's saying?"

"Why, sir," Elizabeth said hastily, fearing her plan was about to fall apart, " 'Tis just a case of nerves. But being a male, you couldn't possibly understand." Then, turning to Raena, Elizabeth put on a sympathetic smile for her benefit.

Raena was close to crying, and not wanting Valor to see her that way, she ran out of the hall. Part of her hoped he would come after her, but part of her wanted no such thing.

In truth, Valor would have run after her, but Elizabeth grabbed him by the arm and stayed his steps. "Stay, Valor. At certain times, females have a need to be left alone."

"Confound it! Times like what?"

"Raena, poor thing, is just being emotional. Can you blame her after what happened with your father?"

Reassured it was nothing more than female temper, Valor decided it best to leave her be. But they would have to have a good talk, soon. She seemed not to know where she stood with him, although he thought he had made it very clear that he wanted this marriage to go forth.

He'd never been the best of orators, not like Matthew or Avery, but he vowed he would learn how to communicate with his faery bride. He'd reassure her that they were leaving soon. That should make her happy.

Back in her hated bedchamber, Raena flung herself on the bed. She would stay right here until the ordeal was over so that she wouldn't have to face anyone. And she would leave right afterwards, before the whole castle knew what had happened. She hoped she'd never have to face any of them again.

But she would have to face Wiggles, and that was far worse than having to face strangers. Wiggles would be so disappointed in her. She had wanted the protection that Valor could give her. But that was not to be.

Then, thinking about the ordeal ahead of her, she wondered what she should do to prepare herself. Should she strip off her clothes?

No. The thought of being touched so intimately by strange hands gave her the horrors. She'd stay covered. That way, she'd have as little contact as possible.

Of course, of necessity, there would be contact between their bodies, but she didn't want to think of that. She couldn't think of that or she wouldn't be able to go through with it.

Why hadn't she thought of bringing mead or wine to her bedchamber? Verily, she wished she were drunk right now.

Stop it, she commanded herself. *Stop thinking about it.*

Willing herself to think of other, more pleasant things, she concentrated on Sherwood Forest and the happy times she had had there, innocent and carefree, until, finally, she drifted off to sleep.

She was dreaming of a lovely path through the woods which led to a beautiful dreaming-pool. Gazing down into the tranquil water, she saw herself reflected there and, with her, a man who was gently caressing her hair. She felt the adoration of this man and it warmed her heart and soothed her soul. Oh, how lovely it was to be adored.

She wanted to see his face, to know who loved her so, but it was blocked to her. But she had to know. She had to know who he was, for when she did, everything would be as it was meant to be and she would finally know contentment.

A sharp knock upon the door startled her awake, and with pounding heart, she walked over to open it.

Her heart stood still.

It was Ambrose Godwin.

She blinked her eyes, as if warding off another blow from him. Why was he here? Did he mean to do her more harm? Nay, he seemed too friendly. Mayhap, he just wanted to make amends.

"May I come in?"

Drawing in a deep breath, she nodded her head affirmatively. What else could she do? This was his castle, after all, but what an awkward time for him to come calling. Any moment now, the man Valor had chosen to bed her would arrive.

Opening the door wide, she watched him stride boldly in. She started to close the door after him, then thought better of it and left it ajar. "Sir Ambrose, I fear I am not well, so if you'll tell me what you want . . ."

Ambrose laughed wickedly, and Raena's heart lurched.

It was no accident that he was here.

Her stomach churned as the realization hit her, *He was the man she was supposed to take to her bed.*

But . . . but . . . that couldn't be.

Valor would never have agreed to her bedding his father. Surely not. It was too hideous to even think of. Too . . .

Seeing the look of revulsion on her face, Ambrose felt an urge to torment her. Did the bitch think she was too good for him? Did she think Valor the better man? Dispensing with any pleasantries, he decided he wanted it rough. He'd show her who was in command. "Lie down."

Raena backed up, shaking her head in denial. "I can't do this. Not with my husband's own father. Send someone else. Anyone else but you."

"Why should it matter that I'm Valor's father? He won't be your husband much longer, now, will he? And you'll be thanking me for that. After I'm done with you, you'll know what a real man is. I'll warrant, my pure-of-heart son doesn't have the slightest idea what to do with a woman. What a woman can do for him. I'll wager he's never had you take his cock in your mouth."

Raena blocked her ears with her hands, but still his lewd words penetrated her senses, making her sick to her stomach. "I beg of you. Leave me in peace."

Ambrose laughed lustily. "Peace is for the grave. I'd rather leave you begging for more. When I get done with you, you'll be afloat with my juices and so thoroughly reamed, you won't be able to walk for a week. Now, do as I say. If you fight me, you'll still end up with your feet in the air and a stiff rod up your—"

"You bastard! You can't take me by force. Everyone will know you forced me because I'll fight you 'til my last breath."

"Have it your way then." Ambrose lunged for her and drove her to the floor.

Raena screamed.

Ambrose swung his fist, slamming it into her chin and she knew no more.

Fifteen

Raena awoke to a loud ringing in her ears and a painful throbbing in her jaw. She didn't know where she was until the hushed murmur of Caroline and Mellicent's voices brought it all back to her and shame washed over her.

How could she face them after what had happened? She prayed the women would go away so that she would be spared, for a time, having to tell them of her ordeal. When it became obvious they were not going to leave, she reluctantly opened her eyes. Instantly, tears welled up and spilled onto her cheeks, though she tried to hold them back.

Caroline responded by sitting on the edge of the bed to comfort Raena with a gentle caress on her brow, which only succeeded in making Raena cry all the harder. It was Mellicent who said the words that dried her tears.

"Hush, child. Nothing happened. There was no rape."

Raena heard but could barely believe it. No rape? Could it be true? "Please don't lie to me. I have to know the truth, no matter how painful."

"I always speak the truth, child. Surely your own body will confirm that no harm was done if you will but listen to it."

Raena closed her eyes and evaluated the condition of her body. She was surprised to find the only pain she felt was in her head and neck. *It was true.*

Taking in one deep shuddering breath of relief, she cried, "But why did he stop? I was completely at his mercy."

"Mercy?" Caroline said with great passion. "I would hardly call it that. He didn't stop for mercy's sake, but from a good whack on the head. Valor heard you scream and came to your rescue."

"Valor?" A flutter of hope feathered through her body. Was it possible Valor hadn't chosen his father to come to her? Could his father have decided of his own accord to be the one to lie with her? Oh, let it be true, for anything else would be unthinkable, anything else would be unforgivable.

Then, remembering Mellicent was Valor's mother and Ambrose's wife, she pleaded, "You must believe me, Lady Mellicent, I didn't welcome your husband to my chamber. I swear to you, I didn't."

"Child, of course, you didn't. No one blames you for this."

"Not even Valor?"

"Least of all he. He knows the evil in his father's heart and he almost killed him for it. I fear he would have succeeded if Matthew and Stephan hadn't stopped him. They locked Valor in the storeroom until he can calm himself."

Shame washed over Raena once more. "Upon my life, I swear if I had but known what troubles would befall your family because of me, I would never have forced him to marry me. You must believe me. My heart aches for what I've done to him. And now this. I'm responsible for this as well. I hardly dare ask . . . how badly did Valor injure his father?"

Mellicent looked almost happy when she replied,

"Let's just say he's in no shape to prey on helpless women at the moment. Thank heavens for Elizabeth. Somehow, she guessed what Ambrose was going to do and warned Valor in time."

Raena was taken aback. The gall of that woman, pretending to be innocent. She and Ambrose had probably plotted it together. But if that were true, why did she change her mind and stop it? One thing was certain, it wasn't compassion that had motivated Elizabeth. But . . . mayhap, it had been a shrewd move. In warning Valor that his father was going to her bedchamber instead of the man Valor had chosen, Elizabeth looked like a compassionate angel.

"My lord received a nasty gash on the head," Mellicent continued, "and is recuperating in bed. But methinks it's shame that keeps him there, for 'tis hard to believe even he could act so despicably. I can only fathom that he must have been very drunk."

Raena understood Ambrose's shame, for she felt it herself. Because of her, Valor's family was torn asunder. It was imperative she get out of his life before anything else happened.

Knowing in her heart it was the right thing to do, she said, "Lady Mellicent, I needs must leave here right away. Tell Valor I'll not stand in the way of a divorce. It's the only way I know to make up for what I've done to him."

Mellicent struggled for the right words. " 'Tis true. I cannot deny it. My dear, I know much more about you than ever you might think. When you were young, we visited Caldwell Castle many times. I'm well-aware of the circumstances of your birth and what motivated your mother's tragic end. Though you are innocent of any fault in all of that, still it is the faery blood in your veins that attracts great tragedy. In truth, my son would be better wed to Elizabeth."

Caroline stared in awe at Raena. "You are faery? How splendid! Then, it must be true. You did enchant Valor. Oh, I envy you that wondrous gift."

"You wouldn't think it so wonderful if you were the one being enchanted. Valor hates me for it. Lady Mellicent, I understand now why you've treated me so coldly, and I blame you not at all. In truth, I agree with everything you've said. Valor will be better off with Elizabeth."

"Oh, no, that isn't possible. Forgive me, Lady Mellicent, but I fervently believe Valor would be much happier with Raena as his wife. She is sweet and kind and gentle, attributes sorely missing in Elizabeth."

Caroline's words brought a lump to Raena's throat. "And you are so very good and innocent that you see only the best in people. I'm going to miss you terribly."

Caroline paled. "Oh, no, please. You must let me accompany you. Just for a short visit, please, I beg of you."

Mellicent stared at Caroline in astonishment. "Caroline, what's gotten into you? Surely, you don't mean to leave Stephan now? Your husband is grievously wounded and just returned from war. Surely you want to be with him."

Caroline lowered her gaze to the floor, unable to look her husband's mother in the eye. "I do want to be with Stephan. More than anything in the world. You know how much I love your son. But . . . there is something I must do before I can be a good wife to him again, and I beg you not to question me about it. I must go with Raena; I have no choice."

"My dearest child. I would not think of doubting

your great love for Stephan. Your devotion to my son has been a comfort to me. I'll not question you on the matter, for I trust there is a good reason for what you do. If you must go, then it is done. But I know it won't be easy leaving here once Stephan and Valor know what you are about."

Raena was surprised to find Mellicent so obliging and she realized there were still things to be learned about Valor's mother. As for Caroline, although she knew the true reason why she wanted to accompany her, still she was happy for her gentle company. She truly liked her new sister and hoped they could become friends despite the fact that once Valor had his way they would no longer be related.

Mayhap, when she had more opportunity to talk in private with Caroline, they could think out the predicament she was in and find a better solution than killing an innocent babe.

She wished she were surer of that, for the answer to the dilemma would not be easily found, but there was no time to think about that right now. First she must get back to the sanctity of Caldwell Castle.

If they were to leave, then it must be by subterfuge. They'd have to act as if they were just going out for a short ride so no one would be suspicious; for one thing was certain, Stephan would never agree to his wife's leaving. Who could blame him? It was even possible that Valor might object and, out of some misplaced sense of duty, insist on escorting her home.

She couldn't bear that. Better to sever the bonds that tied them together swiftly and cleanly. Mayhap, it wouldn't hurt so much that way.

Less than an hour later, they were on their way, accompanied only by Esther and Viola, the two attendants who had come with her to Godwin Castle.

The poor women had no idea where they were going until almost an hour into the ride; but if they were surprised or dismayed, they kept it to themselves. They had always been devoted to Raena and accepted her decisions without question, and she was grateful.

Soon enough, they would learn that Sir Valor would not be their new lord and master, but it was too painful to tell them now. She needed time to adjust to that herself.

Several times she turned in her saddle to look back at the road, alternating between fear and hope that she would see him riding after her; but the road was lonely, save for the occasional oxen cart loaded down with produce, headed back to Godwin Castle, no doubt.

It must have been an unusual sight for serfs and villeins alike to see four ladies upon the road, riding with great purpose. She had no fear of them, for they were harmless and on foot, but she did fear to come upon a band of brigands or thieves, for the country did abound with them.

Luck was with them, and they made it safely to Caldwell Castle by sunset. What a welcome sight it was, the familiar old keep and the colorful banners of lavender and blue flying from the ramparts.

And there was the crest that had been made especially for her upon her birth, a rampant unicorn on a field of gold-and-white stripes. It was an unofficial crest, to be sure; but, nonetheless, her father had proudly displayed it from the ramparts of his castle.

Oh, Father, I miss you more than I thought possible. How can I regret marrying Valor, no matter the trouble it caused, when it gave you such a peaceful death?

Arriving at the keep, they dismounted and walked

through the arched door to the coolness inside, a coolness that was reflected, unexpectedly, in Wiggles's greeting.

"Child, what are you doing here? Has something happened to Valor?"

"No, Wiggles, he's in perfect health," Raena said peevishly. " 'Tis me you should be worried about. Are you not glad to see me?"

"Of course, I am, Gosling. But lesser so without your husband. Don't tell me he tires of you already, for I cannot believe you don't know how to keep him entertained."

"Oh, Wiggles, you won't believe what happened to me in that wretched place. I'll never set foot on Godwin land again."

Raena told her the awful circumstances that had driven her back to Caldwell, and Wiggles listened attentively, her eyes traveling back and forth between her and Caroline. In truth, she seemed very interested in Caroline's welfare, and Raena wondered if she suspected that Caroline was pregnant.

Knowing her wise Elven ways, she wouldn't be surprised. After listening to Raena's story, Wiggles ordered a chamber prepared for Caroline; then, seeing her comfortably settled, she took Raena by the hand and led her to a seat by the fire in the great hall.

"You've told me what's happened, but you haven't told me how you feel about all this. Do you wish your marriage to end?"

"Valor is everything a woman could ever ask for in a husband, but he wasn't mine for the taking. His heart is not in this marriage, Wiggles. It never will be."

"Are you so sure of that?"

"Yes. No. Oh, Wiggles, I don't know. You are so much wiser than I; what are your thoughts?"

"I think there's a fair chance you're wrong. Valor is a noble knight, but he's a man just the same. It takes awhile for men to accept new ideas. They're not half as complaint as we women."

"I'd like to believe that, but 'tis much too hard. You weren't there. You didn't see the cold way he acted toward me, the warmth he had for Lady Elizabeth. Oh, I'm tired of thinking about it. Let him have his wonderful Elizabeth; he'll soon find out what she's truly like."

"What's gotten into you, child? 'Tis not like you to be so sullen. I'm thinking you need some cheering up. How would you feel about meeting your true father, Ohreinn, Prince of the People of Dawne?"

Raena's hand clutched at her heart. "You can't mean it. But why now, after all these years?"

"Why not now? You're a woman grown. Old enough I think to handle it. In truth, when he found out about your wedding to Valor, he wasn't pleased; he had another bridegroom in mind for you, as did I. But once I explained to him the urgency, what with the baron so close to death, he agreed that it had been a wise thing."

"Wiggles, I didn't know you had any concourse with my father. Why have you never told me?"

"Hmph. Do you think you know everything that goes on? Of course, I have concourse with Prince Ohreinn. I report your progress to him regularly."

"But why did you never tell me?"

"Because you weren't ready to hear. Have you not blamed him for your mother's death? Have I not told you over and over that there is more to the story than you know, that in time you will understand that he was blameless. And have you not always responded by blocking your ears and your heart to my plea?"

"Not true. I always heard you; it was just easier to go on hating him, for then I wouldn't have to acknowledge that he was my father. After all this time, does he want to meet me?"

"When you are ready, so will he be."

"When I am ready? Oh, Wiggles, I've lost my adopted father and now my husband; he's all the family I have left, except for you. I want to meet him, for 'tis terrible to feel so alone."

Saera smiled warmly. "Never alone, child. You have more family than you know. In time, you'll see that. But for now . . . I was going to the faery circle this very eve to visit with your father. You may came along if you wish."

Raena was sure her heart stopped beating as the shock reverberated throughout her body. "Now? I can meet him now?"

"Unless, of course, you're too weary."

"Oh, no, I couldn't sleep now, not after all you've told me. I do want to meet him, and suddenly I have a thousand questions. Does he have faery wings? Is he tall or short? Do I look like him?"

"He has extraordinary wings. And as for his looks, you'll soon see for yourself."

Raena had hardly gotten over that astonishment when Wiggles presented her with yet another. Instead of leaving the castle grounds by way of the drawbridge, she led her out through a hidden door in Raena's own sitting room behind an ancient tapestry of frolicking unicorns. It led down to a narrow, damp, and ominously dark passageway that seemed to go on and on forever.

When at last they emerged on the other side of

the castle walls, Raena found they were inside a stone vault in the burial ground.

With one of the many huge keys Wiggles carried with her at all times, she unlocked the door and they stepped out into the night.

Raena was afraid to ask if anyone was buried in that spooky vault. She didn't want to know. But, indeed, it was a clever place to hide a secret entrance to the castle. 'Twas surely the most lonely spot in all the land.

"Did my adopted father know of this secret passageway?"

"No, child. If ever the need had come for him to use it, I would have shown it to him. But in all the years we've occupied the castle, we've never been attacked. I use it to travel back and forth to the faery circle so that no one knows my comings and goings. The only others who know about it are John Barrows, the huntsman, and Robin Hood. Have you not wondered how Robin managed to visit you without fear of being discovered?"

"Wiggles, I can't believe how many secrets you've kept from me. Are there more? I'm most curious to know."

"Mayhap, one or two that will be told to you in good time."

Raena felt a shiver of excitement snake up her spine and knew there must surely be more exciting revelations forthcoming, but she didn't pursue the matter with Wiggles. She had enough to think about for the time being.

Wiggles led the way out of the burial ground to a cottage nestled on the fringe of the forest just outside the castle walls. They would share the back of a black gelding saddled and waiting for them there.

Excited and big-eyed with wonder, Raena gazed at the little cottage. "John Barrows lives here. Is he a friend of yours, Wiggles? What a foolish question. Of course, he must be a friend or you would never have told him about the secret passageway."

"Would you be shocked to learn he's much more than a friend, Gosling? John Barrows is my beloved."

"Oh, Wiggles, no, it pleases me to know you have someone to love you. I should like very much to meet him. I have only seen him from a distance."

A deep masculine voice answered, "Then, 'tis done."

Raena whirled around to see a huge man dressed in hunter green standing behind her. "Oh, you startled me."

"Sorry, me lady, didn't mean to scare you. I'm John Barrows, chief huntsman for the baron these past five years. Your huntsman now, if you have use of my services."

"Of course, I do. You shall continue as you did when my father was alive." Raena was pleasantly surprised by John's appearance. He had a golden beard much like Valor's, but was built far more ruggedly, with a ruddy complexion and a rather large nose. All in all, though, he was pleasant to look upon. But he could be no more than in his mid-thirties. Much too young for Saera. 'Twas odd to think of him as her lover.

"Your new husband may not wish me to continue on as huntsman."

"My new husband will not care. He has little interest in the goings on of Caldwell Castle. His heart lies elsewhere, I'm afraid."

"Me lady, forgive my saying so, but I think you're wrong about that. Lord Valor strikes me as the kind of man who'll take an active part in the running of Caldwell Castle."

"You've met my husband?"

"Aye. The day you left for Godwin Castle. He introduced himself, saying he wanted to get to know the good people of the hamlet."

"Most likely, he was just being polite. In any case, it matters not; he'll not be coming here any time soon. Now, if you'll excuse me, I'm on a most exciting venture and am eager to get started. Wiggles . . ."

Gazing at her nursemaid, Raena was astounded to find her looking as young and as beautiful as she had in the magical mirror. Only now seeing her in flesh and blood was even more astounding. The transformation was truly amazing.

Wiggles—Saera—in this incarnation, she could only be called Saera—was lovely, with long red tresses that curled around her face and eyes the color of leaves newly sprouted on the trees. Her lips were rather thin, but sensuous; and like Raena's, her cheekbones were exceedingly high. But most amazing of all was the transformation of her body from old crone to lithe young woman.

Saera took her lover's hand. "I'll not be gone long, John."

John kissed her hand and smiled warmly at her, and Raena realized the transformation had been for him, that that was how she must always appear to him. A surge of jealousy rushed through her.

Why had Saera not offered her the same privilege? She had never shown her true self to her. Wiggles had been like a mother to her; and yet, Raena knew little about her.

Sensing Raena's jealousy, Saera spoke to her softly after they were on their way. "Gosling, you must trust me now as much as you ever did when you were a babe. I thought 'twould be easier on you to see me but one way. In truth, it was easier for me to look one way for everyone. It was certainly much safer."

"I can understand that. But what about John Barrows? Why did you reveal your true self to him?"

" 'Twas an accident. I thought I was by myself at the dreaming pool near the faery circle. I was bathing there and let my true self show, for I feel the need every once in a while. I was looking at myself in the pool when he happened upon me. He'd been out hunting for the baron and thought to take a drink of water."

"What happened then? Oh, tell me, Wiggles."

Saera smiled. "What happened? Exactly what you think happened, and it was lovely. Isn't life strange? I spent the whole of my life disguised so that I wouldn't attract the attention of human males, then fell in love with the first human to see me as I truly am. But John is unlike any male I've ever known. He cares not for the way of village folk or castle folk, preferring to live by himself. He feels uncomfortable around people of his own kind, I do believe."

"Then, I'm happy he's found you, Wiggles. So happy you've found him."

"I know you are, child, and I'm glad you've finally met him. But not a word of him to Prince Ohreinn. I'm not sure he'd approve of my relationship with John."

There was much to learn about intermingling with elves and faeries, Raena realized. 'Twas much more complicated than relating one human to another. But she was eager to learn all she could and it thrilled her to think that her birth father might be the one to teach her.

Arriving at the path that led down the ravine to the faery circle, they tied their horse to a tree and started down the entangled route. Wiggles walked ahead of her, and it was almost as if she could see in the dark, for she never veered from the narrow, overgrown course.

There was naught but a crescent moon in the sky, making it hard for Raena to see anything but the dark shadowy images of the giant stones.

Suddenly, when they had almost reached the bottom, the faery circle took on a pale-green, luminescent glow, growing brighter and brighter until it nearly dazzled her with its brilliance.

Peering between the stones, she made out fleeting streaks of light that seemed to dance about the circle, and her heart beat wildly in anticipation. Following Wiggles's lead, she stepped inside the circle.

Immediately, the light diffused to that of daylight and the streaks of light became magical beings who leapt about in a strange, exotic dance.

Their scent was strong, but very pleasant and somehow familiar to her, and she realized they smelled faintly of the erotic aroma that was compelling to humankind, mixed with an earthier smell of ferns and moss.

Just then, they became aware of her presence and their dancing ceased. They became still, staring at her as if she were the most fascinating of creatures.

Strangely, Raena felt no fear, but rather a strong restlessness which she could not fathom. It was a wild feeling that leapt inside her like a deer in flight from hunters. And she felt something else, as well. She suddenly felt stronger, lighter, and intensely superior to all who stared at her.

All but one.

When her eyes focused on the beautiful faery queen who stood in the midst of the creatures, Raena felt her power.

This was one to be feared.

Sixteen

Wiggles whispered in her ear. "She is Queen Edainn. Give her homage on your knees."

Raena obeyed quickly, not wanting to offend the faery queen.

But Queen Edainn barely deigned to look at the girl, speaking instead to Wiggles. "Saera Ni? Why did you bring this creature to us?"

"As you know, your majesty, she's Prince Ohreinn's daughter. I thought it time she met her father."

Walking over to Raena, the queen circled her, looking her over as if she were a cow being considering for her herd. Then, cupping Raena's chin with her hand, the queen lifted Raena's head so that she could look directly into her eyes.

Staring back at the queen, Raena was astonished at the deep-purple hue of her eyes. They were so much more vivid than her own. In truth, everything about the faery queen was wondrous to behold, from her curly raven black hair to her revealing gown.

And oh, her wings were amazing to look upon. Never had she seen anything so lovely. To say they were colorful was a vast understatement. She couldn't even begin to count the colors, but most notable were the luminous purple and the iridescent peacock-green accented with black. No winged creature on earth could rival the beauty displayed there so proudly.

As for her clothing, it was made from some diaphanous material of subtle muted hues. No loom in all the land could have woven such a fabric as that. And around her neck was a gold torque decorated with strange symbols.

If that were not enough splendor, around her ankles and wrists were thick gold and copper bracelets and on her head—ohhh, on her head—was a crown made entirely of crystals.

But, above all else, it was her face that was the most compelling. Never had Raena seen the like. It was a wild countenance of such profound beauty that it hurt to gaze upon her. Surely, with such comely features, she had no need of faery glamour to capture any man's heart.

Raena was suddenly grateful Valor wasn't there, for she feared if he ever saw this enticing being, he would never want to leave her presence.

"Rise, child." Wiggles nudged her in her back to get her to move, for, verily, Raena was so entranced by the faery queen she had forgotten even to breathe.

Standing up, Raena saw that Queen Edainn was the same height as she, although that seemed impossible, so imposing was her presence.

"So, you are the one with such great promise for our people."

Great promise? She? Why had Wiggles never told her? How could she have great promise when she had such little knowledge of these people? She opened her mouth to question the queen, then thought better of it. No sense in letting Queen Edainn see just how little she did know.

"She seems strong and healthy, I'll give her that, but she's untried of yet." Tweaking one of Raena's breasts, the queen continued, "Are you with child yet?"

Astonished, Raena answered, "I—I don't know." Raena turned to Wiggles for support, but found her lovely form disconcerting. She wanted her old, familiar Wiggles back to comfort her.

Sensing her unease, Wiggles spoke for her. "Your majesty, 'tis quite possible she's breeding already. Valor is as virile a male that ever walked the earth. He'll make strong babes, to be sure."

"Where is this virile male? I wish to see for myself how very potent he is."

Saera Ni was certain of that. Edainn had a large sexual appetite and would devour Valor if he ever crossed her path. But 'twould all be a waste, for the queen was sterile, her womb barren of any life. It was a fact that could not be denied, and one that put her at a disadvantage in dealing with the fertile Princess Raena.

"Will you summon Prince Ohreinn now? The night grows short."

Edainn felt a twinge of anger at Saera Ni for daring to give orders, but her curiosity over the first meeting of father and daughter overrode it and she clapped her hands together once. Immediately, Prince Ohreinn made his way to her side.

Raena stared at the faery prince who had fathered her, overwhelmed by the awesome sight of him. She instantly recognized him as kin, for she resembled him greatly, and with that recognition came a powerful surge of love for him.

Ohreinn gazed at his daughter with an objective eye. He had seen her many times throughout the years when she had come to the faery circle, though he had kept himself hidden from her sight within the deep recesses of the underworld. He had not wanted to complicate her young life, for she had much to contend with in the human world.

Now that the time had finally come when he could make himself known to her, he accepted her cordially, but coolly, for it wasn't in his nature to show great emotion.

"She favors me. A good sign, don't you think?"

"Good enough to claim her as your daughter, Ohreinn? Is that your wish?"

Ohreinn spread his arms apart in a welcoming gesture. "It is my wish."

Raena felt herself being propelled from behind and realized that Wiggles was forcing her into her father's embrace.

Prince Ohreinn took the soft bundle of his daughter into his arms, surprised at the strange warmth that swept through him. "You are indeed my Dew Drop."

Raena smiled tentatively, for though his words were strange, they were spoken in a friendly tone. Dew Drop. Then, sensing a deeper meaning in the words, she blushed. Since her marriage to Valor, she had become familiar with the dew drops of a potent male. But she took no offense at her father's words, accepting his pronouncement as the faery way of identifying offspring.

Relaxing, she felt a strange contentment wash over her, and it pleased her to know this exotic and lovely being was her kin. Blood of her blood. For that reason, she could accept him without reservation.

He released her from his embrace shortly, and Raena became aware that she was the object of intense curiosity. She stood silently whilst the faery people gazed at her with interest that seemed to grow with each passing moment. One small, child-like faery actually knelt before her and sniffed her feet.

She looked to Wiggles uneasily.

Saera Ni ordered the creature to leave her alone, then addressed Ohreinn. "Raena has many questions for you. Go to the dreaming pool where you can enjoy a moment of privacy with your daughter. With the queen's permission, of course." Saera lowered her head in deference to Queen Edainn.

The queen granted her request with an impatient wave of her hand, and Ohreinn bowed low.

Then, turning to his daughter, he gazed into her eyes and saw the love that shone there. He was flattered she should feel such honest emotion for him, and he was surprised to find it pleased him. "Would you like that, Dew Drop?"

"Time spent with you would be very welcome, Father."

"Then, hold tight to my neck and I'll take you there."

Raena's eyes opened wide, but she obeyed, trusting her father completely. She felt herself lifted into the air and looked over her father's shoulder to see the earth move away from them in a rush.

She felt as though she were dreaming some wonderful exotic dream, for the prince was more like an imagined being than her actual father.

His beauty rivaled the queen's, and she was certain it would take a long time to get used to gazing at him. She only hoped she'd have the chance, for exotic though he certainly was, he was her true father and she wanted to be a part of his life.

He took her up the far side of the ravine in the blinking of an eye, and the experience left her breathless with excitement. If that weren't enough, knowing the astonishing strength and agility her father possessed gave her great pride in him. She had had no idea how powerful faeries could be.

He flew her to a small, almost perfectly round pool of water, and they landed smoothly on the mossy bank. "This is the dreaming pool. Faeries like to linger here. The water is necessary to our survival. In sooth, we rarely travel any farther, for 'tis too risky."

"I never knew this place existed. Do you come here often, Father?"

"Aye, as often as I dare. I sit and dream of the time when we'll be able to live in the upper world once again, when we are free to walk about in the bright light of day. Ah, but enough melancholy. The dreaming pool also has another more frivolous purpose. 'Tis said that on the night of the full moon, if you gaze into the water, you'll see the face of your true love reflected there."

"Whom do you see when you gaze into it, Father?"

Ohreinn laughed bitterly. "I dare not look."

"Oh, Father, be brave, for surely you will see my mother's face reflected there."

Ohreinn opened his mouth as if to speak, but closed it again, and Raena wondered if he was embarrassed to talk of her dead mother. She tried to rekindle her resentment over her mother's death, but the few remaining embers of her hatred were fast a-dying.

Feeling the need to share her thoughts with him, she said, "Strange, but I've dreamt of looking into this very dreaming pool, but I couldn't see my true love's face, for it was blocked from me."

"You dreamt of this pool? What else do you dream of?"

"I dreamt of Wiggles as she truly is long before she ever showed her true self to me."

"Wiggles? Is that what you call our beautiful Saera Ni? You give me hope when you tell me that, for it makes me dare believe she's right, that you do have a fey, faery nature. And you give me hope that you may be the one to save our kind."

"But how, Father? How?"

"Why, in the only way it can be saved. Make a healthy, winged faery child and you'll win the adulation of your people—for then, our future will be assured."

Raena's eyes opened wide. She never dared dream that she might actually be able to produce faery children. But here, in this magical place, anything seemed possible. Ah, but there was one problem in that optimistic vision. She couldn't do it alone.

"Wiggles . . . Saera Ni has told me of your plight, and I wish I could help; but I must tell you that it isn't likely I'll become pregnant, since I vowed never again to use faery glamour on my husband. Without it, I fear he'll not want to bed me."

"Is he a fool? Why any man would want you for his own."

"Oh, Father, 'tis not his fault, but mine, and I can't stand it any longer. Let me come and live with you at the faery circle. I want to live far away from all the hurt and grief of the human's world."

"That cannot be, child. There is no future in the kingdom below. You and others like you are our only hope, and for that, you must live above ground. You must bask in the life-giving rays of the sun—for without it, all living things wither and die."

Ohreinn saw compassion in her eyes and continued, "Faery and elven folk are doomed. We cannot endure much longer. You and a few others have blended well with humans, and through you, our people may once again be able to live above ground instead of in the earthy denizens below.

"It was our hope that you half-lings would seek out your own kind and mate, enriching the blood-line until it became strong again. But it seems fate has played us for fools. Your actions have all but made that an impossible dream."

"I don't understand."

"You see, my child, you were supposed to marry a Godwin, that much is true; but thanks to the intervention of your human father, you were mated with the wrong one. We intended for you to mate with Avery."

"Avery? Valor's youngest brother? But why him? Why not Valor? What difference can it make which brother I am wed to?"

Prince Ohreinn never as much as blinked his eye when he said, "A great deal of difference, Dew Drop, because—you see—Avery, *Prince Avery,* is my son."

Seventeen

In shock, Raena sank to the velvet carpet of green beside the dreaming pool and gazed into the dark water. *Water the color of Avery's eyes.*

"I don't understand. Wiggles told me that you can know faery by the purple hue of their eyes. I've noticed that Avery's eyes change colors most peculiarly, but never have I seen them change to purple."

"I know. 'Tis most disconcerting. When he was a babe, they were the most vivid purple and I had great hopes that he should inherit all my faery attributes. But that was not to be. As he grew older, everything about him that was faery disappeared one by one. 'Twas very odd. No one had ever witnessed such a thing before. Something is at work within him that we have no understanding of. Saera Ni still holds out hope that his faery qualities will return as he reaches manhood, but I am not so optimistic."

As he knelt beside his daughter, Ohreinn's voice took on a plaintive note. "At one time, we had high hopes for both of you. We were so sure you and Avery would mate and produce a perfect faery child."

Raena gasped. "Mate with my half brother? And break so powerful a taboo?"

" 'Tis a taboo only amongst humankind, although at one time it was amongst the faery folk, too. Desperation has made us resort to whatever means possible for the survival of our race."

Raena was shocked by her father's words, but she understood his desperation. It would be a great shame if people as glorious as her father and Queen Edainn ceased to exist.

"But, alas, it seems the human side of both you and Avery is stronger than the faery side, for not only have you each sought a human mate, you love them as well. Avery loves Caroline. You love Valor."

Caroline!

Of course! That was how she came to betray the man she loved more than life. It all made sense now.

Avery must have known when she was fertile and used his faery glamour to force her to mate with him. But she couldn't condemn him for that. Not now. Not knowing that his motivation was the survival of his kind and not selfish lust. Not knowing she had done the very same thing to Valor.

And Avery's enchantment had worked all too well. Caroline was pregnant.

Did Avery know? And what about Ohreinn, did he know Caroline carried his grandchild and possibly the future of his race?

As if in answer to her unspoken question, Ohreinn said, "Love. How it doth complicate matters. Avery's greatest weakness is his capacity for human love. What a heavy price it carries. He's loath to force Caroline to his will, fool that he is. Never before has a male of my tribe ever shirked his duty to procreate, no matter the circumstances. He disappoints me greatly."

Raena couldn't believe what she heard. *He doesn't know. Prince Ohreinn doesn't know.*

Avery was more faery than his father knew, for he had most certainly overcome the human part of him and forced Caroline to his will. But why had he kept it a secret from his own people? What reason could he have?

"You see, Dew Drop, faeries have not the fatal weakness of conscience. It is in their blood to put survival above everything else, even above the precious love you humans prize so highly."

"Oh, Father, do you not feel love in your heart?"

Ohreinn grimaced. "We feel every emotion that humans feel, but we have the ability to override them with reason when we must." Seeing Raena's reaction, he said, "Do not look disapprovingly upon that trait, for it may be necessary to your own survival someday."

It came to her then that she was more like her father than she realized, for she had certainly inherited that very trait—although when she had used it, she hadn't recognized it for what it was.

But now that she knew that it existed, she realized that the day she forced Valor to make love to her, her true faery nature had overridden her desire to release him from his enchantment—and she had felt no remorse whilst it was happening.

Although she now understood the why of it, it didn't make her feel any better. She had strong faery traits, but evidently, she also had strong human traits.

And right now the human part of her regretted deeply that Valor and Caroline were innocent victims in the faery tribe's struggle for survival. Thinking about the child Caroline was carrying, she wondered if she should tell her father. How happy he would be to hear of it.

What a dilemma. Faery folk were responsible for

the tragedy Caroline was going through, but on the other hand, the precious faery child she carried could be the one that could save the tribe. Knowing that, how could Raena even consider helping Caroline?

That was the question that haunted her soul.

Back at Godwin Castle, a distraught Stephan paced the floor outside the storeroom. He wanted to free Valor and hoped he'd calmed down by now, but he knew he'd surely lose his temper once again when he found out Raena had gone back to Caldwell Castle, taking Caroline with her.

Stephan couldn't understand why Caroline had so willingly left him. Surely she must be deeply troubled about something, and he feared what that might be. Did she not love him anymore? Was that it? Had she found someone else to love in the long months he was gone?

He would never have thought that possible just a few short days ago, but then he would have thought it impossible for Valor to wed anyone but Elizabeth, and that had certainly happened.

Since his return from The Crusades, the world seemed to have shifted and changed, and he was not at ease with those changes. All the long, lonely months away from Caroline, he had thought of nothing else but to return to her, to live the harmonious life they had led before the war. It had never once entered his mind that that might not happen. What had changed it all?

He wanted his wife and his happy marriage back, and he would do anything to make it happen. Gritting his teeth, Stephan unbarred the door and opened it, expecting at any moment to be punched in the mouth by his brother.

Peering cautiously inside, he saw Valor sitting on a sack of wheat, an apple in his hand. Glaring up at Stephan, he crunched down hard on the apple, biting off a huge chunk.

Swallowing hard, Stephan braved Valor's anger.

"A matter of grave importance has arisen; otherwise, I'd leave you to sulk in here all night."

Valor's face hardened. "If it concerns Father, I don't want to hear it. You'd best lock me in again, for I'm not certain I'm calm enough yet to keep from running him through with my sword."

"It's Caroline and . . . Raena. They went for a ride, or so I thought; but when they didn't return, Mother told me they had gone to Caldwell Castle."

Valor groaned and ran his fingers through his hair. "What idiot let them out the castle gate?"

" 'Twas me. But I never suspected Caroline would lie to me. She told me they were only going for a short ride. How was I to know? They carried no baggage with them, and none but two attendants accompanied them."

Springing to his feet, Valor said, "God's teeth, that woman will be the death of me yet. Why would she do that? And why would Caroline go along with it? She's always been so sensible. It doesn't make any sense at all."

"I don't mind telling you, I'm worried, Valor. You're right, it is unlike Caroline, unless . . . unless she doesn't love me anymore."

"Don't be a fool. Caroline loves you more than life, but it wouldn't surprise me if Raena used her faery glamour on Caroline to bend her to her will. The woman is diabolical, I tell you."

"I don't believe that."

"You would if you had been the recipient of her faery glamour. Be thankful your wife is so sweet and saintly. Exactly the opposite of Raena."

"Caroline is flesh and blood," Stephan said fervently. "Exactly as I want her. I'm not like you. I have no desire to put my wife with the angels. I much prefer her at my side where I can hold her, love her, share life's joys with her. But enough of this, time is of the essence. I'm going after her. Will you join me?"

Valor's face turned somber as he gazed into his brother's eyes. "You must know I have to leave Godwin Castle for good after what's happened. I'll not have anything to do with that monster who fathered us. I want Mother to join us, too. I don't want to leave her here with Father. You talk to her; she'll listen to you. You've always been her favorite. Father's favorite, too, for that matter."

Throwing the apple core against the wall, Valor declared vehemently, "God's teeth. I used to envy you, but I pity you now. You have to return here. You have no choice if you mean to inherit from him. But thankfully I do have a choice."

"Does that mean you'll not seek a divorce?"

"I had already reached that conclusion before this happened; and now locked here in the dark, in the quiet, I've had a chance to think it over endless times and I know that I made the right decision. I'm not so sure marriage to Elizabeth would have been a good thing."

"Can this be my brother talking?"

"Aye, I am talking now, not Father. Oh, I could put my wife aside legally if I wanted to live strictly by man's laws, but that's not my desire. I choose to live by God's laws; and by His law, Raena *is* my wife."

"But surely God wouldn't hold you to a marriage made whilst you were under a faery spell?"

"Don't you see? It doesn't matter that I didn't willingly choose her to wife, for it seems that God did, and I must accept His will."

Stephan laughed nervously. "I think it is more than God's will that compels you, Valor. I think it is your will. I've seen the way you look at her."

"Come." Valor said gruffly, trying to hide his feelings from his brother. "We're wasting time dallying here." Striding past Stephan, Valor stepped out into the brightness of the great hall and saw the stricken face of his mother.

"Sweet Jesus, Valor, what have you done to your brother?"

"For God's sake, Mother, I wouldn't harm a wounded man, and I certainly wouldn't harm my own flesh and blood."

"Wouldn't you? You hit your father."

"Can you censure me for that?"

"No. As God is my witness, I can't; but you were acting so crazy, I feared you might still be possessed." Stephan appeared in the doorway then, and Mellicent breathed a deep sigh of relief. "When do you leave for Caldwell Castle?"

"Immediately."

"I'm going, too," she responded. "Don't try to stop me. You'll have need of me there; there's no mistake about that. You'll need a cooler head than yours to make things right with your wife."

Stephan and Valor exchanged looks, then laughed out loud.

"By all means, Mother, come along," Valor said. "Did you think I'd object? You'll be much safer away from that evil man you're wed to."

"Good, I'm glad we're in agreement. However,

I'm not prepared to leave before morning. I've no desire to be traipsing across the countryside after dark, even if my sons are the bravest knights in all the land. I've heard whispers that Robin Hood and his bandits have wandered beyond the borders of Sherwood Forest."

Valor started to protest, eager to leave, but he knew his mother was right. Why risk it? Stephan would have one more night of healing before he took to his horse, and that could only be for the good, and it would give him the chance to gather some of his personal belongings. He'd take nothing else with him to his new home.

No sooner had the cock crowed next morn when Caroline came to Raena's bedchamber looking forlorn and pale, her cheeks streaked with dried tears. "Forgive me for disturbing you so early, but I could wait no longer. You must help me now. I pray you take pity on me and give me something to abort the babe. Stephan must never know that I've been unfaithful."

In truth, Caroline hadn't really been unfaithful, for she had no choice but to give in to Avery's powerful faery glamour; but Raena couldn't tell her that. Avery's secret must be kept—at least, until she'd had a chance to think further on it.

An idea came to her then, a way to put Caroline off for a time. Time could be the key to everything. Caroline was a deeply loving person. Once she felt life stir within her, she wouldn't be so eager to be rid of it. Surely that would happen soon. But, meanwhile, Raena had to keep her from doing anything drastic.

"I've . . . decided to give you what you want,

Caroline," she hedged. "You must take a pinch of the special herbs I'm going to prepare for you each morning in a cup of mead."

Raena felt great guilt at the raw relief on Caroline's face. The herbs she would give Caroline were harmless and would have no effect on the babe at all. But she didn't know what else to do. "You must do this every morning for twenty days. On the twenty-first day, you'll abort your child."

Taking Raena's hand, Caroline kissed it fervently. "I can never thank you enough for this. I am forever in your debt."

"Please, don't carry on so. I cannot bear it." No, she couldn't bear it. She couldn't bear the thought of how Caroline would react when she found out it was all a trick.

May the gods and goddesses forgive me for what I do.

Eighteen

As fate would have it, Valor and his family did not get an early start the next day. A torrent of rain beat against the castle in a fury, and for his mother and his wounded brother's sake, Val delayed the journey.

But as morning turned to afternoon, he feared that if they didn't begin riding soon, it would be too late, for he was reluctant to expose his mother to the dangers of a night ride. Just when he thought he couldn't stand another moment of waiting, the weather began to calm, the hard rain turning to a light drizzle, and they all agreed to chance it.

Setting off for Caldwell Castle, they wrapped themselves in woolen cloaks for protection against the rain; but in a short time, they were soaked to the skin.

Despite the miserable conditions, they rode steadily forward, his mother and brother as determined as he to arrive at Caldwell Castle as swiftly as possible. It was as if they each had some secret knowledge of the need for urgency.

Valor told himself it was just his imagination, that their hurried ride was because of their desire to get out of the inclement weather and for no other reason. Still, something nagged at him . . . something that hovered at the corner of his mind, torturing him until, at last, he was forced to face it.

'Twas guilt that rode beside him, guilt that he had not treated Raena better. Guilt that she had felt the need to flee his father's castle. If anything happened to her because of him, he knew he could never forgive himself.

She was so vulnerable, despite her powers to enchant. Indeed, there was a great innocence about her that put her at great risk. Ah, but thanks to his father, she had lost some of that trusting, childlike innocence, for she now knew that men could act as beasts. 'Twas a lesson he wished fervently she had not had to learn.

Glancing at his mother and brother, he saw that they, too, were deep in their own thoughts. Neither seemed inclined to converse. In sooth, the only sound to be heard was the pounding of hooves on the hard-packed road and the wind-driven rain splattering against their faces and clothing.

'Twas just as well, for Valor was in no mood for talking, his mind so full of thoughts it jumped here and there, conjuring up memories he'd much rather forget.

Avery had chosen to stay at the castle with father and Valor found that odd, considering the strained relationship between the two. Avery had always been rebellious, his spirit as wild and free as Raena's. God help them if she had put her enchantment on Avery instead of him, for by their very natures they'd have ended up living in some cave, bereft of any worldly goods.

Aye, Avery was different from his brothers and had suffered mightily because of it. Father had always treated him badly, ridiculing him for his small stature and his strange ways and beating him whenever he didn't obey.

But Avery seemed somehow impervious. He was constantly changing, taking on new attributes and casting off old ones he found useless in his struggle to survive. Nay, not to survive, but to *prevail*. For there was something in Avery that made him strive to be the best in anything he undertook.

It was strange, but Avery had never cried as a child, no matter how harshly he was treated. Not as a child, and certainly not now as a young man. Valor couldn't help but admire him for that fierce, brave spirit.

Despite everything, Avery was amenable and good-natured, and everyone in the castle adored him; yet . . . there was something about him that spoke of power yet unleashed.

As he drew closer to Caldwell Castle, Valor's thoughts turned to Raena and the new life forced upon him. It was not one he would have chosen; but free of his father's influence, he realized that it was a life he was more suited to. Married to Elizabeth, he would have been at Prince John's beck and call, and it was not the way he wanted to live.

If he must be slave to someone, than let it be to his beautiful faery bride. He had to admit it did make his heart sing to gaze upon her. Even now, far away from her faery glamour, he desired her greatly. Ah, yes, but it was possible he was still under the effects of her faery enchantment, even now. For who was to say how long it lasted?

He wished he knew the answer to that, for it bothered him greatly to think he had no free will to love her as any man might love his wife. It was the thorn that pricked at him whenever he thought that he truly loved her, for he could never know if what he felt for her was genuine. Not as long as she had the power to enchant.

'Twas enough to drive any man mad.

Caroline paced the floor in her bedchamber, wringing her hands and biting her lip whilst she waited for Raena to give her what she needed to abort the baby. What was keeping her? Surely she knew the urgency. She had promised her the herbs this morning, and here it was almost dark and still no sign of her.

She had sought her out several times during the day to no avail. No one seemed to know where Raena was, and she was beginning to think Raena was deliberately avoiding her.

Making her way up the spiral staircase to Raena's bedchamber one more time, she rapped impatiently on the door.

Raena knew who it was and decided she could delay the inevitable no longer. With a heavy heart, she opened the door.

Her nerves stretched tight, Caroline cried, "You promised to give me the herbs this day."

Feeling great remorse for betraying Caroline's trust, Raena fetched an earthen jar of harmless herbs and handed it over to the tortured woman without a word. What could she say? What could she do to make things right?

Caroline clutched the small container to her chest. "Thank you, oh, thank you, Raena. You have truly saved my life, for I don't mind telling you now that if you had decided against helping me, I was going to end my life."

Raena's stomach coiled tight. "I can't believe you'd do that."

With a strange, wild gleam in her eye, Caroline answered, "If you knew me better, you'd understand how serious I am. You'd know I couldn't bear to look into my husband's eyes and see his agony when he learned the terrible truth about me."

Raena felt a moment of panic. In three weeks time, Caroline would find out that she still carried her baby. What would she do then? "Caroline, you're not thinking clearly. Don't you realize it would hurt Stephan even more if you were to die?"

"But at least then I wouldn't be there to see it. I'm such a craven coward when it comes to Stephan. I love him so much, I cannot bear to see him suffer."

"Methinks, you have too little faith in your husband's love for you. Think how he'd feel if you left him without even giving him a chance. For that's what it would mean if you killed yourself."

"But why are you so upset, Raena? You've given me the answer to my problems. I have no reason to end my life anymore. Why speak of it now?"

Raena blanched. What was she to do? Soon, Caroline would know she had been tricked. How could she stop her from taking her life then?

She wished she could confide in Wiggles and rely on her wisdom, but she couldn't. Wiggles would think only about the faery child Caroline carried and would most definitely want to preserve its life, no matter the consequences to Caroline. But Raena couldn't be that cold-blooded. Caroline's life must be considered, too.

Raena smiled reassuringly. "You're right. No sense in speaking of such a dismal subject. Everything will be just fine, you'll see. Take a pinch of the herbs each morning, but don't forget: Nothing will happen until the twenty-first day, so you must be patient."

"I shall, now that I know that at the end of that time my worries will be over. Then I'll be able to return to Stephan and all will be well."

Raena couldn't bear to see the hope that lit Caroline's face. Making her way over to the window, she gazed out at the landscape beyond the castle walls. The rain had stopped and the western sky was stained a brilliant orange by the setting sun. Mayhap, it was a sign that all would be well. Oh, how she wished that were true.

A distant movement caught her eye—a small party of riders heading for the castle. She knew immediately who it was, for she recognized the Godwin colors even in the dim light. Stephan. Here to claim the wife he loved so much. But what about Valor? Did he accompany his brother?

Nay, not he. What reason would he have? She had no claim on his heart. He would stay at Godwin Castle with his precious Elizabeth.

"What is it, Raena? You've turned as white as a ghost."

Joining Raena at the window, Caroline looked out and gasped. "Oh, no. He's here. I knew he'd come, but so soon? So soon? How will I face him? What reason can I give for abandoning him like that?"

Raena embraced Caroline. "Here, now. No reason to panic. You can tell him you felt a sisterly need to accompany me here. He'll understand, knowing your kind nature. You have nothing to fear."

"But I never thought he'd come so soon. Not in his condition. He's still not well. He might injure his wound before it's fully healed."

"Nay, he's a Godwin. They come from strong stock." Drawing Caroline away from the window,

Raena implored, "Come, prepare yourself so you can greet him warmly. Act as if nothing is wrong, and he'll be so relieved that he'll not suspect a thing."

"Oh, I wish that it were so."

"Trust me, Caroline. Go out to my rose garden and wait for him there. In that soft setting, Stephan will forget about everything but holding you in his arms."

"Oh, no, not alone. You must stay with me or I'll not have the courage to face him."

Raena's heart went out to the gentle woman. "I'll stay as long as you need me," she promised.

Lighting a torch, they made their way outside. Walking quickly to the rose garden, they sat on a graceful bench carved with delicate Celtic knots.

Raena loved it here, surrounded by nature's beauty. In truth, she felt stronger whenever she was outside the confines of any walls.

She'd need that strength now to face Stephan, for she felt such great guilt at keeping what she knew from him. She wished with all her heart she could tell him the danger Caroline was in and feared she was doing the wrong thing by deceiving him.

Then, Stephan was rushing toward them and Raena had no more time to think. Stephan fell to his knees in front of Caroline and buried his head in her lap.

Caroline stroked his hair, murmuring to him softly, and Raena was struck by the fact that Stephan's head was nestled up against her belly, a belly that was home to a child fathered by Stephan's own brother. Oh, what a tragic situation the young lovers were in.

Stephan looked up just then, gazing at his wife with such a loving expression, Raena couldn't bear to see it. She stood and busied herself at a rose bush profuse with red roses as bright as the flame of love that burned between Caroline and Stephan.

If only she could be loved like that. If only . . .

Hearing footsteps, she looked up to see Valor making his way over to her, running a hand through his rain-dappled hair. She blinked her eyes, disbelieving what she saw, but no, he was truly there.

Forcing herself not to panic, she swallowed hard and, on impulse, picked one of the roses. Gazing into the eyes of the man she loved so much, she kissed the rose softly; then, with a curtsy, she handed the flower to her husband.

"I bid you welcome, my lord."

Valor was surprised and touched by her sweet demeanor. Taking the offered rose, he gave in to a sudden compulsion to brush it across his lips and found the bud as soft and dewy as Raena's own rose-petal lips.

Raising his head from the fragrant flower, he gazed at her. A sweet ache engulfed him at the very sight of her, and he wanted to take her into his arms and crush her to his chest. Instead, he just stood there, the smell of the rose still in his nostrils, wondering if she was sending out her own faery smell to him.

He tried to tell himself it didn't matter, that he was committed to her whether she used her faery glamour or not; but it did bother him. He wanted the right to love her on his own, for surely it wouldn't be so very hard to do.

Raena stared at her husband, a large, hard, lump in her throat. Every time she saw him, she loved him more; and right now, she couldn't imagine ever loving him any more than she did this moment.

But the specter of his father loomed before her,

and she wanted to retreat, to turn and run from her husband. How would Valor treat her after that horrible scene played out with his father? Would he hate her for it? Could he ever forget that because of her he had bloodied his own father?

Forcing herself to stand her ground, she spoke. "My husband, what can I do for you? Would you like meat or drink? A soothing bath or—"

"All that . . . and more."

Valor's voice was deep and husky, resonating through Raena's body every bit as sensuously as if he had touched her in some intimate place. "You have but to command, my lord."

"I shall; but first, will you see to my mother's comfort? She's soaked to the skin and in need of a warm bed."

"Yes, of course, my lord; I didn't know she was with you. I'll see she has a nice warm bath and have a chamber prepared for her. Are there any others who need a bed?" She held her breath as she waited for an answer, suddenly afraid Elizabeth might have come, too.

"And just who else did you expect would come along? Surely not my father?"

Raena felt a stab of pain in her heart. The last thing she wanted was to be reminded of the terrible ordeal with Ambrose. But 'twas obvious it preyed mightily on Valor's mind. "I was thinking of Matthew or—or Avery."

Or Elizabeth.

"Nay, I'm thinking you've captured enough Godwins already. Do you have any idea how much anguish Stephan felt when he found Caroline missing?"

Glancing at Stephan and Caroline sitting side by side now on the bench, she saw that they hadn't heard, so absorbed were they in each other. "She was never missing. Your mother knew exactly where she'd gone."

"Aye, that's another thing. What faery charm have you used on Mother to make her agree to that? Would you make slaves of all my kin?"

"No more than I have of you, Valor. I promised never to use my faery glamour on you again, and I give you my word I've not used it on them."

"The words trip from your soft lips so easily. But Matthew warned me that faery people have no conscience."

"That may be true; but remember, I'm only half-faery. The rest of me is as human as you."

Valor had to admit that she did have a conscience, for she had turned off her faery glamour in the chapel the eve of their wedding. He owed her a debt of gratitude for that much.

Bitterly, he thought about his father and decided he owed her no gratitude at all. He had tried to put all thought of that unholy scene from his mind, but it was impossible. He had to know the truth, or go mad. "See to my mother, then join me in your— our—bedchamber. I wish to speak to you in private."

"Yes, my lord." Raena bowed her head, then turned and left.

Valor was shocked at how easily she acquiesced. Glancing at Stephan and Caroline, he saw them stand and make their way out of the garden arm in arm. Of certain, they'd be going to their bedchamber now. He envied Stephan his loving wife.

Making his way up to Raena's tower room, he opened the door and stepped inside. A subtle fragrance wafted gently in the air. Even when she wasn't present, her faery smell lingered.

Moving about the round tower room, lit only by the faint light coming through the windows, he felt a stirring in his loins. With its commanding view of the countryside from the many windows, the room fit her to perfection. Valor sensed that her wild spirit needed to see the outdoors so that she wouldn't feel so closed in.

He smiled at sight of the scraped hide window coverings rolled up and tied over each window. From the dust and cobwebs, he was certain Raena hadn't used them to cover her windows since early spring.

Walking over to the bed, he pushed down on it with his hand and it sprang back, so full of down was it. A bed fit for a princess. He laughed softly. But then, she was a princess, wasn't she? A princess of the people of Dawne.

Feeling a sudden chill, he stripped off his wet tunic and dried his hair and chest with soft toweling he found draped over a chair.

Hearing the door open, he felt a tightening in his groin and slowly turned . . . to face his wife.

Raena felt her mouth grow dry at the sight of her half-naked husband. She hesitated before entering the room, thinking it too small a space to share with all that masculinity. Closing the door behind her, she placed the candle she carried on a windowsill then, gathering her courage, began to speak. She wanted him to hear her out before he had a chance to reprimand her. "Before you say anything, I want you to know I don't hold you responsible for your father's actions and I don't believe for a moment that you sent him to my chamber."

"What are you talking about? Of course I didn't send my father to you. How could you even think that?"

Surprised at his anger, Raena said, "I believe you. No need to defend yourself so vehemently. It's just that when Elizabeth told me you wanted me to bed another man—"

"What!" Valor roared, so incensed he could barely keep from striking her. "What can you hope to gain by telling me such an evil lie?"

Raena's eyes opened wide with surprise and bewilderment. " 'Tis not a lie. Elizabeth told me you wanted me to take a knight to bed because it was the only way you could legally be rid of me. She told me you had gone so far as to pick out this adulterer yourself."

Balling up his fists, Valor raised his arms over his head, pleading, "God give me strength."

Raena took a step backward, overwhelmed by Valor's passionate display. Was this the man who had always expressed an inordinate amount of self-control?

"Have you faeries no sense of morality at all? How can you stand there and lie like that?"

"Valor. I—I don't know what to say. You act so innocent, I'm beginning to think you had no part in it. Oh, Valor, is it true? It wasn't your wish to catch me in adultery so that you could more easily be granted a divorce?"

Valor shook his head in helpless denial. "Never!" Her words were finally sinking into his brain and, with them, the certainty that she was speaking the truth.

God's blood! He wanted to believe it was all lies, wanted to believe that his father couldn't be that depraved, but in his heart he knew—he had always known—how truly evil his father was. He and Elizabeth had concocted a diabolical plan to destroy his marriage.

But Elizabeth? That was the hardest to believe. How could she have gone along with it? What kind of evil power did Father hold over her?

And yet . . . he knew it was true. Wasn't it she who had told him to go to Raena's chamber? Wasn't it she who had told him that his father was going to ravish Raena? She couldn't have known that unless she was part of the plot. What must Raena think of him, believing that he wanted her to commit such a heinous act?

Still holding the rose in one hand, he drew his sword from its scabbard with the other. Lifting the blade to his lips, he kissed it, saying, "Upon my sword, I swear to you I had no part in planning that abomination."

Raena leaned back against the door for support as a torrent of tears blinded her. "Oh, Valor, Valor! I thought it was your wish. I was willing to do it for your sake, though the thought of it made me sick to my stomach. If it had been anyone but your father, I would have done it."

Unaware of what he was doing, Valor dropped the sword from his hand whilst at the same time crushing the bright rose between his fingers. A thorn pierced his thumb, sending a rivulet of crimson down his hand, but he never noticed, so overwrought with emotion was he.

His face contorted in pain as he pulled his wife to him, crying, "Thank God it was my father who came to you! Thank God it was he; otherwise, you would have gone through with it." Burying his face in her neck, he took a long, shuddering breath.

Raena wrapped her arms around his back and stroked him, soothing him as if he were a child. "Oh, Valor, I thought you wanted to be rid of me. I thought it was what you wanted."

Kneeling before her, Valor took her hand and pressed it to his lips, saying, "Lady Caroline once knelt before you as I do now, in gratitude that you had saved her husband's life. But her gratitude is nothing compared to mine."

With shaky voice, Raena asked, "Gratitude, my lord?"

"And so much more. I am in awe of you and your loving nature. You held our marriage vows sacred despite the dismal way I treated you, despite my family's pressing you to give me up. That means more to me than I can ever say. From this day forward, you hold my happiness, my very life, in your hands."

As if in a dream, Raena heard her husband's words, and a warm rush of happiness swept through her. "Oh, Valor, I never dared hope that you would ever truly want me."

Rising, Valor took her in his arms and crushed her to his chest. "Want you? From the moment I first saw you standing at the top of the stairs, I've wanted you."

Kissing her passionately, Valor lifted her in his arms and carried her over to the bed, gently laying her down. "No man but I shall ever lie with you. Promise me that, Raena."

Raena gazed into luminescent blue eyes and murmured, "You and no other."

Nineteen

Light faded into darkness as the creatures of the night awoke. The chorus of their mingled voices drifted up to the tower room, meshing with the soft, slippery sound of two bodies entwined, moving against the bed covers in slow, languid motions. The lovers were content, for now, to take it slowly, knowing they had the length of the night to enjoy each other.

Raena's heart was bursting with happiness as she reveled in the gentle caress of her husband, basking in the glow of love that emanated from his touch. Nothing could possibly feel as good as his hands moving over her, and she wished—oh, how she wished!—it had been this way the first time they had made love.

In sooth, she felt as though this were their first night as husband and wife; and in a way it was, for this was the first time they had come together freely, each wanting to give to the other instead of only taking, each wanting the other to know how magnificent it could be with nothing between them but the purity of love's flame.

A faint beam of light from the rising moon shone on Valor's face, revealing an expression of such love that she wanted to capture it forever in her heart.

Incandescent blue eyes gazed down at her as if she were the most beloved of women. And at that moment, she truly believed she was.

His hands continued moving over her as she gazed deep into his eyes, her heart and soul captive to this noble knight she adored. Every inch of her body was keenly attuned to his presence, sensitive to the softest of caresses. Her breasts tingled with erotic sensations at his touch, and her nipples hardened and stretched, reaching toward the man who had her in his thrall.

The private place between her legs throbbed to be joined to him again, and as if reading her mind, Valor sent one searching hand down between her legs, exploring her most intimately. She gave a little cry, and her body arched in pleasure at the exquisite feeling that rose inside her.

She wanted to cry out to him that he had more power than she to enchant, for she was willing—nay, more than that, eager—to do anything he asked of her.

But all he wanted, at the moment, was to give her great pleasure. And oh! how he was succeeding. She felt his finger slide into her moist opening and almost fainted from the intense pleasure it evoked.

Seeing the sensual way she reacted to his touch, Valor was encouraged to continue his exploration. Probing deeper, he delighted in the touch of liquid-velvet walls. Raena was the only woman he had ever made love to, and that only deepened the pleasure of discovering the wonderful secrets of her femininity.

God had surely been at his best when he designed woman, for Val couldn't imagine anything as compelling and wondrous as the gentle contours of his wife's lovely body.

To his joy, the question that had haunted him since first he met her was answered to his deep satisfaction. Raena was not meant to be his punishment, but his most treasured reward.

After making slow, sweet, unhurried love, they surfaced from their rumpled bed and drank thirstily from a shared goblet of wine. Then, with his arm wrapped 'round her waist, he walked her over to the nearest window, and together they gazed out upon their domain.

The circle of windows afforded a view in every direction, looking out to the road to the hamlet from one window; a wide meadow from another; and from where they looked out now, the ramparts of the castle and, below that, the sea.

Kissing the tip of her nose, he murmured, "I've never slept in a tower room before. 'Tis odd to stare out at the roof of a castle."

"My lord, if you're not pleased, I can have another bedchamber prepared for . . . us."

Valor's eyes twinkled wickedly. "You mistake my meaning, wife. I'm very pleased with your round little tower room, for we're closer to the heavens here."

Raena sighed contentedly, knowing Valor was happy. But then, unexpectedly, he moved away from her, saying, "There's something I must do."

Puzzled, Raena watched as Valor wrapped himself in the cover from the bed and walked out the private door that led to the ramparts of the castle. Peering through a crack in the door, she saw him talking to the night watch.

The man nodded his head, then turned and left, going down the winding staircase. Seeing they were now alone, Raena opened the door wide and called out to Valor. "Come to bed, my husband. I'm lonely for you."

Instead of coming to her, Valor opened his arms wide, still holding tight to the ends of the blanket. It moved like a banner in the night wind, flagging out behind him to reveal the splendor of his maleness. Needing no other encouragement, Raena ran into his arms.

Cocooned in the blanket, they walked the ramparts, whispering words of love to each other, gazing up at a sea of bright stars, as if seeing them for the first time.

Then, as the need to mate came once again, Valor pulled her into his arms and nuzzled at her neck. "I want to make love to you right here—right now—with the heavens as our witness."

Raena's lovely eyes rivaled the stars with their brightness as she replied, "My lord, I was thinking the very same thing."

Valor felt a deep stirring in his loins. It was as if he had some ancient need to make her his—with the earth and the sky, the stars and the trees, as witness. A need for the cosmos itself to know that she belonged to him.

Raena lowered the blanket to the rough surface of the stones, spreading it out for them to lie upon, but Valor had other plans. Taking her hand, he pulled her to her feet; then, locking his legs, he lifted her up until she was suspended over his steel-hard rod.

Raena needed no instructions. She knew what he wanted and was more than eager to please him. Sliding over him, she found what she was looking for, what he was waiting for. She closed her eyes and the sweet wanting began.

Afraid of falling from her lofty perch, she held

tight to his neck, but he held her in place as if she weighed no more than a delicate butterfly. In truth, she was in awe of the great strength he possessed and pleased that he used it now for their mutual pleasure.

For a long time, he stood, not moving, just enjoying the feel of her, the joy of her, the need of her, as the heavens twinkled their approval. It was a waking dream, standing there washed in the faint light of the stars, and he reveled in it and counted himself blessed.

Raena, too, moved very little, content just to feel him deep inside her, so very deep that she imagined his manhood reaching up into the very center of her being. She felt herself open up even more at that thought, and the part of her that held him captive convulsed involuntarily and the loving began.

Valor arched his back and thrust upward whilst Raena moved herself back and forth on his manhood. She was already beginning to know his natural rhythm and made it work for them both most rapturously.

Hindered by the unnatural position, Valor had to leave most of the work up to his wife, and that was frustrating, whilst at the same time it gave him a great sense of power. He stood rooted to the very roof of the castle, confident in his potency, his strength, receiving all the love that she had to give him with great relish.

As he stared up at the sky, the rapture took him away and he immersed himself completely in the act. A strange sound escaped his lips with each erotic thrust, a sound halfway between a cry and a moan, halfway between heaven and earth, and it en-

hanced the ecstasy greatly, escalating in volume as
he came closer and closer to his release.

Raena was in tune with her husband's cries, in
tune, too, with the earth and the song of the heavens, all of it sweet music to her ears. She concentrated on pleasing her husband, but, oh, she was
sure it was she who received the most from their
loving.

She hung on tight to her man, the night wind at
her back, the sky her sparkling mantle, and her
faery spirit reveled in this unusual form of lovemaking. She wanted it to go on forever, but at the same
time, she wanted it to end, desperate for release
from such great want.

Then, it was happening: She was soaring up to
the stars, taking them all inside her body as the
white heat exploded and she became one with Valor
and with the earth and sky.

Valor staggered backwards, drained of all his
strength, coming to rest against the rough surface
of the parapet. Fearing he would fall, Raena separated from him and slid lightly to the ground once
more.

Valor pulled her into his arms and kissed her
hard. His tongue searched her mouth, delving deep
as if in continuance of the perfect union of their
bodies.

Raena welcomed it, still needing him, wanting
him to go on and on, loving her, pleasuring her.
She could not get enough of him.

Groaning, Valor lifted her into his arms and carried her back into the tower room. When he reached
the bed, he suddenly smiled mischievously and let
her fall into its downy softness. Then, straddling her,
he playfully growled, "Again?"

They made love once more, then fell into a deep

sleep, regaining their strength to start all over again before dawn's light turned their eagles' nest room rosy and pink.

Twenty

Valor and Raena spent the next five days in bed, arising only long enough to take meals and relieve themselves in their own private garderobe before escaping once again to their love nest.

Not all of that time was spent in lovemaking, but oh, it seemed so, for Raena's body tingled constantly from the touch of his hands. Even when he was not touching her, she felt him still.

Using his hands and his tongue, his mouth and his exploring manhood, Valor gained intimate knowledge of Raena's body, memorizing every curve, every crevice, every mole upon her body. He even took the time to count her long dark lashes, but lost count each time he tried. In truth, he never tired from his efforts, never tired of touching her, tasting her, never tired of making love to her.

In all the days they stayed in bed, no one interrupted them, no one even so much as knocked at their door. The usually raucous everyday noises of the castle seemed gentler, quieter, as the castle folk tiptoed around as if they were trying not to disturb a sleeping child.

But instead of a sleeping child, 'twas an awakening love they protected. A worthy love that would strengthen and grow in time, protecting the sanctity of their home, their castle, and every living soul within their domain. In the aura of that vibrant love, all would benefit.

On the sixth day, they made a great effort to stay out of bed. Though the steward was exemplary, Valor knew it was time he took his place as lord of the castle. After making love to Raena, he reluctantly devoted the rest of the day to administering to the castle's most urgent needs.

Feeling suddenly shy and embarrassed at her lengthy stay in bed with her new husband, a red-cheeked Raena sought out Mellicent and Caroline in the great hall, knowing it had been rude to ignore them so long.

She found Caroline sitting by the fire as if it were the dark of winter instead of a delightful summer day, and it pained Raena to see her looking so miserable, so restless and afraid.

Caroline glanced up at her just then, and Raena tried to reassure her with a smile; but Caroline looked through her as if she didn't see her. Raena realized the troubled woman was barely aware of anything around her.

Raena longed to see the sparkle back in Caroline's eyes, but was well aware that there was only one way that could happen.

The time was drawing closer when Caroline would discover she still carried the faery child, and Raena feared what she would do when she found out.

Feeling shame that she had selfishly ignored Caroline's plight in all the days with Valor, she knew it was time to discuss it with someone who could look at the problem objectively. But whom? She dared not broach the subject with her husband.

Nay, she didn't want to take the chance of destroying the closeness they had so wondrously gained.

Any mention of faery enchantments could make him remember what she wanted so desperately for him to forget: That he was with her by her choice and not his own.

She wasn't sure he could help, in any case. He held strict ideals of what was right and wrong and would most likely feel the need to tell Stephan all. And why not? Surely Stephan had every right to know his wife was contemplating suicide.

Oh, it was all so maddening. It was becoming clear that there was no answer to the problem that would be fair to everyone. And she hadn't even begun to think about Avery's part in this. The child was his; surely he should have some say in whether it lived or died.

Hearing her name called, she turned to see Stephan making his way toward her, an intense look upon his face. Her heart sank. He was the last person she wanted to talk to.

Speaking softly so no one could hear, he said, "Raena, I beseech you to tell me what troubles my wife. Why won't she return to Godwin Castle?"

Seeing it useless to deny the obvious, she answered, "Stephan, your wife spoke to me in confidence and I am not at liberty to tell you what she said."

Stephan rolled his head in anguish and glanced back at his forlorn wife before continuing. "Then, 'tis true. Something terrible has happened. You know what troubles her. Tell me. I beg of you. I have to know. I cannot go on like this any longer, pretending that nothing's wrong whilst all the while my insides are being torn in two."

Raena's heart went out to Stephan. How could she keep the terrible secret from him any longer? He was the one person who could keep Caroline safe, but he was also the one person who could drive her over the edge. "I wish I could tell you, Stephan, believe me, I do; but I can't. All I dare say is do not think she has foresaken you, for she has not. She loves you as much as ever she did. In truth, it is because of her great love for you that she suffers so now."

Stephan turned white. "I can only think of one reason why she would insist on staying here, one thing that would cause her to suffer so. But I don't want to believe it. I cannot believe that she would be unfaithful to me."

Raena's heart lurched. "Then do not believe it. Believe in the love you share. Believe in a happy future with your beloved at your side. There's no reason to think any different."

"Then you give me reason to hope?"

Hope. How she wished there were reason for hope; but if there was, she was blind to it. Still, for Stephan's sake, she would be optimistic. "Be patient, Stephan. Let her work out her problem in her own way, and when she's ready, she'll tell you what is troubling her. I'm sure of it."

Raena felt great pity for Stephan and wished with all her heart that she could tell him about Caroline's baby, not just for his and Caroline's sake, but for her own. Selfish though it might be, she wished the burden off her shoulders. Let the decision about the baby be between the two of them only.

In truth, if Stephan had pushed her any harder, she would have told him everything. But as luck would have it, Stephan turned and left, leaving Raena alone to ponder what she should do.

Desperate to sort it all out, she decided to go to the faery circle. Within the circumference of those magic stones, she had always felt serene and wise.

But she'd have to wait until the cover of night, for she daren't let Valor know where she was going. Protective husband that he was, and growing more so every day, he'd want to accompany her.

Since that could prove dangerous for him, she wasn't willing to take the chance. 'Twas dangerous for any human to set foot inside the circle. Not to mention the imminent danger of Queen Edainn's putting an enchantment on him. She had made it clear she liked strong, virile, human males to mate with, and Raena knew the queen cared not whether the object of her desire was wed or not.

Valor belonged to her. She'd not share him with any woman.

She regretted now that she had shown Valor the secret passageway in a playful moment in between their lovemaking. He had seemed not surprised at all to learn of it, and all would have been fine if she hadn't told him that she had actually used it one dark night.

She had tried to explain that there was no danger with Wiggles at her side, but that placated him very little. Still, she had no complaints; she welcomed his concern. A few days ago she had thought there no chance that she and Valor would become so close, and here they were, acting like any married couple.

Feeling a sudden need to speak to Wiggles, Raena was dismayed to find that she had left the castle. It wasn't like her nursemaid to go off alone, save when she visited the faery circle.

Could that be where she had gone? John Barrows would most likely know.

Setting out for the cottage at the edge of the wood, Raena made her way over the drawbridge, her steps growing lighter as the sunshine seeped into her body.

She found John sitting on a stool outside his home, working at a strap of leather he was fashioning into a bridle. When he saw her approach, he put down the leather and started toward her.

"My lady, I had no idea you'd be coming to my humble cottage, this day. Saera Ni never told me. . . ."

"Forgive me, John, but 'twas on an impulse that I came. I can't find Wiggles . . . Saera Ni . . . anywhere and thought you'd know where she's off to."

"She didn't tell you? Queen Edainn sent a message ordering her to appear before her. I don't mind telling you it has me worried. I fear it portends something ominous."

"Do you have any idea why she was summoned?"

"None at all. It took Saera Ni by surprise. I've a good mind to ride there myself and find out."

"No, please, Saera would never approve of that. You know the danger. But there's no reason why I can't go. I had planned on going there anyway . . . tonight; but if you'll saddle a horse for me, I'll go this very moment."

Seeing the relief on John's face, Raena embraced him, patting him on his broad back. "No need to worry. I'll bring your Saera Ni back to you."

Riding with his steward, Miles Kendall, Valor gazed at the passing landscape and felt a surge of satisfaction that it belonged to him. It surprised him to find he had no regrets about the wealth he would have attained from Elizabeth.

Prince John was a volatile man. What he gave could be taken away just as easily. History had already proven that. Better to live in contentment on a smaller parcel of land that was more secure from the whims of fickle royalty.

He would work hard to improve the land and the lot of his people; and with that in mind, he was sharing his plans for the future with Miles. "And over there would be the perfect place for an orchard."

"Aye, my lord, that would be well placed."

"And . . ." Sweeping his gaze toward a cottage on the edge of the woods, Valor forgot what he was going to say. Raena was there, standing very close to a tall, well-muscled man.

Seeing Valor's distraction, Miles looked at the cottage to see what had caught his master's attention. "That's John Barrows, my lord."

"John Barrows? Ah, yes, the huntsman. I remember speaking to him the day I left with Lady Raena for my father's castle. Tell me about him."

'Twas obvious to Miles that Sir Valor was jealous of his wife's attention to another man and, hoping to assuage his fears, he said, "At one time he was the castle's steward. He resigned his position, but the baron let him stay on as his huntsman. Some say he's the baron's bastard son; but if he is, the baron never claimed him openly."

"Is Raena aware of that? Does she look upon him as a brother?"

"I doubt she knows, my lord. It's rarely spoken of."

Valor barely comprehended what Miles was saying, so intense was his concentration on Raena and the virile man she was speaking to so intimately. What was Raena doing standing so close to the huntsman?

Feeling exceedingly possessive, he spurred his horse on and made his way to the cottage.

John saw him first and smiled so genuinely, Valor's fears were immediately put to rest. Whatever there was between John and Raena had to be innocent. Of course, it was; he had no reason to think otherwise.

It was only natural to feel so proprietary, considering the long days and nights he had just spent in her bed. And, indeed, they had accomplished much more in bed than just getting to know each other's bodies. It pleased him to think that their hearts and spirits had bonded as well.

Raena heard the pounding of hooves and turned to see her husband bearing down on her. Taken by surprise, she knew not what to say, but 'twas obvious she couldn't leave for the faery circle now. She'd have to wait until Valor fell asleep that night.

Feeling as if she were caught doing something she shouldn't be doing, Raena greeted her husband awkwardly.

Valor sensed her nervousness with a stab of uneasiness. All the positive thoughts of their bonding disappeared in a flash. What was she up to? And what did it have to do with this all-too-thoroughly-virile huntsman? Trying to sound indifferent, he addressed John Barrows. "I understand from Miles that you used to be the castle's steward."

John nodded his head. "Aye, my lord. 'Twas a long time ago. I left because I thought myself better suited to being a huntsman."

"Commendable, I'm sure, yet it seems odd anyone would give up such a high position for such a lowly one."

John accepted the insult without rancor. "It depends on your point of view, I'd say. I'm not one to be closed up tight in a castle. I like the outdoors and the freedom to come and go as I wish without anyone to answer to."

"Not even a wife?"

John smiled without humor. "Not even a wife, my lord."

Fearing where this conversation would lead, Raena interrupted, "Valor, you came along just in time. I'm suddenly weary. Pray, ride me back to the castle so I have no need to walk."

Without another word, Valor took her by the arm and began leading her over to his steed. Raena turned to wave goodbye to John and mouthed the word *tonight*.

John nodded his head in understanding and stood watching as Valor lifted his wife onto the saddle and climbed up after her. As they rode away, he wondered why his new lord seemed resentful of him.

Valor kept Raena within his sight the rest of the day. He had no wish to confront her with his worries, for until he had a better idea what was going on, he didn't want to risk hurting the delicate bond between them. For the first time in his life he was truly happy, and he couldn't bear for anything to interfere with that.

They made love quickly but urgently that night, and afterward, it took only a matter of moments before Valor fell into a deep sleep. Raena listened to his steady breathing until she was sure he wouldn't awaken, then slowly extricated herself from his arms. He stirred and she held her breath, waiting to see if he'd wake up, but thankfully he was deep in dreamland.

Breathing a sigh of relief, Raena dressed and tiptoed down the stairs to her sitting room, where she pulled an end of the unicorn tapestry away from the wall and slipped behind it into the secret passageway.

Her heart pounded with fear as she entered the dark well and started down the staircase, feeling her way with her hands along the cold, narrow walls.

At the bottom of the stairs, she descended through the long, dank-smelling tunnel; and when, at last, she saw a glimmer of light, she breathed easier. To think that Wiggles used that dismal passageway all the time!

When she emerged inside the vault, she had a moment of panic, remembering that Wiggles had used a key to open the door; but when she put her hand to the latch, it opened easily. Evidently, Wiggles had left it unlocked. Raena feared she must be deeply troubled to be so careless.

Once outside the cloying tunnel, she took in a deep, refreshing breath of the fragrant night air, then made her way to John's cottage.

John was waiting for her, with a horse already saddled. "Have you heard from her yet?"

"Nay, and I'm beginning to worry in earnest."

"You needn't. Your Saera Ni knows how to take care of herself."

"I wouldn't worry if she were anywhere but in the faery circle. What power has she against Queen Edainn?"

Raena shivered, suddenly afraid to face the queen of faeries, but what choice did she have? Wiggles had taken good care of her all her life, it was only right that Raena try to take care of her now.

Awakening with a start, Valor reached out for the warmth of his wife's body, but she wasn't there. Sitting up, he stared across the darkened chamber and felt the loneliness.

She was gone.

Jumping out of bed, he made his way down to the sitting room, but she wasn't there, either. His gaze immediately traveled to the door to the hallway. She couldn't have gone out that way, for the door was still bolted. He knew what that meant. She had taken the secret passageway. But why?

He ran to dress quickly, his heart pounding like a war drum, then descended once more and stepped inside the secret passageway, cursing his fate at having such a willful wife.

As he felt his way through the tunnel, he envisioned turning her over his knee and spanking her firm, rounded bottom. But as stubborn and determined as she was, he doubted it would do any good.

At the end of his slow journey, he felt a shudder of revulsion when he found himself inside a burial vault. But he had to admit it was an ingenious place to put the secret tunnel.

Leaving the tomb, he surveyed the lonely landscape. A dim light caught his eye from the direction of John Barrow's cottage. That's where she had gone. He was sure of it.

With grim determination, he headed toward the cottage. Soon he could make out a small, dark silhouette astride a horse, and a larger shadow standing beside it. Without a doubt, the smaller form was Raena.

Clenching his teeth, he started running toward the cottage, watching in frustration as Raena rode away, unaware he was there. He dared not call out, for fear people in the castle would hear. The last thing he wanted was for the populous to know of his inability to control his wife.

John saw Sir Valor and his heart lurched. The young lord looked so angry, he feared he'd have to defend himself against him and wanted that not.

But out of breath, Valor could only pant and hold his side until the pain of running faded away. "By God, you'll tell me what you were doing with my wife or I'll run you through with my sword!"

"My lord, you have nothing to fear from me. Your wife only wanted my horse. She's on her way to the faery circle to find out why Queen Edainn has detained Saera Ni."

"Saera Ni? Why have I not heard that name before?"

"She's Saera Wigglesworth to you, sir."

"Why all this secrecy? I thought Saera was her nursemaid, and now I find she's much more than that. Why didn't Raena confide in me? I'm her husband, I'm—"

"My lord, forgive me for interfering in your private life, but I know something of faery folk. She wanted to keep you from harm. She knew if she confided in you, you would have tried to protect her, and would surely have found yourself in danger."

"So, instead she feels the need to protect *me?*" Valor was furious. "Why in God's name would she need to protect me from some wispy, faery queen? She can't possibly be a danger to me."

"Take me at my word, my lord. She is. One step inside the faery circle and you are in a magical domain such as you've never dreamt. Out here night follows day, but in that magic place, all sense of time is distorted. You might live there a lifetime and think it but a day."

"Superstitious nonsense."

"Is it nonsense that drove you to marry my lady Raena?"

"What do you know of that?"

"Saera Ni is my confidante as well as my beloved. She keeps no secrets from me."

Valor felt the need to laugh but held it back, seeing how serious this huntsman was. "Isn't she just a little too old for you?"

John smiled. "Do not believe everything you see, my lord. Saera Ni is young and beautiful, lithe of form and fair of face. She uses the ancient power to disguise herself, for she does not wish to be attractive to mortals."

Valor had a hard time seeing Wiggles as anything but a stout, ancient woman, but he believed John's words. He was beginning to understand much more about the magical beings who shared this world with him, but he also knew his knowledge was limited. What would he be facing at the faery circle?

He had been warned by Raena—and now by John—of the dangers of the stones, but by hell's fire, he couldn't stand by and do nothing whilst his wife traipsed over the countryside like a vixen fox.

"I'm going to the faery circle and I'd like you to accompany me. I may have need of you."

"I'll go with you, but I fear nothing can save you once you step inside the circle."

"Do you have a length of rope?"

"There is no magic protection in rope."

"No, but if I tie one end around my waist and you hold the other outside the circle, you can pull me out when I've a need."

John was skeptical that it could work, but like Valor, he felt the need to act. He couldn't bear standing around doing nothing when the great love of his life might be in danger.

"It's worth a try, I'm thinking."

Valor slapped John's shoulder. "You're a good man, John Barrows."

Raena made her way inside the faery circle and glanced around. 'Twas a somber lot of faeries and elves who stared back at her. Strangely, that same feeling of superiority hit her once again, just as it had the last time she'd been here. Was it possible she had some hidden magic power she was unaware of?

The only being there to whom she didn't feel superior was the queen, but she did feel her equal. Perhaps the royal blood of her father elevated her above the others.

As she got her bearings, she spotted Wiggles, dear sweet Wiggles, kneeling before the queen, her head bowed low. What was this all about?

Approaching the queen, Raena gathered her courage and spoke much more confidently than she felt. "I demand to know why my beloved nursemaid is being kept from my service."

Quiet reigned as all eyes looked to the queen.

Edainn rose imperiously from her stone chair. "You dare to address me without first paying homage?"

"I give homage only where it's due." Oh, why had she said that? She was in trouble now. And yet, something deep within her told her she had acted rightly.

Edainn stared down the impudent young woman. But she was suddenly uneasy. This girl must be secure in her power to challenge her so boldly. When it came to half-lings, anything was possible.

And . . . truth to tell, fertile royal princesses had precedence over barren queens.

Was the girl pregnant?

Was that what made her so brave?

"Princess Raena, I honor you of noble blood and see no reason why we can't resolve our problem in kinship instead of rancor. You seem to be misinformed as to why Saera Ni is here. No one is holding her captive. She's free to leave whenever she wishes. Isn't that right, Saera Ni?"

Saera Ni blinked her eyes to clear the awe she felt for her young charge. Never had she seen her act so bravely. Truly, Princess Raena had more faery powers than anyone was aware of. She took command as regally as if she were used to ordering queens about.

"That is not exactly so, my queen. I was summoned here to heal Prince Ohreinn's infant son; and when that was done, you told me I must stay."

Prince Ohreinn's son? Raena was shocked to discover she had yet another sibling. How many brothers and sisters did she have? Excited, her gaze sought out her father and found him standing over a small babe nestled in a reed basket.

Forcing her attention back to the matter at hand, she spoke again. "Why were you ordered to stay?"

Looking to the queen for approval, Saera Ni answered Raena when Edainn nodded. "Because you have outgrown your need of me. The queen wants me to become nursemaid to another half-ling child. I tried to tell her that, any day now, you would discover you were with child, that I was needed to help you raise the precious royal one."

Murmurs of approval rose around her. Shocked and pleased to discover the other faeries were on her side, Raena felt her power increase. "Indeed, that may be so, for I have not bled since my marriage."

The murmurs increased, sounding even merrier.

Of course. They all had a vested interest in her ability to reproduce. Was that the strange power she felt? Was she, indeed, pregnant already? Instinctively, it came to her that fertility equalled power in this domain.

Her hand went to her belly as if to feel the power deep within, and her hand suddenly throbbed with warmth. It was true. She carried Valor's child. She was sure of it.

Edainn did not miss the gesture, and a sadness washed over her. She would give anything, endure anything, if she could bear a child. Turning to Saera Ni, she said, "Are you sure this is what you want? You know the consequences."

Saera Ni answered softly. " 'Tis what I want, your majesty."

"So be it. I'll not interfere with your sentimental attachment to the Princess Raena. You may go."

Raena felt a rush of raw relief, for she had little idea how to make use of this unaccustomed power. But what consequences was the queen talking about? Was Wiggles in danger?

Saera Ni stood up and made her way to Raena's side. She was about to urge Raena to leave quickly when out of the corner of her eye she saw Valor step inside the faery circle.

Mother of Goddess! No.

A loud noise like the drawing in of some giant's mighty breath filled the air, and everyone turned as one to stare at the brave knight.

Raena had no idea what was happening until her gaze fell upon her husband. For a moment, she doubted what she saw. Let it be an illusion brought about by the queen's magic, she prayed silently; but from the excited reaction of the faery beings surrounding her, she knew he was truly there and she sank into the depths of despair.

Valor's fate was in the hands of Queen Edainn. No one could help him now.

Twenty-one

Edainn's gaze turned slowly to the handsome mortal caught inside the boundaries of her circular realm, and a surge of energy coursed through her. She couldn't believe her good luck. "So, this is the virile knight you wed. No wonder you've kept him to yourself, Raena, for he's certainly a tasty morsel."

A small cry escaped Raena's throat.

Saera Ni grasped Raena's arm tightly, whispering under her breath, "Gather your wits about you if you want to save your husband from Edainn."

Her words gave Raena hope, for, verily, she had thought there no chance at all of saving him.

Valor stood just inside the circle, afraid to take another step. From the moment he walked between two of the standing rocks, he had had the uneasy feeling that the world as he knew it had disappeared and he questioned his wisdom in entering this magic place.

Eerie stillness surrounded him as each being within the circle gazed at him as if he were a fascinating curiosity. He supposed he was.

Feeling more than a little insecure, he dropped his hand to his waist, seeking the hidden rope tied around him under his surcoat. It seemed flimsy to him right now, and he wondered if he were foolish to think of escaping this magic place with the mere tugging of a rope. He was unsure if the laws of nature even applied here.

His eyes sought his wife. Raena was standing before an exotic creature who could only be the feared queen of faeries. If he had been uneasy before, seeing the horror on his wife's face confirmed that he must, indeed, be in great peril.

"Queen Edainn, the tasty morsel you speak of is *mine.*"

"Never fear, you can have him back when I'm finished with him. 'Tis been too long a time since a handsome knight has wandered into the faery circle, and I will not be denied the pleasure of his company."

All the power Raena felt but moments ago vanished with the queen's words. All Edainn had to do was turn on her faery glamour and Valor would be compelled to mate with her. The thought of witnessing her husband making love to another woman was too much to bear. Near panic, she turned to Ohreinn and pleaded, "Father, will you not intervene?"

Ohreinn sighed sadly. There was not much he could do to stop Edainn; it was her right as queen to take whatever male came into her realm, but for Raena's sake he would try. "My queen, quell your ravenous appetite for this young knight. 'Twould not be wise to interfere with the bonding of my daughter and her new husband."

"And pray tell me, why is that?"

"If she's not with child already, you may prevent it from happening in the future. Remember that humans are squeamish about sharing their mates. It upsets them greatly. Should Valor mate with you, he and Raena might shun the act of procreation in the future. We cannot take that chance."

"What matter?" Edainn scoffed. "If not this one, some other male will crawl between her legs and plant his seed."

Valor's anger knew no bounds, hearing those hateful words. "Not if I have anything to say about it. Raena has sworn to have no man but me. You could learn from her. What kind of pleasure can you have forcing me to fornicate with you? Have you no pride? Save your lust for one who wants you."

"You speak so bravely, knight. But your words are wasted on me. Have you not heard that faeries have no conscience? And as for love, 'tis a foreign notion. I know not what it's like to be joined to a beloved mate. But don't pity me, for I can enjoy the body of any male I like, and when I am done with him, I can toss him aside as easily as if he were naught but a shard of broken pottery. Shall I demonstrate my powers or will you come to me of your own free will?"

Just as Raena feared, the queen's sexual appetite was powerful. It wouldn't be easy to dissuade her from taking what she wanted, but for Valor—and the precious, fragile love between them—she had to try. "Queen Edainn, I bow to your power. Please take pity on me and do not use my husband."

"Look who speaks, the princess who would be queen. Too late to do homage now. I'll take your man and use him until his seed is dried up and there's nothing left of his body but an empty husk. 'Tis my right. And why should you object? 'Tis a family tradition, after all. For both your mother and Valor's have been seduced by the Faerie."

Valor cried out his outrage, straining at the taut rope that kept him from going any farther into the circle. "You lie!"

Edainn's bell-like laughter filled the magic circle. "Didn't you know your brother Avery was fathered by Prince Ohreinn?"

Stunned by her words, Valor could think of nothing to say.

"Enough, Edainn," Ohreinn said. "You've tortured the man enough."

The queen spun to face Ohreinn. "Be quiet or be gone. I'll not stand for any insubordination from my subjects."

Raena heard the fury in Edainn's voice and knew she would be merciless. Nothing could save Valor now.

Edainn turned back to Valor and let loose her faery glamour in one hot flush of wind. It was so very powerful that it could be seen as a pale-violet cloud.

Valor jerked backward under its power while desperately reaching for the rope. He had time to pull on it but once before his strength to resist was taken from him.

Befuddled by the mist inside his head, he staggered toward the queen; but at that moment, John answered his tug with a hard yank on his end of the rope, pulling Valor off balance.

Valor struggled against the tug of the rope, compelled now to go to the queen; but in his weakened state, he had not the power. At one more swift jerk of the rope, he tumbled backwards out of the circle.

At first, Raena thought her husband's disappearance a magical rescue by her father, but, for sooth, he seemed as astonished as she.

As for Edainn, she fell silent, fearing that Raena's magic was, indeed, more powerful than hers, for how else could the knight have so easily flown out of the magic circle?

Sensing Edainn's fears, Raena took advantage of the moment and in an arrogant voice declared, "You see, 'tis useless to fight me. I'm more powerful than you. Take care, I don't challenge you for your throne."

Saera Ni groaned. Raena had gone too far. Grasping her by the arm, she led her away from the queen, her hand shaking mightily, afraid of Edainn's retribution.

Raena struggled with Wiggles, wanting to stay and taunt the wicked queen some more, but Wiggles pinched the skin of her arm, whispering, "Leave now, while you still have the chance."

As she regained her senses, the fight went out of Raena and she stepped outside the magic circle.

Meanwhile, Valor and John had already started up the path leading to the road. They had no idea how far the queen's powers extended and feared she'd reach out for them at any moment.

Halfway up the course, they heard Raena and Saera Ni behind them. Valor turned to look down at his wife as the wind caught at his mantle, causing it to flare out behind him.

It took all the courage Raena had to look him in the eye, for, verily, she was afraid of what she'd see. Would he hate her now, knowing just how ruthless faeries could be?

In answer to her unspoken plea for understanding, Valor's face took on a look so mournful it nearly broke her heart. She lowered her gaze and continued up the slope.

They rode back toward the castle in silence, stopping at John's cottage to dismount. They would have to enter the castle as they had left it, through the secret passageway, for, of course, the drawbridge was closed for the night.

Saera Ni tried to comfort Raena with a sympathetic smile. "Take heart, Gosling, things are not as bad as they seem."

Raena smiled at her nursemaid, and a thought came unbidden to her head. *Saera Ni is not well.*

"I'm fine, Wiggles, but what about you? Would you like me to brew some special herbs to help you sleep?"

Saera Ni brushed the hair from Raena's face. "No, child, the only medicine I need is to be with John. I will see you in the morning. Don't be worrying about me, now; I'll be fine."

A lump came to Raena's throat. I'll not worry about you whilst you're in John Barrow's care."

Waving goodbye, Raena made her way to the burial ground and followed her husband, engrossed in thought.

She wouldn't blame him if he hated her now. 'Twas hard enough for him to accept his own enchantment, let alone his mother's.

In the darkness of the tunnel, Raena heard a barely discernible sob, and her heart went out to Valor, knowing he was suffering. She wanted to embrace him, comfort him, but dared not touch him, for fear he'd reject her. When they emerged into her sitting room, she searched his face, but saw no sign that he'd been crying. Could she have imagined it?

After climbing up to their tower room, Valor stripped off his clothes and lay down on the bed that had been witness to so much loving. Without a sound he turned his back to her.

She slid into bed beside him, hoping he would roll over and take her in his arms, but he did not. Hurt by his rejection, she had a sudden desire to use her faery glamour to bend him to her will, but remembering her oath, she closed her eyes and waited for sleep to take her.

Valor wasn't so lucky. He couldn't sleep at all; his mind in a turmoil of anguish. He felt like a pawn in a war between humans and faeries, and he didn't like it one bit. He had tried very hard to accept that he was a slave to Raena's will, but to find out that his mother shared his fate was too much to bear. His manhood was slipping away from him, and he knew no way to salvage it.

Twenty-two

A few days later, Raena sat next to Lady Mellicent in the great hall, trying to appear lighthearted, but in truth, her heart ached. Valor was deliberately avoiding her; even now, he was off riding with Stephan, though the day was extraordinarily windy.

Would there never be peace between them? She didn't doubt his love for her; though he had never actually said the words, he told her in a thousand different ways how much he loved her. Not only with their fierce lovemaking, but with the fervent way he looked at her, the soft timbre of his voice when he spoke only to her.

No, she doubted not his love, but she was beginning to realize that there was more to a happy marriage than just love. There must be something lacking in her, she fretted, else her husband would be more content.

Forcing a smile, she turned her attention to Lady Mellicent. "Have you seen the new fire roses blooming in the rose garden? I thought I might pick a bouquet before the wind does damage to them. I'm thinking they'd brighten your bedchamber."

"They would be a welcome addition, but to Caroline's chamber, not mine. The poor child's not feeling well and has decided to stay abed this day."

Raena didn't like the sound of that and decided to see for herself how Caroline was. Excusing herself, she went out to the garden and picked a large bouquet of roses. Arranging them nicely in an urn, she climbed the stairs to the second floor landing over the great hall.

It was here that all the bedchambers but hers were located. She had arranged for Caroline to have her mother's bedchamber, just beyond the little-used narrow stairs to the ramparts. It was close to her own sitting room and she had hoped Caroline would feel more at home there. And since the main staircase to the ramparts was far away, the location afforded Caroline greater privacy.

She rapped softly on Caroline's door, and when there was no answer, elected to leave her alone—not just because the poor thing needed her sleep, but because, in truth, she was greatly relieved not to have to face her. Feeling very much the coward she was, she walked down the hall to her sitting room.

Opening the door, she was astonished to find Robin Hood within. He placed a finger to his lips, and she closed the door behind her before crying out his name. "Robin! What are you doing here? How did you get in?" She shook her head foolishly. Of course. He'd used the secret tunnel. He confirmed her guess with a nod toward the unicorn tapestry.

" 'Tis the only way I can be sure no one knows when I'm here. I do fear bumping into your husband on one of my clandestine visits; I wouldn't want him mistaking me for your lover. I cherish my neck too much for that."

Raena placed the urn of roses on a small table, smiling sadly. "You're not likely to find him here. He's been avoiding me as if I had contracted the plague. But I'm sure you didn't come here to hear about my marital problems." She cocked her head, studying him curiously. "Why *have* you come?"

"Brace yourself, Raena, I have someone I want you to meet. Someone very special to me."

Robin pulled aside the tapestry that hid the secret door and out stepped a petite, redheaded woman. "Raena, this is my wife, the lady Marian. I pray you'll forgive me for bringing her here unannounced, but in truth, we've a great need for someplace to be alone. She has been traveling with me and my men, and as you know, those conditions are not the most favorable for, shall I say, a romantic interlude?"

Lady Marian turned a deep red.

Raena smiled warmly at Lady Marian, liking her immediately. "Lady Marian, I'm so happy to meet you, at last. Your name has become almost legend in these parts. You are adored by all for your great sacrifice in giving up everything you have to be with the man you love. That kind of love is so very rare."

Marian smiled brightly, and the warmth of it lit up the small, dark room. "I thank you most kindly. Robin has told me so much about you that I feel as if I know you already. I hope you will forgive us for showing up so unexpectedly. I pray we do not inconvenience you, too much."

"You could never do that, my lady."

Robin beamed. "I can't tell you how good it is to see my two favorite ladies together. I only wish our meeting could be more open. You understand, no one must know we're here."

"No one shall, Robin. There's a chamber at the end of the hall with a private garderobe attached to it, so you'll not have to take the chance of being seen when nature calls. Only one other person besides myself sleeps nearby. She's Lady Caroline God-win, but there's no reason to fear her."

"Wonderful, Raena. You have no idea how much your courtesy is appreciated. Though she never complains, I know how much Marian misses creature comforts. I would like her to be pampered for a while."

" 'Tis done. Wiggles shall personally deliver your meals. She and my two attendants will see to all your needs. As you know, Saera is the soul of discretion, and as for my attendants, they need never know your names. I'll arrange for a hot bath in your chamber immediately."

Robin took her hand in his and, after rubbing it across his cheek, kissed it fondly. Raena gave him a hug and then embraced Lady Marian before leaving the two lovers alone.

She was happy that she could provide a safe haven for them and hoped it would be but the first of many visits. In that way she could keep Robin in her life and be friends with the woman he loved so much.

She could foresee only one problem with Robin's visit, and that was making sure that Valor and the rest of the residents of the castle never found out. She would take no chances with Robin's life.

Making her way down the stairs to the great hall, Raena found her attendants and whispered in their ear what they must do. Then having made arrangements for a hot bath for her guests, she allowed her thoughts to stray back to Caroline. The poor thing must be frantic with worry by now, wondering if Stephan would notice the physical changes in her body.

Hating herself for her cowardice, she decided to go back to her sitting room for the roses and then face Caroline, but the thought flew out of her head when she looked out the door of the great hall and saw Avery striding into the castle with a princely air.

Oh, no! His presence here would complicate things considerably. The last thing Caroline needed right now was to see the author of all her troubles.

Making her way to the entranceway, Raena asked nervously, "What brings my husband's brother here so unexpectedly?"

Avery raised one perfect eyebrow. "Your brother, too, my lady. Can you not express happiness at seeing me?"

"Forgive me. Of course, I'm glad to see you, but just a little surprised you'd wish to visit here after the terrible scene at your father's castle."

"Raena, dear sister," Avery said, "no one blames you for that. Not even Father. He's the reason I'm here. I have a message from him."

"Nothing he says can possibly interest me."

"As it happens, the message isn't for you, but for Valor. Father wants him to know all is forgiven and that the castle is lonely without his family there."

"All is forgiven?" Her voice escalated to a high-pitched squeak. "All is forgiven? As if it could be done so easily. What audacity! Well, you can tell him I've not forgiven him and I doubt Valor has either."

"Where is my wronged brother?" Avery questioned, brushing an imaginary speck from his flawlessly cut, blue-velvet tunic.

Raena couldn't fail to notice how self-assured Avery was. But then, she had to admit he had a lot to be self assured about. He struck an elegant figure, and it had little to do with his fine clothing. "Riding with Stephan, but I'm sure they'll be back shortly."

"And . . . Lady Caroline?" Avery said, peering behind Raena to the great hall. "I . . . I don't see her pretty face anywhere."

Raena heard the catch in his voice, and her heart went out to him. Of course, he wanted to gaze upon the one he loved. He was trying so hard to appear casual, but she knew the ache he must be feeling. "Come to my sitting room where I can speak to you in private."

"Family secrets already, Raena? My, my, you do fit in rather well with the Godwins."

They made their way up the stairs to the landing in silence as Raena tried to compose her thoughts. She wasn't sure how much she should tell him, but she would at least let him know she had learned that they shared the same father.

Entering the sitting room, Avery looked around with interest. "I'm honored to be invited into your inner sanctum and cannot wait to hear why. What is this important matter you wish to discuss?"

Folding her arms in front of her, she answered, "A moment ago, you called me dear sister. In what way did you mean that?"

"In the obvious way, of course. You are now my sister-by-marriage."

Lifting her gaze to meet his straight on, she asked softly, "Is that all I am to you, Avery?"

Avery took a step backward to gaze at her curiously. "I'm . . . not certain how to answer that. You are my brother's wife and . . ."

"And your sister-in-blood. Surely you know that. Our father must have told you."

Avery laughed, filling the round little room with the sound of tinkling bells. "I knew, but I wasn't sure you did. Did you know he had intended that you and I marry? Unfortunately, fate stepped in the way."

Elated, Raena cried, "Do you really believe it was fate? I hope 'tis true, for it would mean I was meant to marry Valor. If I could believe that, I'd be so very happy."

"So, you love him. How nice for you—and him. I wasn't so lucky. The one I love is married to another."

"Caroline."

"How did you know? Is it so obvious?"

"She told me in her desperation."

"Her desperation? What does she know of desperation? She's reunited with her beloved husband, has everything she's ever wanted. I'm the expert on desperation. Verily, I have made an art of it."

Raena impulsively touched Avery's cheek with her hand and, without knowing she was going to, blurted out, "Caroline has good reason to be desperate. She's pregnant with your child."

Now why had she done that? Because he was the child's father? Or because he was truly her blood-brother? In any case, she felt a great relief, for the burden had been too great for her to carry alone.

Avery's eyes closed for one long, haunted moment. Then, taking a deep breath, he opened them again and Raena saw that they had turned bright violet.

They *were* violet.

Wild, vibrant violet!

Why, that wily creature, he does have faery eyes! But more than that: He has the ability to disguise the color.

But . . . why should he? Ahhh, yes . . . to hide the fact that he's faery. She was quite certain he had no idea his eyes had changed. He was so overcome with emotion that he had let his guard down and his eyes had reverted to their true color.

That little trickster!

She was beginning to understand a lot more about her half brother. He wasn't nearly as benign as he appeared. In truth, he must be very clever and very, very gifted to be able to change the color of his eyes at will.

So clever that he was able to hide it even from Prince Ohreinn. She could only wonder what other powers he kept hidden.

"How is she? All is well?"

Raena shook her head. "How could you possibly think so? Have you no understanding of what she's going through? She's desperate to abort the child and, if she cannot, to kill herself. She can't face Stephan with her betrayal. *Your* betrayal."

Avery's face contorted with pain. "Abort my child? Does she have the power to do so? Answer me, I have to know."

"No. She came to me for help and I gave her some harmless herbs to stall for time until I could figure out what to—"

A small cry startled them.

Raena and Avery turned to see Caroline standing in the doorway dressed only in a shift. For one frozen moment, time stood still. It was Caroline who broke the awful silence with a heart-wrenching sob before darting out of sight.

Avery started after her, but Raena grabbed his arm. "No. Stay. You are the last person she needs right now. You'll drive her to kill herself for certain."

Afraid that what Raena said was true, Avery reluctantly halted his step. More than anything, he wanted to go after her, take her in his arms, and comfort her; but he had not the right. *Damn you, Stephan. Damn you to hell.*

Raena ran out to the landing, but no one was

there. Leaning over the balustrade, she peered into the great hall, but Caroline was nowhere to be seen. Where could she have gone to so swiftly? She had to find her before it was too late.

Then, as she glanced to the narrow door that led to the ramparts of the castle, Raena's heart turned to ice.

Twenty-three

Valor and Stephan were returning from their ride when a strange sight caught their attention: A small figure on the ramparts of the castle, precariously perched on the parapet itself. They knew what danger that held. One slip and the fool would fall into the sea.

Stephan stared in horror, unable to believe his eyes. Shouting above the wind, he said, "Valor, do you see that? Who in God's kingdom is that up there?" Uneasiness crept up his spine, for there was something uncomfortably familiar about the form.

Spurring his horse on, he galloped toward the castle, knowing, but not wanting to believe who it was.

Riding with the wind, he clattered over the drawbridge and through the castle gate with Valor close on his heels. Jumping from their horses, the two men ran into the castle to the nearest staircase leading up to the ramparts bumping into Raena at the top of the stairs.

Raena wrestled with the two men, trying to keep them from going any farther. "Don't go out there, I beg of you. She'll jump if you do."

Reluctantly, Stephan came to a halt. "Why?" he demanded. "For God's sakes, why?"

Raena's body shook as she said, "There's no time for explanations. Go get your mother. Bring her here. She's the only one who has a chance of saving her."

Stephan stared at her, wild-eyed with fear. The last thing he wanted to do was to leave, but the fierceness in Raena's eyes told him that he must. With frantic urgency, he turned and made his way down to the great hall.

When he was gone, Raena turned to Valor. "Wait here. Whatever happens, don't let Stephan through that door."

"How is it you know what's troubling her? In God's name, tell me what's going on."

"No time now. Just do as I say." Opening the door, Raena took a deep breath and stepped outside. A stiff breeze assailed her, and she feared it was enough to blow Caroline off her lonely perch.

"Go away," Caroline cried. "You lied to me! Gave me false hope. There's nothing left to do but end my life."

Forcing herself to remain calm, Raena spoke softly. "That's not true, Caroline. There's one thing more you can do before you die."

Caroline looked at Raena in shock. The words sounded so cruel spoken out loud.

Relieved to see she had Caroline's attention, Raena continued, "You can go to your grave knowing the truth."

A sudden gust of wind blew up, and Caroline's night shift billowed out like a sail. Raena held her breath, fearful it would sweep Caroline away. But she righted herself, and Raena took hope from that. Mayhap, she wasn't too far gone to be saved.

"I know all I can bear to know."

"Believe me, Caroline, there is much more to

know. If you will but stay just a few minutes longer, you'll understand everything and see that you were blameless."

"You expect me to believe you now? After your unholy trickery? You expect me to believe anything you have to say after what you did to me? I am an adulteress! I betrayed the dearest man in all the world! And if that weren't enough to send me straight to hell, I did it with my husband's innocent, young brother. If anyone deserves to die for their sins, 'tis I."

A soft voice spoke from behind Raena. "No, Caroline, you don't deserve to die. Listen to what I have to say."

Mellicent barely breathed as she faced the tormented young woman so dangerously perched over the sea. She had heard enough to know what was going on.

Avery! He was responsible for this. She should have known. She should have warned Caroline that he was not the innocent he seemed. She could have saved Caroline this terrible anguish. "You do trust me, don't you, child? You know I would never lie to you."

Caroline blinked her eyes, swaying a little and Mellicent's heart lurched.

"My lady, you have always been truthful with me."

"Good, then you must listen to my story. It pains me to tell it, but you'll understand all when I am done. Will you do that for me? Will you listen to me?"

"No! I am too afraid. 'Tis cruel to make me delay death a moment longer."

Raena sobbed loudly. "Please, don't do this, Caroline. I witnessed my mother's death on this very spot. I cannot bear to see another's."

Caroline clasped her hands over her ears. "Stop it! Stop torturing me. I can't bear it any longer."

In horror, Mellicent and Raena watched as Caroline turned to face the sea.

Twenty-four

In the time it took for Caroline to complete her turn, Raena and Mellicent moved swiftly to grasp her and pull her down to the safety of their arms.

As one, the women held tight to her, surrounding Caroline's frail body with the barrier of their own. All three shook uncontrollably, knowing how close the brush of death's black wings had come to sending Caroline hurtling into the tumultuous sea.

Sobbing hysterically, Caroline spoke, her voice choked with emotion. "Why—did—you—stop—me? Why? Why? I'd—be—better—off—dead."

Mellicent tilted Caroline's head up to look into her eyes. "You're wrong, my dearest child, and I mean to prove it to you. Come. We'll go to Raena's bedchamber, where we can speak in private. You'll listen to my story. A story I've not dared to tell before today. Raena knows some of what I have to tell, but only the barest details. For no one but I knows what truly happened."

Taking a ragged breath, she continued. " 'Tis past time to let it out of the dark chamber of my heart and air it before you."

'Twas true, Raena knew only the barest of details, thanks to Queen Edainn's blurting it out to her and Valor at the faery circle. Though the queen had told them in malice that Lady Mellicent had been seduced by the faery prince, her words might yet save Lady Caroline and her precious faery child. For she prayed that Caroline would hear Mellicent's story and realize things were not as bleak as they seemed. *Oh, gods and goddess, let it be so.*

Raena forgot all about Avery until she opened her chamber door and saw him standing there. Caroline saw him, too, and she froze, staring in horror as if at a ghostly apparition. "Make him leave, I beg of you."

Avery's gaze traveled over Caroline's slender form and lovely face as if trying to imprint the memory of her on his brain for all eternity, and Raena was reminded once more of how much he loved his brother's wife. She felt great pity for both victim and seducer, for they both were suffering terribly.

Escorting Caroline to Raena's bed, Mellicent spoke softly but firmly to Avery. "Leave us. Can you not see your presence is upsetting her?"

"I'll leave, but not until I know she's all right."

" 'Tis no concern of yours. She's not your wife. Please, leave by the ramparts door. I don't want Stephan to see you in this state. He's sure to guess the truth."

Knowing the futility of arguing, Avery obeyed his mother. Opening the door, he started outside, hesitating long enough to turn and point a finger at Caroline. "Know this. You and the child you carry are very precious to me and I'll protect you both from death with every means at my command. Fair or foul, it makes no difference to me."

When the door closed behind him, Avery felt his strength drain from him and leaned against the wall for support. Damn her. Damn her for loving Stephan instead of him.

Almost from the moment he first met her, he knew that she was the only woman he would ever love. How could he ever love anyone but her, for who else was as kind and good as she? Who else was so natural and untainted by human frailties? A poignant scene came back to haunt him then, and he let it happen, reliving the magic moment once again.

He had come upon Caroline on a walk through the woods, surprised to see her sitting at the edge of a small footbridge over a pond, dangling her bare feet in the water. Her skirts were hiked up and tucked under her bodice and, unaware that he was watching, she was singing a silly little ditty that a wandering minstrel had taught them the night before at supper.

The sight was so charming, and she so beautiful with the sun casting rays around her fair head, that he could do nothing but stare at her in wonder. It was almost as if she a were a faery creature herself, so free and easy was she in that wild setting; and it came to him that she, of all the females he had known, would make a perfect wife to a faery prince.

Why did she have to be wed to Stephan? He wanted her for himself. He *deserved* to have such an admirable female for his wife, for he was a superior being.

What had Stephan done to deserve her? Not a thing. It was she who had sought him out. Stephan had been too shy to approach her, thinking himself unworthy. And, indeed, he was.

It shamed him now to remember that when he had heard that Stephan and Valor would be leaving for The Crusades, he hoped Stephan would never return. Not that he wished his brother dead; he wasn't that evil. But that something would force him to stay in the Holy Land.

It came to him then that it would have, indeed, been better if Stephan had never returned, for then Caroline wouldn't be contemplating suicide now.

The room was silent after Avery left. His warning had a strangely pacifying effect on them all. For they each had felt the awesome power that hovered just below the surface of Avery Godwin.

Mellicent broke the long silence. "Come, child. Sit beside me on Raena's soft bed whilst I tell you of my own enchantment."

At that moment, Valor opened the door to the bedchamber and started to enter with Stephan right behind him, but Raena warned them away with a wave of her arm.

Reluctantly, the men let the door close upon them, afraid that their presence might cause Caroline further anguish. Though both men were truly puzzled as to the how and why of it, at least the waiting would be easier now, knowing that Caroline was safe.

Stephan stood white-faced and unsteady on his feet, and Valor tried to comfort him. "Take heart, Stephan. All is right with the world, for Caroline still resides in it."

"*All right*? How can you say that after what just happened? Something is terribly amiss and I have no idea what it is. How could she have tried to abandon me like that? What kind of evil spirit resides on the ramparts of Caldwell Castle to entice two women to commit the same deadly act."

" 'Tis not the castle, for it's but made of stone and mortar. Methinks it's what resides in the hearts and souls of mankind."

"But what reason can she possibly have? Dear God, she knows how much I love her. What could be so terrible that she cannot face me? What can be so bad that she would choose death over life with me?"

"We'll know soon enough, methinks."

Inside Raena's bedchamber, the two younger women looked expectantly to their husbands' mother for the story to begin. While Raena had some idea of what was coming, Caroline was completely in the dark about Mellicent's seduction. It would be a great revelation to her, for Caroline had once told her that she admired Stephan's mother greatly.

Clearing her voice, Mellicent began speaking, very low at first, and then louder as it all came tumbling out of the dark recesses of her mind.

"It began innocently enough, or so I thought at the time, when I came here to Caldwell Castle to visit with Raena's mother, the lady Eleanor."

"My mother?" Raena exclaimed in a voice filled with awe. It wasn't often that anyone dared mention her name, and it seemed odd now to hear it spoken.

"That's right, my dear. Word had come to me that she was with child and very ill, and I thought she would have use of my friendship. My two loyal attendants, Eloise and Leah, came with me. It didn't take long for us to discover how truly disturbed Lady Eleanor was; and wanting to help her, we settled in for a long visit.

"In truth, it was almost more than could be borne, for Eleanor was completely out of her mind. It was unnerving to see her pacing the floor endlessly, wringing her hands together over and over and talking gibberish to herself. She barely ate, barely slept, and she couldn't abide anyone's touch. At times, I doubted she even knew we were here.

"Her only relief, and ours, was when Saera Wigglesworth gave her a draught of some potent brew twice a day. It had a calming effect on her and made it possible for her to be lucid for a short time. It was then that she would speak to us of the faery prince she loved.

"She told us how beautiful he was to gaze upon and how exquisite was his lovemaking . . . over and over until I thought I, too, would go mad. But her description of him was so detailed that I eventually saw him as she did in my mind's eye. And I must admit I felt a great yearning to meet him. That's when I knew I had to get away before I became as obsessed as Eleanor.

"Saera Wigglesworth kindly offered to take me and my two women for an outing, and I was eager for the change. Mayhap, a picnic in the woods would clear my head and put me right again.

"Saera thoughtfully prepared a tasty meal to take along and two large containers of wine, and we rode away from the castle to a strange, deep ravine. We dismounted there and then walked down to a circle of rocks."

"The faery circle!"

"Aye, Raena, the faery circle. It seemed strange that Saera would bring us to such a lonely spot, but she calmed my fears and, indeed, I did begin to relax, charmed by the absolute stillness of the place.

"Right away we ate our meal and drank two full goblets of wine, and, oh dear, I do hesitate to say what happened next, for 'tis still painfully real in the remembrance."

Closing her eyes, Mellicent took a deep breath and relived that fateful day.

"Enjoy," Saera Wigglesworth said, pouring more wine into Mellicent's half-filled goblet.

"Oh, dear, this had better be my last cup, else I'll not be able to set a horse." Mellicent burped, then giggled like a young girl. "I'm surprised the baron would be so generous with this extraordinarily rich wine."

Saera Ni smiled at Mellicent. " 'Tis my wine, not his. Aged under our very feet, right here in a cavern underground."

"How very convenient." Mellicent giggled again. "You've certainly kept your promise. I feel more at ease than I have in a long, long, time, but methinks it's time to go."

"Aye, we'll go . . . after we've finished the fine wine. 'Twould be a shame to waste it."

Mellicent had to agree. In sooth, she felt compelled to drain her goblet of the delicious stuff. "Mmmm, 'tis an enticing draught, I must admit. I think I'll just sit here for a moment and . . . and . . . what was I saying? I . . . don't remember."

Saera smiled a cunning smile, but Mellicent was too befuddled to attach any importance to it. She turned to talk to Eloise and found her lying on the ground asleep.

'Twas so unlike Eloise to take a nap that she turned to Leah to tell her so and found her asleep, too, curled into a ball on the barren ground.

But rather than being alarmed, she thought, why, what a good idea, I think I'll lie down for just a moment.

A moment . . .

A mo . . . ment . . .

Ahh . . .

Feeling a strange sensation in the region of her breasts, Mellicent opened her eyes, surprised to find it was almost dark out. How long had she slept?

Then, feeling a tugging on each of her nipples, she looked down to see two small, childlike winged beings sucking at her.

She tried to sit, but her head was still too filled with mist. She felt drugged and realized that, in truth, she was. But why? Who would do such a thing?

She moaned, and the creatures stopped their sucking long enough to gaze at her curiously. Mellicent was astonished to see wild, little purple eyes staring back at her.

Drawing in her breath, she thought, I must be dreaming. Yes. That's it. I'm dreaming. These strange creatures aren't really here. This isn't really happening.

Believing that, she let her head fall back once more, and the creatures began their nursing once again. She didn't mind, for her breasts were so full of milk they hurt. Indeed, there was milk aplenty, for she was still weaning Valor from her breast.

No wonder she dreamt of creatures nursing. It was only natural. But that reassuring thought vanished when she felt a hot touch upon her most private part. Looking down, she saw a man kneeling between her legs, fondling her with his hand.

This was no ordinary man, for no mortal looked like he. This male had magnificent wings unfurled. They floated behind him like some gigantic, brilliantly colored dragonfly. Prince Ohreinn! It could be none other. She'd heard so much about him these past few days, she was dreaming of him now. 'Twas a lovely dream, for sure, for never had she seen such a beguiling male as he. No wonder Eleanor was so enamored of him.

The creature, seeing her gaze at him, stood to his full height, and she saw he was naked with a man part so wondrous to look upon, she could do nothing but gape at it in surprise. She giggled, thinking, Ah, yes, we cannot blame Eleanor for being obsessed with him, for what woman wouldn't want a lover so wondrously endowed?

He smiled wickedly at her then, and she knew what he was thinking. The same thing she was thinking, she was sure. She tried to raise herself up on her elbows to see him all the better, but her head was still clouded and her limbs so weak she could barely lift her arm. And all the while, the two small creatures at her breast sucked away.

She knew she could never confess this wicked dream to her priest—or to anyone else, for that matter. But, oh, she wanted it to go on and on and on.

As she became more and more aroused, she realized that the two tiny creatures at her breast were not children at all, but tiny mature beings enjoying her most lustily. She was surprised to find that she minded it not at all; in fact, it made her arousal all the more enjoyable.

But it did puzzle her why the maternal act of nursing should arouse her so. It had never happened to her before. But, then, of course, she had never had a faery prince attending to her needs before this day.

If that were not enough, there was the fact that it had been a long time since her body had been touched so intimately. She had chosen not to share her husband's bed for quite some time now; and being still in the full bloom of womanhood, she was well overdue for a good romp in bed with a lusty, attractive male.

But even that didn't explain how quickly she became aroused. 'Twas much too sudden, and much too exquisite, to be explained away so easily.

Looking up at the magnificent male part of the faery, the why of it suddenly mattered little to her. All that mattered was to mate with the sensual creature before he disappeared and left her in great need.

The faery prince suddenly snapped his fingers. "You've had your fill, gluttons. 'Tis my turn now." The two at her breast reluctantly stopped nursing, lapping up spilt droplets of milk with their tongues before leaving with a sullen expression on their strange little faces.

Mellicent's heart began to beat with a wild rhythm, knowing she would soon have what she craved.

She took a deep breath, inhaling the exotic fragrance that he projected, and her desire for him grew to a sweet agony of wanting.

"Oh, come to me. Why do you wait?"

Bell-like laughter echoed from stone to stone to stone, escalating in volume. It was as if a thousand silver bells were pealing out, and she delighted in the sound. Nay, more than that, her spirits rose to the mountaintops at the magical music of his voice. Oh, what heaven it was to be in his company!

"I'll come to you since you ask so sweetly, but I want to enjoy your body first. It's very beautiful to look upon."

Mellicent was suddenly aware that she was completely naked. What had happened to her clothes? She did not remember taking them off. How drunk had she become on Saera's wine?

Saera.

It was she who had drugged her. But why? Looking around for the old woman, she saw her kneeling beside Leah, undressing the sleeping woman.

Shocked, she turned to look for Eloise and saw her lying on the ground, naked, a male faery between her legs.

She felt a rush of heat then, and a scent such as she had never smelled before fogged her brain so that she could no longer think clearly.

The faery prince now knelt before her once more and used his great long tongue to lap at the juncture of her thighs.

She spread her legs wide, wanting to receive all of him, squirming and squealing as he relentlessly tasted her; and she knew by the soft noises he made, he was enjoying it, too.

He took her to the edge, over and over, teasing her unmercifully until she could bear it no longer. Then, at last, knowing she was more than ready to receive that great man part of his, he lay down upon her, saying, "Fareah likes to straddle his females and sit upon them as if riding a mare, but I like to feel the length of my woman's body. Skin is made of such erotic stuff."

He called her his woman, and she liked that, for she could think of no other reason for existence than to be with him.

Grasping his male part, she was eager to feel it inside her and maneuvered it to her opening, now lubricated well by his incredible tongue.

"Ah, that's the problem with human females; they're always so impatient for the act to begin."

"Then do it, do it please, I beg of you. I can't wait a moment longer."

No sooner had she got the words out, then she felt a tremendous thrust and he was inside her, tight and hot.

She grunted in surprise and then held tight to his shoulders, knowing she was in for the ride of her life.

In bliss, her mouth opened wide, as if she were receiving him there as well—and, indeed, she prayed he would fill that orifice, too, for she was greedy for more and more and more of him.

He obliged by thrusting his tongue into her mouth, and it reached down her throat, plunging deeper and deeper, much deeper than any human tongue could go; and her desire for him grew unbearably.

She heard Leah cry out and, out of the corner of her eyes, saw her gentle friend in the throes of passion with another faery. Her arms and legs were wrapped 'round him as if to make sure he didn't escape before she was satisfied and it astonished her that Leah could act in such a feral way. Her gaze shifted to Eloise, and she saw that she, too, was ferociously engaged in the act of mating.

And then Mellicent lost all conscious awareness of anyone but Ohreinn. Never in her life had she been so thor-

oughly plundered, never in her life had she enjoyed the act of mating so very much. The magical power of faeries was a wondrous thing to experience, and she considered herself amongst the most privileged of females to be chosen for this mating of a lifetime.

She climaxed four times before her need slackened, and still he pumped away mightily while she begged for more. When at last she was completely sated, he spewed his seed into her in one long, convulsive rapture and she went careening out of her mind with the immensity of the ecstasy that swept over her.

Then, drained of her strength and her very breath, she started to close her eyes in a swoon when there suddenly appeared a magnificent female faery looking down at her. She became instantly alert.

"Ah Ohreinn, my virile brother, you did well. She's ploughed and seeded so well, I'm sure she'll produce a fine crop for us."

"Thank you, Edainn. It's not often you approve of anything I do. I think my brothers and I performed our duty well. 'Tis our sexuality, and ours alone, that's kept our tribe from becoming extinct like all the others."

Mellicent listened to the two magical beings talking casually, as if she weren't present; and verily, she felt that now that he had achieved his goal, she no longer existed for him—even though he was still embedded inside her.

But she soon learned that he was, indeed, aware of her, for she felt his man part harden and lengthen once again. But, oh, she had not the strength left to go through another mating and feared she'd not survive it.

But Ohreinn must have realized that, for the second mating was much shorter, though certainly no less intense, taking her to a higher plane than she had ever gone before. She was sure this mating was for his pleasure alone and not to plant his seed in her, for he had done a thorough job of that the first time.

But she wasn't complaining. Let him have his pleasure. He deserved it after all he had given her. To think she might have gone the rest of her life without knowing such bliss.

When he was done with her this time, he stood up and gazed at the scene around him with great satisfaction.

" 'Tis done."

Astonishingly, at the saying of those words, the faeries disappeared, leaving three naked women to gaze around the circle in bewilderment.

Saera helped them dress, all the while avoiding their gaze, then led them out of that wild, pagan place of stones.

They climbed to the top of the ravine, emerging at the road to Caldwell Castle, and mounting their horses, rode back to a much tamer world.

Mellicent was grateful she still had her sanity, that she and the others had not gone mad like Lady Eleanor. But she feared she still might, for the remembrance of that passionate faery prince would haunt her the rest of her life.

Twenty-five

Done with her story, Mellicent gazed at Raena and Caroline, her eyes sparkling with life at the telling. 'Twas obvious to Raena there were still lingering effects from that extraordinary day. Obvious that Mellicent had enjoyed her seduction, despite everything. And what was wrong with that?

Surprised at her own reaction, Raena suddenly wondered if being half-faery had warped her point of view, for, indeed, she wanted Mellicent to have enjoyed her rendezvous.

But, no, mayhap, it was the human part of her that wished it, for if Mellicent had received great pleasure from the act, then enchanting her couldn't have been completely wrong. Hearing Mellicent's voice, Raena listened to what she said.

"I soon learned that it was not a dream at all, for all three of us were impregnated that day. I was the only one, though, who brought a baby to term. Leah lost her child at five months. A perfectly formed, male faery child with the budding of wings already begun.

"Eloise's pregnancy ended after only a few weeks, and it was in such an early stage it could not be determined if it was a faery child or not."

Looking into Caroline's eyes with a steady gaze,

she continued, "As you must have guessed by now, the faery child I gave birth to was Avery."

Caroline had listened in rapt attention, unaware of where the story would lead. When she heard Avery's name proclaimed, she gasped out loud. "Dear God, are you telling me that Avery is part faery?"

"Aye, the male part of him, for sure, for didn't he seduce you just as his father seduced me?"

Jumping from the bed, Caroline cried, "Then, I was under an enchantment just as you were? Just as Valor was to Raena?"

Pulling Raena to her feet, Caroline hugged her tight. "Oh, Raena, you can't possibly know what a great relief it is to hear that, for I had truly believed I was a wicked woman. But it wasn't my fault. *It really wasn't my fault.* All this time I blamed myself, thinking Avery but an innocent boy; and all the while, he planned it, making sure to catch me when I was most fertile."

Then realizing what she had said, Caroline's face took on a somber look. "That's diabolical."

Raena nodded her head in agreement.

"Are you ready to face Stephan, child?" Mellicent asked. "For by now, I'm sure he's out of his mind with worry. I'll stand beside you. I'll tell him of my own seduction; he'll have to understand then."

"No, Lady Mellicent. I won't ask that of you. I'll face my husband alone. No need for him to know we both suffered the same ordeal. I'd like to spare him that much."

"If you're sure that's what you want . . ."

"I'm sure. I'll face him now, this very moment, before I lose the courage, and pray he'll understand."

Raena pressed Caroline's hand, then turned and

left with Lady Mellicent. Descending the spiral staircase, they entered the sitting room where Valor and Stephan waited anxiously.

"She wants to see you alone, my son."

"How is she?" Stephan asked fearfully. "Is she all right?"

"Go see for yourself."

Stephan climbed the stairs and stepped into the bedchamber warily, relaxing when he saw Caroline sitting quietly on the bed.

Lifting her to her feet, he hugged her tight, crying, "Don't ever do that to me again. Don't you know I wouldn't want to live without you?"

"Nor I without you, and truly, today, I thought that I might have to."

"What in God's name have I done to make you think that?"

"It isn't what you've done, but the terrible thing I've done."

"What are you talking about? What have you done?"

"Oh, Stephan, I can hardly bear to tell you."

Caroline gazed deep into his eyes and with a tremble in her voice said, "Whilst you were gone to war, I was put under an enchantment by a male faery and am carrying his child."

"You jest. Surely . . ." Seeing the serious expression on her face, Stephan paled. "Oh, God, you mean it, don't you? You really mean it."

Staggering backward, he bumped into the wall, then turned to pound his fist against it. He needed the pain to block out the agony in his heart; but, oh God, nothing could compare to that. In truth, he wished that she had never told him, for it was too hard to bear.

Caroline was shocked at Stephan's display of vio-

lence. Never in all their time together had she seen
him like this. He must surely have broken his hand,
so brutal was the blow. "Dearest husband, I wish
with all my heart that it hadn't happened, but I will
not ask for your forgiveness. Not now, not knowing
I was helpless to resist the fierce magic that faeries
have. I am as guiltless as you, for I was completely
unaware that this—this—*creature* was anything but
the innocent male I had assumed him to be."

Stephan blocked his ears with his hands, crying,
"Enough! I don't want to hear any more!"

"You must. If we are to survive this, you must hear
me out. When he put me under his spell, I was completely helpless. Surely you can understand that,
knowing of Valor's enchantment by Lady Raena.
Surely you understand that neither Valor nor I had
any choice in the matter."

The alien words his wife spoke were like the buzz-
ing of so many insects. He was in the midst of a
nightmare. He had to be, for what else could explain how his life had turned so bad, so quickly?
But this was his wife who spoke. The woman he
loved more than life. He couldn't risk losing her
forever.

"I'm trying hard to understand, Caroline. Be patient with me, for 'tis difficult to accept that there
are beings so powerful that they could turn a loving
wife away from her husband so easily."

Holding his head in her hands, she cried, "No,
Stephan, no. Look at me. Understand what I say.
My seducer has not the power to make me turn
from you. I could never stop loving you. Not in this
lifetime or the next. This has nothing at all to do
with love. Nothing whatsoever."

"And yet Valor doth truly love the faery creature
who seduced him."

"But don't you see? He wasn't in love with someone else. He had no feelings for Elizabeth. I truly believe he would have fallen in love with Raena whether she used her faery glamour on him or not."

"Agreed. But this seducer of yours, tell me his name so that I can protect you from him in the future."

Caroline went pale, and Stephan knew there was more to the story than she had told him.

Escaping to the window, she looked out over the ramparts, seeking the spot where she had almost jumped. Her eyes widened in shock. Avery was standing there! It was as if he had known before she herself did that she would appear at that very window.

She blinked her eyes; and when she opened them again, he was standing upon the parapet in exactly the same place she had stood.

Was he mocking her? Could he be that cruel?

Stephan grasped her by the shoulders then and turned her around to face him. He hugged her tight to his chest, bracing himself, knowing that what she had to say would be terrible to endure. In a heated whisper he pleaded, "Tell me the villain's name. I have a right to know."

Caroline tried to forget that Avery was out on the parapet just a few feet away, but she was keenly aware of his eyes staring at her like bright purple beacons that gave off such energy she could feel it pulsate through her body. His omnipotent presence was almost more than she could bear.

Averting her eyes from Stephan, she moaned, "Don't ask me for his name, I beg of you. Let it rest; we'll all be happier for it."

Stephan held her at arm's length so that he might

gaze into her eyes. "No more secrets. Do you understand? If we're to have any chance of overcoming this, there can be no more secrets between us. My God, because of a secret, you almost killed yourself."

He was right. She knew he was. It was their only chance at happiness. In a resigned voice she said, "I'll tell you, but not until you promise me you will not hurt him in any way."

Her words hit him like a blow to the stomach. Why was she protecting him? Did he mean that much to her? "You ask too much of me."

"Then, I cannot speak."

Stephan's heart sank. "Why? Sweet Jesus, if you do not care for him, why do you protect him? Are you still under his enchantment? Is that it?"

"Yes. No! Oh, Stephan, I cannot tell you because . . . because . . ." Tears welled up in Caroline's eyes; and acting on a compulsion she could not deny, she swiveled her head to look through the window at Avery, still standing on the parapet. He looked for all the world like some dark angel against the bright sky, and a shiver of fear climbed up her spine.

Stephan's gaze followed hers to see what had distracted her, and a sickening feeling washed over him. He tried to push the horrible thought out of his head, but it was too late. He knew. Dear God, he knew. *It was Avery.* It could be no one else.

Releasing his hold on Caroline, he started for the door that led out to the ramparts. Caroline grabbed his arm and tried to hold him back. "Stephan! No!"

Stephan turned to look at her, but Caroline wasn't sure he really saw her, for his eyes were glazed with pain. Unable to bear his stricken face, her arms fluttered helplessly to her side and she slumped against the wall.

Striding over to the door to the ramparts, Stephan

opened it, stealing himself to face his brother. Stepping out into the wind and sun, he sought Avery, but . . .

. . . he was nowhere to be seen.

Avery was gone. He had disappeared.

Following Stephan outside, Caroline cried out, "Oh, God, no!" Running to the parapet, she leaned through a rugged stone crenel and peered down to the sea.

"Don't be a fool, Caroline. Avery would never jump."

In a daze, Caroline turned to face her husband. "But—but then, where did he go? One moment he was standing right here, and the next he was gone. Was it just an apparition or was it just my guilty conscience that made me see him there?"

"I saw him, too, Caroline. He was here. There has to be some explanation for this. There has to be." Stephan tried to reassure himself that Avery hadn't jumped. He couldn't believe his brother would take the cowardly way out when he was about to be confronted.

But . . . how could he be completely sure? If he had learned anything the past few horrible days, it was that it was impossible to know what was in another's heart.

In truth, he hadn't known Avery at all. But this was not the time to think about Avery's being faery, because then he'd have to think about his mother's part in his conception. Dear God, was his whole family entangled with those deceptive creatures?

Trying to make sense of it all, he ran to the door leading to the main stairwell and flung it open. Halfway down the stairs, he met Raena and Valor on their way up. "Did you see Avery come out this way?"

Raena blinked her eyes in surprise. "No, Stephan. Is everything all right?"

"I think so. I pray so. I have to find out." With that, he grabbed Caroline's hand and fled down the stairs.

"Do you know what that was all about?" Valor asked.

"I have no idea, but by the way he was holding tight to her, I don't think we have to worry about Caroline anymore."

Raena dared herself to look into her husband's eyes. She saw no anger, but that was far from reassuring, for she knew it would come. It was inevitable. "I think Caroline will be all right now. Stephan loves her; he'll do right by her."

"Thanks to your cool head, she's all right. She might have died if Stephan and I had barged out there."

Raena shuddered, thinking of how close Caroline had actually come to killing herself. "You thank the wrong person. 'Twas your mother who saved Caroline's life."

"But how? She has no magic."

"Truth, Valor. Truth was the only magic she needed. Truth about her own seduction at the hands of Prince Ohreinn."

Valor stiffened, and Raena spoke as gently as she could. "Have you not accepted it yet?"

Speaking more harshly than he intended, Valor answered, "I've accepted it. What choice do I have? But I still don't understand what it has to do with Caroline."

"Oh, Valor, I wish I didn't have to tell you this, but Caroline is yet another innocent victim of enchantment. She, too, was seduced by a faery, just as your mother was, and a for the very same purpose, to plant a faery child inside her."

Valor gripped her arms tightly and, overcome with anger, shook her. "Damn you and all your kin! What is it with your tribe that you should prize Godwins above all others? Is it some ancient curse? Are you determined to ruin the lives of every last one of my family?"

Swallowing her hurt and her pride, Raena answered, "I'll forgive you for saying that, since I know how angry you are. I just ask that you reach deep within your heart and find the compassion to forgive your mother and Caroline, for they are innocent in all of this."

Valor released his hold on her. "Forgive them? Of course, I forgive them, since I, above anyone, know how very powerful faery glamour can be. *I live with it every day.*"

Raena shook her head sadly. "I've told you and told you that I no longer use my faery glamour on you, but you refuse to believe me."

In a choked voice, Valor cried, "How can I, when I desire you so?"

"Well, there's nothing more to say, is there? If you'll excuse me, I have a great need to be alone."

She pushed past Valor, then stopped a few steps away and turned to face him once more. "I leave you with but one thing to ponder. Consider, I beg of you, the possibility that 'tis not an enchantment that has afflicted you, but . . . love."

Valor watched as his wife walked farther and farther away from him when all he wanted was for her to come closer and closer. When she disappeared from view, he felt empty and alone. He wanted to be with her so much that it didn't matter to him whether he was under an enchantment or not.

But . . . it seemed that it did matter to her.

Would he ever understand his faery bride?

Twenty-six

Stephan and Caroline ran down the stairs and out into the bailey, searching anxiously for Avery, but he was nowhere to be found. Caroline was beside herself with worry, certain he had plunged into the sea, but Stephan couldn't believe that of his brother. Avery had too great a sense of survival.

But if he didn't jump, then how did he escape from the ramparts so swiftly? There was no reasonable explanation. There was no reasonable explanation for any of this, for in his darkest nightmare he could never have envisioned his brother seducing his wife. Even more, he could never have conceived that Caroline was capable of being seduced. She had always been an exemplary wife and he had always trusted her completely.

But that was before he had gone off to war.

That was before she had been exposed to Avery's faery glamour.

Faery glamour. How easy it was to say those words. As if they were familiar. As if they had been a part of his vocabulary all his life. Was there really such a thing as faery glamour? Or was it nothing more than a feeble excuse the wicked and the weak used to try and excuse their sins.

But if that were true, then it meant that Caroline

was lying, and he didn't believe that. He *couldn't* believe that. Deep in his heart, he knew that she would never have willingly let another man touch her, and so he must believe that she had been under a powerful spell. Faery glamour *did* exist and Caroline was its innocent victim.

Because she was innocent, he could forgive her. But how could he ever forgive his brother? Avery had deliberately set out to seduce his wife.

Suddenly too disheartened to continue the search, Stephan took Caroline by the arm and led her back inside the keep. He had to take his mind off Avery or lose his mind.

Saera saw Stephan and Caroline enter the great hall looking very distressed. "What's going on? Why is everyone acting so strange? Avery was just here, and—"

"Avery was here? Just now? You're sure of it?" Stephan asked incredulously.

"Do you doubt my word? Why shouldn't he be here?"

"Where did he go?" Caroline asked in a small voice. "I have to see for myself that he's all right."

"Of course he's all right. Have you had an argument with him? Is that why he left so quickly when he saw the two of you come in?"

Looking down at Caroline's relieved face, Stephan grinned. "You see. He's fine." A great burden was lifted from his shoulders, knowing that Avery was safe, and Stephan realized that, despite his brother's betrayal, he didn't want him to come to harm.

Valor stood a long time, thinking about what Raena had said, letting the words sink into his heart as well as his brain. Could it be true? Was it love alone that bound him to her. Was her faery glamour just incidental?

He thought about his life with her, all that had transpired since first he laid eyes on her, and he knew his life had been richer, more meaningful ever since. And it wasn't just the gratification he received from their lovemaking, wonderful though it might be.

Aside from his great passion for her, he enjoyed a calmer, deeper feeling as well: A sense of well-being and fulfillment, the desire to make her happy, to have children born from her womb, nourished from her sweet breasts. No enchantment, no matter how powerful, could ever make him feel that way.

It was true. He loved her despite her powers, despite his inability to master her, despite everything and . . . he knew it was time to tell her. Pray God, it wasn't too late.

Making his way to her tower room, he tried the door, but it was locked. Rapping softly, he said, "Raena, let me in."

He waited, his head pressed against the door, listening, but silence greeted him. "Raena, please, I want to talk to you. Will you let me in?"

He heard her soft step, and then, the door opened and Raena's pale face appeared. It was a Raena he had never seen before, somber and quiet, staring soulfully into his eyes. Without a word, she turned and walked back into the room and sat quietly on the bed, gazing up at him listlessly.

Valor gently took her hands and pulled her to her feet. "Can you ever forgive me for being such a fool?"

With one long, shuddering breath, all the hurt she had been feeling drifted away and she stepped into the comforting fold of his arms.

With tears glistening in his eyes, Valor lifted her into his arms and carried her to their bed.

Night came, gently sweeping over the hills and vales as, one by one, the lights in Caldwell Castle were extinguished. In the farthest reaches of the keep, Robin blew out the many candles set around the room in ornate wall sconces, then climbed into the soft down bed to lie with his wife.

After a warm fragrant bath made all the lovelier by endless stroking and teasing of each other's body, they were more than ready to make love. The long nights in the company of a band of rugged men had taken its toll on them and they were hungry for a rapturous night in their cozy love nest.

It was hard to live without a shred of privacy, to be alone only for stolen moments. Most of the time, they had to be content with longing looks and dreams of a day such as this when they would have long, tender hours to satisfy their needs.

Robin lovingly stroked Marian's naked body 'til she fairly purred like a kitten, until the sweet touching caused an urgency in him for more than could be felt with just his hands.

Running his fingers through the thick patch of curly red hair between her legs, he feasted his eyes on the feminine beauty of her freckled body. She groaned at his intimate touch and reached over to boldly grasp his manhood.

Robin removed her hand very gently and pressed it to his lips. "Not yet."

Marian blushed prettily and spread her legs apart, inviting his touch, and Robin shifted position so that he might taste the offered honey with his mouth. Gently spreading her with his fingers, he flicked his tongue into her opening and Marian shuddered from the mighty sensation. "Ohh, I fear I won't be able to wait. It's been too long a time."

Robin smiled to himself, happy to know that he could make his shy Marian turn into a wanton female with such little effort. Spurred on by her words, he renewed his effort at pleasuring her and laved her with his tongue until she was wet and willing and squirming with delight.

She held on tight to his head, encouraging him to continue, and he obliged, circling her opening and thrusting his tongue inside her as far as it would go, then nibbling at her with tiny little love bites until he had her digging her fingers into his hair and writhing against his mouth in a frenzy.

The playful kitten was gone now, and in its place was a sensual tigress seeking gratification. She thrust her hips up closer to the source of her pleasure, begging him to take her before it was too late, but still he answered, "Not yet."

But Marian could wait no longer. She had been stroked and teased, fondled and nibbled so long she was ready to climb the very stone walls of the castle. Then, thinking of how she might get her way, she straddled Robin and settled over his hardness.

"Not fair." Robin groaned.

Marian laughed joyfully and began to wriggle her body. "You've told me many times that in the game of love and war there is no right or wrong, no sense of fair play, so watch out, my fine sir, for I mean to have you any way I can."

Robin groaned again, unable to hold back thrusting his hips. Marian squealed her pleasure, then set about having her way with her husband.

Robin couldn't believe the change in her. Never before had she taken the advantage in their lovemaking, never before had he seen her so energetic. She was young and lithe and rode him like a wild mare as he bucked beneath her, and oh, he did delight in it. Their lovemaking had never been so expressive, so sensuous, and he worked hard to keep from coming too soon, wanting to prolong the sheer ecstasy of their union as long as he possibly could.

"Now! Oh, God, now!" she cried and he obliged, pulling her down on top of him. Rolling her over until he was on top, he worked at giving her the release she craved. They climaxed simultaneously, their hearts and bodies joined in harmony, and when they were done, Robin wasted no time in beginning the process all over again. There would be no sleep for them tonight.

In the bedchamber next to theirs, Stephan blew out the lone candle that lit the room and took his wife to bed. She spooned up against him, as she always did, and his hand cupped her round buttocks as was his habit, then moved up to caress her belly.

He suddenly stiffened, feeling the delicate contours, a soft roundness that reminded him a baby grew there. All was not as it had been before. He wondered if it would ever be so again.

As if reading his mind, Caroline took his hand in hers and moved it back over her roundness again, surprising him. It was not like her to be so bold. She held his hand tightly, and he realized she was determined to make things right between them. A hard lump formed in his throat as a rush of love enveloped him. Removing her hand, he turned her over to face him.

Staring into her eyes, he deliberately stroked her stomach until it brought a sweet smile to her face.

He smiled back, then took her breasts in his hands, saying, "I like the extra weight of them. For certain, I'm going to enjoy a more-rounded wife."

Caroline gave out a shuddering sigh and pulled his head down to meet hers. Just before she kissed him, she murmured, "I cherish you, Stephan Godwin."

Their lips met in a passionate kiss, and all the tension between them vanished like a summer wind moving through the trees. Taking a taut nipple into his mouth, he began to suck on it.

Caroline closed her eyes and ran her fingers through his hair, and Stephan forgot everything but the beautiful woman in his arms. The wife he had always adored, would always adore as long as he drew breath.

With bodies entwined, they fell into the familiar pattern of lovemaking they had always enjoyed, but it was not enough to satisfy either of them. Something felt different tonight. In sooth, Stephan felt a wildness he had never felt before, a restless need to prove to Caroline and to himself that though the intimacy of their relationship had been violated, it would *thrive*.

His need drove him to a frenzy, as if with each thrust of his body he could pump the great love that he felt for her into her. He was trying to show her that she belonged to him, that no one could ever give her what he had for her, that no one could ever make love to her as he did.

Caroline noticed the change in his lovemaking and suspected what motivated it, but said nothing. The reason mattered not to her, for though his hard thrusting was unfamiliar, it gave her exquisite pleasure and—much to her surprise—she found herself responding in kind.

Although she had certainly always enjoyed their lovemaking, she had never been the aggressor. Her role had been more of a congenial, receptive companion. But not this time. Holding tight to him, she gave in to the high emotions that swirled around them in the darkness of their room; and as he pounded into her, she thrust back, timing her movements with his, giving as good as she got until the passion carried her away to some foreign place she had never been to before.

Never before had she felt so out of control. Never before had there been such a need to become one with her husband. She wanted him to believe in their love, and this was the one way she could prove that it would endure.

The sheer pleasure of their frantic lovemaking escalated, peaking at an impossible height; then exploded in a sea of red-hot rapture. Caroline bit down on her lip to keep from screaming out her ecstasy, but still it burst forth, leaving her gasping for breath.

When his wife climaxed, her body shuddering mightily, Stephan pulled her buttocks up tight against his body and spewed his seed into her in one long, powerful torrent, then collapsed on top of her, relieved of all the heartache he had known that day.

He fell asleep still inside her, and Caroline was content to keep him there.

Upstairs in the round tower room, the tiny flames from candles set on the windowsill danced to the tune of the night breeze, then fluttered out one by one; but Valor and Raena took no notice. They slept entwined in each other's arms after making tender love.

Raena stirred and sighed in her sleep as a dream unfolded in her head. She was at the dreaming pool again, gazing deep into the sparkling depths as a full moon cast its golden light on the surface of the water.

"Who is my beloved? I want to see his face. I need to know that I am truly loved."

Her father appeared at her side just then and with a smile pointed down to the image that was forming in the depths of the water. The image of a man floated up toward the surface until it stared up at her, looking directly into her eyes. Through the rippling waters, she saw Valor's handsome face.

Content, Raena fell into a deep sleep, whispering the name of her beloved in the dark. Valor woke at the sound of his name; then, pulling his wife tight against his body, he held her close throughout the long night.

Twenty-seven

Raena awoke at dawn to the hot touch of Valor's tongue between her thighs. Wriggling into position to receive him all the better, she luxuriated in the lovely sensations that rippled through her. She would have loved to have had it go on and on, but Valor's beard was tickling her legs, and she squirmed and giggled and tried to push him away.

Valor was having none of that. He didn't take kindly to rejection and tried again to pleasure her, but her giggles soon turned to full-blown laughter and she cried out, "Stop, I beg of you."

Thoroughly dejected, Val sat up and glared at her. "Confound it, woman, a man doesn't like to be laughed at in bed."

Raena tried to refrain from laughing further, knowing she was hurting his feelings, but she couldn't help it if she was skittish this morning. "I'm sorry, but your beard sometimes tickles me. I've been meaning to tell you that for some time now, but your lovemaking doth distract me too much."

Valor set about distracting her again, and soon they were both too busy for conversation. But later, when he had left and her attendants were dressing her, Raena was sorry she had hurt his feelings. She'd make sure to tell him later how much she adored his golden beard, for she did enjoy the sensation of his dear whiskers against her skin.

Making her way down to the great hall, she searched for his wonderful face amongst the castle folk but could find him nowhere. But that wasn't unusual. Castle business kept him more than a little busy these days.

Remembering her secret guests, she made sure they were being taken care of; then, spying Stephan and Caroline sitting close together at a table, Raena smiled, thinking how lovely it was to have a castle full of loving couples.

Deciding to join them at their table, Raena started toward the couple with a charger full of food when suddenly she was distracted by Valor entering the hall. One look at him and the wooden charger fell from her hands, clattering to the floor.

Valor stood there sheep-faced, bereft of his beard.

In shock, Raena stared at him a long while before finally bursting into tears.

Making his way over to her, he said, "What is it? I thought you'd be happy. Damn it all, I hacked it off for you."

"Oh, Valor, I loved your beard. Truly I did. You look . . . so . . . different now. I—I don't know what to say."

Valor caressed his sore, stinging face with his hand saying, "Now you tell me. Confound it, woman, I—"

He got no further, for suddenly the air was rent with the shrill blare of a horn. Exchanging surprised glances, Valor and Raena started toward the door when a yeoman entered, shouting, "Me lord, me lady, 'tis the prince!"

In disbelief, they ran out to the bailey and stared at the large party of men and horses that waited at

the castle gates, recognizing the colorful banners
that identified the regalia of Prince John.

Raena felt her knees give way, and Valor quickly
circled her waist to hold her steady. "Don't weaken
on me now, wife. We'll face the prince together."

"Oh, Valor, why is he here? What can he want of
us?"

But she knew the answer to that when she saw
the woman at the prince's side. A woman dressed
in a gown of blood red. A woman who smiled triumphantly at them through the gate.

Elizabeth, the prince's daughter.

In a matter of moments, the castle was a hive of
frenzied activity as everyone prepared for the royal
visit. Fortunately, the castle steward had on several
occasions put them through their paces, preparing
for a royal visit such as this. Everyone knew what
was expected of them, exactly what to do, even
where to stand when greeting the prince.

On pretense of needing to change her dress for
the prince, Raena flew up the stairs before Val could
object. She had to let Robin and Marian know that
their royal enemy, Prince John, was here, for it suddenly occurred to her that the prince might be
there because of them.

Fear constricted her chest until she was barely
able to breathe. If the prince knew Robin was being
sheltered in Caldwell Castle, they were all doomed.

Raena started down the landing to Robin's chamber, but halfway there she heard her name called
and whirled around to face Valor.

"For God's sake, woman, come back here. I want
you at my side to greet the prince."

Raena's head swiveled back to look down the hall
to the chamber where Robin and Marian lay unaware of the danger they were in. She had no

choice; she had to go with her husband. If she
didn't, he'd suspect something was wrong, and that
was the last thing she wanted. He must remain ignorant of Robin's presence, for his ignorance was
all that stood between him and death.

With her heart in her throat, she composed herself as best she could and descended the stairs at
her husband's side. In a moment she was standing
at the door to the keep, watching as the royal entourage made its way up to the door of the great
hall.

God and goddesses, could there be a more vexing
turn of events than this untimely coincidence? But
then . . . mayhap this untimely visit wasn't so coin-
cidental after all. It was possible there was a spy in
their midst, one who had gotten word to Prince
John that his nemesis, Robin Hood, was in this very
castle. If that were true, no protestation of ignorance could save Valor from being strung up beside
Robin.

That frightening thought did little to help her
already-nervous state. If anything happened to Val
because of her, she would never forgive herself.
She reconsidered the wisdom of keeping him in
the dark. If he had no idea of what was going on,
how could he protect himself?

But it was too late to tell him now. The prince
was dismounting from his horse, and Caroline and
Stephan were joining them at the door. And then
the king was striding toward them and Valor was
propelling her forward to meet him.

Curtsying low, she held her position until the
prince gestured for her to rise and she found herself
staring into Lady Elizabeth's smug face.

Raena wanted nothing more than to slap that expression from her face, which must have been quite

obvious to Valor, for he dug his fingers into her arm, warning her to behave.

As if she needed to be reminded. She was no fool. She knew the danger they were in, for the prince had absolute power.

But not as much as she.

Where had that thought come from?

It could be dangerous to think that way, and yet, she was glad to have remembered that she was not helpless, that she was armed with the greatest weapon of all, faery glamour.

Spitefully, she wondered how much power she could wield over the great prince and she pictured him groveling at her feet. That amusing thought calmed her, for it reminded her that he was just a man like any other, and she gained enough composure to face the prince unafraid.

Her husband's voice broke through her reverie. "Your grace, you honor us greatly with your visit."

"An honor I'm sure you'd prefer to be spared. I'm well aware of the expense of feeding and bedding my large entourage, so let me assure you, we'll be staying only one night. We'll be continuing on our way tomorrow morning after breaking the fast."

Raena was vastly relieved to hear that. She could endure one night, couldn't she? She'd get word to Robin and Marian to keep their door barred, and no one would be the wiser.

Elizabeth's eyes suddenly opened wide as she gazed at Valor's naked face. "Oh, what a wondrous change you've wrought. You are much handsomer without your straggly beard."

"I'm glad you approve, my lady." Valor gave Raena a pointed look. "I only wish my wife, was as enthusiastic about it."

"Ah, yes, *your wife,*" the prince said. "Indeed,

that's why we've made this unexpected visit. I would have passed by without stopping at all, but my daughter reminded me that we have news for you. I've arranged to have your marriage to Lady Raena annulled."

Raena heard the words through a black mist. Though she was relieved that he wasn't there to capture Robin, still she could find no comfort in knowing the real reason for his visit.

She looked at Valor, but his face was made of stone, and revealing nothing.

"Your grace, I don't know what to say. This comes so unexpectedly. Surely, you know that I've been living intimately with my wife. Under the circumstances, I can hardly see how—what I mean is, in the eyes of God and man, she is truly wed to me."

"Not necessarily so. I understand the priest was forced to marry you at sword point. The details escape me, but one thing is certain, the circumstances were highly unusual and, I might add, decidedly illegal."

Valor started to speak, but Prince John cut him off, his words causing the hair on the back of his neck to rise.

"I've chosen to forgive you for the heartbreak you've caused my daughter and would be loath to hear an argument from you on the matter. 'Tis done. The official declaration will be forthcoming."

The prince turned his gaze to Raena, lingering overly long on the delicate swelling of her lovely breasts, and his demeanor changed once again. "I suppose you cannot be blamed for bedding this luscious creature."

Valor quickly changed the subject, having no wish to encourage the prince's bawdy speech. Acknowledging Elizabeth, he said, "My lady, you astonish me with your devotion. A lesser woman would have given up her claim on so base a knight as I long ago."

"Base knight? Do not speak so harshly of the man I love. The man I am determined to wed." Elizabeth slowly and deliberately turned her gaze to Raena, smiling like a cat with a mouse between its paws.

Raena smiled back at her in a knowing way, hoping to convey with a look what she dared not say in front of the prince, that Elizabeth would never get her hands on her husband.

Elizabeth took her meaning, for her face suddenly turned sour. "My lord, will you not escort me inside your cozy little castle? I'm overly weary and would like to rest in privacy for a bit. We were forced to ride with great speed when it was reported that Robin Hood and his band were in the vicinity. That loathsome creature has the whole of England in an uproar."

Holding his arm out for her, Valor answered cordially, "By all means, my lady, do come inside. You'll find it warm and inviting, methinks, for the lady of this castle has a way of making the most humble of places a home in every sense. I'll see to a bedchamber for you myself." Bowing low, Valor addressed the prince. "With your permission, my liege."

Prince John waved him away and Valor took his leave, escorting Elizabeth inside the keep. Raena was touched by the way Valor defended her, but it was a risky thing he did, and she prayed he would desist. She had no wish for him to feel the wrath of the powerful prince.

Oh, if only it were Richard who sat upon the throne, instead of this evil man. Valor had been one of Richard's most favored knights. But it was useless to dwell on that. She couldn't count on being rescued from her plight so easily.

In a daze, Raena turned her attention back to the prince and saw that Miles Kendall, the castle steward, had taken command of the situation and was escorting the prince inside.

Feeling a great need to be comforted, Raena looked for some one to give her succor. Alas, with Valor occupied with Elizabeth and her attendants, poor things, engaged in preparing the great hall for a meal fit for a prince, she found herself quite alone.

Seeing Avery standing by the entrance to the hall, she approached and said, "Will you stay by my side, brother? I'm not feeling very steady."

Avery took her trembling hand in his and, hiding the rush of emotion that swept over him, murmured, "Lean upon me all you wish."

"Do not be so generous with your offer, for you may be forced to give me much more support than you expect."

Seeing the anxiety and concern in her eyes, Avery's heart went out to her. "Dear sister, I'm at your command. In truth, it makes me feel more like a real brother, knowing that you turn to me for help. I'll not let you down."

Hearing a small cry, Avery turned to see Caroline and Stephan behind them.

Making sure no one was within earshot, Stephan spoke in a low voice. "What kind of faery trickery did you use to escape the ramparts? Caroline was beside herself, fearing you had jumped."

Avery's gaze turned to Caroline. " 'Tis she who sought suicide, not I."

Caroline cringed.

"Do not dare to speak of that to my wife. She is guiltless."

"Stephan, I had no wish to hurt you. I swear to you. But I had an obligation to—"

"Obligation?" Stephan's voice was no more than a whisper, but it conveyed great emotion. "You were obligated to take care of my wife, not seduce her."

"Stephan, I beg of you, don't speak of the matter here where we may be overheard," Caroline said, trying to keep from crying. "Wait until Prince John leaves. Until we can be sure of privacy."

Stephan unclenched his fist. "Agreed. We'll speak no more on the matter until the prince is gone."

Stephan took his wife by the arm and led her into the keep, followed by Raena and Avery. One glance up at the landing over the great hall and Raena froze. Valor was leading the prince and Elizabeth past her sitting room, past the stairs to the ramparts, toward the room she had given to Robin and Lady Marian.

"What is it, Raena? Why have you turned so pale?"

Raena couldn't speak, so tight was her throat. Instead, she lifted her skirts and ran up the stairs, but she was too late, Valor was trying the very door where Robin was lodged. She prayed that it was locked and almost fainted when she saw Valor open it and escort Elizabeth inside.

Making her way swiftly down the hall with Avery following at her heels, she drew to a halt at the door and, bracing herself, peeked in. Robin and Marian were gone. But where? How had they escaped unseen?

Valor saw the fear on his wife's face and tensed. He tried to smile reassuringly, though he knew not what was wrong.

Raena's heart pounded. Frantic at how close he had come to being arrested by the prince, she realized all the more how much she loved him. The intensely personal look he gave her made her heart leap with hope, for it conveyed such warmth, such love, she knew that he felt the same way.

Without speaking a word, he was telling her that things would be all right. Smiling, she said, "I wanted to make sure the linens were fresh."

Taking a couple of steps toward the bed, she gave it a cursory glance, then declared, "It's as I feared, no one's changed the linens. If you'll pardon me, I'll see to it straight away."

She turned to leave, but Valor caught her by the arm. "Calm down, my love," he said under his breath. "Stay here with Elizabeth and try to be civil whilst I see to the prince. I'll send an attendant to change the linens."

Raena forced a smile and nodded her head. Valor gave her a questioning look as if he were trying to understand something, and then, shaking the cobwebs out of his head, he left to join the prince.

It occurred to him halfway down the hall that the bed had been rumpled, indeed. Knowing it was Raena's mother's room, it surprised him to find it had been used. Hmmm, Raena was up to something, but he had no time to wonder what it was. Not with the prince breathing down his neck.

Raena drew in a deep breath, relieved her husband had left and eminently relieved that there was nothing out of place in the chamber aside from the rumpled bedcovers, That was enough. That was quite enough.

She wondered again where Robin and Marian had gone and uneasily settled her gaze on the tapestry hanging on the wall. "I think you'll find the chamber comfortable enough, Lady Elizabeth, though certainly not as luxurious as you're used to."

Elizabeth turned her back to her, and she seized the opportunity to peek behind the tapestry. There was no one there. She almost giggled out loud from the tension. Where were they? How could they have disappeared so suddenly?

Walking over to the window, Raena looked out at the sun-drenched fields beyond the castle walls and saw two figures, garbed in green, riding away from the castle. She watched as they disappeared from view and breathed a sigh of relief.

"What is it you are gawking at out there?"

Lady Elizabeth walked up to the window and pushed her out of the way. "Do you find it so hard to look me in the eye that you must stare out at empty fields?"

Raena turned to face Elizabeth. "And why should I find it hard to look at you? 'Tis true, you're not the handsomest woman I've ever looked upon, but you're not so ugly as all that."

Elizabeth fumed. "You know very well what I mean. You feel shame at stealing my betrothed from me and find it hard to look me in the eye now. Admit it."

"I'll admit no such thing. Knowing what I do about you, Elizabeth, I find it hard to believe that you care one whit for Valor. You forget, I overheard you in your bedchamber having a lusty tryst with your lover."

"So, we're back to that, are we? Are you threatening to tell my father about my relationship with Sir Ambrose? Well, it'll do you no good. He'd never believe it, and neither would Valor."

Raena was stunned. Valor's father was her lover? Great stars in heaven, if Valor ever found out, he'd be devastated. "Lady Elizabeth, I have no intention of telling anyone about your sordid little affair. Your secret is safe with me."

Elizabeth's eyelids flickered in surprise. "I don't understand. You have every reason to hate me, seeing that I have made sure your marriage to Valor is annulled. Why will you not take revenge upon me?"

"For a very simple reason, Elizabeth, though I'm not sure you'll understand it. Because I love my husband and want to protect him from hurt. He'll never know from me just how truly evil his father is."

Elizabeth's face distorted with pain. "Will you find it hard to believe that I, too, love my father and wish to spare him any hurt?"

"Indeed, I do believe you, Elizabeth. You have a woman's heart, the same as I."

Elizabeth stared curiously at Raena, searching for some hint of sarcasm on her face, but there was none. Swallowing hard, she answered, "Yes, a woman's heart doth truly beat inside my chest. We are not so different, you and I—or so I hope most fervently, for I needs must believe that it's not too late for my salvation."

Raena was surprised at the emotion in Elizabeth's voice and realized how truly tortured she was. Something akin to pity grew and blossomed inside her. Elizabeth had wealth untold, a position in life to be envied, and yet Raena envied her not: Despite her riches and status, Elizabeth had no confidence that she could love or be loved.

How truly sad.

Twenty-eight

That evening, Raena took her seat at the high table, where dozens of candles burned. She gazed around the hall in satisfaction, knowing how festive it looked with lengths of fabric secured to stanchions, draped from ceiling to floor in a colorful display. Raena was sure Prince John's own castle could look no grander.

Her gaze scanned the surrounding tables for the magical being who had pulled this all together so quickly and found Saera Ni sitting against the wall, looking pale and tired. She remembered noting that Wiggles wasn't well, but wrapped up in her new husband and Caroline's terrible problem, she had let it slip her mind.

Angry at herself for neglecting her beloved nursemaid, she vowed that as soon as the prince left, she'd make sure Wiggles got proper rest. She would see to her needs herself. Oh, why did the accursed prince have to come today?

"Lady Raena, you seem so very far away. Do not leave us, I'd hate to think my company so tedious that you had to escape into a waking dream."

Raena smiled sweetly at Prince John. "Your grace, I was only thinking of how I might make your stay

more pleasant. I would not have you want for anything."

"Hmmm, I can think of several things I want, but
never fear, I can be patient until you're no longer
wed. 'Tis a pity, though, we can't stay longer so that
we might get to know each other better."

Elizabeth chimed in with a pout. "Must we leave
so soon? I've seen so little of Valor since he returned
from The Crusades and we have so much to discuss,
so many plans to make for our future."

"Elizabeth, have you no manners at all? Surely it
is ill-bred to discuss your plans with your future husband in his present wife's home."

Raena thought that remark rich, considering that
the prince had all but announced his intention to
bed her as soon as her marriage to Valor was annulled.

"And why not, Father?" Elizabeth asked peevishly.
"Was it not ill-bred to seduce my betrothed in the
first place?"

Raena wanted nothing more than to walk away
from the table as quickly as she could, but she stayed
rooted to her chair. To think she had pitied this
irritating, spoiled, and utterly infuriating woman.

Her foot tapped against the leg of her chair in
rapid succession as frustration and anger took its
toll on her, but she was unaware of the noise it
was making until Valor reached over to touch her
knee. Glancing down the length of the table, she
saw that everyone had noticed the unusual sound.
Smiling sheepishly, she turned her attention to her
husband.

Valor seemed tranquil enough at first glance, but
gazing deeper into his eyes, she saw the anger there
and knew she wasn't the only one who wished this
awful meal to be over.

She smiled, hoping it would convey a calming effect, and he rewarded her with a smile of his own. That reassured her considerably. No need to worry about him. Of all men, this one was capable of controlling his emotions. Didn't she know that firsthand?

Elizabeth saw the interplay between Raena and Valor and snapped, "Look at the way she simpers over him. Does she think a pretty smile will keep him at her side?"

Raena tried to emulate her husband's self-control, but it was hard. Too hard. She opened her mouth to speak, but feeling Valor grasp her hand under the table and squeeze it reassuringly, she chose her words a bit more carefully. "My lady, how wise of you to realize I do love my husband dearly. I'll carry him in my heart forever, and though he may not be free to say so, I know I'll always be in his heart, too. No legal document can change that."

Valor felt his chest tighten, squeezing the very breath from his body. Never had he felt more helpless. He had battled and killed more men than he cared to think of, had bravely stood his ground against every enemy, but all that skill was for naught here in the presence of the prince. How he wished he could stand proudly and proclaim his love for his wife, but he must heed the prince's warning. It would not go well with him if he did.

A terrible silence followed Raena's words. Everyone at the table waited to see how Prince John would react, fearing what he would do.

Prince John looked first at the impudent but lovely young woman and then the white-faced Valor and burst into laughter. "My lady, how clever of you to put words into your husband's mouth! I cannot take offense, since he did not utter them, yet, methinks you do speak his mind most truthfully. 'Tis a pity my daughter is so taken with him, for I do believe he would much prefer to stay with you."

Valor jumped to his feet, not knowing until he did so that he was going to speak. "Your grace, my wife doth speak truthfully. I do love her with all my heart and wish to honor our marriage. My life truly began the day I met her, and without her, life would hold no meaning for me anymore. I beg of you to find some other way to make your daughter happy than sacrificing the one I love beyond reason."

Avery silently cheered his brother on, though he was certainly shocked at his brother's speech. He never knew there was such passion in Valor's heart.

Raena looked terrified, as shocked as everyone else that Valor should act so boldly. He wanted to do whatever he could to help her and . . . and . . .

. . . it suddenly came to him just how that might be accomplished.

Recovering his surprise at Valor's bold stand, Prince John spoke in a voice much softer than expected. "Sir Valor, I can't help but admire your bravery in speaking so passionately of the woman you love. 'Tis quite moving. I envy you your great love and wish I could grant you that favor, but you ask the wrong person. If Elizabeth wishes to set you free of your obligation to her, than 'tis done."

Raena held her breath; hoping against hope that the Elizabeth she had seen in the bedchamber would return. That she would see what an empty marriage she'd have to a man who loved another. Surely pride alone would force her to set Valor free.

Elizabeth rose to face Valor, and the hall became

suddenly quiet. "You speak of love so prettily, Valor, but I speak of honor and duty and obligation. Love has little import in their company. There is nothing to discuss."

With that, Elizabeth stalked from the table.

Avery dared not wait a moment longer. Excusing himself from the table, he started walking very slowly, as if to leave the hall, whilst at the same time releasing his faery scent to Elizabeth. He let it out quickly, giving her no time to fight it.

Before he was halfway to the door, Elizabeth cried out his name and started toward him.

He pretended surprise and turned to face her, whilst at the same time letting out even more of his faery scent. Elizabeth undulated her body, looking altogether like some great green snake about to strike. Her eyes became glassy and wet, her mouth slack, and he could only wonder at the emptiness of her soul that she should fall under his spell so easily.

He stood there, looking like the innocent boy everyone thought him to be, and watched as she made her way to him. He had no idea what she would do, but he was sure it would be entertaining.

Prince John watched the scene, puzzled as to why Elizabeth was so anxious to speak with the young lad, and an uneasiness came over him. She was acting very peculiar. Was she drunk?

That hardly seemed possible in the short time they had been at the table; but if not that, then what? He watched as she made her way to young Avery and, like everyone else gathered there, waited to see what she would do next.

A loud gasp filled the hall as Elizabeth kneeled in front of the young man and groped for his private parts. Her hands moved inside the flap of cloth that protected his manhood and pulled it free.

Before anyone could comprehend what she was doing, she took it in her mouth.

Twenty-nine

The great hall became hushed as if some mighty sorcerer had put a spell upon every soul there, turning them all to a stone. Cups half-raised to lips halted. Voices in the midst of speech paused as everyone watched the lady Elizabeth's vulgar act.

For an uncomfortably long time, no one made a move to stop her.

Who amongst them dared?

She was Prince John's daughter.

The prince himself was too frozen with shock to do anything, thinking he must surely be dreaming this, for it couldn't possibly be happening.

But seeing the shock on young Avery's face as he tried to disengage Elizabeth from his person, the prince knew it was not a dream, but a terrible, living nightmare.

And still he could not move.

Elizabeth's movements, however, were anything but frozen. Under the great compulsion she felt to mate with Avery, she was using her mouth and hands to harden his member so that he could pleasure her. In truth, she was so completely under his spell she lost all awareness of anyone else in the hall. It was as if she were in the midst of an erotic dream from which she could not wake.

Nay, it was more than a dream; it was a frenzy, a desperate need she must satisfy no matter what it took to do so. It was all she could think of, all she lived for, all she needed. She couldn't understand why Avery was trying to push her away, for surely he must be feeling it, too. She would surely go mad if he didn't respond to her soon.

It didn't take Valor long to figure out that Avery was using his faery glamour, for nothing else in this world could explain Elizabeth's bizarre behavior. God's blood! Didn't Avery know the risk he was taking, using the prince's daughter so sorely?

And the prince, why wasn't he ordering his men to stop this—this unholy debasement? Turning his attention to the most powerful man in the kingdom, Valor saw the stunned expression on the prince's face and knew he was in too much shock to act.

It was up to him to stop it.

Clenching his jaw, he strode to Avery and Elizabeth and gently tried to remove her, but she resisted him violently. She lashed out and scratched his cheek with her sharp fingernails, then seeming to forget he was even there, turned her attention back to Avery.

Her momentary distraction gave Avery time enough to cover his manhood, but that didn't stop Elizabeth. Losing access to one part of his body, she worked on another.

Leaping to her feet, she began tearing off his tunic, going after him like a deranged creature whilst all the while crying out her need for him in language unbefitting a lady.

Miles, the castle steward, joined Valor in trying to control Elizabeth, and between the two of them, they managed to pry her away from Avery, whereupon Valor lifted her over his shoulder and carried her out of the hall. Elizabeth pounded on his back with her fists and tried to tear the hair from his head.

Wide-eyed and dazed, Raena stared at the awful spectacle. Avery appeared so embarrassed and distressed, she could almost believe he was truly innocent. But she knew better. No one in her right mind would ever act that way in public. Not even Elizabeth.

But still, she was relieved to see him looking so genuinely innocent, for if the prince had any inkling that he was the cause of Elizabeth's humiliation, he would surely have Avery killed on the spot.

Though she detested the humiliating method he had chosen, she was grateful he would risk his life for her. For, indeed, she knew he was doing it for her.

Prince John rose to his feet and, without a word, started out of the hall after Valor and his daughter. He found them in the chapel, where Elizabeth stood banging her forehead over and over against the wall. He feared his daughter was completely mad.

Taking a deep breath, the prince spoke to Valor. "I thank you, sir, for having the presence of mind to remove my daughter and end that awful scene. God help me, I was too shocked to do anything at all. Never in my life have I seen such a thing as that, and never care to again. That it is my own daughter who behaved so despicably is more than I can bear."

"Your grace, no need to speak of it."

"This changes everything, of course. I don't expect you to marry a madwoman. You're free. I only regret you had to witness that humiliating scene. Under the circumstances, I think it's best we leave right away."

Avery chose that moment to make an appearance,

inspiring Elizabeth into action again. "I won't go! Give me one night with him."

She pointed to Avery, who looked for all the world as though he were, indeed, nothing more than an innocent child. Caressing her own breasts, she undulated her body, murmuring, "Oh, yes, one night with him and I'll be much recuperated. That's all I need. That's all I want. One night with him."

Prince John gaped at her as if she had two heads. "Elizabeth, control yourself. It grieves me to see you this way. Do you realize the object of your desire is no more than a boy? Have you lost your mind entirely?"

Elizabeth's face contorted as if in pain. "What's the matter, Father? Do you want him for yourself?"

Prince John slapped his daughter's face so hard, she staggered from the blow. Then, turning, he strode out of the chapel without another word.

Avery grinned and turned off his faery charm, leaving Elizabeth to sink into total despair.

Realizing what she had done, she stared after her father in horror. She hadn't meant to say that.

God help her, she hadn't meant to say that. He could have her head for that. People had died at his hands for far less.

What was happening to her? Was she going mad? What had ever possessed her to attack the boy like that? She tried to tell herself it wasn't as bad as she thought, that it had happened so quickly no one had even noticed; but when she turned to face Valor and saw him make the sign of the cross, she knew. It was much worse than she'd thought.

The first pain stabbed through Caroline's abdomen as she sat next to her husband, watching Elizabeth degrade herself before a hundred pairs of eyes; but she was so shocked at what she was seeing she barely noticed the pain. If she had ever had any doubt about Avery's powers of seduction, she had none now. Nor could Stephan now fail to see that she had been helpless against Avery's magic.

Seeing the horror on his face, she was grateful he had not had to witness her own humiliation. But, in sooth, Avery had not been so callous with her, and for that she was grateful. At least, he had acted like a genuine lover and seduced her in privacy, treating her with compassion.

Memories of their time together suddenly flooded her, and with the remembrance came a sweet sadness. Their mating had been delicate, sensual, and yes, loving. If she had never met Stephan, she would have been content to have had Avery for a lover. In many ways, he was very much like his older brother. But watching his cruelty now, she knew that in many more important ways, he was not.

Another pain stabbed through her, and this time she couldn't ignore it. Was it just the excitement or was there something genuinely wrong?

Stephan noticed her wince and asked, "What is it?"

"I—I don't know. I've been experiencing some sharp pains. I'm sure it is nothing."

Stephan's brow creased. He was out of his domain when it came to female troubles. But still, he didn't want to take any chances. "I think I'll ask Saera Wigglesworth to look at you. She's wise in such matters." He stood to leave, but Caroline stopped him with a touch of her hand on his arm.

"Are . . . are you sure you want Saera to help? Mayhap, it would be best to let nature take its course."

Stephan looked at her solemnly. "Best for whom?"

"For you, my dearest husband. If the child is aborted, you'll not have to be reminded of my infidelity every time you look at it."

Removing her hand, Stephan placed it gently at her side. "Methinks you're the one who wants no reminders. This child is part of the woman I love, and I can accept it and love it because of that. It may not be mine, but 'tis certainly Godwin blood that nourishes its heart. I can live with that. Can you?"

Caroline stepped into her husband's arms and held him close, her head pressed against his chest. "Oh, Stephan, that's all I wanted to hear. It won't be hard for me to love this child, knowing you can, too."

Stephan's eyes closed in pain for just a moment, then swallowing hard, he murmured, "Let's find Saera."

But Saera Wigglesworth was nowhere to be found. Stephan walked right past the beautiful young woman leaning against the stable wall.

Saera Ni was very weak and could barely stand. She was too weak to disguise her true form any longer, for it took too much energy from her.

She waited whilst John Barrows fetched a horse for her from inside the stable. It was imperative that she leave the castle immediately to escape the throng of people. It was they who drained her of the energy to use her faery glamour.

She had always known this day would come.

The day when she could no longer sustain her false image as a stout old woman, for it was too hard

to do with more than just a few people at a time.
So many years of having to keep up her shield had
slowly drained her of her strength.

Now, she would have to rest somewhere quiet to
regain her dangerously dwindling health.

Standing in the portcullis, Raena waved goodbye
to the prince as he hurriedly rode over the drawbridge and away from the scene of his daughter's
humiliation.

Valor rode with him, accompanying the prince's
entourage to the boundaries of his property in a
sign of fidelity. Thinking quickly, he had arranged
for the people of the hamlet and castle to line the
road with lit torches to show the way for the prince.

Raena thought the plan brilliant and knew that it
would soothe the prince's ego. Watching as the entourage disappeared from sight, she sighed and re-
entered the castle grounds. Truly, today had been
the most trying of her life.

Walking back inside the bailey, she saw Saera Ni
standing near the stable and her heart fairly stopped,
seeing her in her true form.

Something was wrong.

In all the years she had known Wiggles, the nursemaid had never revealed her true self to anyone but
Raena and John.

Saera Ni saw Raena coming and cried out, "There
you are. I was hoping I'd see you before I leave."

"Leave? Are you going somewhere, Saera Ni?"

"I must. I pray you understand, John and I depart
straight away for the cottage where you and I dwelled
so many years."

"But why? I don't understand. At the faery circle

you told Queen Edainn, told everyone you were needed here with me, and oh, 'tis true. You are.''

"Nay, you have no need of me anymore, child. Not with brave Valor by your side. In truth, the queen was trying to spare me when she ordered me to stay. She knew my strength was dwindling and wanted me to stay and regain it in the quiet of the faery circle; but fool that I was, I thought I was stronger—that I could last a few years longer amongst humankind. But it seems, I cannot."

Brushing a tear from Raena's face, she said softly, "Will you understand and make this easy for me?"

"I have no choice. But . . . promise you'll let me visit you there. I couldn't bear never to see you again."

"My dearest, sweetest little Gosling, of course you may. I'm not going to the ends of the earth, now, am I? You and I have made the journey to Sherwood Forest before, have we not? You'll see, it will all work out for the best."

"Raena! Thank God, I've found you."

Raena spun around to see Stephan with Caroline in his arms. Her heart stopped at the sight of the bright-red spot of blood on her pale-colored garment.

"I've been looking everywhere for your nurse-maid Saera, but she's disappeared. I fear Caroline is about to lose the child."

Looking at Caroline suspiciously, Raena asked, "Isn't that what you wished for, Caroline?"

"Not any longer. Stephan and I want this child. Help me, please. Where is Saera?"

Raena looked into Saera Ni's eyes for a moment, long enough to see how truly weak she was. "Saera is gone. I'll help you. Everything that Saera knows, I know. She taught me well."

Saera Ni nodded her head. "Aye, she did that. But I'm thinking in this case, neither you nor Saera is powerful enough to stop her from miscarrying. You need another's help."

"Whose? Tell me whose?" Stephan cried.

"Someone you are not acquainted with, Sir Stephan. Someone who may not be willing to help."

"But who could be so callous? Who would deny an innocent child its life?"

Raena knew immediately whom Saera meant, and the dreaded name escaped her lips. "Queen Edainn."

Thirty

Power was a heady thing, Avery thought, gloating. He had brought a mighty prince to his knees without much effort at all. Thinking of all the mischief he could cause in London if he had a mind, he walked up to the ramparts to be alone, the better to fantasize and revel in his victory.

Leaning through a crenel, he stared down at the bailey and the portcullis through which the prince had ridden just a few moments earlier. *How very trusting humans were.*

Faery folk knew better than to believe everything they saw with their eyes, for in their world, magic was as commonplace as the humans bustling around down there in the bailey, gossiping, he was sure, about the strange behavior of Lady Elizabeth.

Oh, how amusing that had been, watching her make a complete fool of herself. But then, it wasn't solely for his own amusement that he had done it, but as a way to help his sister and her husband. Raena was blood of his blood, and that was more important to him than wealth or power or even great sport at Prince John's expense.

Ah, yes, blood of his blood.

Caroline's child was blood of his blood.

An icy chill traveled up his spine as he recalled

how close death had come to denying him his child. His people were struggling for their very existence, doing everything they could to survive, yet Caroline had selfishly decided to end not only her own life, but that of his precious child.

And they thought faery folk were ruthless!

Was it ruthless to try to protect his people from extinction? What he did was no more than any intelligent being would do to survive. It was imperative that faeries procreate, that they let nothing stand in their way, for that was the only chance they had.

Considering how easily humans bred, bringing so many unwanted children into the world, it was no wonder they couldn't understand how precious life was. Look at them down there, scurrying around like prolific little rats. Look at . . .

Avery focused on Stephan carrying Caroline in his arms, and melancholy settled in his heart like a comfortable, old friend. He had always taken great pride in his superior faery powers, yet it was Stephan who held Caroline in his arms, Stephan who captured her heart without the help of faery glamour. What good was all his power when it couldn't make Caroline love him?

He ached to be the one holding her now, carrying her . . . but what was that? There, on the front of her clothing? It looked like . . .

Blood!

His heart lurched.

She'd done it. Mother Goddess, she'd done it!

Rage overwhelmed him at the thought that she had willfully harmed his child. Racing down the staircase, he made his way outside, forcing himself to calm his anger, else he couldn't be responsible for what he might do.

Raena saw him, and her face lit up as if he were

her savior. "Oh, Avery, thank goodness you're here. I needs must get Caroline to the faery circle immediately. The faery queen is the only one who can help Caroline keep her babe."

"Keep the child?" Eyes glistening, he seized Caroline's hand. "You . . . want to keep the child?"

Stephan couldn't bear to see the hope shining on Avery's face. Hope he didn't deserve to have. Hope that had little chance of being realized, for it would take a miracle to save Caroline's baby now. "Don't just stand there. For God's sake, Avery, can't you see we're in need of horses? Hurry!"

Grateful for something to do, Avery helped the groomsmen saddle horses and in but a few moments they were on their way, riding like the wind toward the faery circle.

Dismounting at the top of the ravine, Stephan reacted angrily to Raena's plea that he remain outside the faery stones. "I won't let her go in there alone. Surely you exaggerate the danger. What harm can come to me from fragile, fey creatures?"

"Stephan, you must trust me on this," Raena said. "It would be far better for everyone if you waited outside. The faery circle is a treacherous place."

"If it's as treacherous as you say, I'll not let Caroline enter it without me at her side."

"Listen to Raena," Avery said, tethering the horses. " 'Tis not just for your sake, but for ours. You'll be too great a distraction to the queen, believe me. She won't help Caroline if she has you to prey upon. Edainn eats men like you as if they were sugared plums."

"Then, for God's sake, Avery, you must go in with

her. You're half-faery; surely you're in no danger there."

In truth, Avery had never been inside the faery circle. Everything he knew about Queen Edainn came from his father. But he wasn't about to tell Stephan that—the fool would insist on accompanying his wife and would end up being more of a hindrance than a help.

"Of course, I'll go. The queen will listen to me. Am I not a prince of the people of Dawne?"

Stephan shook his head wearily, thinking, "Has the whole world gone mad? Or is it just me? Am I the only one who had no knowledge that faeries actually exist?"

Swallowing hard, he fought to keep his emotions in check, but they were so strong he couldn't contain them. His face contorted with pain, he burst out, "I rode to the ends of the earth to fight an enemy only to find upon my return, an even greater enemy on my very doorstep. 'Tis too much to bear."

"Faerie are not the enemy of man," Avery answered. " 'Tis man who is the enemy to faerie. If not for humans trying to rid the world of those they cannot understand, we'd all be living peacefully side by side, learning from each other, sharing the beauty of the earth. Instead, my people are forced to live in the bowels of the earth where they sicken and die."

"Stop it!" Raena shouted. "There's no time for bickering now. We've got to get Caroline to the queen quickly."

Stephan lifted Caroline into his arms. "Lead the way. I'll carry her down."

The moon was bright and full, shining upon the path like a heavenly torch to light their way. Still,

Stephan stepped cautiously on the steep slope for fear of falling and causing Caroline more injury.

Avery caught up with them at the bottom of the ravine, blanching at the sight of the swirling green mist inside the ominous dark circle of stones. " 'Tis exceedingly awesome," he murmured. "I can see why humans fear to venture inside. The mist is to keep humans away, is it not? It must be very effective, for I admit I feel some small amount of fear myself just gazing at it."

Raena looked at him in surprise. "Yes, of course, the mist is a protective device, used only when the queen feels the need to shield what's inside from prying eyes. Sometimes, when it's absent, humans wander inside and are trapped. Surely you knew this already?"

"I fear not," Avery confessed sheepishly. "This is my first time here. You see, Mother filled my head with awful tales of the faery circle when I was small. She told me it was an evil place where wicked witches were waiting for juicy young boys like me to come along so they could eat them. I've never been tempted to come here, even after I was old enough to know her stories were but inventions."

"But surely you must have been curious to meet others like yourself?"

"Curious? Oh, yes, I was very curious; but you see, I've always been gifted with a strong sense of survival. 'Tis hard to understand, I know, but I thought if I had no concourse with my people, I'd be immune to their frailties."

"Oh, Avery, I've never seen anyone with so strong a sense of self-preservation. Mayhap, you should stay outside the circle, too. If you've never met Queen Edainn, you can't possibly know how to deal with her. She can be most formidable."

With a sad smile, Avery replied, "Don't you think it's time I learned?"

Before she could stop him, he stepped into the mist and disappeared from sight.

Caroline gasped, and Stephan held her tighter. "God's blood! He's—he's disappeared! This powerful magic frightens me. Are you certain Caroline will be safe in there?"

"Very certain. She carries a faery child. They'll not harm her."

"Then, I suppose I have no choice but to let her go. She and the child will surely die if I don't." Lowering his wife to the ground, Stephan took Raena's hand in his. "Protect my wife. Bring her safely back to me."

"Upon my life, I vow that she'll be fine."

Caroline echoed, Raena's words. "I'll be fine. Don't worry so, dearest one. Avery will be there. Do you think he'd let any harm come to his child?" With one last, longing look at her husband, Caroline took Raena's hand and stepped into the green vortex.

Queen Edainn's sexual appetite was stronger than usual this night. Though she was barren, she still experienced the same cycle as other females, and this was the time when she would normally have been fertile.

She clung to the hope that she might yet conceive a child. It might still happen. *It must. It would* happen. All she needed was the right male.

Standing naked before the altar rock, she gazed at three equally naked male faeries standing eagerly before her, each hoping to be the one she chose this night.

Suddenly, a soft roar filled the faery circle and she knew outsiders had entered. Hoping the intruders would be worthy of an evening's sport, she turned in delighted anticipation and saw . . .

. . . oh, Mother Goddess, she saw a male of such great beauty walking toward her, she fairly fainted from the sight.

Who was this luscious creature? There was something very different about him, something that did speak of majesty.

Her faery playmates were forgotten as her gaze traveled over the young male's form. He was very young, but not too young. Nay, he was most definitely of an age when he could be of good use to her.

"My queen, we come to you on an urgent matter."

Princess Raena's voice rudely interrupted Edainn's lusty thoughts, and the queen's brow furrowed with disapproval. "What are you doing here again so soon? Why doesn't your virile young husband use his cock to keep you nailed to your marriage bed? Has he lost interest in his new bride so soon? If you have no use of him, then send him here to me. I'll use him well."

Raena wanted to answer the queen with a sharp retort, but that wouldn't have helped Caroline. Instead, she spoke respectfully. "Your majesty, this is Lady Caroline, wife of my husband's brother. She carries a faery child within her and is about to lose it. Knowing of your healing power, I've brought her here to you."

"To me? What do I care if she loses the babe? It would be just one more feeble half-ling with no faery traits at all. The world will be better off without it."

Avery had a hard time controlling his temper, but

following Raena's lead, he spoke much more softly than he wanted to. "The faery child you speak of is mine."

"Yours? I see nothing that doth speak of faery in you. 'Tis true you have great beauty, but there is beauty in every race." She sniffed at the air, then frowned. "I cannot even smell the faery scent on you."

"Clever of me, isn't it, to hide my faery half from the world? But I assure you, Queen Edainn, I am born of royal faery blood."

"And now he claims royalty. What gall! I am familiar with all the offspring of nobility and have no report of any royal males outside my realm save for Prince Ohreinn's son."

Bowing low, Avery said, "At your service, your majesty."

"You are Prince Avery? How astounding! You do not favor him at all, save for your arrogance." Turning to one of the naked male faeries, she said, "Go. Bring the prince to me so we may settle this."

Seeing the queen was more interested in Avery than in helping Caroline, Raena said anxiously, "Time is of the essence. The child Lady Caroline carries is of royal blood. For that reason, I'm certain you'll want to help."

"The child's parentage changes nothing. I've seen too many of these half-faery creatures sicken and die. Faery and humankind were not meant to meld."

"Are you so sure of that?" Avery asked.

Raising an eyebrow exceedingly high, she answered, "I have only to look at you to see 'tis true. Though you are a fine specimen as humans go, still you are bereft of any of your father's superior faery traits. Bringing more humans into the world is not the way to help my people. 'Twould be much more helpful to get rid of a few."

Avery smiled wickedly. "So, I've fooled even you."

"Fooled me? How so? I can see with my own eyes that there's nothing about you that speaks of my kind, most certainly not your dull, colorless eyes."

Avery laughed out loud and said, "Look again, my queen, look again."

Growing angry at the manchild's impudence, she drew closer and stared deep into his eyes. "And what am I to see? You do have dull eyes for one so otherwise good-looking."

Avery willed his eyes to change to their natural color until they shone like vibrant, purple gems. Edainn's own violet eyes grew large with wonder at the transformation. "It cannot be. This is some trick of the light or . . . or . . ."

"Ah, I see you've met my son, Prince Avery." Ohreinn said, appearing suddenly.

Spinning around, Edainn said, "Ohreinn, you have much to answer for. Why did you never tell me your son had faery traits? 'Tis treason to withhold such important information from your queen."

"Faery traits? You know as well as I that Avery lost all his faery traits when he was very young. If there had been any encouraging news, I would have gone to you straight away."

"Encouraging? With eyes like that, how could you possibly think I would not be encouraged?"

Ohreinn looked at his son's eyes and was astonished. "I—I didn't know. I swear to you, I didn't know."

"It's true, my queen. I never let my father see my faery eyes. Nor any of my other faery talents."

"Other talents?" Edainn's pulse quickened, for she suddenly dared hope this exquisite male faery would be the one she had waited a lifetime for, the one to be her faery king, the one to quicken her womb. "What other talents do you have?"

Avery was enjoying himself. After all the years he had held his secret, it felt good to expose it to the very ones who would be most impressed. "Tell me, my queen, what talent would please you most?"

"Don't play with me. Any talent will do. I have no preference."

Avery opened his mouth, but instead of talking, he slid his tongue out farther and farther until it was an impressive length. No human had a tongue such as that. From the rapt expression on the queen's face, he doubted any faery could match his size.

Edainn stared in rapture at the wondrous sight. Amongst her people, only Ohreinn could rival Avery. Her heart beat madly. Oh, surely, this was the one she had been waiting so long for.

"What other faery talents do you have? I am most eager to learn of them."

Avery was sure of that. He could smell her musk growing stronger by the moment. "I'll be pleased to show you all my talents, but first . . ."

"Yes, yes, tell me."

"First, heal the Lady Caroline. Stop her pain and her bleeding, and I will continue."

Edainn looked over at Caroline, and her eyes narrowed to tiny slits. This pale, sickly creature had had the privilege of mating with Prince Avery first. The last thing she wanted was to stop her pain. She preferred to let her die as punishment.

But one look at Avery's face and she knew that if she hoped to make him hers, she'd have to please him on this matter. "Very well." The sooner it was done, the sooner she could send the puny creature back to the upper world.

Edainn stalked over to Caroline and, placing her hands on either side of her head, drew her face up against her mouth. Caroline's arms fluttered at her side in protest, but Edainn's superior strength held her tight.

Pressing her lips against the fetid, human female's, Edainn parted her mouth with her tongue and blew into it. Immediately, Caroline stopped struggling and accepted the healing breath.

Raena watched in astonishment at the unexpected sight. She had had no previous knowledge of this method of healing and wondered why Wiggles had never told her about it. But she had no doubt that it was, indeed, healing, for Caroline immediately stood straighter, free of her pain, the color flowing back to her cheeks.

Avery watched as the woman he loved became healthier and healthier, and his heart rejoiced. Until this moment, he had thought the exceptional healing powers of faery queens just a myth.

"There," Edainn said, wiping the horrid taste of the female from her mouth. "I've granted you your boon, now grant me mine."

Avery's gaze swept over Caroline. When he was assured it was no trick, that she and the child were healthy once more, he bowed low to the queen. "Your wish is my command."

"Then, show me. I want to see everything about you that is faery."

"For that, I'll have to remove my clothing, but I'm reluctant to do so in front of Raena and Caroline. Send them away."

"Very clever, Avery, to try to trick me into letting them go; but they'll stay until I'm sure I have no need of them anymore. If they are offended by your nakedness, they can turn their heads. *I* will watch with great relish."

Caroline's head was still filled with mist, but even she was curious. She had seen Avery's body when they'd made love, but had noticed nothing that was anything other than human.

As for Raena, she was impatient to leave the circle before anything untoward happened. Edainn was so unpredictable. But 'twas obvious the queen wasn't about to let anyone leave until she was done with Avery. What was it about him that fascinated her so?

And then, oh, then, she had her answer.

Standing naked now before them with a wide, knowing grin upon his face, Avery very slowly spun around; and as he did so, faery wings budded and grew from his shoulder blades. Glorious wings that blossomed into things of such beauty that everyone who gazed upon them felt humbled by the experience. And if that was not wondrous enough, *he could grow his wings at will.*

Never had Raena seen such an incredible sight, and it thrilled her to know this magnificent creature was her half brother. Both Caroline and Edainn were awestruck as they gazed at Avery's male glory.

And no wonder. In truth, she didn't think there was a female alive who could resist his great beauty. He had no need of his faery glamour to enchant.

Eager to see her father's reaction, she glanced his way in time to see tears fall from his eyes. At last, his dream of the survival of his race was assured through this powerful, young, and virile, faery prince.

The significance of his ability to hide the faery part of him from everyone was not lost on her. It was the most incredible talent of all. One that obviously neither her father nor the queen had ever dreamed possible. One that assured faery folk might once again walk freely upon the land, for if they were as gifted as Avery, no one would even guess they were faery unless they wished it known.

Ohreinn embraced his son warmly, then went down on one knee and kissed his son's hand. "That I might live to see this day is the greatest gift you could give me. You are the future, my son. Our bright and shining future."

Touched and embarrassed by his father's words, Avery suddenly felt a weight lift from his soul. He hadn't known it until this very moment, but he loved his father and wanted to please him. "I've almost told you a thousand times, wanting to share my accomplishments with you, but something always held me back. Now, I know why. I wanted to wait until I could perfect my talents so that you would be proud of me."

Standing once again, Ohreinn said, "Proud? That doesn't begin to describe what I feel. Knowing you are free to walk the earth as any human male frees my spirit and gives me great joy."

Turning to the queen, he said, "I thank you for saving my grandchild, for 'tis possible you have saved a perfect faery child. Surely, Edainn, you're as pleased as I?"

In a husky voice, the queen answered, "More than you can ever know, Ohreinn." Overwrought with emotion, Edainn ate Avery up with her eyes. This was the one. The perfect mate for her. She'd have no further use of inferior lovers now. "So pleased, I mean to make him my king."

She said the words proudly, raising her chin to show there was no question that it would be done, and waited in happy contentment to hear Avery's acceptance.

But why was he not speaking? Why was he looking at his father and his sister as if there were some doubt in his mind? This was intolerable! "The ceremony will take place tomorrow eve when the moon is at its fullest."

At last, Avery spoke. "My queen, though you are without a doubt the loveliest female that has ever graced two worlds, I will not marry you. You above anyone should know what a great sacrifice it would be to give up my freedom to walk the green earth. And for what? This stifling stone prison and the dark, sunless caverns below?"

Edainn was speechless. She had no weapon to use to force him, for without a doubt his faery glamour was more powerful than hers; but she must have him. *She must.*

Surely there was a way to force him to her will.

Thirty-one

Torches lit the road from Caldwell Castle as far as the eye could see, brightening the night most spectacularly. Valor was sure the splendid sight had taken away the sting of the terrible scene with Elizabeth and would leave the prince with good thoughts toward the people of Caldwell Castle.

Scores of people had lined the long, winding road, even bringing along their children to hold their own little torches. Prince John had seemed quite taken by the outpouring of support, and rightfully so, for 'twas a most impressive sight.

To think he had wanted nothing to do with this land, these good people. To think he might have traded it all for a larger castle, and a colder wife. Truly, he had been a fool most of his life.

Now, sitting atop his mount, Valor watched as the king's entourage disappeared into the darkness ahead. It could have ended quite differently, for the prince was known to be harsh. But now, he felt quite sure that Prince John would not hold him or his people responsible for Elizabeth's act of madness and that when he thought of them it would be with fondness.

Feeling lighter of spirit than he had since his return from The Crusades, he turned his horse and cantered down the road, waving to the few stragglers along the way. Most of his people had already dispersed. Dots of lights, like tiny fireflies, grew smaller and smaller as the serfs and villeins returned to their homes, still carrying the flickering remains of their torches.

Soon, there was no one left but Valor and the bright moon, and that was good enough for him. He enjoyed the solitude of the night, for it gave him the opportunity to savor his newfound contentment. He was, indeed, a lucky man and wanted nothing more than to love and cherish his wife forever, knowing only death had the power to part them.

Hearing a murmur of voices somewhere in the darkness ahead, he slowed the pace of his horse and moved cautiously down the road, his gauntleted hand closed round the handle of his sword.

He saw them then and relaxed. It was naught but a group of hooded monks walking down the road. So, even the good brothers of the monastery had come to help light the way for the prince. Good. Good.

He was halfway past the holy men when it occurred to him that he knew of no monastery nearby.

Too late.

Two of them attacked, grabbing his horse's bridle and bringing the animal to a stop whilst the others pulled him from the saddle before he had time to gather his wits. He struggled in vain, for there were too many of them to fight.

The leader of the knaves stripped off his monk's robe to reveal a tunic of hunter green underneath, and Valor knew it must be the notorious Robin Hood.

"My lord," Robin Hood said, bowing low. "What a splendid exhibition for the prince. My men and

I enjoyed it immensely. We were about to leave when, lo and behold, you suddenly left the prince's side and headed back this way. What is it? Did the prince discover he had left some trinket behind for you to fetch for him? 'Twas unwise of him to send you alone. The land is full of knaves and cutthroats waiting to deprive you of your worldly goods. Best hand over your valuables to me so that I might better safeguard them."

Laughter rang out as Robin Hood's men enjoyed their victory over the evil prince's minion.

Valor gritted his teeth and endured the mirth at his expense. 'Twas obvious they thought him part of the prince's entourage. "Alas, I have nothing worth taking, so, if I can be of no further use to you, I'll be on my way." He struggled against the tight grip of the burly men who held him.

"We'll judge for ourselves whether you have anything of value. John, search our impatient friend."

A giant of a man stepped in front of Valor, blocking his view of Robin Hood, and the other men relaxed their hold on him whilst the giant searched under his tunic for a money belt.

The band of thieves seemed so merry, 'twas hard to believe they were so successful at their game. Trying to distract them, Valor pretended to be ticklish at the giant's rough touch and began to squirm and laugh like an idiot.

Struck by the amusing sight, Robin Hood and his men started laughing, too, until some were practically rolling on the ground with merriment.

Seizing his chance, Valor broke lose and moved backward out of reach whilst at the same time pulling his sword from its scabbard.

The laughter came to an abrupt stop as the thieves reached for their own swords and the sound of metal on metal rang through the darkness of the night.

"Don't be a fool," Robin Hood shouted. "No need to make so much of it. We'll but deprive you of whatever coin and valuables you have and leave you none the worse for wear. If you insist on resisting, your life will be forfeit."

Robin Hood's words were lost on Valor. He had never backed away from a fight, and God help him, he couldn't do so now. How could he live with himself knowing he had acted the coward? How could he ever be worthy of Raena if he slunk away into the night?

Backing farther away, he said, "Easy for you to say, but, alas, not easy for me to do. I could more readily give up an arm or a leg than give up my manhood. I ask but one thing of you. If I'm killed, see that my wife knows that I died bravely."

Robin shook his head in amazement. Who was this romantic knight? He was greatly outnumbered and yet he still chose to fight? "If that's the way you want it, who am I to dissuade you? Tell me your wife's name, and I'll see that she gets a true account of your brave and noble death."

"Lady Raena Godwin of Caldwell Castle. 'Tis her land you violate now."

Robin's eyes opened wide with amazement. Raena's husband? Robin dropped his sword arm, and his men followed suit. But 'twas too late, for the knight was raising his sword, ready to charge them.

Valor gave out a war yell and started for the band of thieves when, before his very eyes, they scattered, disappearing quickly into the surrounding woods.

Coming to a halt, he stared in bewilderment, looking for some sign of them, but there was none.

They were gone, leaving the night as silent as the grave.

Valor was completely bewildered. Why had they run? He was certain it wasn't from cowardice, not with the reputation that Robin Hood and his men had earned. And not when he was so vastly outnumbered. Then why? Why had they refused to fight him?

Frustrated, he tried to remember what had happened just before their disappearance. *Raena.* He had said her name. Valor's face flushed with anger. Once again she had deprived him of his free will, nay of his very manhood! Damn her! Did her powers reach beyond the castle walls to the very ears of a roving band of thieves? His old resentment came back to haunt him once again.

Climbing back on his horse, he rode down the dark road in a rage that he should be deprived even of his God-given right to defend himself.

Somewhere ahead; he heard the nicker of a horse and, heartened, rode faster, eager to face whoever it was. Eager to fight a foe, any foe, to prove his worth.

Rounding a bend in the road, he saw four horses tied to a tree and recognized where he was. The faery circle.

Curse Satan. That could mean but one thing. Raena was there. But with whom? Who were the fools who accompanied her to this wild place?

Dismounting, he made his way to the bottom of the ravine, determined to show her and the world that he was a man of free will.

Thirty-two

Overhead the moon shone down upon the eerie circle, casting long shadows of the standing rocks across the ground. If Valor had been a superstitious man, he might have thought they were reaching out to him, for they seemed to swell and ebb with life. But surely he imagined it.

Ah, but what to make of the pulsating green glow that emanated from the very heart of the circle? Of all the nights to prove his manhood, did it have to be this night?

Aye, it had to be now, for Raena was inside. If he didn't prove himself here and now, he might as well shrivel up and die.

He took long strides toward the stones, but was suddenly jerked violently backward. A strong arm was choking the life out of him. He struggled with his assailant and, cursing his carelessness kicked backward, connecting with someone's knee.

"Argh! Stop it, Valor. You're hurting me."

Hearing his brother's familiar voice, Valor stopped struggling. "Stephan! God's blood! You scared me out of a full year of life. Why did you attack me like that?"

"To stop you from entering the faery circle.

Raena made me promise to keep you out if you came."

"So, she made you promise, did she? And what about you? Did you promise not to enter, too?"

"I did."

Valor started toward the circle again, a determined look upon his face. "Good. Then, you'll be able to keep one of your vows."

"No, Valor! Avery warned me how dangerous it is for humans there. You don't stand a chance."

"I refuse to believe that. Don't you understand? I have to know I'm capable of defending myself and my family, or lose my manhood forever."

"So, for the sake of male pride, you'd risk everything? God's teeth, Val, Raena has no need of your protection in there. And, besides, she has Avery with her. He'll protect her and Caroline."

"Caroline is in there, too? And you wait out here like a craven coward?"

Stephan suddenly fell apart, and Valor knew he must have been agonizing over what to do.

"Blast it! I've been out here trying to talk myself out of going in when I crave more than anything to be with my wife, no matter the danger. I'm going with you." With that, Stephan started in, and it was Valor's turn to hold him back.

"No. Wait. We've got to think this out. No use in both of us risking our lives. How long have they been there?"

"Too long. I can't wait a moment longer. Caroline was bleeding. She could be lying dead on the cold, stone floor this very moment. I have to know. I have to see."

Valor wrapped his arm around his brother's shoulder. "Then, we'll do it together. Remember our creed from The Crusades? United, Godwin men can defeat any foe."

Buoyed by his brother's bravado, Stephan took a deep breath, as if he were about to plunge into bottomless water, and then stepped inside the circle with Valor at his side.

When the mist cleared and the roar of wind died down, Stephan and Valor found themselves confronting a beautiful tableau. The queen of faeries stood on a platform made of rock, bereft of clothes, her arms outstretched as if waiting for an embrace, and before her stood . . . *Avery.*

No, not Avery. He could never be just Avery again, for this magnificent creature was no ordinary boy. He had been transformed into a regal faery prince, naked to the world save for the adornment of his exquisite dragonfly wings.

Stephan and Valor exchanged puzzled glances. This was the last thing they had expected to see. It was as if they had entered some fantastic painting.

Edainn saw the two men enter shoulder to shoulder, and a surge of energy coursed through her. She might yet gain Avery as her husband this night, with the help of these two romantic fools.

Indeed, they were fools to think they might rescue their wives through brute strength alone. They would learn a great lesson this night and she was most eager to teach them. "Welcome, my lords. You have no idea how happy I am to see you."

Raena stifled the cry that formed in her throat. Oh, why did Valor have to come? They were all doomed now.

Ruffling her brilliant wings, Queen Edainn let out a trill of raucous laughter and the faery circle became as still as a tomb. "I despaired of finding excitement this evening; but look what the gods have brought me—two strong and handsome knights to do my bidding. What an exciting change of fare you'll be. Ah, but shall I take turns with you or have you both service me at the same time? I warrant that will be a new one for you. Or did you share your camp whores whilst on your so-called Crusades?"

Avery stood calmly watching his brothers, though he was sure they were squirming inside at the queen's harsh words. 'Twas no more than they deserved, barging in where they knew they didn't belong. The queen would use them sorely, and if they were lucky, let them go, a little sadder but eminently more wiser. How amusing to see them trying to look so confident whilst all the time they were ready to lose their piss.

In truth, there was nothing he could do for them. Edainn had the sovereign right to take any male she wished. Any male, save for those of royal faery blood. He was grateful for that, for he chose not to be any female's love slave.

"Nay, I believe I'll take you on one at a time. But, which of you to try first? The one who got away last time or this new delectable shy one who was cuckolded by his own brother?"

Stephan felt the heat rise on his face, but he kept silent. All the battles he had fought with his sword had ill-prepared him for a battle of words with a naked faery queen. He hardly knew how to react.

Edainn's words angered Raena, too; but, unlike Stephan, she couldn't keep it to herself. "How dare you speak that way to a member of my family?"

"Be quiet, she-wolf." Edainn's eyes glittered with raw power. "As long as I am queen, I speak and act exactly as I wish and there's nothing you can do about it."

Raena found herself completely at a loss. 'Twas true. There was nothing she could do to stop Edainn—not because she was defenseless against the queen, but because Valor and Stephan were. "Father," she called out plaintively, "is there nothing you can do?"

Prince Ohreinn, in fact, remembered an obscure and ancient law that might obligate the queen to let the men go, but he chose not to divulge it. He had weighed the consequences and had come to an extraordinary conclusion. Indeed, if what he thought was true, then it would be wise to let the scene play out.

"Nay, daughter. There is nothing I can do, but there is something *you* can do."

"What? Tell me what to do."

"Use your faery glamour on Valor. 'Tis more powerful than Edainn's. He'll be compelled to go to you instead of the queen."

Raena's throat tightened. "Oh, if it were only that easy." She turned to Valor, her eyes glazed with tears. "I promised on my father's grave never again to use my faery glamour on you, and my dearest husband, I cannot break that promise now. You taught me the meaning of honor, Valor, and I fear you were too good a teacher. Can you ever forgive me?"

Valor gazed at his wife, his eyes bright with love. He finally knew the answer to the question that had plagued him since he first laid eyes on Raena, the truth that had always been there for him to see if he hadn't been so blind.

He was under no faery spell. What was between them was real and wonderful. "Raena, there's nothing to forgive. I know that now. Let the queen do her worst, she hasn't the power—no one has the power—to change the way we feel."

Edainn watched the two lovers, and a strange twinge of regret twisted through her, but she couldn't back down. She was queen, after all. "Prince Avery, see the love between Raena and her husband. You and you alone have the power to keep it pure. Become my king and I'll send this gaggle of feeble-minded knights home with their wives."

Avery's amusement vanished. He wanted to tell her to use the knights and be done with it, but that was before he saw the fierce love between Valor and Raena, before he realized how devastating it would be for Raena and Caroline to see the husbands they loved so much used in such a sordid way.

Valor and Stephan deserved their fate, but Raena and Caroline did not. These were the people he loved most in this world, and he didn't want them to suffer heartbreak or cause them to lose their spirit.

And yet . . . if he did give in to the queen, he'd be shackled for life. It would be like having his wings clipped, and he could never willingly do that. Was there no other way out of this? After a long pause, he answered, "I . . . might consider a compromise."

Edainn's face lit up. "Yes? Go on."

"I would consider becoming king if I still had the freedom to come and go as I please. Who knows? You may be so enticing a lover that I'd have no desire to leave. Will you take that chance and agree to those terms?"

"You ask too much," Edainn said. "It would not be in the best interest of the realm to have an absent king. I deny your request. Choose this very moment to be my king or . . . as consolation, I shall keep these two knights here to amuse me until I tire of them. They are so handsome and virile, I fear their wives will be deprived of their services for many years to come."

"Take them then," Avery said arrogantly, "if you think they can keep you satisfied. I have no wish to be king of your barren domain."

Devastated by Avery's refusal, Edainn suddenly experienced a strange sensation. 'Twas as if she had a stone lodged in her throat. With a shock, she realized it was a desire to cry. Never in all her life had she ever felt the need to cry and she dared not give in to it now. She must show no weakness to these humans.

What was wrong with her? What was this alien emotion? Then, looking at the handsome faery prince, she knew the reason. She wanted him as she had never wanted anyone before. Not just for the pleasure of his body, but for his powerful magic. She had dreamed all her life of living in the company of such a man as this.

But he would never know that. She'd show him by her actions that his rejection mattered not at all. "Very well, Prince Avery. Two virile males are better than one. Go in peace."

Caroline sobbed despairingly and clutched at Stephan's tunic. Raena, on the other hand, started for Edainn in a rage to do her harm, but her father held her back. "No, Dew Drop. The punishment for harming a queen is death!"

Looking around helplessly, Raena struggled for some unseen answer to her terrible predicament. She couldn't just give up. She had to do something.

Valor saw his wife's stricken face and knew it was up to him—and that was just the way he wanted it to be, the way it was meant to be. He'd use all of his God-given strength to fight the queen's faery glamour. Raena depended on him now, and for her, he must succeed.

Avery watched the scene in consternation, wondering where and how he had lost control. He should have been relieved that he was free to untangle himself from this mess, but he found himself reluctant to leave. Did she really think two human males were better than he? Fah!

"Did you not hear me, Prince Avery? I said you may go."

Trying to save face, Avery proclaimed, "And miss the entertainment?"

"Very well, stay if you wish. The *entertainment* provided by your brothers should, indeed, be amusing."

Avery glanced at Valor and Stephan, then quickly looked away. No, it wouldn't be amusing. His brothers were great warriors. They didn't deserve humiliation at the faery queen's hands.

With a lithe, sensual gait, Edainn stepped down from the stone platform and approached Valor.

"I'll have you first," she purred, running a finger down his chest. "And it will be long and slow so that I can enjoy your suffering."

Ever so slowly, she let out some of her faery scent, but Valor had no trouble resisting it. 'Twas not like with Raena, whom he had wanted even before she had used her glamour.

Seeing her efforts had no visible effect, not even the evidence of an erection, Edainn heightened her aura until her body pulsed and throbbed with its sexual power.

Still Valor resisted. He felt a small tightening of his stomach muscles, but forced himself to relax. He wanted to taunt her, tell her how undesirable she was to him, but he knew that would only make things worse. He stood silently, not moving a muscle, until . . .

Damnation. Her faery scent was getting stronger, and he felt himself grow hard. Oh, God in heaven, it was growing stronger yet, and he felt the need to take her. No. He wouldn't do it. He couldn't bear to do it. He must think of Raena and fight it with all his might.

Edainn saw the sweat upon Valor's brow and was relieved. For a moment she had feared he was immune to her glamour, but that was ridiculous. No living male was immune. Still, she had better work faster before she wearied and her glamour weakened.

Closing her eyes, she gathered up all her strength and let loose all she had.

Valor's body jerked involuntarily, and his erection grew painfully hard. He wanted her and had a hard time remembering why he shouldn't take her. His mind was filled with purple mist and he couldn't think anymore. He was capable only of reacting to the need that overpowered him, the need that engulfed every fiber of his being, causing him to sway back and forth as the mist worked its magic.

He wanted desperately to take her, to spill his seed inside her, and he would. He would. He had to.

No. Fight it. Fight it.

Oh, God, no, he couldn't. He wouldn't. His need to mate was more powerful than his need to breathe, and the pain of holding back was more than he could stand. Squeezing his eyes shut as the ache became overpowering, he stumbled forward, his arms reaching out blindly for the object of his terrible desire.

There was no need for sight, for he followed the trail of scent, though now it was a more subtle and delicate strain that directed him, not the overpowering scent that had choked his throat and nasal passageways. But it didn't matter, all that mattered was becoming one with the object of his desire.

His hands came in contact with a soft body, and her touch was so erotic that his need became ferocious. Crushing her in his arms, he pressed his lips on hers in a passionate kiss that escalated his deep need beyond all reason.

A loud, feverish wail suddenly penetrated the purple mist inside his head, and he halted in confusion. For although the voice was surely the queen's, it was coming from too far away.

Opening his eyes, he saw that it was Raena in his arms.

He let out a cry and, overwhelmed with raw emotion, kissed her again, then buried his face in her neck. "You and no other."

Sobs shook Raena's body as she held on to Valor for dear life. "Oh, my dearest husband, it has always been, will always be, you and no other."

Edainn stood frozen, trying to contemplate what had gone wrong. She had used all of her glamour to capture Valor, but it had been in vain. He had gone to his wife instead. She was certain Raena had not used her faery glamour to attract him, for that wasn't something that could be hidden, and yet . . . "How can this be?"

Ohreinn was jubilant. He had been right. It had happened just as he had thought it would. "How, Edainn? I'll tell you how. 'Tis well known that whatever you are outside this place, you are doubly so betwixt the faery stones. Valor is a true and noble knight. His honor is stronger than all your faery magic."

Turning to Valor, he said, "But even more, you, my son, are under a spell, the most potent spell of all—true love. You loved Raena greatly outside this faery circle, and doubly so inside. Instead of responding to the queen's powerful scent, you instinctively sought out the natural scent of your wife—a scent so faint as to be almost undetectable beneath the queen's glamour, but even so, more powerful because it is the scent of your beloved. No faery magic can compete with that."

"True love," the queen spat out. "You knew all along, didn't you, Ohreinn? You let me humiliate myself just so you could prove a point. But did you forget there's yet one more knight to do my bidding?" Edainn suddenly stopped, as a thought occurred to her. "Mother Goddess give me strength. Is it as I fear? This one's love for his unfaithful wife is just as powerful?"

Caroline started shaking all over. She didn't want to put their love to the test. Not now, when she felt so unworthy. Valor had the strength to reject the queen's glamour, but she had given in to Avery's. Did that mean she didn't love Stephan enough? That she was undeserving of his love?

But Stephan's answer was bold and assured. "I love my wife more than life, as she does me. If Avery had used his glamour on her here in the circle; she would have had the strength to resist. But he made sure to seduce her where she had not the power to repel his powerful magic."

"Enough!" Edainn roared. "I don't want to hear any more. Go away, all of you. I have no patience for sniveling, love-struck humans."

Raena was surprised the queen was letting them go so easily. Was it possible she had been affected by the love demonstrated here tonight?

"My queen," Ohreinn said, more deferentially

than usual. "One more thing before you dismiss them, if you please."

"What is it, Ohreinn? My head pounds and I'm in need of quiet."

"Before my daughter leaves, there's someone here very anxious to meet with her. You agreed it was time."

"Why not? 'Twill be the perfect way to end this wretched evening. Get it over with now so I'll not have to witness it later. Have your little family reunion, Ohreinn; but as for me, I've had enough of human sentiment for one evening."

With that, the queen was gone.

Unexpectedly, Raena's heart went out to her. Edainn wasn't evil, just bitter and lonely. A fate Raena might have shared if Valor hadn't come into her life. Then, remembering her father's words, she asked, "Father, who wishes to meet me?"

Ohreinn nodded to someone in the shadows and a dark form walked timidly out into the moonlight. It was a woman, with two young boys beside her and a small infant in her arms. The woman approached Raena with a beautiful shy smile upon her face, a smile that tugged at Raena's heartstrings. Who was she? Who was this lovely, serene woman?

"This is your mother, Raena."

"My . . . mother?"

The words were said with such wonder and reverence, they brought tears to Lady Eleanor's eyes. "Raena, oh, Raena, how I've longed for this moment!"

The voice sang through Raena's senses, and she remembered it, though she had not heard it since she was a babe. "Mother, oh, Mother, I thought you dead!"

"I know. I'm sorry for that, but it was the only

way to keep the secret. Too many people saw me jump from the ramparts. 'Twas most fortunate no one saw Ohreinn fly up to catch me in his arms before I tumbled into the sea. He braved being discovered by humans, having left the safety of the faery circle to find me, and he saved me from death."

"Everyone thought you had plummeted into the sea. Everyone . . ."

"I know. I was out of my mind with grief and longing; I didn't know what I was doing. I didn't want to live without him. And so he came for me, but there was a price to pay. A very dear price. I was banished to the faery world to live. If humans learned how I had been rescued, they would have known that faeries still exist, and that would have been dangerous for the people of Dawne. It was imperative that I remain dead to humankind."

"But—but, Father, why didn't you tell me? I would have kept the secret. I wouldn't have endangered you. And what about Wiggles? How could she have kept such a secret from me?"

"She is blameless. It was my decision. Mine and Queen Edainn's. If I could have but foreseen how you'd turn out, I would have trusted you with the secret. But you must remember, we were very new at mating humans with faeries then and had misgivings as to your fitness. And . . . what if you had demanded your mother back? We couldn't take the chance."

Raena understood, but it was still very hard to take. Staring into her mother's eyes, Raena swallowed her hurt. She had her mother, and that was such a wonderful gift that she would be content forever. Reaching out, she embraced her mother and the small, baldheaded baby in her arms.

A strange, wonderful, alien feeling came over her at the touch. It was the special love between mother and daughter.

She held onto her mother for a long, long time, enjoying that special feeling, and didn't release her hold until she heard a boy's voice whisper, "Mother."

Raena looked down at the two young boys and saw their resemblance to her. They were, without a doubt, her true brothers, for they certainly shared the same mother and father as she.

Eleanor pushed her sons gently toward their sister. "Aaron and Daemon, this is your sister, Raena. Will you not greet her?"

The boys looked up at her with their beautiful purple eyes, so much like hers, but were too timid to speak. In truth, she was sure this was the first time they had met anyone from outside the faery stones. "I'm so happy to meet you." She turned and beckoned Valor to come closer. "And this is my husband, Sir Valor. A brave and noble knight."

The boys looked up at Valor with awe. "Sir knight," said the older one. "Will you show me your sword? I've naught seen one but once."

Valor pulled out his sword and handed it to Daemon. "Handle it carefully; for 'tis very sharp and heavy."

Daemon struggled under the weight of it. "Have you killed many people with it, Sir Knight?" he asked, touching the blade very carefully.

"Just enough and no more. If your father allows, I'll show you and your brother how to wield a sword when you're a bit older."

Daemon handed the sword back to Valor. "I would like that very much."

"Indeed, their instruction would be welcome." Ohreinn said contentedly. His family was all here together, and from the looks of it, they'd get on together quite well.

"This is a momentous day, is it not? I learn that my son is gifted with talents much greater than even mine, and a mother and daughter are reunited."

" 'Tis momentous for yet another reason, Father. I learned this night that my husband truly loves me."

Valor tightened his grip on Raena, "And that love is the most powerful force in or out of this world. I'm grateful for that knowledge, for it arms me as no other weapon can."

"Leave it to a man to think of love as a weapon," Raena said. "Methinks you need some gentling. You've been at war too long."

Raena spoke the truth. He had been at war too long, though not the war she spoke of. He had been at war with his heart, fighting too hard to be free of an enchantment that didn't exist. For he knew now, it wasn't faery glamour that kept him captive to Raena, but his deep and abiding love for her.

The faery circle took on a soft glow, the culmination of all the love it contained. Deep love between husbands and wives, mothers and daughters, fathers and sons. Love such as had not been felt in this place for a long time. And in that glow, a healing began that would make the future brighter for faery and human alike.

Epilogue

Valor wiped away the sweat that beaded his brow and ducked under a low-hanging branch. 'Twas risky riding through Sherwood Forest without an escort of armed men, but they had no choice; 'twas imperative they keep the location of Saera Ni and John Barrows's cottage secret from the world.

Ahead of him, Caroline and Stephan led the way. They knew it well, by now, having traveled there many times to visit Caroline's faery daughter. Little Faith had lived with Saera Ni and John since her birth a year and a half ago.

This was Valor's first time, however, and knowing the dangers this wild place held, he kept himself alert.

But there was no stopping Caroline and Raena from this journey. If he hadn't agreed to go, he knew his stubborn wife would have sneaked off when he wasn't looking.

Moving his horse behind his wife's, Valor gazed at the cherubic face of his baby daughter strapped to her mother's back, and a great surge of love enveloped him. He was grateful Merry could stay with them instead of being fostered to Saera Ni's care, like little Faith. It would grieve him not to see her angel-face every day.

But Caroline's child had been born with budding wings and, though it was a joyful sign to Prince Ohreinn and Avery, it was a problem for Caroline and Stephan. It would be impossible to hide Faith's faery features from humans very long. That's why the babe had been sent to the safety of Sherwood Forest and the loving arms of Saera Ni. And that was why Caroline spent so much time traveling back and forth.

Valor could not think why they hadn't been accosted or robbed by now—if not by Robin Hood, then by other knaves. It was almost as if Caroline and Stephan had a guardian angel watching over them, for their trips had all been without incident, so far.

Valor was relieved when they finally came to the path that led to the little cottage. They had to dismount and walk their horses the rest of the way, for the trees were very thick here and the branches lying low, but it offered them a degree of protection from curious eyes.

Coming to the end of the path, Stephan dismounted and tugged at the base of the large shrubbery that blocked their way.

"What the devil are you doing?"

"It's in a wooden container, Val. Help me move it so we may continue. It hides the secret pathway to the cottage."

Amazed, Valor made his way over to the large bush and helped Stephan set it aside. Once on the other side, they set it back in place before continuing down the path.

After traveling awhile longer, Valor asked, "How far is it from here?"

"Shush," said Raena. "Listen, and you'll hear your answer."

Valor came to a halt and tilted his head, listening for what, he didn't know. Then it came to him, the sound of tinkling bells. No, not bells, but Avery's laughter. He smiled and hurried faster along the path.

In a few moments they came to a large clearing that held a thatched-roof cottage hewn of rough timber. Raena had told him it was the same cottage where she had lived for so many, many years. No wonder she was such a wild little thing, raised in such a rustic location. But, in truth, he wouldn't have her any other way. He loved her earthy, un-spoiled ways.

As they drew closer to the cozy cottage, Valor saw that a long table had been set up, laden with food enough to feed a legion of hungry yeomen. Things must be going very well for Saera Ni and John to have such an abundance to lay out. "Just in time for supper," he cried out.

Saera Ni looked up from placing a jug of wine on the table and cried for joy. In an instant she was surrounded by the weary travelers. All but Caroline, who went immediately to her daughter, held lov-ingly in Avery's arms.

Seeing her coming, Avery set the child down and whispered in her tiny ear. "Go to Mama."

Lifting the child into her arms, Caroline kissed her sweet little face, crying, "Oh, my darling, you've grown so much in the past two months."

Avery watched with a lump in his throat. Then, shaking himself free of the emotion that threatened to overtake him, he made his way over to Stephan and nervously held out his hand. This was the first time he had been in his brother's company since

Faith's birth. Until now, he had made it a practice
to visit Faith only when Caroline and Stephan were
away.

Stephan hesitated but a moment before taking
Avery's offered hand, and the two brothers stared
into each other's eyes a long time, their hands
clasped together in fealty. The poignant silence was
broken when little Faith cooed, "Da. Da." The two
men looked down at the darling child and smiled.
Instantly, they were both on their hands and knees
playing with Faith.

Caroline sighed with happiness. With two such
awesome men in her life, Faith was a fortunate little
girl.

Saera Ni, eager to see baby Merry, circled around
Raena and lifted the child from her nesting place.
"Oh, Raena, she's beautiful. Methinks she looks just
like you, though I can see some of her father peek-
ing out from her eyes, for certain."

"Oh, Wiggles, you have no idea how happy I am
to be here. I've wanted to bring Merry since the day
she was born, but my cautious husband would have
none of it. Her birth did weaken me far longer than
I expected."

"He was right to wait until you had all your
strength back. But look at you! I can see you're completely recovered from the birth; you glow with good
health."

"And you, Saera Ni. You're even lovelier than I
remembered. Which reminds me, I've brought you
a present. My magic mirror, so you'll always know
how truly beautiful you are."

"My sweet Gosling, I couldn't take it from you.
'Tis part of your family treasure."

"Hmmm," Valor said, his interest piqued. "What
treasure do you speak of?"

Raena and Saera Ni exchanged knowing glances; then, laughing, Raena said, "I suppose it's safe to share that little secret with you now that I know you truly love me. 'Tis my birthright gifts from the faeries and the elves, but you'll have to wait until we return home to see them."

Val gave her a puzzled look, then shrugged his shoulders. 'Twas probably naught but feathers and rocks and other useless things faeries deemed valuable. Whispering in her ear, he said, "I know one thing worth waiting for, though I pray I won't have to. 'Twould be too cruel to make me wait 'til we go home before I can make love to you."

Raena's eyes twinkled with delight as she pushed him away and went on with her conversation with Saera Ni. "You'll keep the mirror, Saera Ni. 'Tis my marriage present to you. Now, tell me all about your wedding to John."

"Ah, yes, my wedding. I would have waited 'til you could be here, but John was in a hurry to make it binding. You can't imagine the reason why." Saera Ni laughed heartily.

"He said that now that I show my beautiful true self, he wants to make sure no one else steals me away. Now, I ask you, isn't that a silly reason? It's not as if the woods were full of suitors."

"Sounds like a man very much in love to me," Raena answered.

"He had a friend of ours actually kidnap a priest on his way to Nottingham to perform the ceremony. Can you imagine that. A Christian wedding for me?"

"You have friends here in the forest? Then you're not too lonely?"

"How could I be lonely with John by my side? And little Faith. That child gives us great joy. And Avery is here so often, he practically lives here. He dotes on Faith and brings her sweet treats, which she adores. And as you know, Caroline and Stephan visit as often as they can—and always with news of you and your little family. I miss you terribly. I only wish you could visit more often."

"She may, now that her strength is back." Valor said, circling Raena's waist. "For we've decided we want Avery to instruct our daughter in faery ways, too. I have a feeling little Merry may have more faery traits than she's shown so far and 'twould be good for her to learn how to hide them from humans."

"Avery will be pleased to have another pupil."

"What pupil is that?" Avery asked, appearing at Raena's elbow.

Raena smiled at her brother. "Merry. Look, see how vivid her purple eyes are. The castle folk call her their shy little violet. They accept the color of her eyes without question, thinking only that the unusual color runs in my family."

Avery took Merry from Saera Ni and held her aloft to get a better look at her. "What have you been feeding this child? She's as heavy as Faith, yet half her age."

"She does love to eat. Just like her father."

"Speaking of which . . ." Valor said, pointedly. "I'm famished, and the food on yon table is too tempting to ignore."

"Well, you'll not have to wait any longer, Val," Saera Ni said. "See, John is bringing home some very special guests for supper."

Hearing John's booming voice, Raena turned to see him coming down the path, a group of green-clad men behind him.

Valor's hand closed over his sword, but his tension

eased when he saw that Robin Hood and his men were obviously friends with John.

Raena hugged John tight, and the embrace he gave her in return nearly squeezed the breath out of her. "Look who's here to see you, Raena. He tells me you were betrothed once."

Val pricked up his ears at that. "My wife betrothed to another?"

John laughed. "When they were children."

Robin Hood clapped John on the shoulder, saying, " 'Twas surely the most short-lived betrothal ever known, for we argued over who should keep the fledgling hawk we found that very day. The matter was settled when the hawk found its wings and flew away. Raena blamed his escape on me and declared the betrothal broken."

Laughing merrily, Raena threw herself into Robin's arms. "I had almost forgotten about that." His familiar scent washed over her, and she buried her face in his shoulder in contentment. Robin would always have a special place in her heart.

Then, turning to Valor, she said, "Robin, this is my husband, Val."

Robin gazed at Val with a twinkle in his eyes. "We've met."

Valor stared back, then slowly held his hand out to Robin Hood. "Not formally."

Robin took Valor's offered hand and each man clasped the other's, squeezing overly hard.

Raena looked at them in wonder, wanting to hear more, but 'twas obvious the two men were going to keep their meeting secret from her. Men. They were such mysterious creatures. "Robin, where is your lady wife? I yearn to see her."

Val released his hold on Robin Hood's hand, and Robin flexed his fingers, trying to uncramp them from Valor's painful grip. "Lady Marian is lying in at her sister's house. She's just given birth to my son."

"You have a son? Oh, Robin, I'm so happy for you. Did it go well?"

"She's doing fine, and as for the babe, he's healthy and strong. I'm thinking he'd make a fine match for your daughter. Do you think Merry would mind a younger man?"

Robin Hood laughed, and the sound of tinkling bells filled the air. Then, suddenly, Robin's eyes turned the color of purple silk as he solemnly proclaimed, "Wouldn't that be a wondrous thing to behold? Our families joined by marriage."

Saera Ni smiled knowingly.

Dear Reader,

I adored fairy tales as a child and spent many happy hours reading them. I searched the library for every one I could find, enthralled by the plight of beautiful princesses and the handsome knights and princes who did battle for them. The stories inspired me to write my own when I was ten or eleven years old. Little did I know that my childish writing would be my first step toward a career in writing. Little did I know that I would one day seriously set about writing a highly imaginative and sexy adult fairy story.

The Enchanting is such a tale, complete with faery princess and handsome knight. It was great fun to write and I gave my imagination free rein. I conjured up a tribe of faeries with vivid purple eyes, and they truly came alive for me—and I hope for you, too. I was thrilled when Zebra trusted me to write this unusual story, for it truly pushes the boundaries of romantic fiction.

THE ENCHANTING is my sixth book for Zebra.
My other titles are:
ROSEFIRE, A LOVE FOR ALL TIME,
THORN OF THE ROSE,
ONE SHINING MOMENT, and
THE HEART REMEMBERS

If you enjoyed this unusual story and would like to read more adult fairy tales, I'd love to hear from you.

Sandra Davidson
PO Box 3634
St. Augustine, FL 32085-3634

ROMANCE FROM HANNAH HOWELL

MY VALIANT KNIGHT   (0-8217-5186-7, $5.50)

ONLY FOR YOU   (0-8217-4993-5, $4.99)

UNCONQUERED   (0-8217-5417-3, $5.99)

WILD ROSES   (0-8217-5677-X, $5.99)

Available wherever paperbacks are sold, or order direct from the Publisher. Send cover price plus 50¢ per copy for mailing and handling to Penguin USA, P.O. Box 999, c/o Dept. 17109, Bergenfield, NJ 07621. Residents of New York and Tennessee must include sales tax. DO NOT SEND CASH.

PASSIONATE ROMANCE
FROM BETINA KRAHN!

HIDDEN FIRES   (0-8217-4953-6, $4.99)

LOVE'S BRAZEN FIRE   (0-8217-5691-5, $5.99)

MIDNIGHT MAGIC   (0-8217-4994-3, $4.99)

PASSION'S RANSOM   (0-8217-5130-1, $5.99)

REBEL PASSION   (0-8217-5526-9, $5.99)

Available wherever paperbacks are sold, or order direct from the Publisher. Send cover price plus 50¢ per copy for mailing and handling to Penguin USA, P.O. Box 999, c/o Dept. 17109, Bergenfield, NJ 07621. Residents of New York and Tennessee must include sales tax. DO NOT SEND CASH.

ROMANCE FROM JANELLE TAYLOR

ANYTHING FOR LOVE (0-8217-4992-7, $5.99)

DESTINY MINE (0-8217-5185-9, $5.99)

CHASE THE WIND (0-8217-4740-1, $5.99)

MIDNIGHT SECRETS (0-8217-5280-4, $5.99)

MOONBEAMS AND MAGIC (0-8217-0184-4, $5.99)

SWEET SAVAGE HEART (0-8217-5276-6, $5.99)

Available wherever paperbacks are sold, or order direct from the Publisher. Send cover price plus 50¢ per copy for mailing and handling to Penguin USA, P.O. Box 999, c/o Dept. 17109, Bergenfield, NJ 07621. Residents of New York and Tennessee must include sales tax. DO NOT SEND CASH.

DANGEROUS GAMES (0-7860-0270-0, $4.99)
by Amanda Scott

When Nicholas Barrington, eldest son of the Earl of Ul-combe, first met Melissa Seacort, the desperation he sensed beneath her well-bred beauty haunted him. He didn't realize how desperate Melissa really was . . . until he found her again at a Newmarket gambling club—being auctioned off by her father to the highest bidder. So, Nick bought himself a wife. With a villain hot on their heels, and a fortune and their lives at stake, they would gamble everything on the most dangerous game of all: love.

A TOUCH OF PARADISE (0-7860-0271-9, $4.99)
by Alexa Smart

As a confidence man and scam runner in 1880s America, Malcolm Northrup has amassed a fortune. Now, posing as the eminent Sir John Abbot—scholar, and possible discoverer of the lost continent of Atlantis—he's taking his act on the road with a lecture tour, seeking funds for a scientific experiment he has no intention of making. But scholar Halia Davenport is determined to accompany Malcolm on his "expedition" . . . even if she must kidnap him!

Available wherever paperbacks are sold, or order direct from the Publisher. Send cover price plus 50¢ per copy for mailing and handling to Penguin USA, P.O. Box 999, c/o Dept. 17109, Bergenfield, NJ 07621. Residents of New York and Tennessee must include sales tax. DO NOT SEND CASH.

SAVAGE ROMANCE
FROM CASSIE EDWARDS!

#1: SAVAGE OBSESSION   (0-8217-5554-4, $5.99)

#2: SAVAGE INNOCENCE   (0-8217-5578-1, $5.99)

#3: SAVAGE TORMENT   (0-8217-5581-1, $5.99)

#4: SAVAGE HEART   (0-8217-5635-4, $5.99)

#5: SAVAGE PARADISE   (0-8217-5637-0, $5.99)

Available wherever paperbacks are sold, or order direct from the Publisher. Send cover price plus 50¢ per copy for mailing and handling to Penguin USA, P.O. Box 999, c/o Dept. 17109, Bergenfield, NJ 07621. Residents of New York and Tennessee must include sales tax. DO NOT SEND CASH.